THE DEVIL'S BAIT

THE DEVIL'S BAIT

Jeffrey J. Mariotte

MALEVOLENT BOOKS
Santa Monica, California

FIRST EDITION

Library of Congress Cataloging-in-Publication-Data is available on file.

ISBN: 978-1-936573-05-9

Malevolent Books, in association with Global ReLeaf, will plant two trees for each tree used in the manufacturing of this book. Global ReLeaf is an international campaign by American Forests, the nation's oldest nonprofit conservation organization and a world leader in planting trees for environmental restoration.

10 9 8 7 6 5 4 3 2 1

For Maryelizabeth, as always.

Acknowledgements:

No book writes itself, and no writer writes alone. A lot of people had a little something to do with this one, and I can't name them all here. But I can mention my family, who put up with me sharing fascinating tidbits from the world of money laundering, my parents, who took me to New York, France and Switzerland in the first place, and the author Thomas Gifford, who taught me what thrillers were made of. Also, great thanks to Jim Strader, Dianne Larson, and J. Carson Black.

THE DEVIL'S BAIT

Worldly wealth is the Devil's bait; and those whose minds feed upon riches recede, in general, from real happiness, in proportion as their stores increase, as the moon, when she is fullest, is farthest from the sun.
—Robert Burton

The bank is something more than men, I tell you. It's the monster. Men made it, but they can't control it.
—John Steinbeck

Chapter 1

There were two rules about banking that Jessie Dawn Cutler kept in mind at all times.

Well, there were really more than two rules—a *lot* more, banking being probably second only to the law in the sheer crushing quantity of statutes and regulations, voluntary and otherwise, imposed upon its practitioners.

But the two to which Jessie paid the most stringent attention had to do with money, and the banker's personal relationship with same. The first commandment of the Gospel According to Jessica was this:

All that money? It's not yours.

The second commandment went pretty much hand-in-hand with the first. Jessica phrased it thusly: And neither is the guy it *does* belong to.

Which commandment, the second one, that is, Jessie sometimes had a hard time persuading herself to live by. Especially when the guy who had the money, and plenty of it, was Richard Steele. Mid-thirties, built, well dressed, richer than sin, and, not to put too fine a point on it, gorgeous. Drop dead knock your socks off stone cold wow. Richard Steele was an inch or so over six feet. Combine George Clooney's jaw and Paul Newman's eyes with the bone structure of Redford—the young Redford, not that the older one was any slouch, mind you, and you'd be heading in the general direction of what Richard Steele looked like...when he just woke up. As the day wore on, he only got better looking.

Jessie was guessing on this last point, having never yet had the opportunity to wake up with Richard Steele. Not that she was opposed to it, in principle. Even though it would violate Commandment Number Two. But sitting across from him at a grill at the corner of 73rd and Columbus, with a candle on the table and a fireplace roaring behind her back and a few drinks and an excellent fettuccini Alfredo, preceded by a green salad and followed by a slice of flourless chocolate cake (an extra hour in the gym this week, she figured), in her stomach, looking at the dimples that formed at the corners of his mouth when he laughed, it was more and more difficult to keep in mind that she was his private banker, his Relationship Manager, in the official terminology of MetroBank, and that to sleep with him would probably, at some point, result in her being dismissed, or, in the terminology of Jessie, who wasn't one to mince words, in having her ass kicked to the curb, employment-wise.

And as hot as Richard Steele was, as much as she could feel the mutual attraction that arced between them, a tingle that started below her waist and worked its way over the rest of her body like a low-grade electric charge, Jessie loved banking more.

Hard to believe, she knew. But there it was. In the contest between getting laid by the best-looking, wealthiest man she had ever met, and keeping her job, the job won out.

Thinking about it now, she shook her head, swallowed a sip of her French roast.

"What is it?" Richard asked.

She shook her head again—consciously this time, since she didn't even realize she was doing it before.

"Nothing," she said. "You don't even want to know."

He laughed. "I like that," he said, raising his cup toward her. They'd both switched to coffee from Chardonnay when...well, when the bottle was empty, come to think of it. "It's nice to think that my banker has layers of mystery about her."

"I might as well," she said. "It's not like they'll ever match yours."

He laughed again. She liked it when he did. His teeth could have had their own career, at dental schools, as the "after" example of proper hygiene and excellence in orthodontics. "Nothing particularly mysterious about me," he said. "I'm just a lucky guy."

"Is that what you call it?"

"No other word for it. I'm successful, sure, but it's not really from anything I did. I mean, it's not like I was a genius at school, or invented anything brilliant, or made any special contribution to the world. I just do what I do and I'm well compensated for it. If that's not lucky, I don't know what is."

"I think you're underestimating your skills, but whatever," Jessie allowed. "Have it your way."

"I usually do," Richard said. She knew he was right on that count.

Jessie had asked him once, over iced double nonfat lattes at Starbucks, where he made his not inconsiderable money. It was cash, mostly, or at least that part of it that Jessica saw was. Of course, the source of his income should have been among the first questions she asked, even before accepting him as a client. KYC was the first official rule of private banking—*Know Your Customer*—and MetroBank emphasized that rule to all of its relationship managers on a near-daily basis. But Richard had been passed down to Jessie by her boss, Barbara Slonaker, who had vouched for him, said he was a great client, and warned her not to ask questions that might spook him. She wanted the Steele millions to run through MetroBank, and who was Jessie Cutler to argue with Barbara Slonaker, who had, after all, practically invented private banking in the modern age?

So Jessie took Richard Steele on, and only after he had been a client for almost a year, and she had run more than sixty million dollars through his accounts, had she bothered to ask him where it all came from.

"Here and there," he had said. Seeming to realize the evasive nature of his response, he had set his clear plastic cup down and leaned forward, a rare, serious expression on his face. "I own some contracting firms up and down the coast. We build homes, repair them when they break, you know. Real blue-collar stuff. And then I have an interest—a small one, really, but it's a profitable gig—in a casino down in Atlantic City. The Kasbah. Maybe I can take you down there one of these days, comp you a room, a few dollars in chips. I'd like to watch my banking queen try her hand at some gambling."

"Not really my thing, Richard. To me, shoving quarters in the washing machine in my building is a gamble. And one I'm always nervous about losing."

"I'm sure I could change your mind, Jess," he said. "You just let me know when you're ready to try."

"I'll keep it in mind," she said. And, knowing she was prying but not willing to stop herself, she pushed a little. "But let me ask you, why take such precautions with your cash, then? I mean, there are easier and more liquid ways to manage your cash flow than what you've got me doing for you."

"A huge portion of my income is cash—you know that better than anyone," he said. "Some of our contracting clients pay in cash, and most of what I get out of the casino is cash. I'm concerned about it because...well, to be honest, you know what kind of people you meet in the casino business, right?"

"Not personally," she said. "By reputation, sure."

"Well, the reputations are true, in many cases. It was worse in the old days, I'm sure, before gaming commissions and the like. Still, I'm in business there with some people I wouldn't want to be on the same side of the street with, if I had my choice. Nasty customers. I don't want any of them deciding that they'd like to get their hands on my cash. So I figure it's best if I keep all my accounts secret, so they can't 'accidentally' find out what I'm really worth."

"Are these guys dangerous, Richard? Mafia types?"

"Some of them could be mobbed up," he replied. The words sounded awkward in his mouth, like he was repeating something he'd heard on TV. "I don't really know, for sure. I don't want to. The less our paths cross, the better. Though I have to say, they sure keep the casino running smoothly."

"I bet. I'd hate to think that you were in any danger, though."

"Oh, I'm not. I keep my distance from those guys, and they don't have any reason to bother me. They bought in after my partners and I did—one of my partners had a cash crunch, a few years ago, and had to sell his interest. The guys who bought it, as I said, are not guys I'm totally comfortable with. But as long as I don't have to break bread with them, I'm okay."

She had dropped the subject then. But the conversation came back to her every now and again, especially on occasions when she thought about waking up next to him, and the thought occurred to her that she might be waking up next to a horse's head at the same time.

Which had happened more than once, during this dinner. The part about waking up with Richard, which naturally enough would have to follow going to bed with Richard. The part about the horse, only once. Tonight.

But now dinner was over, coffee gone, dessert already a happy memory, and he had paid the bill and was helping her on with her coat, his hands brushing the back of her neck as he straightened her collar. She nearly melted right then, a sticky puddle on the restaurant floor, but somehow she maintained her proper viscosity and led the way out of the restaurant and into the cold early December night. She pulled her coat more tightly around her, and tugged gloves from its deep pockets.

This had been a business dinner—teasing and flirting aside, it had been a strategy session to talk about Richard's financial plans for the upcoming year, and to go over some of the tax law changes that would affect him if she couldn't manage to shelter every dime he made. But it was the teasing and flirting and the feel of Richard's fingers touching the fine hairs at the nape of her neck that she would remember, she knew, more than any details of offshore accounts and commingled funds.

They said their goodbyes, wished one another happy holidays in the nonspecific manner that had become traditional, shaken hands, and shared a quick, overcoat-bulky hug, and then she had headed down Columbus to look for a cab while he had disappeared around the corner, to where he said he had parked his car. He had offered her a ride, but he was going the opposite direction and she figured if she had him in a car within a mile of her actual bed, it would all be over for her resolve.

She actually had her hand out and a cab in sight when she remembered that she had forgotten to give him the holiday card in which she'd written her new phone extension and the hours she would be working over the next few weeks. Not a big deal, she knew, but she wanted to be considerate, and since she didn't have many other clients with his kind of weight—like, *none*—she wanted to make sure he knew when he could and couldn't expect to reach her. It would only take a minute, she knew, to go around the corner and catch him before he got to his car. She dropped her arm, turned, and walked briskly for the corner.

And as she rounded it, she saw him, walking toward the three-story parking garage a block away. But he wasn't alone. Another man walked with him, a taller man wearing a black trench coat and one of those furry Cossack hats. His long legs moved like a robot's, fluttering his coat with every step, while his upper torso remained almost still. She thought he walked like a stork.

She headed that way. She didn't want to interrupt what seemed to be a fairly serious conversation between Richard and the stork—and where had he come from, anyway? Had he been waiting outside the whole time? But there might be an opportunity to catch Richard, after the stork got into his own car or went in some other direction. So she held back, standing in the shadows of buildings and low, leafless trees, and didn't call Richard's name.

The men entered the garage, and it looked like maybe they would be driving away together after all, so Jessie thought, fuck it, manners are nice but they're not everything, and she started to run.

When all hell broke loose, she had almost reached the entrance to the parking garage. She was still in the shadows, outside the staircase that led up to the second and third floors, and she could see Richard and the stork standing near Richard's Jaguar, but there was no way, unless they were looking for her, that they could see Jessie.

They weren't even close to looking for her. They were looking up the ramp, as Jessie was, because from up the ramp came the growl of an engine and the screaming of tires, and then before it seemed like it should have been possible, the car lunged into view, and the windows were open and there were guns, like quills on a porcupine, bristling from every window.

Jessie's heart stopped.

Richard and the stork didn't run, didn't shriek, didn't dive under the car—all of which would have been Jessie's reactions, if she had been able to do anything other than stand there in terrified shock. Richard and the stork reached under their coats, and when they pulled their hands out there was metal in them, and Richard and the stork stood their ground, firing at the oncoming car.

One of them hit the driver.

The driver—probably not surprisingly, since he had one or more bullets in him—lost control. The car slammed into one of the concrete support posts and came to a noisy stop. Only then did Richard and the stork take cover behind Richard's Jag. Firing over the top of the car, they tried to pick the gunmen off as they emerged from the wreck. A couple went down right away, but two others got out the far side of the car and darted behind nearby parked cars.

They returned fire, and the noise echoed in the confines of the parking garage. To Jessie, standing outside, it sounded like all the fireworks shows she'd ever seen rolled into one. The garage boomed with flashes of light and the thunder of gunfire.

Richard and the stork seemed invulnerable. A bullet blew the stork's Cossack hat from his head, revealing a shock of curly copper hair. He wasn't hurt, though. Within a couple of minutes, the gunfight was over.

Richard and the stork were still standing. Nobody else.

Jessie breathed, finally, blowing out a huge lungful of air that she hadn't realized she'd been holding. She didn't understand any of this, had never known that Richard carried a gun—though with the kind of cash he carried around, and the kind of business associates he had, it made a certain amount of sense. But *this*?

Then, as she watched, still shielded by the trees and the shadows and the dark December night, Richard and the stork did something else she didn't expect. Something she couldn't have expected, couldn't believe even though she was watching it happen.

Calmly, almost casually, Richard and the stork walked to each body that sprawled on the concrete slab floor of the parking garage. One of them, either Richard or the stork, would lean in close to the fallen man, press his handgun up against the man's head, and pull the trigger. Brain and blood and fragments of skull skidded across the garage floor with each blast.

Jessie could taste her Alfredo, fought to keep it down.

One by one, the two men cold-bloodedly finished off each of the men who had emerged from the car. Then, a job well done, they put their weapons back underneath their coats, climbed into Richard's black Jaguar, and drove away.

Jessie watching.

Sick.

In the distance, sirens wailed. Someone had called the police.

Jessie turned and ran, for Columbus and a cab. She didn't want to have to answer any questions about this. Not until she'd sorted it out for herself.

If she ever could.

Chapter 2

Jessie folded the *Times*, tossed it onto the to-be-recycled stack. Nothing.

She had skipped her run that morning, that's how upset she was.

Fitness was a ritual. She would be thirty-five in four months. Then downhill to forty. But she liked the way she had looked at twenty-five, and every year it took more effort to maintain that.

She was proud of what she had done, though. She was five-eight; her weight ranged from 122 to 130. Ass tight and high. Belly flat. Legs strong and toned. Hips under control. Breasts maybe a little large for her frame, but she wasn't complaining about that.

She ran five days a week: two miles on Tuesdays, Wednesdays, Thursdays and Saturdays, five on Sundays, instead of church. Three gym nights during the week. Spinning, stepping, aerobics, Nautilus. A longer session on most Saturdays.

Fitness was key.

On this morning, she skipped the run. Showered quickly. Toweling off, she had a brief flash of Richard's fingertips grazing her neck, and shivered, but then she remembered the guns, and the skull fragments bouncing across the garage floor like stones skipped over a still lake, and the vision faded.

She pulled dark blonde hair into a ponytail, secured it with a blue scrunchy. No makeup.

Then she put breakfast together—also ritual: one cup of strong coffee, a tall glass of O.J., a muffin from Muffins Galore, half a block away on 83rd, and the *Times*. Never online—she loved the feel of the paper in her hands, the noisy crinkle when she folded it. Normally the finance section first, then the front page, then the local news. She skipped sports, skipped the classifieds. She loved her job and she loved her apartment, 14th floor with a doorman and laundry in the building, so why bother with the classifieds? She would stay put until she could afford to buy. Another year, maybe two, for that.

But this morning, she started with the front section, skimmed it fast and went to local, and there was nothing. A shootout in a parking garage, five people dead...you'd think it would generate a headline or two. But no. She flipped through the rest of the paper, then back to the beginning, page by page, column by column. It wasn't there.

* * *

She hadn't slept well. Images kept strobing back at her—the calm set of Richard's face, illuminated by the muzzle flash as he pulled the trigger. The way he and the stork-looking guy methodically finished off each of the gunmen. The way his eyes crinkled when he laughed. It was hard to reconcile the two ideas of Richard Steele.

But she had known there was something not quite right, hadn't she? In the still quiet hours of the morning, she sat in a chair in the darkened living room of her apartment drinking water from a Pottery Barn glass and thinking about how she had come to be his private banker. He had been Barbara's customer first, and when Barbara had been promoted up to management, he had landed in the metaphorical lap of Barbara's protégé.

Barbara had indicated that she had fully screened him. A private banker's job was to help wealthy customers, whose financial needs were more complex than most people's, through the tricky warren of financial rules and regulations in order to make the best use of their money. The law was meant to be obeyed, if occasionally stretched. Used, really, like a woodworker's favorite tools, to achieve the desired ends in the most precise fashion possible.

Since Richard was her biggest customer, she was pleased that he had avoided the pitfalls that had devastated so many investors over the past few years. The credit default swaps, the collateralized debt obligations, bundled mortgage-backed securities—if he had hinted at any interest in those, Jessie would have had no choice but to get involved in them, to start selling him junk investments that could have wiped him out, as they did so many others. Those had mostly hit institutional investors, but Richard moved so much money through the bank that he might as well have been an institution. Most of the fiasco had fallen out by the time Barbara moved Jessie into relationship banking, and Barbara had emphasized that Richard had dodged those traps of his own accord. He didn't want to play games with his money, Barbara said, he just wanted to protect it and build his wealth.

Sounded good to Jessie, at the time. But if Richard was in fact a criminal—which the incident in the parking garage seemed to virtually guarantee, since murder still, last she'd checked, ranked higher on the forbidden list than greed, and for sure more people did hard time behind it—then what Jessie was doing was helping him launder money.

Which the government frowned upon. Laundering money could cost an institution its banking license. She was sure MetroBank, a billion dollar plus business, would have serious issues with that outcome. MetroBank had come through the crash without taking government bailout money, which its top execs still crowed about. But since then, there had been more talk than ever of banking regulation, of oversight and Wall Street cops who would bring the financial industry under stricter control. The banking industry had successfully fought and lobbied for years to replace restrictive regulation and enforcement with voluntary compliance, and—though the degree was a topic of constant debate among industry insiders—their victory in that crusade had led, at least in part, to a national financial catastrophe. A big laundering scandal at a major bank would invite the sort of scrutiny that bankers wanted to avoid.

Her own career was at risk, too. She paced the hardwood floors of her apartment, exploring and discarding one option after another.

By the time she'd finished her fruitless hunt through the newspaper, Jessie had decided what she had to do. On the theory that Barbara Slonaker knew full well she was laundering illicit funds—and it seemed almost impossible that Barbara could not know—she had to go over Barbara's head. Jim Mackie was Barbara's boss, and Jessie's oldest friend at MetroBank. She knew she could speak to him in confidence, lay the whole thing out for him, and let him take whatever action was called for.

Only one problem remained—the parking garage. She hadn't done anything at the time, which she now realized was a big mistake. She should have called the police right away. Since she hadn't, she could be charged as an accomplice. She had assumed the incident would turn up in the papers and there would be a police investigation, clues would be found, Richard and his friend arrested, and she could avoid the whole mess.

But it hadn't, and she didn't know if that meant the police didn't know about it, or if there was more to it than she could tell from the outside. Whatever the case, getting involved now seemed like a bad idea. She would tell Jim that she had misgivings about Richard, and how he earned his money, but she wouldn't mention the shootout. If it became necessary at some later time, she would go to the police with it.

* * *

MetroBank's corporate offices were on Fifth Avenue, between 34th and 35th. Branch office downstairs, corporate offices on floors twenty-one through fifty-five. Jessie dressed for work, went to her office, dealt with some e-mail and voicemail. Her office was on thirty. Interior, no windows, but at least it wasn't a cube. Barbara had assured her that within a year or two she would be skipping floors and moving up into the big leagues.

About nine-fifteen, she called Jim Mackie's office and asked for an appointment with him. She told Claire, his admin assistant, that the nature of the requested meeting was personal. She was given a slot at eleven-thirty, only because Claire knew she and Jim were old friends.

The morning was a waste. She could barely focus on work. Finally, wired and anxious, her scheduled time arrived and she rode the elevator up to the forty-sixth floor.

The word "sumptuous" came to mind when she looked at the corner office where he spent his workday. Floor to ceiling windows let in the light and the Manhattan skyline, blocked on one side by the looming Empire State Building. An expensive-looking Persian rug covered part of a polished wood floor that looked like poured honey.

His Louis XVI desk stood at an angle on the rug. Two matching visitor's chairs faced it, straight-backed and stiff-legged.

If Jim wanted you comfortable, he directed you instead to the sitting area in front of the tall windows. An Italian leather sofa faced two butter-soft black leather chairs, placed casually around a cherry wood coffee table. A credenza nearby always held an ice bucket, a silver water pitcher, and crystal glasses. The stronger stuff was kept inside the credenza.

When Jessie walked in, Jim rose from his desk, crossed the long room toward her, and took her hand. He was in his sixties, short and round, but perfectly dressed and coifed in a manner befitting both his age and his station in life. He wore a double-breasted gray wool suit with fine pinstripes, a white shirt with understated diamond cufflinks, a matching tie-tack restraining a silk tie that added a splash of vibrant purple to the ensemble, highly polished black shoes. His short hair was silver. An understated cologne clung to him, smelling as traditional and masculine as brandy and cigars at a men's club. He held Jessica's right hand between both of his, which were small and soft.

He had occasionally performed as Santa Claus for company Christmas parties that included the children of employees, and Jessie suddenly flashed on him, wearing a cotton beard and the traditional red suit, eyes shining with a distinctly Santa-like twinkle, sitting with a kid on his lap and a crowd gathered around his chair.

"It's so good to see you, Jessica," he said. "You've been a stranger."

"Well, I have work to do, you know...a few floors down. In the salt mines."

"You'll be up here in no time," Jim Mackie said. His voice was as silky as the tie. He had a gift for acting like he had known you forever, listened enraptured to your every word, and cared what you had to say. It had taken him far in the banking world, Jessie knew.

They exchanged a few pleasantries, and then moved to the sofa and chairs by the window. Jessie was glad he'd opted for comfort, but felt oddly exposed sitting in front of the huge expanse of glass. By now, he could tell there was something wrong, and his jovial, Santa Claus expression changed to one of concern.

"Is something wrong, Jessica?" he asked. He always used the formal version of her name—had, in fact, since she was a child. He was almost the only one who did.

"As a matter of fact, Jim, I think there might be."

"What is it? Anything I can help with?"

"I sure as hell hope so. I'd hate for you to think I only come to see you when there's a problem," she began. "But I don't know where else to go with this one."

"You can tell me anything, Jessica." He mimed pulling a zipper across his lips. "In absolute confidence."

"I know, Jim, and I appreciate it," she said. "This is just..."

A cloud crossed his kindly face, the sort of face the word "avuncular" was coined to describe. "It's bad, isn't it?"

"I think so, yes. I think it's bad. It's a customer of mine, a very wealthy customer. I think...I think he's a crook."

Jim was quiet for a long moment, head bowed, rocking ever so slightly on the sofa, fingers pressed together at his lips. Just at the point where she started to wonder if he'd forgotten she sat there, he opened his eyes, put his hands on his knees, leaned forward. "So how bad is it? Are we laundering for him?"

"The idea has crossed my mind."

"What about KYC?"

That old devil *Know Your Customer*.

"I didn't," she admitted. "I don't. I mean, I thought I knew him, but I didn't check him out as...thoroughly as I might have."

"Why not?"

"He was recommended. Highly. And he was already with the bank, I just took him over."

"From who?"

Jessica stared at the floor. "Barbara Slonaker."

"Hence your problem," Jim said, grasping it right away. "She's your boss. She recommends a client to you, you take him on without checking him out, then you find out he's up to something unsavory and you're concerned about your position. As well as the bank's, of course."

Nail on the head. She smiled a little. For the first time in about fourteen hours.

"That pretty much sums it up, Jim."

"First of all, don't worry. I know, I know, Jessica, this is a serious and delicate situation. But don't worry. We'll make sure this doesn't bite you on the rump, no matter what."

"Thank you."

"And at the same time, we'll do whatever we can to make sure it doesn't bite MetroBank on its significantly larger rump."

"That would be good too."

"Very important, if we're all to keep our jobs, right?"

"Always a concern of mine."

Jim Mackie rose, went to stand before the window. He looked out at Manhattan like he owned it. Which, come to think, maybe he did. The longer Jessie spent around money the more she understood that she'd always been naïve about it; about how much a person could amass, and what could be bought.

"What makes you think this client is a 'crook,' as you put it?"

"I'd rather not say, if that's all right," she hedged. "I've had a weird feeling about him for a while. He moves a lot of cash, through some pretty roundabout means. I've asked him where the cash comes from, and he's been evasive. I mean, he would answer the question, but never very specifically. The 'here and there' kind of answer."

"I know it well."

"So anyway, now I've become pretty convinced he's not on the up and up."

"Can you prove it? In a court of law?"

"I...I'm not sure. I might be able to. Would I have to?"

"You are more familiar with the comings and goings of his money than anyone, with the possible exception of him, Jessica. If you can't prove that he's engaged in criminal money laundering, no one else will be able to."

"My concern is that the money is derived from illegal activities, Jim. I mean, I haven't broken the law in how I've manipulated it."

"Of course not. And you're not legally at fault unless you know the money is dirty. If you just think that maybe it's dirty, that's a different story."

"If I suspect that it might be—"

"Then you're supposed to tell someone. Which you have done."

"I haven't even told you who it is."

"All right." He turned around to face her, hands clasped behind his back. Behind him, a pigeon fluttered to a landing on the window ledge. "Who is it?"

She hesitated. No going back now, she thought. But she had come this far, so what the hell. "His name is Richard Steele."

"Of course," Jim said. He would certainly recognize the name, Jessie knew. Everyone in the bank knew the names of people with Steele's kind of account activity. Even the tellers downstairs probably knew him by sight. "Steele. He was with Barbara for, what, three years or so?"

"A little over," Jessica said. "I've had him for almost eleven months."

"I'll do some poking around, Jessica," he said. "Quietly. Discretion assured. We're good at this sort of thing. MetroBank, I mean. Trust me. You will be fine."

"I really appreciate that, Jim."

"The least I can do, Jessica. Barbara's a hell of a banker, and if she felt okay about Steele, I'm sure he's aboveboard. I'll let you know personally, in a few days, what I find out. I'm ninety-nine percent sure everything will be copacetic, and you'll continue on as his Relationship Manager until you get promoted out of the spot, just as Barbara did. But if you're uncomfortable with him, for any reason, just let me know and I'll have his account reassigned."

"I'll go along with whatever you decide, Jim," she said.

"That's fine, Jessica. You know I'll take care of you."

He put his hands out, helped her out of the chair. She almost hated to give up the feel of the leather. But she felt a hundred pounds lighter, with the weight of this thing off her shoulders. He walked her to the door.

"Got plans for the holidays this year?"

"Nothing firm yet," she said.

"Why don't you come over for Christmas dinner?" he asked. "The kids are coming in, and Marjorie would love to see you."

"The kids" were older than Jessica. "That sounds lovely, Jim," she said. "Can I let you know in a week or so?"

"Any time until Christmas Eve," he said. "The door is always open."

He gave her a hug, properly avuncular, she thought, and a light, dry kiss on the cheek. "Thanks, Jim," she said. "For everything."

Chapter 3

As the elevator dropped, Jessica's spirits fell with it.

Jim had made her feel better, in his usual comforting fashion. But this wasn't the end of it. Jim Mackie hadn't been in the parking garage. For all his soothing words, he didn't know about what she had seen Richard Steele do.

Nobody did.

She hoped she could keep it that way.

The longer she went without telling the police, the worse it would look for her. She had hoped that part would take care of itself. Then she thought that somehow, magically, Jim Mackie would know and deal with it. Neither of those had happened, but she had promised Jim that she'd let the whole matter lie while he investigated.

If she kept that promise, she couldn't go to the cops. If she didn't, she might be kissing her career goodbye, not to mention destroying her relationship with one of her oldest friends.

She skipped lunch. She had been useless all day. Now she forced herself to concentrate on her work, and she managed to forget, for stretches of up to fifteen minutes at a time, the problems that weighed on her.

At six, she thought about leaving for the night. But before she did, she knew the Steele issue would continue to plague her into the hours when she should be sleeping. She had tried to avoid it during the day, but it couldn't be avoided forever.

She went to her filing cabinet, slid open the third drawer from the top. There were several files for Richard. She pulled out the first one, containing all the original documents Barbara had handed over and her notes from her initial meetings with Steele. The second was the first three months of their relationship. She took that one too, slipped both files into her Gucci briefcase. From her desktop, she downloaded all the electronic records of his account onto a flash drive, and dropped that into the briefcase as well.

Jessie didn't think she had actually committed any crimes. But the law was a tricky beast, not as cut-and-dried as one might like it to be. And while she believed her activities on Steele's behalf to be totally legal, a prosecutor might be able to shade them differently. In the end, what was okay and what wasn't could be decided by a criminal jury composed of people who knew no more about banking than how to balance their checkbooks. If that.

Would they understand how and why you could deposit millions of dollars into commingled accounts, mixing that money, more or less literally, with the money of hundreds or even thousands of other people, and then move it out again, effectively erasing any trail of ownership? Would they appreciate that an individual could create a corporation in the Cayman Islands, the directors of which were other corporations also created by that individual, none of whom had to be identified to authorities in the United States? Was there a way to convince a jury that not only was it legal, but there were legitimate reasons one might want to hide his money in such a convoluted fashion? Or would it automatically look criminal to the jury? Rich people doing their best to abuse the system and rip off the tax man.

Hell, if she were a juror with an overdrawn account she'd probably convict herself.

She would go over the files tonight, at home, with an objective eye, and try to find any instances in which she might have inadvertently broken the law as she understood it.

She thought herself innocent, but she would sleep better if she knew she really was.

She left the office at twenty after six. In the marble elevator lobby, she said goodnight to John, the watchman, and headed through the big glass doors onto Fifth. The city was already decorated for Christmas, and she always enjoyed the store windows, the energy, the bustle of this time of year. Maybe she'd visit Macy's on the weekend.

Her subway station was just a block away. She descended the steep flight of stairs into the city's humid underbelly, trying to watch all the people carrying packages, dressed for the cold in heavy overcoats, mufflers, and hats, in hopes that it would take her mind off the Steele matter. One of those ever-present, unshaven men stood by the wall with a priest's collar on, though at a glance you could tell he'd never been a priest. He had a bucket in his hand. Collecting money for some not-quite-specified charity. Jessie had dropped pocket change into such buckets before, earning herself a muttered "God bless," but today she was distracted and just glanced at him. He met her glance with pale gray eyes that carried a hint of madness, and she looked away.

On the crowded train platform, she stood near the edge. Doing so never failed to take her back to her childhood, and early subway rides with her parents. She loved the rumble of the approaching train, the way it pushed air ahead of itself as it sped through the tunnel, a physical sensation of wind shoving into her that sometimes preceded even the light from the train's nose.

She felt it now, tasted the ozone-flavored air, and closed her eyes to let the sensation take her back. Then she felt another push, this one from behind. The kind of feeling you get when someone bumps into you, unaware of how much space her purse or his shopping bag really takes. But it didn't go away, the person didn't back off, and it wasn't a bag, it was a hand, pressed against the small of her back, and she opened her eyes and tried to turn her head but then there was a stronger shove and she was going over.

* * *

Barbara Slonaker sat on the couch in Jim Mackie's big office, her knees pulled up with her arms wrapped around them, bare feet on the soft leather. Her pumps lay on the carpet below.

Jim rushed through the small talk and got to the point. "Did you know that Jessie Cutler's been to see me?"

Barbara could feel her jaw drop. "About what?"

"I think you know the answer to that one, Barbara," he said.

"Fuck," she said.

"Yes," Jim said. "Exactly my reaction."

"What'd you tell her?"

"What could I? I told her we'd take care of it. I told her that the bank was used to taking care of delicate issues involving our larger depositors."

"Which is true."

He nodded. He was sitting over at his big desk, and Barbara wished he would move away from it. It was so far away; when he sat there and she was over here, she always felt like the loser in some kind of vague power struggle.

She was, she guessed. Not many people could make her feel that way, but Jim Mackie was one of them. That was one reason she had kept her old office, instead of moving up to this floor. It was, she recognized, a passive-aggressive kind of reaction to her promotion, but it was the only kind she could think of, the only way to maintain her identity and her power base.

If she were on the same floor as Mackie, nobody would look twice at her. Downstairs, she remained a big wheel, just because she had chosen to stay with the others. The common people.

Her subjects.

"Which is true. As far as it goes, anyway. I'm sure that what I have in mind is not the same thing that she has in mind."

"God," she laughed. "I hope not."

"I wanted to make sure that you're aware, Barbara. Until this is cleared up, one way or another—and I believe it's being cleared up right about now—you'll need to watch your step. If you have any documents that might incriminate you in any way, shred them. Burn the shreds. Wipe your hard drive. You need to be cleaner than clean for the next little while."

Cleaner than clean, she thought. Tough to pull off. All anyone had to do was look at her rent, her credit card bills, and her tax returns to know she was living far beyond her salary.

"Will I—will the bank—be under any official scrutiny?"

"I don't think so, Barbara, but I really can't be sure yet," Jim said. "I expect we'll be done with Ms. Cutler by tomorrow. She might decide to accept what I told her—that we would deal with it—and we'll all go back to business as usual. She might not. She might not even have that opportunity. This is a rough patch, Barbara, that's all. Stay on your feet and you'll skate past it."

Which was easy for Jim Mackie to say. He hadn't brought Richard Steele into the bank in the first place. His name wasn't on the documents. He hadn't opened offshore accounts for Steele. He wasn't the fucking treasurer of Cielo Holdings, for God's sake.

It was Barbara, not Jim Mackie, who was required by law and MetroBank policy to exercise due diligence when bringing a customer in. She had applied due diligence, all right—she had diligently looked at Steele's ass, at how he looked naked, at how he made her feel beautiful and desirable when he made love to her.

She had met Steele at a party. A very A-list party. Two major editors-in-chief, from Harper's and Cosmo, were there. The Governor sent his regrets and his wife. A couple of Cuomos, a Clinton, one of the lesser Kennedys, two former mayors, and Lady Gaga. The Donald made a brief appearance.

And she had wangled an invite. Barbara Slonaker, middle-class girl from Rhode Island, high school honor student who had never made the cheerleading squad or student government, who had gone to a state university instead of an Ivy League school, had managed to get invited to this upper west side penthouse bash.

She made the most of it. Maxed out a credit card for new clothes, and ran up another one with a purse and shoes. Her hair was perfection. She worked out with a personal trainer once a week, but in the two weeks before the party she upped it to four times, so the skin her new dress revealed would be tight and toned.

And at the party, she was introduced to Richard Steele. Who, she was told, was very very wealthy.

She knew the expression about charming the pants off someone. She had never experienced it in the flesh.

As it were.

But she did, that night. She would have jumped him there in the penthouse, but he, at least, had enough presence not to move on her right there.

In the limo afterwards, though, she had unzipped him, taken his cock out of his black tuxedo pants with the stripe down the leg, and gone down on him. It occurred to her that she'd never had someone this rich in her mouth.

After, they talked about banking.

He needed a new bank. One that was aggressive.

She laughed. "I'm that," she said.

"Can't argue," Richard Steele said. "I also need a bank that's flexible. Willing to bend a little."

She pointed to the floor in front of his seat. "I wasn't flexible," she said, "I never would have fit down there."

"Are we talking about you, or MetroBank?" he asked.

"Honey," she said. "I *am* MetroBank."

He took her back to his place, a penthouse apartment on Central Park East that made the party penthouse look shabby. This, he explained, was his town home. He also had an estate in the Hamptons, and another in Miami Beach.

Barbara had never known money before. Not this kind of money. As a banker, you got used to money as an intellectual concept. The idea of money. You moved it around, you invested it, you hoped it would grow.

But only those at the top of the game got to experience it first-hand. The power of it. The things you could buy, if you had enough.

You could buy anything.

Anyone.

Absolutely, she decided, without fail. Anything and anyone.

All it took was the right price.

Hers was lower than she'd ever expected.

And she didn't feel bad about that at all.

Chapter 4

Jessie wore inch-and-a-half heels that day, and they probably saved her life.

Because when she went off-balance, the right heel snapped off, and she dropped an inch and a half on that side before she went over the edge of the platform. Instead of falling as far out as she might have, the angle of her descent was almost straight down.

Seeing the train's light as she fell.

Seeing the driver, fear etched on his face, behind the glass.

Seeing the track rushing toward her.

Jessie put her arms out, purse and briefcase slung over her shoulders. The briefcase was slipping; it landed before she did and absorbed some of the impact. Her arms and legs absorbed most of the rest, though not enough to keep her face from striking the rail.

She'd have a bruise on her right cheekbone.

It wouldn't mean a thing if she didn't move.

Give the mortician something to practice his makeup skills on, maybe.

She pushed off with arms and legs, not caring where she went.

Slammed herself, hard, against the concrete base of the platform. Flattened there.

The train shot past.

Wind-whipped, bruised, cut, aching, she watched it pass and jerk to a stop. Crap flew into her eyes from the tracks.

She *loved* the pain, because it meant she was alive.

Now she could hear again—the shrill screech of the train, shouts from the platform, blood rushing in her own ears. She couldn't stand up—there wasn't enough space between the train and the platform. She stayed where she was, pressed against the cold, hard concrete, and waited.

The train backed away.

It couldn't have taken more than a minute or two, but it seemed like hours. Finally, it was clear of her, and she was able to stand, dust herself off, check herself. Nothing broken.

Onlookers reached down for her. A transit cop, gray mustached, belly hanging over his belt, crouched at the edge. She took his strong hands and he hauled her back up.

"Were you standing too close?" he asked.

"I was pushed," Jessie said when she got her breath back. "Deliberately pushed."

"Are you sure? Did you see who did it?"

"No," she said. Then thought about it. Had she seen anyone?

Panic had erased all memory of what had happened before she fell. Was pushed, she corrected herself.

"You okay, lady?" the cop asked her. "Need to see a doctor?"

"Bruised," she said. "Embarrassed. Not hurt, though."

"Good, I'm glad. Let's go into the office and you can file a report. Do you think you see whoever might have pushed you?"

She scanned the crowd, uncomfortable at being the center of attention. She just wanted out of there.

That wasn't happening, though. This guy was doing his job, going by the book. She should have just said she fell. But she had insisted that she'd been pushed, and that ratcheted his responsibility up a few notches.

His office was tiny, cramped, barely room for her legs when she sat in the gray metal chair in front of his gray metal overflowing desk. He'd fallen behind in his paperwork, if the stacks on his desk were any indication. How, she wondered, could a transit cop generate so much paper? A small coffee pot sat on a hot plate on a corner of the desk, black tarry-looking stuff cooking at the bottom. The little room smelled like burned coffee.

She was surprised the hot plate hadn't ignited the stacks of paper.

He asked her questions off a form, she answered. He copied down what she said, verbatim, as far as she could tell, on a different form. Explained some of the paperwork.

There was nothing she could tell him that would possibly help. He said there might be video, but then there might not be. It was rush hour, the platform was crowded, there might be no way to distinguish whose body parts were whose on the screen.

Finally, he promised to let her know the results of the investigation and escorted her upstairs to a waiting police car he had called. Two officers sitting inside. She got into the back, and the transit cop shut the door behind her. No handles on the inside, she noticed, and a heavy metal screen between her and the cops in front.

"Where to, lady?" the driver asked her.

She gave her address. "Some cab," she said. "But where's the recorded seat belt message?"

"We don't bother with that," the officer in the passenger seat said. "We just arrest you if you don't buckle up."

Jessie buckled.

They rode the rest of the way in near silence. The driver asked a couple of questions about her ordeal, but she answered in mono-syllables, and they realized she didn't want to talk about it.

But her mind was racing, and she was pretty sure she had figured out who pushed her.

Not *who*, exactly. She had never seen him before today. But she knew the face. Thinking about it, she realized she had seen a man on the street, before she went down to the subway, when she had been watching the shoppers and business people out on Fifth Ave.

Then she had seen him again, close to her in the crush of people on the platform.

And when she had come back up from the tracks, he had been gone. Most of the people were still there—the train had backed up without opening its doors, so they hadn't had anywhere to go, and anyway, everyone wanted to see if she was okay or smeared all over the tracks.

But this guy was gone.

He had a baby face, she remembered. Big brown eyes with thick lashes. Soft round cheeks, round chin. Curly brown hair, cut to a medium length. Wearing a camel trench coat.

It could have been a coincidence—or a series of them. Sometimes you notice a person, and then you notice him again.

But she didn't think so.

She would remember him if he turned up in the future.

She didn't mention him to the cops. Keeping secrets from the police was becoming a regular habit, she realized. The problem with keeping one—they multiplied.

Fucking rabbits, secrets were.

* * *

The squad car stopped across from her building. The cop in the passenger's seat got out and opened the door for her. "Thanks for the lift," she said as she got out. Her legs didn't feel steady.

"You gonna be okay from here, ma'am?"

Ma'am. The cop was almost a decade younger than her. When had that happened? She had once dated a guy who told her that he felt old when he realized that the centerfolds in *Playboy* were young enough to be his daughters. This was like that.

She had broken up with the guy, just because the whole image creeped her out.

"I'm fine, thanks," she said.

The officer climbed back into the car, and it pulled back into traffic.

Her building looked like it was a long way off. All the way across the street.

And she felt like she was being watched.

Paranoid, Jess, she told herself. Get a grip.

When there was a break in the traffic she crossed. Mark, her building's doorman, saw her coming and a smile split his dark face.

She felt better. Mark had been a fullback in college, down at Auburn. Never made pro. He had returned to New York, and found a job as a doorman. Been at this building for seven years. His friendly bulk was comforting. As long as Mark was on the job, she'd be fine here.

"How you doing, Miz Cutler?" he asked as she reached the sidewalk.

"Just fine, Mark. You?"

"Couldn't be better. Got that Christmas spirit, you know?"

"That's great, Mark," she said. "I'm trying. Maybe in a week or so."

"Don't wait too long." He opened the door. "Christmas'll come and go before you know it."

"I'll keep that in mind, Mark. Good advice."

"I'm full of that," he said. "You have a good night, Miz Cutler."

Inside the lobby, Jimmy sat behind a polished wood counter. He had been with this building for as long as any tenant could remember, as familiar and stable as the counter itself. "Evening, Jess," he said. "Got a package for you."

"A package?" she asked.

"Christmas is coming, after all." He placed a brown paper-wrapped box on the counter.

"So I keep hearing."

She recognized the label—tea she had ordered from a catalog. Coffee in the morning, tea at night. Herbal. She tucked it under one arm and crossed to the elevator.

"Thanks, Jimmy," she said. "Have a good night."

"Same to you, Jess," he said.

The elevator doors opened and she stepped inside. They slid closed with a comforting *thump*, the car gave a small, familiar lurch, and started up.

The fourth floor hallway was the same as ever. Across from the elevator, a small table held a pot of artificial flowers. A gilt-framed mirror hung on the wall behind the flowers.

The wallpaper was peeling in spots, but clean, and the floor was vacuumed. She felt good here. At home.

Safe.

Jessica put her key into the deadbolt, turned it. It didn't offer any resistance. Had she forgotten to lock it? She didn't have any specific memory of locking it that morning, but it was long-ingrained habit. Still, she had been more than a little preoccupied. She inserted another key into the knob, turned that, heard the usual click as it unlocked. She pushed the door open with the box and went in.

The apartment smelled *wrong*.

Someone had been here.

Chapter 5

Jessie stood in the doorway, listening and smelling—hard to do both at once, but she tried—until she convinced herself that whoever had been inside wasn't any more. Certain enough, she stepped inside, flipped on the lights, closed the door.

Was it a cliché to think that the place smelled like a man had been inside? Vaguely musky. Maybe someone who smoked, although he hadn't been smoking inside the apartment.

Whatever it might be, it definitely wasn't her own familiar scent. Her place usually smelled a little like lavender, sometimes like coffee if she didn't rinse the breakfast dishes sufficiently. Never like this.

She gave the front room a quick scan, and didn't see anything that had been disturbed. But no way there hadn't been someone in here, presumably looking for something...and not something easily pawned, since her stereo, TV, and MacBook were still here.

There were things out of place, though. Only slightly—whoever had searched the apartment had taken care. Drawers were closed, closet doors shut. But she had three antique suitcases stacked up, that she used as an end table. A piece of heavy glass protected the suitcases, and there was a dried flower arrangement in a vase on the glass. She kept it so that an Indian blanket, red at the center and white at the tips, faced toward the couch. She liked its suggestion of warmth on these cold winter nights.

Now, however, the Indian blanket faced the wall.

Without warning, tears welled in her eyes. The fear she had been bottling up all day was suddenly unleashed. She went into her bathroom, pulled a handful of tissues from the box.

Sat down on the closed toilet and sobbed.

After a while, she pulled herself together. Thought about why she was so upset.

Decided it made perfect sense.

She had witnessed a man she considered a friend, or at least a close acquaintance, murder several people. Someone had tried to kill *her*, for God's sake.

And now, someone had invaded her sanctuary, the place in the world she felt the most secure. Looking for what? The records of Steele's transactions that she still carried in her briefcase?

Or maybe this had nothing to do with Steele. New York wasn't the crime-ridden city it had once been, but it still had more than its share. She might just have been the latest victim of a prowler, looking for cash or dope. Or a rapist, disappointed that no one was home.

She blew her nose. Shook her head. Random crime was one thing, but she didn't like coincidences. The gunfight, the subway incident, now this? Too hard to believe they were unconnected. If someone had searched her filing cabinet at the office, they would have noticed those Steele files were missing. The next place logical place to look would be her apartment. They would have had to work fast, but there had been plenty of time while she was in with that transit cop.

She had thought she could trust Jim Mackie—her father had mentored him, back in the day, and Jim, then Barbara Slonaker, at Jim's direction, had done the same for Jessie. She had known him most of her life. But for things to have happened so fast, he must have tipped somebody off. She hadn't spoken to anyone else about Steele. Had, in fact, intentionally dodged phone calls and avoided e-mails, since she didn't want to accidentally say anything to friends.

It had to be Jim. And if it was, how high in MetroBank did it reach?

She touched the case of the laptop. It was warm. Whoever had been here had powered it on. But there would have been nothing there to find, she realized. She had no notes here, no files, no records of anything pertaining to Richard Steele.

Having drawn a blank didn't guarantee that the prowler—or prowlers—wouldn't come back. Didn't mean the place wasn't being eyed right now. She had felt like someone was watching her get out of the police car, right? They had been keeping tabs on her, were right there at the subway to shove her under a train.

This had been her safe place. Mark outside, Jimmy at the desk. Whoever got in here got past them.

Or had their help.

She tipped them at Christmas, spoke to them as if they were friends. But what would it take to get one, or both, to betray her? A hundred bucks? More, because they'd be risking their jobs. A thousand? Five?

Nothing, to a man with Richard Steele's millions.

Pocket change. Walking-around money.

For the first time, she realized how serious a mistake it had been not to tell the police right away. She should have whipped out her cell and dialed 911 while the shooting was going on. By keeping quiet, by figuring it would explain itself away, she had made herself part of it. And it was bigger than she was.

Someone had tried to kill her, and failed.

Searched her apartment, and come up empty.

They would try again. Could be on their way right now, if they had her under surveillance.

She had to get out of there.

She went into her bedroom. This was the biggest room in the apartment, which was why she fell in love with the place in the beginning. When you walked in, there was a small kitchen on the right with a pass-through counter into a good-sized living room. Off to the left, the bathroom and her bedroom, which was longer than the living room and kitchen combined, and had windows facing onto 84th or, looking straight down, onto the low roof of the laundry room, which opened off the second floor.

Barbara had promised that within a year she would be making enough money to buy a much nicer home. Jessie had been looking forward to that—had worked her butt off to get to that position, in fact.

When her dad had been in the business, when he had brought Jim Mackie up, bankers were reasonably well-paid professionals, on a par with doctors and lawyers. Since then, things had changed. Some bankers, doctors, and lawyers could become ridiculously wealthy. In her world, if one wasn't grasping for the pot of gold at the end of the rainbow, it meant she wasn't trying hard enough.

She had always expected that she would miss this apartment, this huge, bright bedroom, when she moved on. But she had expected that she would move on, just the same.

Just not quite in this fashion.

No time to mourn now, though. She grabbed the most important and practical clothes she could think of—jeans, T-shirts, underwear, one nice skirt and top, some toiletries—and shoved them into a backpack and the Nike gym bag she carried to the health club. Carried them into the living room and packed her laptop and accessories.

Fortunately, packing was fast because she knew where everything was. She was neat—"meticulous," her last boyfriend had called her, though to him that had been an insult. She liked things to be a certain way. The same organizational skills that made her a good banker allowed her to maintain her home—a place for everything, everything in its place, the saying went.

Not that she had many things that needed places. Her philosophy was that until you owned, you should never have more stuff than you could move in a single day with a small truck. Stay loose, keep it light.

She made a good living from MetroBank. But she didn't put the money into acquiring possessions. She saved much of it, used the rest for various luxuries. To eat well at nice restaurants. To have regular spa days and facials, and to have her hair done by the best once a month. To have a great apartment, and a cleaning woman who came by twice a week to dust and vacuum it. To own the best of everything—expensive furniture, expensive clothes—but not too much of anything.

It had occurred to her that her theory of possessions could also be applied to her theory of relationships. Keep it simple. Keep it loose.

Never hook up with a man you couldn't leave behind at a moment's notice. If it looked like you were getting too attached, cut him loose.

She had lived her whole adult life like that. Sometimes she wondered if she should maybe examine that attitude. But then...

Why bother?

You left them or they left you. Better to be the one who could walk away at any time.

That's where the power was.

She kicked off her dress shoes, stuck them in the gym bag, took running shoes from the closet. Peeled off the dress she'd been wearing, tossed it into the hamper. Pulled on jeans, a T-shirt, a bulky cable-knit sweater from Scotland over that. Put on the running shoes. She tied them, made a circle of her room. Lots of things she felt she couldn't live without, but she wasn't saying goodbye forever, just until this whole mess was straightened up. She'd be back.

From the closet, she took a heavy leather jacket, flannel-lined, and put it on. Checked to be sure her lined leather gloves were in the pockets. She slung the backpack across her back, hung the gym bag over her shoulder with the strap between her breasts, put her purse on the other shoulder and the Gucci briefcase in her right hand.

And stepped outside, toward the elevator.

And stopped.

If anyone was watching the place—or if Jimmy or Mark were involved—they would see her come out the elevator. She looked like a woman on the move, so they'd never let her shake them.

There had to be another way out. There was some underground parking, but Jessie didn't own a car, and the entrance was right next to the front door anyway. If she walked out there, she would be just as visible as if she had taken the elevator.

She went to the staircase, pushed open the door, and started down. Trying not to clomp too loud. When she reached the door with 2 painted on it, she went through. No one in sight. Halfway down the hall, there was another door. The laundry room. She could hear a dryer going, but when she cracked the door, she saw that the room was empty. She went in.

The laundry room was built by itself on top of the lobby roof. It was an afterthought in a building that had no laundry facilities when it was built, set off here where it wouldn't take up any rentable space. People on the second floor appreciated it because it had no common walls with their apartments, so anyone washing clothes at odd hours wouldn't disturb them.

And there was a window at the far end of it, looking out onto the flat rooftop.

The window had been painted shut at some point. Jessie pushed it, hammered at it with the ball of her hand. Finally, the paint cracked, and she was able to shove it open with a loud creak. Couldn't be heard over the dryer's racket, she was sure. She dropped her bags out onto the gravel rooftop, then climbed up onto a dryer, stuck her head through the window.

She couldn't see anyone.

She went out, stinging her palms and knees on the gravel.

Crossed the roof, to the 84th side. Walking as quietly as she could, so as not to alert Jimmy.

Jimmy's apartment was on this side, but no doorway opened into the public areas of the building. This was her best bet to avoid anyone who might be watching for her.

She waited in the darkness on the roof as a couple of cars passed by. When they were gone and the street quiet, she shrugged into the backpack, kept her purse with her, tossed the gym bag and briefcase down to the sidewalk.

It sounded like cannon fire when they hit. She was amazed no one came outside to see.

But no one did.

She lowered herself off the rooftop, hanging at the extreme limits of her fingers. Still several feet from the ground. She hoped she didn't break something, making all this effort for naught.

She let go.

Landed on the balls of her feet, then lost her balance and went down.

On the same stinging palms. First the subway, then the roof. They were taking a lot of abuse today.

But she was alive, so what the hell?

She gathered her things, ran to Broadway.

Hailing a cab, she asked for Times Square.

If you have to lose yourself, she figured, why not do it where there were a lot of people to hide among?

She was right. The Square was crowded with shoppers, tourists, theatre-goers. Everybody bundled up for winter. A sea of dark coats. She was just one more.

She felt better here, safer. No one would be able to find her here. No one would think to look—this wasn't a place she ever came, except on her way through to somewhere else.

She wandered into the big Virgin store, gazed blindly at CD cases while she tried to figure out what to do next. Staying outside overnight was not an option—she'd freeze.

Her instincts had been good, she thought. Running without warning, going someplace she didn't frequent. She had to stay on that track.

Let her feet lead her. She headed out of Times Square, down 43rd to 8th. Turned left. Hotel signs beckoned through the night, and she followed one. The Highland. Red letters shining in the dark.

Pretty tony name for a dump.

The desk clerk sat behind scratched Plexiglas. A small sign, written in ballpoint pen, was taped to the window: NO VISITORS. There was a slot at the bottom of the plastic for money or credit cards, and some slits in it to speak through.

The clerk didn't look like someone she would want to speak to.

Maybe fifty, fifty-five. The years showed in the pounds, the chins, the rolls around his middle. A balding fat man with a little boy's dirty face, wearing a stained blue shirt and watching a tiny television.

"I'd like a room," she said.

He looked at her. Under his gaze, she longed for a shower.

"Never seen you here before."

"I've never been."

"Room for the hour, or the night?"

"The night," she said. "Maybe a couple of nights."

Like hell.

"Room is fifty-five, plus a five buck key deposit," he said. "But here's the deal. You can have it for thirty-five, but you split everything you make with me. Ten bucks for everyone who goes up with you."

She pointed to the NO VISITORS sign. "What about that?"

"I can't read," he said, shoving a registration card under the window. "Can you?"

She took the card, wrote the name Jane Smith on it, and made up an address in Pittsburgh. Took sixty bucks from her wallet and pushed it back under.

"I'll pay the fifty-five," she said.

"Lemme see your I.D., Miss Smith," the man said.

"I lost it," she said. "What's the difference? You can't read."

"Forgot," he said.

She put another ten under the plastic. "Good enough?"

He fingered the bill, folded it, put it into the pocket of his stained shirt.

"Have a nice day." He dropped a key into the slot, and turned his attention back to his TV.

There was a number on the key: 201. She went through a glass door looking for an elevator, found a staircase instead. Started up.

At the top, two women looked down at her. Hookers. They wore long coats, in deference to the winter weather, but the coats were open, revealing short shorts, fishnet stockings, low cut tops. The black one had enormous breasts spilling out of hers. The white one was skinny, no curves, straight brown hair and a gap between her front teeth. Both were smoking.

Jessica started up. They watched her.

"Coffee break?" she said.

"Ooh, she a funny one," the black hooker said.

"Ain't she, though?" the white one said.

"Excuse me," Jessie said when she reached the top.

"You excused," the black one said. "You ain't plannin' to work here, are you?"

"Ummm, no," Jessie said. "I didn't have any intention of doing so."

"Damn straight," the white one said.

Jessica squeezed between them, catching a whiff of strong perfume mixed with smoke and booze.

"Believe me, ladies," she said. "This neighborhood is all yours."

"Got that right," the white one said. They were both still laughing when she closed the door of 201 and hung the chain lock on the inside.

If anyone could find her here, they deserved her.

The room was shabby. A threadbare yellow carpet barely covered the floor. There was a bed, with cigarette holes in the red cotton spread. A nightstand next to it with a yellow pages on the shelf. On the wall with the door in it, a scarred wooden dresser held a TV, which was bolted down. No telephone, but she had her cell.

She was sure there were cockroaches, unless they'd checked out on account of not having enough amenities. Or been chased away by the bedbugs.

She turned on the TV to drown out the sound of the whores laughing outside—they had been joined by friends—and sat on the sagging mattress. She slipped the Steele files out of the briefcase, booted up the laptop, and immersed herself in his finances.

He did enormous cash business. In seventeen cities—Tallahassee, Birmingham, Tuscaloosa, Athens, Atlanta, Savannah, Charleston, Charlotte, Greenville, Richmond, Arlington, Baltimore, Pittsburgh, Philadelphia, Atlantic City, Newark, and the Bronx—she and Barbara had set up systems so that people could make cash deposits, without showing identification. The deposits were never big ones, always less than five thousand dollars, but they were frequent and regular. This money went into a New York concentration account—also called a commingled account, because the net effect was the same as taking a big pile of cash and throwing it into a pot that also contained cash belonging to other MetroBank branches and other customers.

From there, the money was shunted into an account that bore only the name Cielo Holdings.

Cielo was a company incorporated in the Cayman Islands. Richard Steele was the only executive who actually existed, if you didn't count Barbara, whose treasurer role, Jessie believed, was largely titular. Steele's identity was protected under Caymanian law. To further complicate the trail, Barbara Slonaker had created, also in the Caymans, two shell companies that functioned as the "board of directors" for Cielo. Steele, the only actual officer, was supposed to hold an annual director's meeting in the Cayman Islands, but that meeting could be held by proxy. Barbara had arranged for Barrett Fowles, a local man, to act as "secretary," keeping such records as Caymanian law required to be kept, and Richard apparently had used him as a proxy to hold his annual meetings. Richard had mentioned him a couple of times, giving the impression that he liked and trusted Fowles. Jessie had seen no indication that Steele had ever been to the Islands in person.

After taking over the account, Jessie had opened two additional investment accounts for Cielo, in Paris and Geneva. The Paris account didn't bear the name of Richard Steele anywhere. The Swiss one had to, by law, but also by law the Swiss bankers were very close-mouthed about with whom they did business, and Steele's involvement was totally confidential.

The primary reason for a concentration account was to create a disruption of the paper trail. Funds were moved from the commingled account into one of the Cielo accounts in Paris or Geneva, and ultimately transferred to the Caymans, so they were exempt from taxation.

From there, Jessie didn't know where it went. Presumably he or his agent there cashed it out and shipped it to him in Manhattan so he could afford bullets, dinners, and body work on Jaguars. If it were her, she would have the Cayman branch of MetroBank pay it out in Cayman Island dollars, which she would take to another bank and convert to U.S. dollars in the form of bank checks. The bank checks would be written for small dollar amounts—a practice too-cutely called "smurfing" in the banking world—so that each deposit would be under reportable levels. Then she would deposit the bank checks in a third bank, and have that bank wire the funds to an institution in New York. Richard had never talked to her about that end of things, but if he had taken advice from Barbara, that's what he would have done.

Close to the edge of legality, she knew, but she believed she had not gone over the line.

Except by not knowing for certain where the cash came from, and not reporting the murders in the parking garage, and lying about being pushed from the subway platform. She didn't know if lying to the desk clerk was against the law, but it probably was.

Trouble behind, trouble ahead.

Chapter 6

Sleep wasn't happening.

Jessie watched TV late into the night, willing her eyes to close and her body to drift off.

The whores outside wandered away, came back with tricks, left again. The building never seemed quiet—there were always doors opening and closing, water running, laughter, arguments. At 2:14, by Jessie's watch, someone stomped down the hallway pounding on every second door and demanding cigarettes. He missed her door, but it hardly mattered.

A shitty night, overall.

By morning she had decided what she needed to do. She woke up, took a shower, dressed in her nice clothes. Outside, she found an Au Bon Pain, ordered a coffee and a scone.

If you're changing your identity, you might as well lose the old rituals, she thought.

No more Muffins Galore.

She drank two cups of coffee, finished the scone, then headed back outside. Stopped at a MetroBank ATM. She was going to get this mess cleared up, but it might take a couple of days to straighten out all the details and make the appropriate arrests, so she might be in hotels for another night or two. She withdrew two hundred dollars—should be enough, she hoped.

Then she went back to the Highland, relatively quiet now that the sun was up, brushed her teeth. She wanted to present herself as a solid citizen and a responsible banker—as solid and responsible as she could, running on almost no sleep, fear and caffeine.

Back outside, she hailed a cab.

Took it to 26 Federal Plaza. The Jacob K. Javits Federal Building. Lower Manhattan, between Worth and Duane.

This complex of Federal offices was the second largest Federal office building in the country, behind the Pentagon. Most United States government branches that had offices in Manhattan had them here. The building directory was almost mind-boggling, as was the line of immigrants along Worth, waiting to get in. Finally, she located the Treasury Department's Enforcement Division on the directory, and took the elevator up.

The reception area looked like that of any other large office, with the exception of the Treasury Department's seal on the wall behind the desk. A pleasant-looking young woman sat at the desk, talking quietly into a telephone headset. After a moment, she glanced up at Jessica.

"May I help you?" she asked.

What Jessie really wanted was FinCEN, the Financial Crimes Enforcement Network. FinCEN was the body that investigated money laundering. But FinCEN's offices, she knew, were in Vienna, Virginia. As a banker, she had on a few occasions filed SARs—Suspicious Activity Reports—with FinCEN.

However, FinCEN worked in concert with a number of investigative agencies—Treasury, the FBI, the IRS, even Interpol, to track the movements of ill-gotten cash. Employees of those agencies were assigned to FinCEN on a case-by-case basis. People here at the Treasury office would know how to reach someone connected with FinCEN locally.

Then, with the full weight of the United States government behind her, Richard Steele would no longer be her problem.

She only hoped MetroBank would survive. Without, she figured, Jim Mackie and Barbara Slonaker employed there.

"I hope so," she said. "I'd like to report some money laundering. Is there someone here associated with the Financial Crimes Enforcement Network?"

The woman blinked twice. Apparently her approach was a little more direct than most visitors off the street. "One moment, please," the receptionist said. "Please take a seat."

As Jessie settled into one of the visitor chairs, the receptionist spoke softly into her headset. She listened for a second, then took her headset off, pushed her chair back from the desk, and caught Jessie's gaze. "Please, come with me."

She led the way through a heavy wooden door into a hallway. Offices lined both sides of the hall, some doors open, others not. She ushered Jessie into a conference room. Big oak table, nine chairs, white erase board on the wall. Next to the door was a floor-to-ceiling strip of glass.

"Mr. Garland will be right with you," the receptionist said. "Just have a seat in here."

"Mr. Garland?"

"Jake Garland. He's assigned to FinCEN. He's very anxious to meet you."

The woman left, and Jessie sat in a fabric-covered chairs facing the doorway. She wondered why she hadn't been allowed to wait in the reception area, but figured that most people reporting major money-laundering schemes were probably happier out of sight of the general public.

She felt good. She felt like she had tried to do the right thing, but it had turned out wrong at every step. This time, though, she was doing what she should, and things would be taken care of. Things would—

—oh, shit.

She had glanced out the window, down the long hallway. Coming down the hall was a tall man with long, thin legs and a mass of copper curls on his head.

The stork.

She slid from her chair and stood right behind the door, so if he glanced inside he wouldn't see her.

If he came in, the door would slam right into her—but she'd be screwed then, anyway.

From this angle, she could see part of the hall but she couldn't see the stork. Another man stepped out of an office, between him and the conference room, and looked down the hall in the stork's direction.

"Jake," the man said. "Come in here a second. I got something I want to show you."

"Sure thing," the stork said. He went into the other man's office, and the door closed behind him.

There couldn't be two Jakes in the office, Jessica thought. And even if there were, she didn't want to take a chance on this one finding out about her. He didn't know there was a witness to the gunfight, but since he seemed to be in league with Steele, it was entirely possible that they'd figured out by now that it was the shootout that had tipped her off.

Probable, even. They wouldn't have taken such extreme measures to ensure her silence unless they guessed she had seen the gunplay.

She pulled open the conference room door, dashed up the hall to the big door into the reception area. The receptionist was on the phone, but looked up at Jessie with raised eyebrows. Jessie smiled and crossed to the elevator, punched the down button.

Waited, fingers tapping her skirt.

Waited.

The elevator bonged and a door slid open. The down light stayed illuminated, though. This one was going up.

Up was okay.

Better than staying where she was. As the doors moved together, she stepped between them.

The elevator closed, and started climbing.

She got off on fifty-four, with a clutch of other people. She let them disperse and then pushed the down button.

A different car came, after a minute. She got on.

This one made four stops, then reached the ground level.

She exited the elevator in the middle of a pack, stayed with the pack as well as she could to the street. A line of cabs waited there. She hailed one.

"Times Square," she said.

Familiar turf, now.

In the cab, she buckled her seat belt, put her head back, inhaled and exhaled a few times. The cab pulled away from the curb, shoved its way into traffic.

She risked a glance back toward the Javits Building.

And saw the stork, standing in front of the main doors, his neck twisting as he tried to look in every direction at once.

Jesus, she thought.

How big *was* this?

Richard Steele, she thought she could deal with. But the bank? The federal government?

Into what kind of miasma had she submerged herself?

She got out of the cab on Broadway at 42nd. Times Square was, as usual, busy and noisy and rank. Cars honking, pedestrians babbling, the shuffle of hundreds or thousands moving from where they were to where they needed to be.

Perfect.

She took her phone from her purse and dialed MetroBank. Punched the extension of Nicole Gedrick, whose office was across the hall from hers.

Nicole picked up right away. "This is Nicole Gedrick."

"Nic," Jessie said.

"Mother of God, Jessie, where the freak have you been?" Nicole asked. "What's going on?"

"Slow down, Nic. What do you mean?"

"What do you mean, what do I mean? You must know that *something's* going on. Where are you?"

"Stop asking that, Nic," she said. "I can't tell you that, I'm sorry. Just tell me what's been happening there."

"I don't have the slightest freaking clue. All I know is, the brass has been looking for you."

"The brass?"

"Barb. Mackie. Some of the other execs. They've been in your office a few times. They took your freaking hard drive, Jess."

"Shh! Don't use my name, Nic. They took my computer?"

"That's right. A couple of goons from security went in with Jim Mackie, and they unplugged it and took it away with them. I tried to ask Barb what was up, but she said it was a personnel matter and she couldn't discuss it with me. Have you been fired?"

"It's starting to sound that way," Jessie said.

"I don't know what you did," Nicole said, "and I don't want to know. But whatever it is, it sure has pissed off some people here."

"No shit. Thanks, Nic."

"Hey, what are you going to do?"

"Nicole," Jessica said. "I have no fucking idea."

* * *

But she did.

The idea had started germinating on the cab ride up from Federal Plaza.

When the government is involved in something crooked, she thought, who do you turn to?

The press.

And she was right here, in midtown Manhattan. Home of the press, in the United States, anyway.

Home of the Gray Lady. The ever-loving *New York Times*.

She walked. Thought about hailing another cab, but decided she could use the exercise. She was having pretty good luck with cabs lately, though.

She was having pretty good luck in general. She had spotted Jake Garland, AKA the stork, before he saw her—and then fate handed her a chance to get out of the building before he got to her.

She had survived being pushed in front of a rushing subway train.

She had missed whoever had been in her apartment.

She was still alive, and she still had the Steele files.

But, she thought, if luck was really on her side, she wouldn't be involved in all this to begin with. She never would have inherited Richard Steele as a customer, never would have gone to dinner with him, never would have followed him to that parking garage.

Luck. Right.

She hadn't realized how complicated it would be to get into the *Times*. She had seen newspaper offices on TV, but they never showed the reception area, the locked doors, the passes required to move between offices. Not bank-level security, but not too far from it, either.

"I'd like to speak to a reporter, please," she told a guy at the front desk.

"Which one?"

"I don't know. I have a story to report."

"Local? National? Sports? Weather?"

"National, I should think."

"Okay, that's a start. Politics? Environment? Business?"

"How about business?"

"Getting somewhere," he said. "Stocks? IPOs? E-commerce?"

"Is everyone a fucking specialist?" she asked. "I just want to talk to a business reporter."

"Just doing my job, lady," the guy said. "You don't know who you want, I'm supposed to figure it out."

"Isn't there some cub reporter you can send me to?" she asked. "Do they still have those, cub reporters?"

"Yeah, and they're all named Jimmy Olsen," the guy said. "I don't think that term is PC anymore."

After going around with the guy for another few minutes, she found herself seated in a cubicle, next to the desk of someone named Paul Fischer. If there were still cub reporters, Fischer was one. He was young, early twenties, Jessie figured, probably just out of journalism school. He had thick black hair, thick black glasses, probably thick black socks, though she couldn't see his legs. His blue cotton shirt hung loosely on his thin frame.

The room was huge, a warren of cubicles just like this one. They didn't contain the noise, the sound of hundreds of fingers clicking on keyboards, voices everywhere, printers grinding out copy. But she didn't mind the noise. Telling this to one person would be hard enough; she didn't want a crowd.

"Tell me a story, Ms. Cutler," Fischer said once they were settled in.

"How much time do you have?" she asked. "Never mind, that's a joke. Not a good one, I admit, but I'm pretty much fresh out of the good stuff."

"Do you mind if I record this?" he asked, tapping a silver digital recorder on his desk.

She did, but she couldn't say why. "I guess not," she replied. "Might as well get it right the first time."

"That's the way I look at it," he said, punching the REC button. "So."

"So." She took a deep breath. "I'm a banker. A relationship banker, at MetroBank. That means I work with very wealthy clients, handling their banking needs for them."

"Okay, and?"

"And I saw one of my clients kill some people."

"Fuck me," Paul Fischer said. He swallowed, then swallowed again. "I mean, *fuck* me. You mean, *kill?* Some rich motherfucker?"

"Exactly."

She continued, telling the whole story. Watching the killings, talking to Mackie, who promised to take care of her. Being pushed in front of a train. Her apartment being broken into. The stork being the FinCEN agent who was supposed to be investigating money laundering, not backing up a practitioner thereof in a gunfight.

She named names.

It took about forty minutes. She had to stop once, while he replaced a battery.

When she was done, he just looked at her.

"This is heavy," he said. Master of understatement. His small eyes blinked behind those thick glasses.

"Yes."

"I mean, really fucking heavy. This is Pulitzer territory, Jessica."

"I don't care what awards you win, Paul. I just want the story out there. I figure that's the only thing that'll save my life now—if the whole world knows it, then there's no reason to kill me."

"That's one way to look at it."

"There's another?"

"Well," he said. "You could figure that once the whole world knows, they'll still want to kill you just because you pissed them off."

"Thanks."

"No, thank *you*," Fischer said. "This could really put me on the map, you know? Make my name in the business."

"Welcome to the Fourth Estate."

"Do you know what it's like, to want to do something your whole life, and then finally get a crack at it, not knowing if you can really do it well, if you really have what it takes? Your whole life's goal in your grasp. That's what this could mean to me, Jessica. The difference between knowing and not knowing."

She knew. His was journalism. Hers was banking.

She had maybe just thrown hers away, giving him his.

She hoped he made the best of it.

* * *

She picked up Chinese takeout, carried it back to the Highland.

A scone had been the only food she'd eaten since a light lunch the day before. She had been moving too fast, been too scared and nervous to be interested in food. But now, she realized, she was hungry. Really hungry.

On her way back to the Highland, she stopped in a corner store, picked up some candy bars and soda, a small container of chocolate chip ice cream. Thought about a bottle of wine, but decided she might need her wits about her.

She stood in the aisle, holding the ice cream. There was no refrigerator in her room.

She'd just have to start with that, work her way to the cashew chicken and steamed rice.

The prostitutes were on the corner, gathered around a streetlight. Last night's pair, plus two others, both white, both dressed in the same style as the first. Evening casual, if by that you meant "lady of the evening." Jessie smiled at them as she approached. "Hello, ladies," she said.

"'Sup, girl," the big black one said. After Jessica passed, she heard whispers and then laughter. Didn't let it bother her.

After what she'd been through, she could deal with people talking about her behind her back. Even hookers.

As soon as she was locked in the room, she switched on the TV. Fischer had promised her that the beginning of his story on her ordeal would be in the paper the following morning. Just in case, though, she tried to catch a news program. Nothing on her, Steele, the Treasury Department, or anything else.

After a while, she took a couple sleeping pills, over-the-counter stuff, knowing that it was important to finally get some sleep.

Finally, she did.

Chapter 7

For the second time that week, she went for the newspaper first thing.

Well, not totally first, since delivery wasn't an option at the Highland. She dressed quickly in jeans and a sweater, ran a brush through her hair a few times, tugged on her leather jacket and went outside. She bought a paper from a news vendor, carried it to Au Bon Pain, bought coffee and scone, and sat at a table. Unfolded the paper. Scanned the front page.

Nothing.

Serious déjà vu.

The story wasn't in the paper. No mention of money laundering, Richard Steele, the Treasury Department, MetroBank.

On her second time through, she found the real story. Page three, bottom.

TIMES REPORTER FOUND SLAIN, the headline said. It hadn't caught her eye the first time. It did now.

The body of New York Times reporter Paul Fischer was found early this morning in a parked car near Battery Park, according to police officials. Mr. Fischer had apparently been shot twice, execution style, in the back of the head at close range. The shooting apparently happened shortly after midnight.

"Paul Fischer had a great career ahead of him," said Edward McCrae, his editor. "He showed enormous potential, and we are saddened to know that he will never have the opportunity to demonstrate that potential."

Mr. McCrae said he did not know what Mr. Fischer might have been doing in that neighborhood so late at night. He had just finished a series of articles on first-time investors who struck gold in the stock market, and hadn't been assigned to any new stories yet. "If he was working up something on his own, I don't know what it was," Mr. McCrae said. "He never went out without his notebook and recorder, but the police said neither one was on the body when they found him."

There was more, but Jessie couldn't bring herself to read about the mother and sister who survived him.

She had killed Paul Fischer, as surely as if she had pulled the trigger herself.

Whatever he was doing at Battery Park, it was related to the story she had sent him chasing after.

Maybe it was just a handy place to dump a body.

"You okay, lady?" the man behind the counter asked. She realized that her eyes were full of tears, and they were dropping off her cheeks onto the newspaper.

"Fine," she said. "Never better." She left the paper and went out into the street, to let the cold breeze dry her cheeks.

But it had started to snow, and instead the snowflakes dotted her cheeks, mixing with her tears. Jessie stood on the corner, looking up at the slate-gray sky hanging low and heavy over the rooftops of Manhattan.

She felt small, lost, alone.

She felt utterly beaten.

Chapter 8

She didn't know how long she'd been standing in the snow when her Blackberry began to ring.

Eventually, the sound penetrated her mental fog, and she fished it from her purse, answered it without checking the screen. "Hello?"

"Jessie, thank God."

Barbara Slonaker. One-time mentor and friend, and the person who had initiated Richard Steele's relationship with MetroBank and then passed it on to her. "Hello, Barbara."

"I've been so worried about you, Jessie. I called you at least a dozen times yesterday, when you didn't show up for work."

That much could be true—Jessie had left her Blackberry off most of the previous day, and she never taken the time to check voicemail, work or home. She would have to do that later.

"Are you sick?" Barbara continued. "Where are you?"

"Try to have more respect for me than that, Barbara," Jessica said. "We both know what's going on."

"I'm afraid I don't understand, Jessie. What do you mean?"

"You weren't there yesterday when my hard drive was taken? You haven't had any conversations about me with Jim Mackie? Or Richard Steele?"

"Should I?" Barbara asked. "You're beginning to worry me, Jess."

"Well, that's only fair, I guess, since I'm plenty worried myself."

"Why don't you meet me somewhere and tell me all about whatever this is? Maybe there's a way I can help you."

"I've had about all the help I can handle, Barb. I don't think so."

Barbara's tone changed; the concerned friend voice vanishing. "It's your call, Jessie. I can reach out to you, but if you don't take my hand there's nothing I can do for you. I don't think you know what you're playing with."

"Why don't you tell me?"

"Why don't you meet me, so I can?"

"Because I don't think I'd come out alive, Barbara. Good enough?"

She ended the call, and switched off the Blackberry. She was concerned about GPS, triangulating cell towers. Stuff she had seen on TV. She would have to be careful about using it.

Barbara's betrayal hurt as much as anything else. When Jessie was new at MetroBank, fresh out of school and dealing with people who thought she had won her job because of her father's legacy, Barbara had been one of the first to recognize her true potential. Barbara had taken Jessie under her wing, taught her most of what she really knew about money—not the technical aspects of banking but the personal ones. How to use money, how to relate to it, to get what was best for your clients and yourself. She taught Jessie how to dress, how to speak, how to act in social settings, in order to fit into her new, high stakes world.

And as Barbara moved up, she pulled Jessie along, fitting her into Barb's own slot. With clients like Richard Steele.

She's probably on Steele's payroll, Jessie thought, as well as MetroBank's. He bought her off to get her to overlook crucial aspects of her job and set up such an effective system of disguising the trail of his cash income. Turning dirty money into clean. Barbara would have known that she was helping him break the law, so she would have needed a good reason to do it.

The nice clothes, the sweet, the corner condo with the river view, the summer place on Cape Cod. MetroBank paid its execs well, but Barbara had started living like she was one of the multimillionaires whose money she took care of.

And now Barbara was dirty too. Laundering money. Breaking and entering. Murder.

How could someone change so much? How did you go from being an upper middle class girl growing up in Rhode Island, daughter of an insurance executive and a housewife, to being a major player in New York banking, to being a criminal—an accomplice, however indirect, to multiple killings? Was it just greed, or did it get more complicated than that?

Jessie would probably never know. She had hoped she was done with Barbara Slonaker forever. But she wasn't—Barbara wasn't going to rest as long as Jessie was walking around out there, knowing what she did about Steele, his money, his crimes. Neither was Steele, or Jim Mackie, or Jake Garland, the federal agent who was supposed to be regulating those sorts of activities.

Jessie had to get out of town, out of New York. There was no place that was safe here.

She had used an ATM just a block from the Highland, she realized. A MetroBank ATM. Stupid. They would be watching for that. They'd be watching for credit card use. She didn't know how big their net was, or how fast they could close it on her. But it was out there.

Could she survive this? She didn't have the street smarts. She was a sheltered girl from the suburbs, playing in the big leagues against guys who hurt people for a living.

She found a pay phone on a street corner, shut herself in the booth. Dug change from her wallet. No credit cards, from here out. Consulted her pocket address book and dialed a number.

Victoria Burrows was her oldest friend. They'd gone to junior high and high school together, in Connecticut. Most weekends, she spent a night at Victoria's parents' house, or Victoria at hers. They had preferred Victoria's house, though. It was a more relaxed place.

Then they had both been accepted at Columbia, and had taken an apartment together, not too far from where Jessie's apartment was now.

Victoria had majored in political science, and her career had taken her to D.C. She worked for a think tank now, and had a home in suburban Reston, Virginia.

She would be at work, so Jessie dialed her direct line. Victoria answered.

"Jess," she said when she heard Jessie's voice. "What's going on?"

"What do you mean, Victoria?"

"Are you in trouble?"

"Yes, as a matter of fact. But how do you—"

"Two guys came to see me. They were asking about you. Showed some kind of government I.D., Treasury agents, they said. Were they for real?"

"Could have been, Vick. God, I'm in such deep shit."

"I can imagine. How did they even know about me?"

Good question. The answer didn't take long, though.

"Ah, Christ, Vicky, they took my hard drive. I had my whole phone book on there. They know everybody I know."

"They, who, Jess? The government? The Treasury? What have you done?"

"I can't tell you, Vick. I shouldn't even be talking to you. For all I know, they've got your phone tapped."

"You think?"

"Maybe. We can't take the chance."

"Can I call you somewhere?"

"No, Vicky. Thanks, but...I'll get in touch with you when it's safe to."

"I'm worried about you, kiddo. You don't sound good."

"That's because," Jessie said, "I'm not."

She hung up. She hated that she had dragged Victoria into it—and who knew how many others? What would those people think of her? All her friends, the men she had dated, her relatives...she imagined Aunt Sheila out in Washington state being visited by men with badges. The poor woman would keel over on the spot.

Jessie had reacted initially by retreating into herself, seeking her own counsel, and now she was trapped there.

Maybe, she thought, she should just go right now. Forget the clothes back in the Highland—she had taken to carrying her purse and briefcase everywhere, so she had the important stuff. She could take a subway to Grand Central and buy a ticket for the first train going anywhere. Maybe in a safer environment she could figure out a first step that wouldn't end up with somebody getting killed.

She found the nearest subway station and went down the escalator. As it dropped, she found herself growing more concerned. The last time she had been under the earth, she'd almost never come out. Could she even stand on the platform again without panicking?

She took a deep breath, straightened her spine. Get back on the horse, she thought. The only way.

She kept her back to the wall while she waited for the train. As far from the edge as she could be. Her head swiveled like it was on a ball joint, back and forth, watching for any familiar faces—Jake Garland, Barbara Slonaker, Richard Steele...

She didn't see any. But she did see two men in black coats. They started at the far end of the platform and worked their way through the crowds, ever closer to her. They weren't waiting for a train; they were looking for someone, and not really making an attempt to disguise it. She had never seen them before, but their type made her nervous—they were big men, powerful, with dark hair and dark eyes and grim mouths, wearing expensive, somewhat flashy suits and polished shoes. They didn't look like T-Men. They looked like thugs. They weren't here to make an arrest; they were here to kill.

She turned away and started for the exit at the far end. Up the escalator, she imagined she could feel their gaze on her, could sense their gun barrels sighted on her back. But she couldn't look back. In case they hadn't spotted her, she didn't want to give herself away.

When she hit the street, panic won over caution and she started to run.

Jessie ran five days a week. She could run for a long time, or she could run fast for shorter stretches.

This time, she opted for distance.

She had only taken a few steps when she spotted a third man, hanging around near the subway entrance. Another black coat, another cruel mouth, small angry eyes. He saw her—hard to miss a woman bursting out of the subway in full flight—and his hand snaked beneath his coat.

She was already moving, almost upon him. No way to stop, to change direction, without slowing herself down so much that he'd have her. She had to rely on the fact that running was one of the things she was good at, that they couldn't take away from her no matter what.

So she used her speed, her momentum. When she reached him, he had his right hand inside the coat, presumably freeing a weapon from its holster. His balance wasn't what it might have been—he was turning, all his weight on his left leg. Jessie stuck her arms out, rammed into his right side as she ran past him. Risky, she knew, but she needed the head start.

It worked. He fell to his left, slamming into the wall. It wouldn't hurt him, but it would slow his ability to draw his weapon, to aim, and it would make it harder for him to catch her.

She didn't miss a step. Her arms absorbed the impact and she kept moving, not looking back, purse and briefcase bouncing against her as she ran. The sidewalk crowd parted before her, and closed up behind her.

She turned the first corner she came to. She wasn't even totally sure where she was—she had been wandering, earlier, without paying attention, and now she wasn't about to take time to look at the signs. This street wasn't as crowded, so she put on the steam. She risked a glance back when she hit the next corner, and there was no sign of pursuit. She made a left, then saw that the light was with her and she dodged across the street. At the next corner, she made a right. This she recognized as Madison Avenue.

And she realized where she'd ended up, without paying attention. The back side of FAO Schwarz loomed ahead of her. She jogged down 58th, paused long enough to compose herself, then went inside, smiling at the doorman.

She had always loved this store. Now she took a few moments, certain that she was not being followed anymore—not sure, in fact, if she ever had been, or if she had just ruined the day of some poor sap who had been fishing for cigarettes or a wallet, to wander the aisles. As she did, she wondered if her imagination had gone into overdrive. They couldn't have people at every subway stop in New York, could they? Was it just a coincidence that they'd been there, or were they in fact not even looking for her? Maybe it was two businessmen waiting for someone at the station. There shouldn't have been any way to know she'd be there—she'd been wandering aimlessly, ending up near St. Patrick's, far from her usual or her new neighborhoods.

She went downstairs and browsed the toy cars and soldiers and action figures, then back up to the street level to see all the stuffed animals. She realized how long it had been since she'd watched children's television—she didn't know Dora or Yo Gabba Gabba, was only vaguely aware of and disturbed by Spongebob. She recognized the Sesame Street gang, of course, and was pleased to see that Big Bird and Miss Piggy were still around.

A bear caught her eye—a small red one, made of something like very soft terrycloth and loosely stuffed. He didn't seem to tie in to any TV show or movie or comic book; he was just a loveable little bear with stitched facial features and a friendly outlook. She knew it was stupid—she was on the run, she shouldn't be weighing herself down with material things—but he was so adorable and so inexpensive.

She decided to buy him.

The hell with what made sense. She was denying herself a normal life. She wouldn't deny this one impulse.

Standing in line, watching the cheerful salespeople ringing up the customers ahead of her—there was always a line at FAO Schwarz in December—she was reminded of one of her earliest memories, of coming here as a child, a toddler, really, not quite three, with her parents and her big sister Joan. She had considered the store to be one of the world's most magical places.

Maybe it still was.

Her sister...

Chapter 9

"Joan? It's me. Jessica."

A long silence.

"Your sister."

"I know."

"But?"

"What makes you think there's a 'but?'"

"I can hear it in your voice. In your general lack of enthusiasm at the sound of my voice."

"I don't hear from you much. I figure it's bad news, or I wouldn't be hearing from you now."

"Only if you consider someone trying to kill me as bad news."

"I'll reserve judgment on that. Tell me."

"Not over the phone. I'm worried. I need someplace to stay where I'll be safe for a while."

"And you think this is the place?"

"Joan, they have my computer, they have my address files. They have every phone number I know, except yours."

"You didn't keep my number in your Rolodex?"

"I didn't even know it. There was no mention of you there. Or on any paperwork they could possibly have access to."

"Good. That's the way I like it."

"I know."

"Where are you now?"

"Manhattan. It's too dangerous here. I've got to get out."

"I have a daughter, Jessica. She's six. I don't want her endangered."

A daughter? Jessie really had been out of touch. Which, as Joan said, was the way she liked it. "Oh, I didn't know that, Joan. Congratulations. But no one knows you exist. I've never put your name down on a form in my life. I've never had you written in my address book, or had your birthday noted on my calendar."

A long pause.

"You'll need identification."

"You're right. Can't get on a plane or rent a car without it these days. I hadn't even thought that far ahead."

"I have."

"I'm sure."

"Here's what you do. There's a check-cashing store on Broadway, at 92nd. Go there and ask for Vinnie."

"Sounds like a joke."

"Only certain people get the punch line. Just do it. After that..."

* * *

It had taken Jessie twenty minutes to screw up the courage to call, once the idea had presented itself inside the toy store. Joan was her big sister, but Jessie had only been five when Joan left the family home, under less-than-ideal circumstances. They had talked a handful of times in the intervening years, reminding one another that they were still alive, but that was about it.

At first, she hadn't remembered how to reach her sister.

She knew the name of the town, Clark's Grove, Iowa, in which Joan had been living last time she'd heard anything. But Joan had been married then, and while Jessie didn't know if the marriage was still on, she knew that Joan would have kept her husband's name unless she had since remarried. It was just the way Joan did things.

She had dialed information to get the area code for Clark's Grove. Then she had stood near the pay phone, at the corner of Central Park, across Fifth from FAO Schwarz, and racked her brain for the husband's name.

Finally, Temchin had come to her, out of the blue. Will Temchin, she thought. She had called Iowa information, and asked for Joan Temchin in Clark's Grove. Joan had always kept her first name, even through a variety of lasts. Astonishingly, there had been a listing.

She'd waited another couple of minutes, and then dialed. Holding her breath.

* * *

The conversation had gone better than expected. Joan had offered solid advice, and invited Jessie to stay with her in Clark's Grove for awhile, asking no questions about the nature of her dilemma. Couldn't ask for more than that from a big sister.

Well, you could ask for one you were closer to, one who spoke to you once or twice a year, maybe even sent a card now and again. But Jessie was used to not having that. She didn't give it a second thought—it was simply the way things were between them.

She was getting a lot of practice at coping with the way things were. Powerful people wanted her dead—that was something to cope with.

MetroBank had sent her to a seminar in money laundering prevention, and in the cab on her way uptown she tried to remember exactly what she had learned. The instructor had been an aging Treasury agent who was uncomfortable speaking to large groups. She remembered the pools of sweat under his arms by the end of a lecture, the way he'd constantly wiped perspiration from his shiny, balding head as he paced the floor. His face had been almost sweet, his voice as rough and raspy as a Harley engine on a cold morning. But he had known his stuff, and had been involved in solving cases totaling many millions of dollars. His name had been Saenz, she remembered. Morris Saenz.

The term "money laundering," he had said, pacing before the class like an anxious monkey at the zoo as he growled out his lecture, came from laundromats, which were a cash-intensive business that criminals— "bad guys," he had always called them—liked to own in order to launder their funds. The point of money laundering was that "dirty" money had to have a "clean" source in order to be put back into the economy.

By which he meant "spent."

Most of what was laundered these days—more than a hundred billion dollars a year, by some estimates, or considerably more than the total economy of many nations—was drug money. But it didn't all come from drugs. There was also money from white collar crime, fraud, insider trading, and a wide variety of other criminal activities. Bad guys, Saenz had said, tended to not specialize too much. Whether they got their initial financing from robbing banks, selling drugs, pimping hookers, or anything else, all but the lowest of street crooks soon found themselves branching out into other criminal arenas.

Moving money illegally was one of the most common criminal pursuits they engaged in—simply trying to use their illegal gains meant they had to break numerous other laws. Once you were crooked a little bit, Saenz said, pacing back and forth in front of the class, wiping his glasses, you found that you were crooked a lot.

Being a little bit criminal was like being a little bit pregnant.

Modern technology, while making it easier to catch the money launderers, was also making it easier to launder money. Online banking, the Internet, electronic wire transfers—these could all be used with some degree of anonymity, which was the most important factor in discreetly shifting around large sums of money.

Not all the money movers had embraced the digital age. There was still simple smuggling to contend with. U.S. Customs officials, mostly geared toward stopping drugs and other contraband from coming into the country, had started taking a look a few years ago at shipments going to the former Soviet Union, and had discovered large crates of hundred dollar bills leaving our shores. Likewise, billions in cash, meant to be spent on the ground in Iraq and Afghanistan, had vanished from sight and now flooded markets across the Middle East and South Asia, in China and Russia and elsewhere.

Dollars were the primary currency of the criminal trade, Saenz had pointed out. Rubles? Who wants them? Colombian drug dealers would sometimes buy Colombian pesos, but only to convert them again into dollars. Currency exchanges, or *bureaux de change*, were, in fact, a favorite way of turning dirty money into clean.

No, the bad guys wanted dollars.

More and more, criminals were becoming sophisticated in their money laundering techniques. This was the category Richard Steele fit into, Jessie thought. Develop a relationship with a big, established bank.

Let that bank help you develop shell companies in a territory with liberal tax codes and strict privacy laws, like the Caymans.

But before the money gets there, move it through a few other banks. This practice, Saenz called "layering," building more and more levels between the money and the person who it ultimately belonged to. Add in the nifty trick of moving it through commingled funds, and it was basically impossible to trace without the assistance of the banker initiating the process.

"Look at this," the cabbie said, interrupting her mental review.

He had halted the cab, on Broadway near 86th, because a Mercedes was stopped in the lane in front of them. The trunk of the Mercedes was open, and there was a man with a thick mustache looking around from inside the trunk. After a moment, he sank from view, except for one arm, which reached up, grabbed something inside the trunk lid, and pulled it closed over him.

The Mercedes drove off.

She hadn't seen whether the man had started out in the trunk, or had climbed in right there in the street. Apparently the cab driver hadn't either.

"What was that all about?" she asked.

"Hell if I know," he said, his accent—Eritrean? Ethiopian? Somali? she couldn't say for sure—so thick it was hard to understand him. "Only in New York, eh, lady?"

Only in New York.

It occurred to her then that she would be leaving New York soon, and for an indeterminate length of time. Maybe forever.

She had always lived here, or close by, in Connecticut. With the exception of a few trips to Europe, Florida, and the West coast, she had always been here. The Connecticut childhood meant she had never developed a strong New York accent, but she knew many people who had them, and it always sounded like home to her.

She looked out the cab's windows for the rest of the trip. People crowded the sidewalks, heavy winter coats adding bulk to make it look like there were even more of them. Up here, more of the faces were brown and black than in her neighborhood, diverse and exciting though it was.

A tall, lean, dreadlocked black man skated down the sidewalk, wearing skin-tight bike shorts and a sweatshirt. He dodged and swirled around the pedestrians.

The shops were all open. Electronics shops glowed with color and energy, bright neon and shining chrome filling the windows. People moved in and out of liquor stores, bookshops, hardware stores, cafes, carrying bags made of plastic, paper, cloth.

The sounds of automobiles were omnipresent, motors, horns, brakes. More horns.

New York, New York. She had been born Jessica Dawn Cutler in a hospital in Queens, had grown up there, never out of sight of the Manhattan skyline until her mother had moved her to Connecticut when she was eleven, after her father died. To the big, quiet house. And even then, it was only a short train ride away.

Soon she would be leaving the area, living under a different name. How did people do it, she wondered. How did you just up and go? How did you get used to being called something else? To not knowing where all the restaurants and shops and services were?

The cab pulled over to the side of the street in front of a storefront with a big yellow CHECKS CASHED sign in the window. "Here you go, lady."

She handed him a ten and a five, for a nine-fifty fare. He thanked her as he pulled out into traffic.

The CHECKS CASHED place looked filthy. She felt a pang of sympathy for those without bank accounts, who had to use places like this—and pay their usurious fees—for their everyday financial needs.

She felt worse for herself, for having to go in there and begin an illegal process.

You can't be a little bit crooked.

She pulled the glass door open and went in.

Chapter 10

"Is Vinnie here?"

The guy behind the thick, scratched windows glared at her. He was a huge guy, Samoan maybe, with thick black hair and bad skin. Muscular, but with an enormous gut.

"Inna back," he said. He nodded toward a door set into the back wall.

There were a couple of other customers in the place, but mostly it was empty space. A long, narrow space, with nothing in the front but long counters along the wall. All the action was at the back, where the windows were, and behind the windows a cage where she guessed the cash was stored.

A sign over the windows said COUNT YOUR MONEY BEFORE LEEVING WINDOW.

The kind of joint where everybody trusted each other.

Jessie glanced at the other customers, but they paid no attention to her. She went to the door. As she reached for the knob, the door buzzed, and it opened under her touch.

She passed through, into a small office. Another guy was back here, sitting at a metal desk. He was looking at her, one hand inside the top right desk drawer. Apparently satisfied that she wasn't a threat, he withdrew the hand, empty.

"Yeah?"

"I was told to ask for Vinnie."

"I'm Vinnie," he said.

He didn't look like a Vinnie. Like the guy in front, this guy looked vaguely Asian, or maybe Pacific Islander of some sort. He was older and much smaller than the other man, with a bulging forehead, wire-rim glasses and short hair, specked with gray.

"I need a new identity," she said. Seemed blunt, but they were the words Joan had told her to say.

"I can do that. Driver's license, social security card, passport. Need credit cards?" He spoke like a machine gun, rapid-fire.

"No, I don't think so."

"Good. That makes it easier for me."

"But I do want one extra. A company ID card. To match this one." She laid her own MetroBank ID on the desktop.

He looked at it, lips pursed. "No problem," he said. "It'll run you fifteen. Is that a problem?"

"I was told seven fifty." Also what Joan had told her to say.

"Twelve fifty."

"Eight seventy-five."

"Split the difference," he said. "One thousand. I can't go any lower, because you want the extra."

"Done."

"I need it up front."

She shook her head. "Half now, half on delivery."

"You've done this before?"

"I have a good coach."

Before heading up here, she had gone down to Greenwich Village, found a MetroBank branch she had never used before and never would again, and made a cash withdrawal. She had the full thousand and then some on her. She was half-surprised that her accounts hadn't been frozen, but then figured that Barb probably wanted her to keep using ATMs so they could triangulate the activity and figure out what neighborhood she was hiding out in.

She had withdrawn fifteen hundred, but the rest of her money was going to have to be off limits. It was a risk going into the bank, and one she couldn't afford to take often.

Vinnie scribbled an address on a Post-it note and waved it toward her.

"Go here," he said. "This guy there will take some photos. Then you bring the photos back to me here and we'll hook you up. What name you want to use?"

Jessie had thought long and hard about this one. Came up with one she thought might prove handy. "Barbara Slonaker."

The rest of the process wasn't especially difficult or demanding. Vinnie's friend—for an extra three hundred dollars—took a series of digital photos in the appropriate dimensions for a passport, driver's license, and the MetroBank I.D. He printed them out, trimmed them, and dropped them into a plain white envelope. Another cab ride back to Vinnie. He had taken her information before she left, so the eye and hair color, weight, and so on, would match up.

Once she was back in his office, he handed over the photos to an underling who had gone through yet another doorway. "The computers are back there," Vinnie explained. "We use Macintosh. You know Macs, or you a PC person? This'll only take a few minutes. Gotta love this technology."

It took more like an hour, during which Vinnie didn't say much but spent a lot of time looking at the way her jeans clung to her thighs. She began to feel happy that he had only wanted money.

When the hour was over, though, the underling came back in and handed Vinnie a stack of documents. Vinnie glanced through them, and passed them on to Jessie.

Who was amazed.

She couldn't tell they weren't legit. Maybe a skilled police officer could, but she had spent years as a teller, looking at people's identification every day, and she would have sworn these were real. Even the MetroBank ID badge, which hung on a length of chain just like her own.

Seeing her picture over the name Barbara Slonaker gave her a chill. But she was half-convinced by the I.D. that she was Barbara Slonaker.

She would be putting it to the test, soon enough.

She caught a cab back to the Highland, waved to the hookers, and took a nap.

Waking an hour later, she showered, dressed in her nice dress, applied make-up. She wanted to look like a professional, out for a night on the town.

Found another cab, and took it to within a block of MetroBank's corporate offices.

As a private banker, there were many occasions when she had to work odd hours. She was counting on being a familiar face to the night security guard, but not on him knowing her name. There was always the chance that the guard would have her picture posted on his counter with orders to shoot on sight—but she was reaching the point where postponing the inevitable didn't necessarily hold a lot of appeal. If he killed her right here, then she wouldn't have to go through with the rest of her plan.

At this moment, it scared her more than dying did.

Approaching the lobby doors, she hung her ID badge around her neck, checking once to make sure it was the badge with Barbara Slonaker's name on it, and not her own.

"Evenin'," the guard said, with a friendly smile.

"Hello," Jessie said. She shook her head, as if frustrated. "These damn clients. When they want something, it doesn't matter to them if you're on a date."

He slid the clipboard across the counter to her, not really looking at her badge. She signed Barbara Slonaker's name to it—she'd seen it plenty over the years, and even signed noncritical documents for her a few times. She couldn't forge the signature, but she could approximate it. She wrote down 1:45 as the time in, which was pretty close. The guard took the clipboard without looking twice. "Have fun," he said as she headed toward the elevators.

On the way up, the icy fingers of terror gripped her. What if Barbara was still here, for some reason? Or Jim Mackie? Or just about anybody—everyone must know by now that Jessica Cutler was no longer employed by MetroBank.

Terror, accompanied by a sharp pang of grief. All she had wanted was to be a banker, and a good one, like her father and his father before him. Not for the money, but because of an intellectual fascination with the idea of money—what it could do, how you could tend it, make it multiply, make it provide for you and yours. It was like being a gardener, she had explained to friends. You take care of it and it takes care of you.

Now, by trying to preserve her position, she had given it all up. Or put herself in a situation where it was taken away from her. She didn't know what else she might want to do with her life—banking had been the goal from an early age, and there had been no second best. She had put her career first, before relationships, men, marriage. Her lie to the guard notwithstanding, it had been a good long while since she'd had a date at all, much less one that it would have pained her to walk away from if duty called. She had a circle of friends, but none she trusted enough to call for help. They were mostly in the business, too. They wouldn't want to risk their own careers for her.

Her days as a banker, she feared, were over. And who was she without that?

She used her card key to get into the offices. She had hoped they wouldn't have changed the locks, and they hadn't, nor had they taken the relatively simple step of canceling her card key. Counting on the downstairs security to keep her out, she figured.

She entered on Barbara's floor instead of her own. Her card key had opened Barbara's office for several years, and when Barbara had changed jobs, she had kept the corner office she loved so much. The key still worked. Jessie slipped inside, closed the door, and turned on the lights.

Barbara could have moved to a bigger space, but she might have had to give up the corner, which had big windows on two walls. She was a plant-lover, and the place sometimes looked more like a greenhouse than a banking office. To move all the plants into an office that might not get as much light was just too much for Barbara to bear, so she had taken the extra cash and change in job responsibilities that came with her advancement, but "moved upstairs" in figurative terms only.

She had probably forgotten the days when she had first taken Jessie under her wing, had her young protégé water her plants, put her mail on her desk when she was traveling, do some of her filing.

Safely in Barbara's office, she went to the computer on Barbara's desk, which she, like most people, almost never shut down. It was on now, the monitor dark. Jessie sat down at the desk, took a deep breath, and placed her fingers on the keyboard. She tapped a key and the screen came to life.

From here, it wasn't that complicated. Jessica had accessed Richard Steele's accounts from her own computer enough times that she knew the necessary codes and passwords. She moved through the screens, opened each account, and made one small change to the account's specifications: adding the name Barbara Slonaker to the list of signatories.

There wouldn't be a signature card to match up with, but she hoped that wouldn't be an issue. Barbara's name was on some of the incorporation paperwork of Cielo Holdings, because she had helped him set up the corporation. So between being treasurer of the company and having her name show up in the computer, Jessica hoped that would be good enough for a branch manager.

After all, she had to get out of town, and she needed to finance the trip somehow. Not to mention her new life. Why not let Richard pay for it?

And she had already made her first giant step into crime. Theft would just be a little baby step behind that.

Her task finished, she closed the files she had opened and left the desktop looking just as she had found it. She was almost to the door when she heard footsteps on the polished stone floor on the other side.

* * *

"Hello, Richard."

Barbara hadn't seen Richard Steele in months, even though they talked on the phone every week or two. Here, in the soft, indirect light of a crowded neighborhood pub, she remembered all over again why she had fallen for him so fast and hard.

It wasn't simply his good looks.

It wasn't just the money.

Richard Steele carried himself with supreme confidence. He spoke to people as he crossed the room toward her—every eye seemed to be on him, and he delighted in that, drew energy from it. Strangers looked at him, and he smiled and chatted, putting his hands on their shoulders, touching them, a god-like figure bestowing his blessings on the masses.

Women wanted him. Men wanted to be him.

Plenty of *men* wanted him.

If he'd set his sights on a screen career, he could have been a star. He had magnetism that Barbara was sure would come across on the screen. He dressed well, wore expensive clothing well, and he took excellent care of himself.

But that confidence—that was the thing that got her.

As if he believed that every woman in the place would go home with him in a heartbeat.

She had known him for more than a year.

He did believe that, and he was generally right about it.

"Hi, Barb," he said, kissing her lips.

She would have swooned, once. Not anymore. She had spent several months with those lips. They were great. Richard was a tremendous kisser. An amazing lay.

But she was over him.

She reminded herself of that every time they spoke.

"It looks like we've got a little problem," he said. "Can we grab a booth?"

For the first time, she was able to tear her eyes off him long enough to notice that he wasn't alone. Two men had followed him in, trailing in his wake like seagulls behind a fishing boat. They wore dark coats, had close cropped hair, plain faces. One man was black, one white.

In the shadow of Richard's radiance, they were almost invisible.

Which, she was sure, was the effect they tried to achieve. It couldn't have been easy for them—the white guy, smaller of the two, was the size of a phone booth. The black guy could have eaten two basketball players.

"You brought company?"

"Couple of friends," Richard said. The black guy flashed her a smile, showing gold.

"Any friend of Mr. Steele's..." he said.

"Charmed," Barbara said.

The white one didn't speak.

They pushed their way through the crowd, found a corner booth that a handful of college students were just vacating.

The students might have been sped along a little by the sight of the two small buildings closing on them.

The two guys let Richard and Barbara sit at the booth while they stood nearby. They didn't look at the booth. Between them, Barbara realized, they could see every other inch of the pub.

"What is this, Richard?" she asked. "I've never seen you running around with thugs like this before."

He put a finger to his lips.

"They're very sensitive," he said. "That word is considered demeaning."

"What should I call them, then? Legbreakers? Enforcers? Hired guns?"

"They're security specialists. As you know, we've had a pretty severe security breach."

"You think Jessica Cutler is coming after you with an army? If she meant to do that, she'd have done it already."

"Let's not use any names, please," Richard said.

"Sorry, I know." She ran a hand through her hair. "I'm tired, Richard. I haven't been sleeping well, you know? Worrying."

"I'm a little worried too, frankly. I was told that this situation would be taken care of, Barbara."

"We're working on it."

"Why am I not relieved?"

A waitress came to the table, and Richard ordered Glenfiddich, rocks, for himself. Barbara ordered a glass of Merlot. The waitress batted her eyes a few times at Richard before drifting away.

Die, child, Barbara thought.

There was a time when she believed she and Richard might be married. Fooling herself, she knew now. Richard would never have settled down with someone her age. She was only a few years younger than him. He'd hold out a while longer, then find himself a trophy, still in her twenties, probably, to help maintain his image and his ego for the next decade or so. When he hit his sixties, he'd trade her in on a new one, older than the first was but not as old as the first had become.

Still, the delusion had been attractive for a while.

That and the money.

She had allowed it to rule her life to the extent that she got deeply involved in his financial affairs—more deeply than was prudent, definitely more than was legal. She helped him set up accounts to move money around, to launder it, if you wanted to get specific. She allowed him—hell, she encouraged him, to be exact—to name her treasurer of Cielo Holdings, the offshore dummy corporation she had set up for him to hide his earnings. After all, she had bills, a mortgage, credit cards, and it was clear that he was going to be cutting off the money he'd been spending on her. She had grown accustomed to the lifestyle, and staying tight with Richard, in whatever fashion, would help her continue to be able to afford it.

She knew he didn't make his money in socially acceptable ways, though she never knew all the details. She knew he moved in circles in which sudden violence was not unheard of. She didn't let that knowledge dissuade her.

But she had never, in her wildest three AM paranoia, imagined that it would be directed at her.

Now, though...sitting across the table from him, she looked at the clenched teeth, the set of his jaw, the narrowed eyes. And she knew that he was a couple of wrong words from striking her.

The legbreakers didn't whisper encouraging words to her psyche, either.

"Richard, what do you want us to do? We took steps. She's gone underground. Disappeared."

"Disappeared isn't good," he said. "That means she can reappear."

"It may be the best you're going to get. If she's running scared, at least she's not here trying to hurt you."

"She's tried, a couple of times. Fortunately, we were able to block her at every step."

"Then what's the problem? She's no fighter, Richard. She's weak. She knows banking, but not like we do, and she doesn't know anything else. She'll give up. We'll never hear from her again."

"The problem is that she's out there. God knows I hate to use a cliché, but she knows just a little too fucking much, Barbara, wouldn't you say? The problem is that every time I start to think she's had enough, she turns up again. The problem, Barbara, is that I let your boss tell me that MetroBank would take care of this, and so far MetroBank has done shit."

"I thought we weren't naming names."

"You don't name names. I'm the one in trouble here, and I'll name names if I fucking well please. You know what else? If I don't see some action—positive, definitive action—happening soon, I'm going to start doing more than naming names. I hold you responsible, Barbara. You and Mackie. You understand what I mean by that, right?"

Barbara glanced at the two bruisers, leaning against barstools that were probably too flimsy to hold their full weight, keeping their eyes open for anyone who might pose a threat to their boss.

"I think I get it, Richard."

"I've let you guys handle this, and you've done nothing. From now on, I'm handling it. My own way."

"Seems like you've been plenty involved from the beginning, Richard." Barbara chuckled. "And where's that gotten you?"

She saw him take in his breath and hold it, as if sucking in the rage that made him want to hit her or pull a gun on her. She didn't like herself for taunting him, but their relationship, she knew, was really over now. He might remove her as Cielo's treasurer, maybe even move his accounts to another bank.

So she might as well have what fun she could.

"It's been real, Richard," she said. "But I think it's time for me to turn in."

"You do that, Barbara," he said. "Just don't worry about a thing. I'm on this now, and I won't rest until Jessie's pretty little head is on a silver plate."

Barbara drained the last of her Merlot and stood. "I think the cliché is 'silver platter,' Richard. As long as you're in that kind of mood."

She walked out of the pub and hailed a cab. She had planned to head back to the office after the meeting, but she suddenly felt exhausted, and she gave the driver her home address. Traffic was light. Forty minutes later, she was asleep.

* * *

Jessie felt her stomach flop. If she were caught in here...she'd be looking at jail time, at best. It wasn't a large office, there was really no place to hide if someone came in. She edged back into the jungle of plants, crouching down behind a big potted fern. Maybe with the lights off she'd be semi-invisible, but she had turned them on, and hadn't made it to the switch before she heard the steps.

The footsteps stopped just outside the door. She heard the knob rattle under someone's hand. There was a pause. Jessie held her breath, felt like she was underwater and had been for some time.

Then the steps moved along. Down the hall, another knob rattled.

Just security, checking to make sure the office doors were locked, then. She blew out the breath she'd been holding, an unbidden smile on her face. She waited a few minutes until she could no longer hear the footsteps or the doorknobs being tested, and then opened the door a crack. Looked out.

Clear. She slipped out, closed it behind her, locked it with her key.

Moved as quietly as she could across the stone floor to the elevator lobby. Pushed the DOWN button.

And the security guard came around the corner. Smile on his face. The elevator reached her as he did.

"You all done, Ms. Slonaker?" he asked, following her into the car.

"Yes, it didn't take too long after all," Jessie said.

He punched the L button. "Funny, I just shook on your door a few minutes ago. All locked up tight. You lock it when you went in?"

"I must have been in the bathroom then," she said. "A little too much wine with dinner, you know?"

"I guess I do at that," he said with a chuckle. "More of a beer guy, but still."

The elevator opened onto the lobby, and Jessie stepped out, followed by the guard. She tossed him a smile as she crossed to the clipboard to sign herself out, and he returned it.

"You have yourself a great night, Ms. Slonaker" he said. "What's left of it, anyway."

"Same to you," she said.

Outside, she caught a cab and went back to the Highland. It was cold enough and late enough that even the hookers were inside.

In her room, she took three pills, undressed, and climbed into bed.

Another long day.
And more to come.

Chapter 11

Times like these, Morgan Byrd felt like nothing so much as a goddamn babysitter.

It wore on him. Patience wasn't his strong suit to begin with. Putting up with a bunch of too-rich, too-stupid Eastern fools would be the death of him one day, he figured.

If only because he would put a gun to his own head and squeeze the trigger.

On this particular occasion, he was in a saloon in Paonia, Colorado, in the company of four men—two doctors, an insurance executive, and the drug company sales rep who was paying for everything. Tomorrow they were going into the wilderness for five days, in search of trophies.

Nothing particular in mind, they'd said. They just wanted to kill some animals that would look manly on their walls.

Shit.

If he didn't need the money...

But he did, of course. There was no percentage in thinking that way. You always needed the money. That was what kept the world going 'round. What kept you working.

Still...

So of course, what they wanted to do tonight was to get drunk in Paonia's biggest tavern, such as it was. Morgan would rather have spent the evening sleeping, getting ready for the next day's long trek into the mountains. But he had learned—take a pack of upper middle class white men away from home and into the wild, and first thing they want to do is act like college kids on the rampage.

It was better if he went with them, because then he could at least try to moderate their intake and get them to bed at a semi-reasonable hour.

They would fuss tonight, but tomorrow they would last longer on the trail, and they wouldn't whine quite so much.

The trade-off was worth it.

The salesman, though—Sniegoski, his name was, a barrel-chested, long-armed, ape of a man—was getting out of control. Morgan braced for trouble.

Sniegoski had been making lecherous comments about, and to, Carmen, the cocktail waitress since his second gin sling. She was a looker, Morgan allowed, with lustrous blonde hair piled up on top of her head, an easy smile, wide hips and a pair of spectacular breasts straining the buttons of her plaid flannel shirt. Made a man proud to be a mammal.

She reminded Morgan of Christie, and he thought he'd have to go pay her a visit back in Ely soon.

But he couldn't let his mind wander in that direction. His concern right now was Sniegoski, who was taking things a little too far. When Carmen brought another round of drinks to the table, Sniegoski eyed her chest and turned to Morgan.

"You sure we're in Colorado, Byrd?" he said. "Because from where I sit, it looks like Texas. Everything seems bigger here."

The men at the table—except Morgan—brayed laughter.

"Let's just check," Carmen said. She leaned close to Sniegoski, breasts against his shoulder, put her hand in his crotch, and held him for a moment. Finally, she released him. "Nope." she said. "This ain't Texas."

The table erupted again, roars of laughter coming from everyone including Morgan.

Except Sniegoski. The monkey-man's cheeks reddened, then turned purple. A vein in his temple stood out, throbbing scarlet.

"Fuck you!" he spat.

"Easy, now," Morgan said.

"Fuck you too!" Sniegoski said. "Fuck all of you. White trash whore thinks she can talk to me like that—"

Morgan was on his feet. "That's enough," he said. "Let's go."

"No," Sniegoski said. "I'm not going anywhere until she apologizes to me."

"Seems to me you're the one ought to apologize to her," Morgan said. "Let's get some rest now. Big day tomorrow."

Sniegoski braced himself against the heavy oak table. "I said *no*."

Morgan leaned in close to his ear. "Listen, Billy boy," he said. "You are gonna tell the lady you're sorry, and then we're leavin'. You can walk out or you can be carried, but your big night is over."

Sniegoski glared at him. His cheeks were splotched with white; spittle flecked the corners of his mouth.

"I'll go outside with you, cowboy," he said. "But only to kick your skinny ass."

"Let's go, then."

The four men followed Morgan out to the parking lot. Sniegoski puffed up his chest like a bantam rooster as he went, rubbing his right fist in his left hand as if he had already used it.

Morgan faced Sniegoski in the crisp night air. The man swung at him. Morgan dodged the blow easily, then came inside his long-armed reach. With the flat of his palm, he pushed against Sniegoski's collarbone. The man staggered back three steps, then the ass of his brand new Levi's scraped gravel.

"You couldn't take me on your best day," Morgan said, "much less drunk. Give it up."

"You're fired, Byrd," Sniegoski said. He pulled himself to his feet.

"You can't fire me," Morgan said. "I haven't worked for you since you insulted that waitress."

"And we want our deposit back."

Morgan went to his dented '86 Dodge Raider, opened the back and started to haul out those things that belonged to his four ex-clients, dropping them unceremoniously on the gravel lot.

"You must not have read the fine print," Morgan said. "The deposit ain't refundable on account of your being assholes."

"Careful with that," Golden, one of the doctors, said when Morgan tugged his soft leather suitcase from the Raider. Morgan dropped it on the ground.

"Oops."

He was just as glad. He hadn't been looking forward to spending the next several days in the mountains with these guys, trying to keep them alive in the face of their own ignorance. Better to dump them now, when they could just pile all their gear back into DeCandido's rented

Land Rover, than halfway up the Rockies. At least the road out of Paonia was paved.

Sleeping bags hitting the dirt almost muffled the click of a weapon being cocked.

But not quite.

Morgan was holding a backpack in both hands—a city backpack, nothing you'd actually want to wear on your back for five days of humping through mountains more than a mile above sea level. When he heard the noise—and he knew what it was—he spun.

Calculating the distance between him and the Land Rover, in which the men had their rifles stored. Too far to cover before a man could pull a trigger.

Even a drunk man.

And at this range, even a drunk man was likely to hit something.

As he spun, he released the backpack.

Dropped.

The backpack sailed through the air.

From the ground, Morgan saw Golden, holding a single action Remington 30.06. Golden saw the backpack rushing at him like a cannonball and raised the rifle to block it.

Morgan propelled himself off the ground, gravel biting his palms. Before Golden could lower the rifle, Morgan slammed into him. He grabbed the rifle's barrel and stock, swept it aside, drove a shoulder into Golden's not inconsiderable belly.

The doctor went down. Morgan kept his footing, wrenched the Remington from Golden's hands. Raised it a foot over Golden and then drove it down, a pile driver into Golden's midsection.

He followed that by swinging the weapon's butt up and into Golden's jaw. He heard bone break. The wooden stock tore skin and hair off Golden's bearded chin.

Morgan knelt on Golden's chest, holding the stock of the gun against the man's throat. "Never point a gun at a person," he growled, "unless you're fixin' to kill him."

He stood, took the gun off Golden's neck. "Now you've learned somethin'. Consider that lesson what you spent your deposit on."

The doctor rolled onto his side, spitting teeth. Morgan stood back, holding the gun on the other men.

Sniegoski, DeCandido, and Nieto just stood there, looking at Golden writhing on the ground. Looking at the Remington.

"There a doctor in the house?" Morgan asked.

Chapter 12

Jessie slept in, killed time in her room, scanning online newspapers, reading, and watching TV until just after noon. Then she took a long, leisurely shower, scrubbing well, shampooing and massaging her scalp. Who knew when she would have another chance to relax and pamper herself?

She dressed and went out for breakfast at about two. After that she walked to a quick printer and had a hundred "Barbara Slonaker" business cards printed while she waited. She made it, by cab, to a MetroBank branch in Brooklyn shortly after four.

She made a point of arriving at the branch office about an hour before closing time. Long enough to be sent to the branch manager, but not long enough to take things further than that.

The teller's reaction was pretty much what she expected when she asked to make a forty-five hundred dollar withdrawal from a corporate account. She kept it under five thousand, because that would set off a whole different set of bells.

"I'm afraid I'll have to get the manager's approval on a withdrawal of that size," she said.

"Of course," Jessie said. "I wouldn't expect anything less."

"I'll be right back, Ms. Slonaker," the teller said. She walked away. Jessie scanned the suburban bank branch—a brick building on the outside, bland on the inside, with cream-colored carpeting and pastel pink walls decorated with outsized black and white photos depicting Brooklyn's turn of the century days.

There was a camera on her, she knew—cameras blanketed the entire floor of the bank. A chance she had to take. She'd count on the withdrawal being just small enough not to send up any red flags, so none of the people she was concerned about would ever see the security tape.

Eventually, of course, the withdrawal would cross Barbara's desk. Unless she had already reassigned Richard's account.

She had a feeling that wouldn't happen for a while.

Her teller, Beth, according to the nameplate on the window, had gone into a glasswalled office, and was bending over a severe looking woman in a charcoal gray suit. The woman glanced up at Jessie, made eye contact.

Jessie smiled.

One professional to another.

The branch manager walked out with the teller.

"Hello, Ms. Slonaker," she said. "I'm Denise Wilson. Have we met?"

"I don't think so," Jessie said. "I don't get out to the branches very often, I'm afraid."

"I'm sure you're plenty busy at headquarters, Denise said. "I'm so sorry for the trouble. Can I see your identification, please?"

Jessie showed her the new driver's license and the employee badge. She also showed her a business card identifying herself as the treasurer of Cielo Holdings.

"You understand that our hesitation is just because this is a business account, and not at this branch."

"Of course," Jessie said. "I was just in the neighborhood, and need some cash to take advantage of an opportunity for a client. If you're uncomfortable..." She let the sentence trail off.

"Oh, not at all," Denise Wilson said. "I'm sure this is all in order." She scrawled her initials on the withdrawal slip. "Beth will get you taken care of right away."

"Thank you."

"My pleasure." Denise went back to her office, and Beth smiled at Jessica.

"How would you like the cash?" she asked.

"Hundreds will be fine," Jessica said.

* * *

Outside, she was waiting for a cab when her Blackberry rang. She answered, momentarily nervous that it would be Barbara again, having discovered that someone had been in her office.

But it wasn't.

It was Richard Steele.

"Jessie," he said. "I've heard from Barbara that we have some sort of problem."

"Yes, Richard, I'd call it a problem."

"What is it, Jess?"

"Not something I want to talk about on the phone, thanks."

"Where, then? Let me buy you dinner and we can talk this over. I'm sure whatever it is, we can straighten it out, Jess. I love having you as my banker, and I'd sure hate to have to train someone new."

"Richard, coy doesn't suit you," she said. A cab was approaching, but she didn't want to get in it while she was on the phone, so she lowered her arm. It sped past.

"I don't know what you mean, Jess."

"Neither does disingenuous, so just drop it."

"How about someplace totally public? The Empire State Building lobby, something like that."

"We really have nothing to talk about, Richard," she said. Except that I've just stolen four thousand dollars and change of your money.

But hey, who wanted to go there?

Another step into crime.

"I'm certain that we do, Jessica."

The thought that had occurred to her when Barbara called came back now. Could he be tracing her location somehow, with this call? Maybe with the power of FinCEN behind him.

"I'm sure we won't be talking again anytime soon, Richard," she said. She ended the call, then turned off the phone. She scanned the curb, spotted a big storm drain. She tossed the phone down there.

With any luck, some homeless person would find it and they would spend a few days tracking him through sewers and alleys.

Better yet, maybe one of New York's legendary alligators would eat it.

* * *

It was almost dark before she got back to the city. She had packed her bags and left them in her room at the Highland before leaving on her errand. She would collect them, and then get out of the city.

She just hadn't quite figured out how yet.

If they were watching subways for her, then they would definitely have people at the airports and train stations. What she needed, she thought, was some kind of theatrical makeup, maybe a wig...

As the cab pulled up in front of the Highland, she saw her answer.

* * *

"How many girls you need?" the black hooker asked, her voice booming. "You think I can't satisfy you by myself?"

"Shh," Jessie said, finger bisecting her lips. "I said I wanted to *hire* a few of you. I didn't say I wanted to have sex with you."

"Well, we ain't paintin' your house or no shiznit like that, girl."

"I understand that. Look, can we maybe go inside and talk for a minute?"

"Your room or mine, honey?"

They went to Jessie's room. She sat on the chair, and the two hookers sat on the bed. They thought the whole thing was hilarious.

Jessie struggled to control the conversation.

"Look, how much do you get for an hour?" she asked.

"You ever met a dude could last an hour without cummin'?" the thin white one asked. She had introduced herself as Cherry, and the big black prostitute called herself Bambi.

"Not me, honey," Bambi said.

"We usually work per the cum, not per the hour," Cherry said. "Sometimes thirty, sometimes fifty."

"Depend on how rich the trick look," Bambi said. "Or what in his wallet when he open it."

"'Sides rubbers," Cherry added with a snorting laugh.

"Well, how many guys can you do in an hour?"

"Maybe three, on a good night." Cherry said.

"Is tonight a good night?"

"Honey," Bambi said, "when it come to gettin' a piece of me, any night a good night!"

Cherry cracked up again.

Jessie waited until they were finished.

"Look, let's cut to the chase. I want you both, and two other girls. I need to catch a train."

"A train? Now you lost me," Bambi said.

"Don't make me spell it out," Jessie said, "or I'll take my business elsewhere. I'm prepared to pay the four of you five hundred dollars to hang out with me for an hour."

The two ladies looked at each other.

"We in," Bambi said.

"Damn skippy," Cherry said.

* * *

Jessie didn't look half bad.

Cherry's clothes were a little tight for her, but that only added to the effect. She wore glittering purple plastic platform shoes. Short shorts of sparkling gold spandex. A red bustier that pushed her breasts up and out. A coppery wig. More make-up than she usually wore in a week.

"I don't look that good in those clothes," Cherry complained.

Bambi stuck her breasts out, waving them in Cherry's face. "Cause you ain't got no boobage," she said. "Barbie here, she got 'it."

"You sure you don't want to stay in town, work with us?" Cherry offered.

"Sometimes we get to do threeways that are pretty fun."

"I'm sure they are," Jessie said. She was unemployed, and it was a job offer, of a sort. But not one she could see herself taking. "And I truly appreciate you asking. But I don't think so."

There was a knock on the door. Bambi opened it and let two more hookers in, the white girls she had seen on the corner a couple of evenings before, with Bambi and Cherry. They were introduced as Lacey and Kendra. After they took turns admiring "Barbie," Jessie picked up her bags, put on her coat but left it open to let the goods show.

They all went downstairs.

Caught a cab to Grand Central.

Jessie was invisible.

Everyone looked at her. Everyone in the terminal looked at all five of them. But no one would have seen Jessica Cutler there. She was just another whore: metallic hair, inches of cleavage, long legs ready to wrap around the first guy who flashed the cash.

They went everywhere together. When Jessie bought her ticket, all five of them were crowded together around the kiosk. Then they all went into the waiting area together, sat around laughing and telling each other stories in loud, shrill voices. Nobody seemed to notice that one of them didn't do much talking.

At one point, Jessie spotted two guys with their hands in their coat pockets wandering through the terminal, looking like people who were searching for someone. But Kendra was telling a story, and Jessie found herself enjoying the woman's narrative so much she didn't pay much attention to the men who might well have been out to kill her.

"So I'm working my usual corner downtown, right?" Kendra was saying. "This is when I was still out in San Jose." This was the third city she'd mentioned working in so far, most of them out West. "I'm keeping an eye out for cops, right, and I look down the street, toward where the college campus is. And I see these white things, objects, right, coming my way. Now this is seven, eight blocks from the campus, and it looks like that's how far away they are, but I can see them, right? I mean, no detail, just big white shapes.

"So a couple of minutes later I look down there again, and I can see that it's these guys, and they're getting closer. But they're still four blocks off, maybe. I give them another couple of minutes, and then I look again. Now they're just a block or so away, and I can see that it's these Japanese dudes. They're all dressed the same, in white shirts and gray pants, and it's the white shirts I was seeing, because these guys are big, right? I mean, I've dated a couple football players. These dudes are way bigger than that.

"So then they finally get up to where I am, and it's like having these smiling buildings in white shirts looking at me. Not all of them are tall, but they're just thick! Wide as refrigerators, right? And they're looking me over, looking me up and down. I smile at them.

"Then one of them, the only one can talk English, I guess, comes up to me and says 'May we rent you?'"

All the women, Jessie included, cracked up. Jessie glanced around, but the suspicious-looking guys had moved on.

"So it turns out they're this judo team from some Japanese college, here to fight the San Jose team. And they decided while they're here, they'd get themselves laid by an American girl. But they're mostly too shy to go by themselves, so they all want to go with the same girl.

"Lucky me, I'm that girl. I was sore for days, right in my thighs, from trying to spread my legs around those monsters!"

The women laughed again. Jessie was starting to feel like maybe she should stick around town after all. These ladies were a lot more fun than a bunch of bankers.

Then her train was called. The five of them rode the escalator down to the platform. They gathered around as the passengers boarded—standing especially close, because at this point Jessie was handing out hundred dollar bills all around.

At the last minute, one of the hookers peeled off from the pack and boarded the train. The others took their cash and headed for the up escalator. Still laughing, enjoying their adventure.

On the train, the solo hooker went straight for the washroom. There, she discarded her wig, washed off her make-up as best she could. Put a sweater on over the bustier, which she had decided to keep. She kicked off the platforms and peeled off the shorts, wadded those up and shoved them into the trash container. Pulled on jeans. The platforms followed the shorts, and running shoes came out of the Nike bag.

A different woman came out of the washroom, found a seat.

Four hours to Boston.

Chapter 13

By the time she reached Clark's Grove, Jessie was sick of traveling.

Four hours to Boston. She got there in the middle of the night, so she took a cheap hotel room close to the train station. The next day, she caught a shuttle to the airport and found a flight to Chicago, which she booked under the name of Barbara Slonaker. During a two-hour layover at O'Hare she ate a slice of pizza and browsed a couple of newsstands, buying some paperback books. Then another flight took her to Cedar Rapids, landing a little after six, local time. She spent that night in a motel just outside the airport. In the morning, she took a Greyhound to Dubuque. Eleven hours on the bus, then a county transit bus to Clark's Grove, since Greyhound didn't go there.

Long trip.

The bus dropped her off downtown, if the term even applied here. There was a town square that might have been pleasant if she hadn't been dead on her feet. It was strictly, she thought, Norman Rockwell country. A wide lawn, patches of snow shimmering silver in the moonlight, complete with a band shell. A twenty-foot pine was decorated with glass balls and tinsel garlands, lit by three spotlights.

On one side of the square stood a building that couldn't be anything but a courthouse. Next to that, a smaller building had a sign hanging in front of it that said POST OFFICE, but it looked like somebody's cottage. Icicles hung from the eaves.

Across from the courthouse, there were some brick buildings housing shops. On the other sides of the park were a schoolhouse and another row of shops, this one in a series of wood-framed buildings.

Trees raised bare branches to the waning moon. Wood smoke scented the air.

Three blocks away, the Mississippi River flowed.

According to the map she had, anyway. Jessie wasn't about to walk the three blocks. She wasn't about to walk anywhere. If there were a hotel here, she'd get a room and wait until tomorrow to see Joan.

As it was, she didn't see anything resembling a hotel. And hadn't, riding through what there was of Clark's Grove on the bus. There had been miles and miles of fields and trees and corn and pigs and more fields. Then there had been a small collection of houses, then a few commercial buildings.

Everything was closed. It was just after eleven o'clock at night. Manhattan would have been booming.

Hell, Manhattan *Kansas* was probably booming.

The bus had stopped in front of the courthouse. That's where she stayed.

There was a pay phone against the wall of the post office. Not a booth, just a phone on a little stand. She walked to it, even though it was almost half a block away. Dialed Joan's number. After a moment, Joan picked up.

"I'm here," Jessie said.

"Where?"

"At the post office."

"Stay there," Joan said. "I'll be right down."

She hung up.

Stay there.

As if there was anywhere else to go.

She stayed.

Twenty-three minutes later, the first vehicle she had seen in motion pulled into the square. It was a full-sized blue Toyota pick-up.

She figured if it was anyone but Joan, it would have been Chevy or Ford. This was "buy American" country. She stepped away from the post office wall she'd been leaning on. Waved.

The truck pulled up beside her. Inside were a woman she didn't recognize and a six-year-old towheaded girl wearing a Cubs cap. Blonde hair spilling out of the cap dangled past her shoulders. She was thin, with petite features and a spray of freckles across her dot of a nose.

The woman bore a striking resemblance to Jessie's mom, so she figured it was probably Joan. She was thicker than Jessie, but she wore the weight well. Her attractive face was full, and when she smiled, dimples creased her cheeks, erasing a decade. Her hair was gray and cut short. She wore a heavy wool coat over a plaid shirt and jeans.

When she stopped the truck, the little girl unlocked the passenger door, then unbuckled her seat belt and shoved over next to her mother. She buckled the center belt around her tiny waist.

Jessie opened the truck's door.

"Joan?"

"God damn," Joan said. "You look so much like me it's scary." She laughed, a loud barking sound that Jessie found infectious. "Like I did, I mean. A few years back, of course. Only better dressed. Get in, girl, you think I want to heat all of Iowa with this little truck?"

"Uhh," Jessie said. "Hi." She tossed her backpack and gym bag in the truck's bed, climbed in. The girl looked at her, looked at the seat belt. Jessie buckled up.

"Cassie's big on seat belts," Joan said. "Cassie, say hello to your Aunt Jessica."

"Hello, Aunt Jessica," Cassie said.

"Hi, Cassie. You can call me Jessie."

"You can call her *Aunt* Jessie," Joan corrected. "Around here, Jessie, kids are still taught to respect their elders."

"Aunt Jessie it is, then." She fished in her purse for the little bear she'd bought in New York. "I brought you this, Cassie," she said. "Maybe you're too grown up for teddy bears, though."

"It's cute!" Cassie said. "Thank you, Aunt Jessie." She took the bear, a smile on her face for the first time, and examined it carefully. "Is it a Beanie Baby?"

"No, not a real one," Jessie said. "I just thought it was adorable, and when I bought it, it made me think of you. Well, your mom."

"A teddy bear made you think of Mom?"

"The store did," Jesse explained. "I was in FAO Schwarz, on Fifth, Joan. Remember how we used to go there with Mom and Dad?"

"I remember when I was little," Joan said. "I can't really remember going there with you along. Maybe once or twice."

"Your mom was just about out of the house by the time I came along," Jessie explained.

"The folks had decided I was hopeless, so they wanted to try again, see if they could get it right."

"I'm sure that's not what happened, Joan."

"I'm sure it is. I even talked with Mom about it, one time."

"And she said that?"

"Not in so many words, but she basically admitted it."

"I'm sorry you never got to meet your grandparents, Cassie," Jessie said. "They'd have loved having a little blonde granddaughter to spoil."

"Cassandra is plenty spoiled," Joan said. "Here we are."

They'd driven maybe twenty minutes through the Iowa night, and Joan was turning down a tree-shaded dirt lane. The house was set back from the road about three hundred feet. Between the house and road was a wide lawn, and scatterings of trees that Jessie couldn't even name. Oak, maybe. Maple?

"Cassandra?" Jessie asked. "What a beautiful name."

"Thanks, Aunt Jessie."

"No hidden meanings, in case you're wondering," Joan said. "We just liked the way it sounded."

The house was whitewashed clapboard, two stories, with dormer windows under the sharply slanted roof. There were two steps up to a door, then a small, glassed-in porch. Beyond the porch was a real front door.

To the left of the house was a carriage house converted to a garage. The doors stood open, and two rutted tracks led inside. It was barely wide enough for the truck. Tools hung on the walls. Overhead, the roof beams supported planks on which cardboard boxes rested.

They got out of the truck.

"This is home." Joan said. "Come on in and get comfortable."

She led the way out of the carriage house and through the porch. The storm door on the porch was unlocked, but Jessie noticed there was a deadbolt on the main door, as well as the knob lock. Once they were inside, Joan locked both, and slipped on a chain lock as well. There was a peephole in the door.

Could have been a Manhattan apartment. Jessie had thought Iowans were more trusting.

The place reminded Jessie of her suburban Connecticut home, the only freestanding house she had ever lived in. Right down to the lack of any distinguishable male presence. "No pets?" she asked. In Connecticut, she and her mother had a dog and a cat.

Mom's allergic to their dandruff," Cassie said.

"Dander," Joan corrected.

"Yeah. But I have fish, you want to see?"

"You'd best get back upstairs to bed, young lady," Joan said. "Aunt Jessie can stop in before you go to sleep, and you can show her your aquarium."

Cassie breathed a disgruntled sigh. "Okay, Mom. And thank you again for my bear, Aunt Jessie."

"You're welcome, sweetie," Jessie said.

When the girl was safely upstairs, Joan took Jessica into the kitchen. It was a sunny room, even at midnight. The walls were yellow, cabinets some blond wood, old and faded. Floor of ceramic tile in black and white squares, counters yellow tile. The house had probably been standing, unrenovated, since the twenties. "Coffee?" Joan asked.

Jessie shook her head. "It's been a long, hellish day. One of many. I have to crash soon, and coffee will just wire me. It won't keep me awake, at this point, but it'll make my sleep lousy."

"Just wanted to offer. We do have to talk."

"I know. I want you to know how much I appreciate this—"

"We're sisters," Joan said. "Not close ones, maybe, but blood is blood. You want to tell me what's going on? Don't have to, but you can if you want."

"I do want to, but not tonight. How about tomorrow?"

"Whenever you're ready. I am happy to help you hide out, but I do have some ground rules." Joan leaned against the counter, arms folded over her chest. She looked like someone who had given this lecture before, and Jessie realized that she probably had.

"Okay."

"Do *not* put my little girl in danger."

"I wouldn't dream of it," Jessie said. She sat at the wooden table. A green linen tablecloth covered it, and she let her fingers play with the fringe at the edge. "She's a sweetheart."

"She's my sweetheart, and I won't lose her. For anything."

"Where's her dad?"

"He went his own way, a few years back. She gets a card from him once in a while. Birthdays, Christmas, like that."

"Great."

"It's his life," Joan said. "Cassie is mine. You understand?"

"Yes," Jessie said.

"Good. You're welcome to join us for meals. You're even welcome to cook some of them, especially if you don't like my cooking. Rather see you do some of the work than bitch about what I make."

"I'm not much of a cook, but okay."

"That's right, you live in the land of takeout. We can't even get a pizza delivered out here. Definitely no Chinese."

"I can cope."

"You'll have to. If I'm doing most of the cooking, which it sounds like I will be, I'll expect you to do dishes."

Jessica looked around the room.

"No, there's no dishwasher," Joan said with a short laugh. "That'll be you." She pointed to a yellow plastic dish drainer, next to the sink. "There's that. And towels. Sponges, a sink, some detergent. Everything you need."

"Great."

"I didn't ask you to come here, Jess."

"I know, Joan. I'm sorry. I'm just tired."

"I hope you don't show any attitude around Cassie," Joan said. "You have any idea how hard it is, raising a child in this world? Trying not to let her be ruined by greed and TV and poisons in the air and water, by fashion magazines and stalkers on the Internet and hatred everywhere?"

Greed, Jessie noticed, came first. Tough spot for a banker's daughter, and a banker herself.

She didn't think it was a rhetorical question, and she considered her answer before she gave it.

"No, I don't. I'm sure it's very difficult, very challenging. But as far as actually knowing, having any personal experience with it, no. I have spent some time with the kids of colleagues, and I dated a single dad for a little while. That's about it."

Joan scooted back a chair, turned it around, straddled it.

"It's fucking hard," she said. "If you've got any values at all, and you want your kid to share them, it's just fucking hard."

"She seems like a great kid."

"She is. I'm trying to keep her that way."

"I'll try not to be a problem, Joan."

"I know. I'm just telling you what's important to me. How long you think you'll stay?"

"I don't know. Hopefully not long. But I have to say, I don't exactly have a plan or anything."

"Just hiding out?"

"Exactly."

"This place is good for that," Joan said. "Not like anyone will accidentally find you here."

"I figured that," Jessie said. She stared at Joan, and finally the older woman grew uncomfortable under her gaze.

"What are you looking at?"

"Myself, I guess. In a few years. According to you."

"Live right, Jess," she said. "And you'll never have to look like me."

* * *

As promised, Jessie dropped by Cassandra's room after her talking-to from Joan. She expected the girl to be asleep, but when she pushed the door open, a strip of light from the hall fell onto an open eye. "Aunt Jessie!"

"Shh," Jessie said. "I've got to get some sleep, and so do you. I can only stay for a minute."

"Okay. Can I show you my fish?"

"Of course."

Cassie rolled from bed. Her nightgown reached her knees. Horses and sections of fence, barns and clouds decorated it.

A table stood by the wall opposite her bed, with a small aquarium burbling gently on top of it. Cassie flicked on an interior light. Fish swam past the glass and darted in and out of artificial coral and plants resting on a bed of marble-strewn gravel.

Those are golden white cloud minnows," the girl reported. "Here, these are diamond tetras. This pretty one here is a sparkling gourami."

Jessie knelt by the tank, breathing in Cassie's pleasure at showing it off. The fish really were pretty, catching the light, moving with easy abandon through the water. Behind the larger of the coral pieces was a small plastic deep-sea diver, a tube linking him to the surface. He stood before a treasure chest, its top wafting open and closed as air bubbled out. A seeming fortune in painted, plastic gold coins filled the chest to overflowing.

"They're beautiful, Cassie."

"Do you want to know their names?"

"Maybe tomorrow, honey. Right now I'm so sleepy I'm not even sure of my own name."

"Okay." Cassie threw her arms around Jessie's neck, gave her a quick squeeze, then shut off the aquarium light and climbed back onto her bed. "Aunt Jessie?"

"Yes?"

The girl slid between her covers, pulled a red comforter up to her chin. "I'm glad you're here."

"I am too, sweetie," Jessie said. She was almost surprised by how much she meant it. "Me too."

Chapter 14

Sitting in Clark's Grove's library, around the corner from the courthouse she had seen the night before, Jessie checked e-mail on her laptop. The library had Wi-Fi, while the only option at Joan's would have been dial-up. Joan didn't have a computer in the house—wouldn't have one, she said, until Cassie was sixteen. Jessie got the impression that her sister was some kind of neo-Luddite who had only recently accepted the necessity of having a telephone in the house, but wasn't about to go as far as a computer, pager, cell phone or videogame system.

DVD? Forget it.

She did own a television set on a satellite system, which surprised Jessie a little. It was a fifteen-year-old Panasonic. Everyone looked a little green.

E-mail was a pointless exercise, Jessie decided. Everything was either mundane—notes from friends she didn't dare communicate with, reminders of appointments she'd already missed, jokes forwarded at lightning speed around the Internet, appeals for money from various interest groups—or disturbing. The disturbing ones included a note from Victoria Burrows, asking if she could explain her mysterious phone call the other day, and a couple of messages from Barbara Slonaker, asking her to please get in touch as soon as possible.

She didn't answer any of it.

Joan had been sitting in another section of the library, reading a magazine. She looked up as Jessie approached.

"You don't look like you feel better," she said.

"I don't," Jessie said. "You were right, I shouldn't even have looked."

"Sorry," Joan said. "Feel like some lunch?" She replaced her magazine on the slanted periodical shelves.

"Sure," Jessie said. She followed Joan from the building.

* * *

She had spent the night on a couch in Joan's living room. There was no spare bedroom, so Joan gave her a couple of blankets and a pillow for the long sofa.

This room, like the kitchen, was full of things. Clutter, to Jessie's mind. The couch, two chairs, a separate piece of furniture holding a stereo system, lamps, bookshelves containing books as well as an assortment of knickknacks: little statues, framed photos, souvenirs of trips. Paintings and a big clock hung on the walls. A coiled rug covered part of the hardwood floor. Toys were scattered on the rug and floor, and a cocked pile of children's picture books leaned next to one of the chairs.

Then there were the dolls.

Every flat surface, seemingly, that wasn't taken by a photo or a clock or a statue or a souvenir mug had a doll on it. Many were in glass cases, and Jessie could tell that some were antiques, probably valuable. There was every type of doll she could think of: baby dolls, Madame Alexander dolls in elaborate outfits, a classic Barbie in her black and white striped bathing suit, a Kewpie, a Raggedy Ann so ancient and threadbare Jessie thought she could almost be the original. Some of the dolls had delicate porcelain or china faces, others plastic or cloth. One was made of what looked like a bunch of rags, loosely knotted, yet the final effect was as convincingly human as some of the more elaborate constructions.

"Nice dolls," Jessie said to Joan. "Cassie's, or yours?"

"Cassie has a few in her room. These are mine. It's a hobby we can share."

"That sounds like a good thing."

"I like dolls," Joan said. "They don't ask you questions."

Jessie was struck by the sense that this was a family's home, and she was not used to family homes.

She was reminded again of the house in Connecticut, the one her mother had moved her to after Jessie's father had died. That was supposed to be a family house. It had all the trappings.

But it was quiet inside, sterile. Her mother, she figured, had already begun the long process of her own dying. She didn't bring any energy to the house, didn't infuse it with the sense of a life being lived that Joan and Cassie's house had.

No wonder she'd tried to escape it on weekends by going to Victoria's whenever she could. Victoria's house was always full of people coming and going—her brothers and sister, her parents, a grandmother who lived in a little room downstairs, friends of the family. It was a crowded but comfortable house.

Joan's house wasn't crowded with people, and it was dark, and there were no views of city skylines, no sounds of cars and people in motion, no sirens.

In Iowa, crickets sang her to sleep.

In the morning, she had wakened to the sounds of Cassie getting ready for school, but she wanted to seize every minute of sleep she could get. She pulled the pillow over her head, and fell asleep again. Finally, a little before ten, she woke up for good.

The house was quiet.

She went upstairs to the only full bath, peed, showered in a big claw-footed bathtub.

When she came back downstairs, toweling her hair—she kept her blonde hair relatively short, low-maintenance: some shampoo, some leave-in conditioner, an occasional brushing, and she was set—Joan was in the kitchen preparing a big country breakfast.

Jessie dressed quickly, joined her sister in the sunny kitchen.

"Breakfast is usually at seven," Joan said. "I figured this once, with jet lag and everything else, I'd let you sleep in. Do it again and you get to fix your own breakfast."

Jessie looked at the spread—bacon, eggs, biscuits, gravy, two kinds of toast, slices of melon, coffee, and orange juice. "I usually don't eat a real big breakfast," she said.

"I can tell that by looking at you," Joan said.

"Thanks."

"Wasn't necessarily a compliment."

Jessie sat down to eat, and found to her astonishment that she was really hungry. She put away at least a little of everything.

Afterwards, they climbed into the truck and Joan gave Jessica a tour of Clark's Grove. It didn't take long.

Included were the town square she'd already seen, McPherson's Drug and Dollar, also on the square, where Joan worked as a sales clerk, and the Mississippi, which was even wider and more brown than Jessie had imagined it. The town's streets dipped toward the river, and small shops shared space with a couple of docks and warehouses at its banks.

The water was full of boats—sailboats, barges, pleasure yachts, even a big paddlewheel riverboat that Joan said was a floating casino.

When Joan drove her into the business district, she was surprised by the number of vacant storefronts, and commented on it.

"Look in the mirror," Joan said.

"What?"

"That's your kind at work. Wall Street, the banks."

Jessie shook her head, drawing a blank.

"Seriously?" Joan asked. "You missed the economic crash? Kind of comfortable there in Manhattan, weren't you?"

"I didn't miss it, but—"

Joan pulled into a slanted parking slot and killed the engine. "We're hanging on at McPherson's, by the skin of our teeth." She pointed toward one of the empty stores. "There used to be a men's clothing store there. Ranch and farm wear, some Sunday church suits, that kind of thing. Hank Milligan, who owned it, he blew his brains out with a shotgun when his house was foreclosed. His business had dropped off to almost nothing, but he stayed solvent by taking a line of credit against the house. Practically overnight, the house lost more than half its value. He couldn't refinance, the bank called in the loans. Hank couldn't stand it."

She indicated two other empty spaces, contiguous to the former menswear shop.

"Beauty parlor there employed five women, three of them single mothers. Two of them are working at a Walmart forty miles away, one's on relief, I don't know where the other two landed. Beside that, that big space there, that was Raley's Tools. Hardware, small home furnishings, that sort of thing. After the store folded up, Glenn Raley's house burned to the ground, and I'd give you five-to-one odds he lit the match."

"That's terrible, Joan, but—"

Joan wasn't finished. Jessie got the sense that she'd had something building inside her for a long time, but the right person to unload on hadn't come around.

Until now.

"Biggest non-farm employer in the area used to be a pipe and tube manufacturing plant, over by the river. They mostly sold to local governments or developers, infrastructure projects. When those stopped, they were hurting. When they couldn't get a bank loan to carry them through, they shut down. Grocery store followed, and the movie theater, Snoopy's Sporting Goods. Families that were getting by on two incomes had to rely on one, and sometimes not even that. People have been unemployed so long, the unemployment's run out. Only place you'll see a line on a weekday now is at the food bank. Most of them still get food stamps, but those don't last long with a family of four. Do you know the symptoms of a child who's chronically hungry, Jess?"

One of those questions in life to which there were no good answers. Jessie didn't try, simply shrugged.

"You'll learn them, if you stay long enough. Sunken eyes. Crusted lips. Hoarding what food they do get. There are probably as many people out of work in this country as live in all of North Korea, Jess. Even here in Clark's Grove, at least one house in five is either underwater, in foreclosure, or abandoned."

"It's tragic. But I hardly think I'm the one responsible."

Joan shot her a stern, sidelong glance. "The generic 'you,'" she said. "People who play with money like it's nothing more than numbers on a computer. They think it's all about the big numbers, the toxic assets that Goldman Sachs and MetroBank and the rest have on the books that they have to unload any way they can. Not understanding that at the core, it's really about people's lives. Debt is a drug, and you people, bankers and financiers, you're the pushers. And the drug is poison."

"I've read the newspapers," Jessie said. She felt she ought to defend herself and her chosen profession, but Joan's barrage of words was overpowering. "Believe me, there's poverty in New York, too. Somehow I thought—"

"You thought we were immune to it, out here in the heartland? Hardly. Voltaire said the comfort of the rich depends on an abundance of the poor, or something like that.

"Well, it's working, the way I hear it. The rich are plenty comfortable, and the poor are plenty poor."

She started the truck again, her piece said. She started talking about the town's demographics and geography. The population of Clark's Grove was a little over a thousand, although Joan suspected that even that number had dwindled since the last real census. They were north of Dubuque, with nothing but a few little hamlets and a lot of cold between them and Minnesota, and then the great expanse of Canada.

"This is mostly hog country," Joan explained. "Some corn and other crops. But hogs drive what economy is left. It's like, what do you want for dinner, ham or pork chops?"

"And bacon every morning."

"You get thrown out of the county if you miss a day."

"What do you grow?"

"My place isn't really a farm," Joan said. "I have a few vegetables— corn, beans, tomatoes—and some herbs. Mostly just for me and Cassie, and some leftover to put up, or give the neighbors. I only have a few acres, and no real interest in working it all. The place is rented; I don't own it."

Jessie looked at the rural landscape as they passed. It seemed like you could see forever, your view broken only by clutches of trees or the occasional neat farmhouse, white barn, or silo. Quite a change from the concrete canyons of Manhattan. And the sky was a vast bowl of clear blue.

"Sure is flat here," Jessie said. She was glad the conversation had turned. She wasn't personally at fault for the economic situation in Clark's Grove or anywhere else, but Joan had made her feel part of the moneyed class, enriching themselves at the expense of their countrymen. She didn't like the feeling.

"Yep," Joan said. "This part of Iowa and Wisconsin is known as the Driftless Area. In the last ice age, sheets of ice scoured the whole region clean."

"So how did you end up here?"

Joan turned her gaze from the road, looked straight at Jessie. "By car," she said flatly.

As they drove, Jessie had tried to ask questions about Joan's life since they'd last spoken, but Joan made it clear that she wasn't interested in talking about anything but the here and now. She worked at the drug store. She dated a man named Frank sometimes. Cassie liked him, but she had no intention of getting married again. Cassie liked school and the friends she had there. That was about as far as she would go.

Then, as if to emphasize the point, she had pulled to a stop before the small town library. "You said something about e-mail," she said. "They have wireless here."

* * *

Lunch was at Danny's Inn, a coffee shop on the main shopping drag, which was two blocks long and extended away from the town square. The decor was strictly 50's diner—long Formica counter, booths with orange Naugahyde cushions, lots of chrome accessories. The two waitresses wore starched white uniforms and little hats.

Jessie thought she'd walked through a time warp.

Joan led the way to a booth, and Jessie followed. She obviously knew the routines here. After a minute, a waitress came to the table bearing one menu. She handed it to Jessie.

"I know you don't need one," she said to Joan.

"Betsy, this is Barb, my cousin from New York," Joan said.

"Hi, Barb," the waitress said.

"It's nice to meet you, Betsy," Jessie said. None of this had been prearranged; she had no expectation that Joan would introduce her to any of the locals, or that she would carry on the Barbara Slonaker charade here.

But it made sense.

Clark's Grove was a small town, not a tourist mecca. People didn't just show up here without a reason. Visiting a cousin was as good a reason as any other, and would help explain why Barb Slonaker had never come up in conversation before.

Joan was good at this stuff.

"Listen, Joan," Jessie said after Betsy had taken their orders. "I want to pay for lunch. And I want to contribute financially to the household as long as I'm here. There's no reason your electricity, water, and food bills should be a problem because you're putting me up."

"That's fine," Joan said. "But I thought you were in hiding."

"Meaning?"

"Meaning you can't write me a check. And you can't exactly go to the bank and make a withdrawal whenever you feel like it."

That was true, Jessie thought.

But Barbara Slonaker could.

Or could she? If Barbara found out that her name was being used to make withdrawals, she would start to track them. She would be able to figure out that Jessie must be hiding in Clark's Grove. Knowing that much, it wouldn't be that hard to find her.

"Good point," Jessie said. Another idea was already occurring to her. "I can't. And Barbara can't. But you might be able to."

"Say what?"

"I need to put some thought into it," Jessie said. "But I think I could arrange to have some funds transferred into your account here. The people I'm worried about have no idea who you are, so the name Joan Temchin wouldn't ring any bells for them. Then you could transfer it to a dummy account I'll create for myself."

"But couldn't they just follow the money?"

"Not necessarily. I mean, there's always a trail of some kind, unless you physically carry cash from one place to another. But there's also something called concentration accounts. Money from various sources is all mixed together—commingled, we call it."

"Why?"

"That's a little hard to explain."

"Maybe," Joan said, "you should tell me everything. From the beginning."

So Jessie did. Told her about being a private banker, about Steele's accounts in various lands, and about seeing Steele shoot people in a parking garage, accompanied by Jake Garland. Over pie and coffee they talked about what she had done since, how she had gone underground in New York and funded her escape with money from Steele's own accounts.

It was easier to tell this time than it had been to the New York Times reporter.

Still, it took a while, especially since it was punctuated with interruptions by Betsy heating up their coffee, clearing dishes, being generally nosy. Finally, she stopped by the table for no apparent reason and said, "I guess you two had a lot of catching up to do."

"That's right," Joan said. "We don't get together very often, I'm afraid."

They took their leave shortly after that. They had left Joan's truck parked by the library, and now walked through the cold, crisp air back toward it. Brown leaves swirled at their feet.

"So," Joan said as they walked. "What do you really want?"

"Meaning?"

"Meaning, do you want to spend the rest of your life running and hiding? Or do you want to take some action against these people, maybe get your life back?"

"Action, I guess," Jessie said. "I don't know what yet. Higher law enforcement authorities, maybe. The FBI?"

"You're not going to make much progress out here in Iowa," Joan said. "If you want to fight this, you can. But you need to stay alive long enough to do it, and as soon as you surface, you'll become a target again."

"That is the challenge, isn't it?"

"It doesn't have to be that hard," Joan said. "There is something you can do. I can't deny that it'll be dangerous. But that wouldn't be any different than what you're going through now."

"True."

"So you need help. You need someone who is also dangerous. If people are going to try to kill you, you need to accept that, in trying not to end up dead yourself, you may be responsible for those other people being killed. Being peaceful is not always an option, unless you don't mind losing the fight. You need someone who can keep you alive long enough to come up with a plan, and implement it."

Made sense.

"Do you have somebody in mind?"

"No," Joan said. "I don't. But I think I know how to find someone."

"Okay," Jessie said. "How?"

"Back to the library."

* * *

Jessie was getting used to the library. This time, Joan sat at her shoulder. She started to figure out what Joan had in mind when she suggested, as a starting point, a site called www.worldsoldier.com.

"Mercenaries?" she asked in a whisper. "How do you know about this sort of thing?"

"Let's just say that people living on the fringes tend to run across each other. I don't have any friends in the business, but I've known people who know people. Anyway, you need someone who knows what combat is like," Joan said. "But someone who won't make fine legal or moral judgments. You've already stolen, after all. You're probably a fugitive from justice by now, and if not, you will be soon. You can't exactly bring in a private detective or an off-duty cop. And people are turning up dead. You're running out of options."

"I guess you're right." She turned back to the screen. With Joan offering input, they followed a couple of links, finally ending up at a kind of classified page, where people who went to war for money promoted their services.

Jessie was uncomfortable with the whole thing, but Joan urged her on.

Together they read a number of ads. They all seemed wrong to Jessie. She couldn't quite overcome her sense of revulsion at the whole concept. These people were killers.

They could call themselves mercs, or warriors, or soldiers for hire, but really they were rent-a-killers, offering up murder to the highest bidder.

Finally, they found one that didn't entirely turn her stomach.

"Soldier/bodyguard/security services," the headline read. Jessie clicked on it, and it opened a link to the body of his ad.

"Experienced soldier (Iraq/Afghan, Africa, L. Amer.) seeking long or short term position. Skilled in all forms of combat, weaponry, demolition, infiltration. Night work, wet work specialties. Located in western US but will travel. Reasonable rates. Email byrd@worldsoldier.com with phone number for further information."

"That sounds like a good one," Joan said.

"I like the fact that he offers bodyguard and security work. Like he's more than just a hired gun."

"Remember, what you probably need is a hired gun."

"Doesn't mean I have to like it," Jessie said. "And I don't."

"It can't hurt to talk to him," Joan insisted. "Send him an e-mail."

Jessie opened an anonymous-sender email program, composed a short note.

"I saw your ad at worldsoldier.com," it said. "Am in need of bodyguard services for an indefinite period of time. Currently in Iowa, but some travel may be necessary."

"Can I put your phone number?" she asked.

"You got a choice?"

Not since she had tossed her Blackberry down a sewer. She typed in Joan's phone number, added, "ask for Barbara," and clicked on SEND.

She almost hoped he wouldn't call.

Chapter 15

Barbara Slonaker's life was consumed by the Jessica Cutler problem. No one knew where Jessie had gone. There had been signs of life—ATM withdrawals, occasional sightings around Manhattan—but then nothing, for days now. Barbara had other responsibilities at MetroBank, but they were going unattended.

Papers piled up in her in-basket. Pink phone message slips littered her desktop. Emails stacked up. She didn't care.

She wasn't sleeping. She was barely eating. She knew she looked like hell. Dark circles ringed her eyes. Her color was pale.

She didn't care.

Jessie Cutler could bring them all down, if she could manage to tell her story to the right people. So far, she had been prevented from doing so, thanks to the protective network Richard had built. But how far did that network stretch? Even Barbara didn't know the answer to that one.

She knew Jessie, however, as well as anyone. Knew the younger woman had determination to spare. Always had.

If she gave up easily, she would have quit banking during her first six months, gone to work at a shoe store or something. Nobody made it easy on her. They said she only got the job because of her father's old connections, his reputation. They didn't just say it behind her back. She heard things. She was tested, over and over. But she never let them force her out.

Barbara had a gut feeling that she would be the same way now.

Her phone buzzed. "Yes?" she said. Snapped, really. Patience was long gone.

"Ms. Slonaker, you have a visitor. Mr. Garland?"

"Bring him in," Barbara said.

Her office door opened a moment later as Julie, her administrative assistant, showed Jake Garland into the room.

"No calls, Julie," Barbara said.

"Got it," Julie said.

Barbara waved distractedly at one of her black leather guest chairs. He sat. She buried her face in her hands.

"I do have a life, you know," she said, her voice muffled by her hands. "I have a job. I'd like to keep it."

"What you have, lady, is a problem."

She looked out from behind the cage of fingers. He sat there, looking awkward in his own skin. Thin as a pencil, with that thatch of copper on his head like new pennies melted and spun into coiled fiber.

"Think I don't know that?"

"I'm sure you do. I just want you to know that you aren't the only one who does."

"Believe me," she said. "Jake, do you know what it could do to me, you coming to my office like this? For God's sake, you're assigned to FinCEN. What if someone recognizes you? You're not exactly unassuming. You know what people would say?"

"It's not that bad, Barbara. Maybe you're making a report to us."

"Yeah, and maybe I'm being investigated. You know what I don't need right now? I don't need the scrutiny, you know? I don't need my colleagues asking lots of questions about me."

"Then let's keep it brief, Barb. We all want Cutler found. You know her best. I need to know if there's anything about her, anything we've been missing, that might point to where she's gone. Family? Friends? Favorite places? Childhood haunts?"

"I didn't know her when she was little, Jake. Jim Mackie did, but I'm sure you've already been over everything with him. Her immediate family's dead. Cousins, aunts, uncles, I don't know any of that stuff. I gather she wasn't very close to any, though, or I'd have heard about them. She always seemed sort of distrustful of family ties to me, so I don't think that's a way to go.

"As far as friends, you've seen her Rolodex. I'm sure you've checked out everybody who was on there, right?"

"As best we could. Lot of dead ends there."

"Then you know as much as me. I liked Jessie. As an aggressive young banker who was willing to take chances to get the job done.

That's about as far as it went. We had dinner a few times, we went out for drinks. She's been to my place. I've been to hers. We weren't bosom buddies, Jake. I do know I wouldn't call her a people person."

"Think about her, Barb."

"Please don't call me that, Jake." As soon as she said it, she knew it was a mistake. You never let a guy like Jake Garland know what you liked and didn't like, because he would exploit it.

"Think. Where would she go? What does she like to do?"

"She likes to sit in her apartment with flannel jammies on and watch old movies on Blu-Ray while she eats ice cream. She likes to run in the park. She likes to work. She truly enjoys banking—the intellectual challenge, manipulating figures. She likes sex, but I don't think she likes men that much. She never seems to get really closely attached to any. I think it's part of the family thing. She never wanted to get married, settle down, so she always kind of kept her men at arm's length, it seems like. Maybe everyone. She builds walls around herself. I don't know what it takes to get in. Maybe nobody ever does."

"That's good, Barbara. What else?"

"I don't know, Jake," she said, frustrated. "The color green, I guess. Starbucks. She likes to read, but seems to have difficulty finding time for novels. She's always got magazines around. She files them by title and date."

"Very interesting, Barb, but it's not helping me get close to her. Where would she go?"

"I don't know!" Barbara slammed her hand down on the desk. "Damn it, I just don't know. I don't see her going back to Connecticut. She hated it there. Queens? Why? I don't know where she would go. She loves Manhattan. It's a big place. What makes you think she's gone anywhere?"

Jake rose from the chair.

"I don't know, Barbara. I'm just trying to figure her out. If you think of anything else, call me."

"Fine. Just...get out. Try not to let anyone see you on the way."

* * *

That night, Barbara stood in her condo, looking out at the Hudson River, a glass of red wine in her hand. She loved the view from here, through the big panes of glass. Even though the river was black, she could see lights glimmering on its surface, watch the occasional boat cruise past.

She had come to think of her life as a river. On the surface, things were orderly, controlled, business as usual. Commerce ruled it, but pleasure craft skittered around the big barges and liners. Under the surface, though—and not very far under—there was a whole unseen world of turmoil. She had become involved in criminal activities. She kept these things hidden from most of the world, disguised beneath the orderly surface. But these were the roiling currents that really ruled her life, though—the traffic on the surface was at the mercy of unseen forces from below.

Now, though, her world had turned upside down. This afternoon, in her own office—once a symbol of business as usual—she had told a federal law enforcement officer everything she could that might help him find, and probably kill, a law-abiding individual whose only mistake was that she was too damn honest.

The river was out of control. The bottom was the top, and the surface was in turmoil underneath.

And she was swimming as hard as she could against the current.

Drowning in thin air.

Chapter 16

Three days later, a beat-up, battered, silver Dodge Raider pulled up outside the house, coughed twice, and died.

Joan and Jessie, who had been reading in the living room, looked out the window.

The driver's door opened and a man unfolded himself onto the ground. He was six feet tall or a little more, long and lean and grizzled looking.

From inside, it looked like he was maybe sixty-five, as well. He hadn't sounded that old on the phone, and Jessie hadn't thought to ask his age.

Maybe his African service had been during the Boer War.

He moved slowly toward the door, as if each step sent shooting pains through his joints. Maybe they did. He wore a heavy denim coat with a leather collar, a plaid shirt with pearl snap closures, jeans, cowboy boots, and in his right hand he carried a big black cowboy hat. He was probably too tall to comfortably wear it inside the car.

Jessie and Joan looked at each other.

"My God," Joan said. "You've hired Clint Eastwood."

"Clint I could live with. I'm afraid I've hired his grandpa."

There was a slow rapping at the door.

Close up, there was an ageless quality about him. He had lived plenty, Jessie could tell, but he could have been anywhere from fifty to seventy. He had short white hair, a lined face, pale gray eyes so small and hidden behind such folds that Jessie was surprised he could see out of them at all. He looked like he hadn't shaved since leaving Nevada, which is where he'd told Jessie on the phone he would be driving in from.

"Howdy," he said.

Of course he did.

"One of you ladies named Barbara?"

"I'm Barbara," Jessie lied.

"My name's Morgan Byrd," the man said. He put his hand out and Jessie shook it. His palm had the dry, callused skin of someone who worked with his hands.

"Won't you come inside, Mr. Byrd?" Joan asked.

"Glad to. Don't mind if I stand for a bit, though. Been sittin' on my ass just about three days straight. Excuse my French."

"Excused," Joan said. "Just watch the language when my daughter's around."

"I'll do that, ma'am," Morgan Byrd said.

"I'll leave you two to your business," Joan said, heading upstairs.

Jessie ushered Morgan into the living room. She sat, while he stood, moving this way and that, looking at the pictures on the walls, the dolls, the books on Joan's bookshelves.

She guessed most rural Iowans didn't have "Soul On Ice," "Das Kapital," and "Steal This Book" in their collections.

He didn't seem to notice, though, or didn't say anything if he did. Instead, he fixed his gaze on Jessie. "So you're Barbara Slonaker."

"That's me," she said.

"I suppose you can show me some identification says so?"

Jessie was taken aback. "Ummm, sure." Since she was sleeping in this room, her purse and bags were here, tucked behind the couch. She grabbed her purse, opened it, took out the Slonaker driver's license.

"I guess maybe I should ask you for something to prove you're Morgan Byrd?" she asked, handing him the license. He took it in a big hand, webbed with wrinkles.

"Guess you should." He tugged a worn leather wallet from his Wranglers, handed over a Nevada driver's license that identified him as Morgan Byrd, of Winnemucca, Nevada.

"Mind tellin' me your real name?" he asked.

"What do you mean?"

"This is a pretty good fake. But a good fake's still a fake, ma'am."

"Thank God you don't work for the airlines," she said.

"I'll second that." He handed her back the license. "Let's get somethin' straight right off the bat. I do a variety of jobs for a variety of folks. Some of 'em ain't exactly within the letter of the law. Yours might not be either, I'm guessin'."

"Uhh..." Jessie said. "There's every chance that it isn't."

"Is, or isn't?"

"I have broken the law. Probably will do so again. If you hire on, you might break it as well. Certainly in terms of being an accomplice."

"Now, that's what I appreciate, ma'am. Straight shootin'." He sat finally, on the edge of a big easy chair. His big hands hung between his knees.

"I'm gonna tell you a little story. When I'm done, I want you to tell me exactly what it is I'm doin' here, and what you want with me. When I'm done, you'll know that you can tell me the truth, whatever it is."

"Okay."

"Do you understand what I'm sayin' here?"

She felt uncomfortable under his gaze. Figured that was the way she was supposed to feel. She determined not to let him see her squirm, stared right back into his eyes. "I think so, yes."

"Okay then. In 1984, I killed a man in Omaha, Nebraska. His name was Anton Barks. Not the kinda name you forget. It wasn't self defense, wasn't a bar fight, nothin' like that. Barks was one of my best clients, in fact. But he sent me out on this one job—I'll spare you the details—and he wasn't straight with me about how it would go down. Put me in an uncomfortable position and endangered the lives of some guys I hired to do it with me. When it was done, I went to see Barks. We had some words. Now he's dead as last week's roadkill."

He paused for a moment, then reminded her, "There's no statute of limitations on murder."

The silence sat there, as big as a city bus in the crowded room.

"Your turn," he said after a moment.

She understood. He had given her something that she could use against him, if need be. If his story was true. So she could tell him about her considerably lesser crimes, and know that he wouldn't use the knowledge against her.

He was, she was starting to realize, a smart guy. Maybe, through sheer, blind luck, she had picked the right man.

Again, if his story was true. She would try to research it later, in the library.

But later didn't help right now. She decided to trust him—decided she *had* to trust him. She sure as hell wasn't going to send him away and try to hire someone else. She needed help, maybe the kind he could offer. She needed someone who could keep her alive long enough to figure out how she could take action against Richard. If he was going to help her, he had to know the score.

She took a deep breath.

Started to speak.

And he put a hand up, silencing her.

"Let's take a walk," he said.

There had been some people in Jessie's life who made her uncomfortable right off the bat, people who threw her off balance. This guy, Morgan Byrd, was one of them. Even that name. Morgan Byrd? What kind of name was that for a mercenary, an admitted killer?

Morgan Byrd.

Jesus.

* * *

Morgan stood, and she followed suit. They went out the front door, walking slowly, casually. He was always leading, Jessie tagging along.

As they walked, he didn't look at her. He looked at everything else. The house, the yard, the road, a hundred yards away through the trees, the fields behind them. When they had put in a little distance, he glanced over his shoulder, making it look casual, and scanned the roof of the house. Clear. No neighbors close by; lights from the nearest house were at least three quarters of a mile off.

Long habit. Learn the lay of the land.

Anyplace can be a battlefield. If it became a killing ground, he would want to know it better than the other guy.

He had learned that at the knees—and fists—of his old man, who might not have been a very good teacher in the sense of setting an example for his son, but was a hell of a teacher in the sense of instilling lessons, however twisted, that were not soon forgotten.

They'd had a spread somewhat like this once, back in Nebraska. Bigger, with crops and some livestock. His father had blown everything he'd managed to save and win at cards on a farm, determined to settle down and become a "gentleman farmer."

That could happen.

The first winter had been hard, as they tended to be in Nebraska. By spring, he needed to borrow money for seed. That summer was long and hot and dry. By fall, the cattle were scrawny and he needed to borrow more to pay workers to bring in the harvest, and when the town's banker said he considered Zachary Byrd a bad credit risk, Zach had decked him with a single punch.

It had been up to Morgan's mother to smooth things over, and when she got home, she got a black eye and a couple of bruised ribs for her trouble. Zach's idea of loving communication.

These days, he would spend time in jail, and probably be sued, for what he'd done. In those days, the mid-fifties, they just moved on. Abandoned the farm.

Life in the Byrd household.

"What is your name?" Morgan asked the woman. "Real one."

"Jessica Cutler. Jessie's fine."

"Okay, Jessie. Tell me your story."

"I'm a banker, in New York," she said. I'm sorry, he thought, but he didn't say it. Somebody had to do it. Anyone else was better than him. "Or, I was, anyway. What they call a private banker. I help very wealthy people with their financial needs.

"I had a client—"

"Named?"

"Do you have to know that?"

"I reckon not. I don't mind drivin' back to Winnemucca."

She blew out a sigh. Her discomfort at his questions was palpable; so was his need to ask them anyway. He didn't put his life on the line without understanding the circumstances. He had, in his younger days, but somehow the more years he managed to tuck away, the more precious the ones that remained seemed. "Does the name Richard Steele mean anything to you?"

"Nope."

"Okay. Anyway, Richard is very wealthy. His financial interests are kind of complicated. He's got bank accounts in New York, Paris, Switzerland, the Cayman Islands—"

"He run drugs?"

"I don't think so, no."

"What's he do?"

"I...I'm not entirely sure."

"Then he might run drugs."

"He might. He doesn't seem like the type."

"The best ones probably don't. Doesn't matter, really. Accounts in those particular places, though. Sounds like maybe he's hidin' something."

"Yeah, well, I think he is. I didn't used to think so, really. But then one night, I had a dinner meeting with Richard—"

"You sleep with him?"

"Does it matter?"

"I don't know yet."

"What if I did?"

"It don't mean a thing to me, Jessie, but it might change how you feel about him. I'm just tryin' to fix the whole picture in my mind, is all."

"Okay, fine. No, I haven't slept with him. We had a business relationship, nothing more. So anyway, we had this dinner, and then I went to get a cab, but then I remembered that I had meant to give him something. So I chased him back toward where he had parked, but he was walking with someone."

"Someone you knew?"

"No. A man I had never seen before."

"Okay. Go on."

"They went into this parking structure where Richard had parked."

"Was there an attendant in the booth?"

"Now that you mention it, I didn't see one. Is that significant?"

"You never know what's gonna be significant, Jessie. Keep goin'."

"They were walking toward Richard's car. Suddenly, a car came down the ramp, with guns sticking out of the windows. They started shooting at Richard and the other guy. Richard and the man pulled guns and shot back. They hit the guy who was driving, and the car crashed. The other gunmen got out of the car, and there was a short gun battle. Richard and the guy with him won."

"Sounds like self defense to me. You know he carried a gun?"

"No, I didn't. But I thought the same thing. Self defense. Thank God he had the gun, I thought. But then something else happened— Richard and his friend went from one guy to the next, firing a bullet into each guy's head. I think they were already dead, but Richard was making absolutely sure."

"Sounds professional," Morgan said. "Or anyway, someone don't like takin' chances."

"At least."

"So you called the police?"

"No." He could see this part shamed her. The downcast gaze, the flush coloring her cheeks. "I should have. I just couldn't. Richard was my customer. I thought, in some way, that he was my friend. I knew there must be some kind of explanation for this. I figured the police would find out, and it would be investigated, and Richard would either be arrested or cleared. Either way, I wouldn't have to admit to him that I'd witnessed it. I guess I just couldn't see it for what it was. Stupid, huh?"

"Yup," Morgan agreed. They had completely circled the house by this point, and were heading toward Joan's barn. The barn hadn't been kept up well—it was white, but the paint was flaked and peeling, and the structure took a definite slant to the left. Maybe seventy-five, eighty yards from the house. "But I ain't here to judge you. What next?"

"Well, there was nothing about it in the newspapers, which surprised me. I decided I needed to talk to someone about it, so I went to my boss—actually my boss's boss, Jim Mackie."

"Why go over your boss's head?" Morgan led the way into the barn. It was dark inside, and minutely warmer than out. The floor was dirt, with hay strewn around randomly. No animals. The property had been much bigger, then subdivided.

"My boss is named Barbara Slonaker—"

"Hah!" Morgan's laugh burst from him like an explosion. "You are a gutsy one."

"Well, sometimes," she admitted. "And the reason I didn't go to her is that she's the one who recommended Richard Steele to the bank as a client. She managed his account, until she was promoted into a different department. That's when I took it over."

"So you figured if this guy Steele was dirty, she already knew about it. And she didn't care." As he walked through the barn, his gaze took in everything: the rafters, the lofts, the ladders, the stalls, the shadows.

Especially those.

People could sense when they were being watched, or so it was claimed. Morgan felt that way pretty much all the time. Only the eyes on him belonged not to the living, often as not, but to the dead. He remembered the face of everyone he had ever killed. Close to it, anyway. And those faces wouldn't leave him alone. Those eyes never closed.

"Or she was in on it from the beginning. She's also named as the treasurer of a dummy corporation he has in the Caymans, called Cielo Holdings."

"That SOP? For a banker to also be an officer?"

"It's not necessarily unusual. A lot of bankers are on the boards of corporations their clients run."

"On the board is different than bein' an officer."

"Yes, I suppose it is."

"So you figured that she might be dirty, but her boss wasn't. And you went to this guy Mackie."

"That's right. I've known him for years. He and my father were friends."

"And what'd he say?"

"He said that he'd look into Richard's accounts. If Richard was laundering money, he said, he'd take care of it. The bank is used to dealing with problems, he said."

"Did he?"

"I think his definition of 'problems' is different than mine. Or at least his definition of solutions is. When I was on my way home after work that evening, someone pushed me in front of a subway."

Morgan stopped in his tracks, looked at her.

"And you're still here. You're lucky or blessed."

"I'm thinking maybe both."

118 - Jeffrey J. Mariotte

"Sounds about right. You see who pushed you?"

"I think so. But I had never seen him before or since. Anyway, I dodged the train. But by the time I finally made it home, someone had been there. Searching the place, I guess."

"Not waitin' for you?"

"No, they'd left. I was worried, though. I figured they'd be coming back, since whatever they were looking for, they hadn't found. I thought maybe they were looking for some of the Richard Steele files I had, but most of them weren't at home or in my office. I was carrying them with me."

"What'd you do then?"

"I got out of the apartment. Went out a window, actually, so no one would see me. I rented a hotel room, with cash, in a part of the city I almost never go."

"Smart."

"Thank you. So that night I had another idea. If Richard Steele was laundering money—and people in my bank were not only aware of it, but helping protect him—I should go to the authorities who are supposed to be investigating money laundering in the first place."

"Can't argue with that."

"There's an agency called FinCEN. The Financial Crimes Enforcement Network. They use people from the Treasury, FBI, Interpol, and other agencies, I guess. Bring them all together in a kind of task force approach. I went to the Treasury office and asked for their agent assigned to FinCEN. Fortunately, I saw him before he saw me."

"Meanin'?"

"It was the guy who had been with Richard that night, in the garage. Shooting those people."

They left the barn, and started walking out along the perimeter of Joan's rented property. White-barked leafless trees lined the eastern and western borders, with empty brown fields beyond the tree lines. The ground was flat and hard. Jessie pulled her jacket tight against the late afternoon chill.

Across some fields sat another farmhouse, small and neat, smoke wisping from a chimney toward the wide blue sky.

"Shit," Morgan said. "Excuse me."

"That's pretty much what I said."

"I bet."

"So I got out of there, before he could see me. And tried another idea. I went to the *New York Times.*"

"If you can't get to them legally, embarrass them in public?"

"Pretty much, yes. I talked to a young reporter there. Gung ho, full of fire. He loved it."

"So why didn't I see it on CNN?"

"He was dead by morning. Murdered. Body dumped in his car."

"Figures," Morgan said. "He wouldn't have wanted to go with a story like that without havin' it confirmed by someone else. Whoever he picked to call on offered to meet with him to talk about it, but then killed him instead."

Jessica looked at the hard brown earth.

"I'm really tired of people dying, Morgan. And I don't want to be added to that list."

"We'll see if we can't do somethin' about that, Jessie."

"I hope we can."

"Keep going. What'd you do next?"

"Decided I needed to get out of town. I went to grab a subway to the train station, so I could just leave. But there were some guys in the train station who looked like they were looking for someone. I panicked, figured it was me they were looking for. I ran. Finally, when it was safe, I called here, asked Joan if I could stay with her. She said sure, but pointed out that I would need identification to get on a plane. She told me where I could get fake I.D."

"She knew that?"

"Yes. Knew exactly where."

"Hmm...curiouser and curiouser."

"So I went there, got the driver's license and some other stuff. I knew I needed some money to finance the trip, so I..." She looked at him, remembering the story he'd told her about the man in Omaha. "I stole it from one of Richard Steele's bank accounts. Using the Barbara Slonaker I.D."

"You are a clever lady," he said. She had already surprised him a couple of times, with her instincts and ingenuity.

"I guess. Anyway, I ended up here."

"And then you got in touch with me," Morgan said. "Why exactly?"

They were at the far side of the property. The line of trees separated this untilled field from the neighbor's. Morgan stood in place, made a slow circle, looking at the far distance. Satisfied, he started back.

"What are you doing?" she asked. "I mean, why are we out here looking at everything?"

"Someone's tried to kill you," he said. "At least once. Maybe more. Other people are dead, too. I'm gonna protect you, I want to know the lay of the land. It never hurts to be prepared and know how things set. Sometimes it hurts if you ain't."

"I see."

"Now, why'd you contact me? What did you want me to do?"

"I was hoping you would have some ideas on that point."

He did, but then he always had opinions on matters that involved people killing people.

Kind of a professional preoccupation, he figured.

"Let's get inside," Morgan said. "You can pour me some joe and we can talk about it."

Chapter 17

"Go after the money."

They were sitting in the clutter of Joan's kitchen. Cassie had come home from school, and she was in the living room watching TV. Joan had made coffee for them. Jessica expected Byrd to take it black, cowboy style, but he surprised her by spooning in two sugars and heavy cream.

"What do you mean?"

"You've already taken the first step, Jessie. You hit Steele once. How much you reckon he's laundered through MetroBank?"

"I'm not sure. I've personally seen about sixty million go through. I don't know how much he laundered when he was Barbara's client, though."

"But you know the reason he has this power—folks who'd kill you, folks who'd break into your place, folks who watch subway stations lookin' for you—is because he's got all this green to throw around, right?"

"Well, sure, I guess. I mean, those people don't work for free, right?"

"It's simple, then. What you've got to do is hit him where it hurts. Which also happens to be the area you're most familiar with. His money."

"I tried hacking into the bank's computers from here, but I can't get in. MetroBank's' firewalls are better than I am, even knowing my old codes."

"Probably changed those by now anyway."

"I'm sure they have."

"Do you still have his account numbers? And know where those accounts are located?"

"Unless he's changed all that."

"He expect you to come after him? Or to run like a scared rabbit?"

Jessie smiled at the image. "Probably the rabbit, I'd imagine."

"Exactly!" Morgan said, slapping his palm on his leg for emphasis. "Never do what the enemy expects you to."

"That makes sense, I guess."

"'Course it does, Jessie. Let me tell you somethin' about me."

Great. Was this going to be another of his murder stories? She wasn't sure she could handle that.

"You saw my ad, but you don't know shit about me 'cept that, right?"

"That, and what you've said today."

"Ninety-five percent of today we've talked about you."

"That's true."

"I'm fifty-two," Morgan said. "Look older, maybe, but for my trade that's pretty damn good. I've seen combat in the Gulf, Angola, Nigeria, El Salvador, Cambodia, and a pile of other places you probably never heard of, much less could find on a map. I'm good at it. You know what makes me good at it?"

"You're diabolically clever?" Jessie ventured. "Excellent hand/eye coordination?"

He smiled at her, a crooked grin that split his unshaven face. "I outlast the bastards," he said. "I survive. The secret to winnin' a battle is makin' it to the end alive. I always manage to do that."

"I see."

"I can do that for you, too. You're havin' a problem because this bastard Steele wants you dead, right? I can see that you survive him. It'll kill him if he can't find and destroy this one lone woman, who's not even a professional, who knows enough to put him away for a long time. He won't rest, Jessie. He's gonna keep comin' after you. But if you can manage to keep survivin', like you been doin', it'll just drive him fuckin' nuts. Maybe you'll get lucky and he'll kill himself."

"You sort of stopped apologizing for the swearing, didn't you?"

"I figure sayin' 'sorry' gets old, but I ain't likely to stop swearin'. It bother you so much you don't want to hire me?"

"Doesn't bother me at all."

"Well then. Reckon we just have to talk about money. You go along with my plan, you'll have plenty to pay me with."

* * *

Over the past four days, while living in Joan's house, Jessie had started to get used to having a kid around.

Some of it was getting Cassie used to her. Once she had, she'd clung to Jessie like a favorite toy—waking her as soon as she climbed out of her own bed and padded downstairs, sitting next to her at meals, sitting on her lap for bedtime stories at night. They'd taken to sitting together on the couch and watching Christmas specials on TV, especially over the weekend. When Jessie had shed a couple of tears over "Miracle on 34th Street"—because it made her miss Manhattan, and Macy's, not because the story, while sentimental, really reached her that powerfully—Cassie's eyes had misted up too.

She'd never given serious thought to having family, and with the exception of visiting some colleagues from MetroBank, her experience with kids was minimal. Her experience with families was, for that matter. Her father had died when she was a young teen. Her mother sank into her own self-imposed oblivion in the Connecticut house, and then followed him in death. Jessie had been in college by then, and eighteen, so she was on her own.

She didn't trust families.

Family left you.

Wasn't the best way to live, maybe, but there it was.

Jessie liked herself, mostly. Thought she was a good person, whatever that was. Tried to live right. She contributed to the United Way, Jerry's Kids, PBS, Greenpeace. Didn't smoke, drink excessively, or use illegal drugs.

If she had owned a car, she would brake for pedestrians, and if she had a dog, she would carry little baggies around with her when she walked it.

So if there were these areas in life where she didn't quite measure up—like, say, trusting that people she loved wouldn't disappear from her life when she least expected it—well, nobody's perfect, right?

It made relationships difficult, sometimes. She had a tendency to break up with men right when they thought things were going well. Took them by surprise.

Morgan Byrd said surprises were good.

Maybe he had something else in mind.

Cassie, though, she could take. The girl was starting to look at her like she was some kind of goddess, and Jessie kind of liked the feeling. She liked the hugs when those skinny arms were thrown tightly around her neck. She liked the dry little toothpaste-smelling kisses before bed.

And now, after only a short while, she was leaving Cassie.

She wouldn't miss Joan, necessarily. As sisters went, they were about as close as the heads of the Ku Klux Klan and the NAACP. Not really antagonistic, but far from intimate. If she needed Joan again, she figured her sister would be there. And she hoped Joan felt the same way. But if they went another six years without speaking, that would be okay too.

Joan was family.

Cassie was family, once removed. Maybe that's what made the difference.

Morgan spent the rest of the evening at the house. He parked his Raider in the barn and closed it up tight, then took a broom and swept away the tire marks he'd made. He left gear stowed in the Raider, which Jessie figured included weapons that he couldn't carry through airport security. Everything else he owned seemed to fit into one leather overnight bag.

* * *

Cassie looked sad as she got ready for school the next morning.

"I'm coming back, Cassie," Jessie said. "See, I'm leaving some of my stuff here. And Morgan is leaving his truck here, so we have to come back here."

"But you don't know when," Cassie said. "What if you miss my birthday?"

Her birthday was in early March, but she was already looking forward to it.

"I might miss Christmas, Cassie. No way will I not be back before your birthday."

"Well, Christmas," Cassie said. "And New Year's. You'll miss New Year's too."

"Maybe."

Cassie wiped her nose on the back of her hand, sniffling. "But you'll be here before my birthday."

"Yes, Cassie."

"Promise?"

"I promise, Cassie."

She might be gone again before then, but she would have to return, however briefly.

"Okay," the little girl said. "Are you going to see the ocean?"

"From an airplane. I'll be flying over it. Do you like the ocean?"

"I've never seen it, except on TV. But I like it. I watch shows about fish and divers and sunken ships and everything. Like in my aquarium. It's cool."

"One of these days you can see it for yourself. You'll love it."

Of course, she'd have to get out of Iowa first, and Joan didn't seem to have any inclination in that regard.

"Come on," she said. "Give me a hug."

Cassie put her arms around Jessie's neck and squeezed tight, once, then let go, slipped her backpack over her shoulders, and went out the door.

Jessie thought her heart would break as she watched her niece walk to the street. She stood in the window, watching, until after the big yellow school bus came to take her away.

Joan drove them to the airport.

Chapter 18

Paris was a dream.

The streets, slick with winter rain, reflected the lights in buildings and trees and homes, the floodlights washing the sides of churches and the neon in shop windows, the streetlamps on every block. Every light in the City of Lights was magnified through the falling water and doubled in the black streets. Jessie understood why Paris had earned that nickname on the short cab ride from the Gare du Nord to their hotel, the Hotel des Grandes Écoles, in the Fifth Arrondissement.

Even the taxi was a pleasure, a Citrôen with clean, plush seats that made her think she would never be comfortable in a New York cab again. It purred through the Paris night, the swish of wheels on wet pavement louder than the engine.

Morgan Byrd had chosen the hotel. For a guy who looked like a broken-down cowboy, he had traveled a lot—occupational necessity, he'd explained on the Air France jet from Chicago. There wasn't much work for a mercenary Stateside.

The trip had been a long one, but Jessie was getting used to that kind. From the airport in Dubuque they caught a commuter shuttle to Chicago's O'Hare. Air France flew direct from there to the Charles de Gaulle airport, outside Paris. A *tres grand vitesse* train covered the distance to Paris's Gare du Nord in thirty-five minutes, the city's outskirts seeming to glow as they sped past the windows in the rainy French dusk.

Morgan wasn't the chattiest travel companion Jessica had ever known. Once you got him going, though, he could spin a tale...leaving Jessie wishing, a few times, that she had just read a magazine instead.

"One time in Sierra Leone," he said, chopping at a slice of Air France chicken, "me and my guys was comin' down the side of a mountain. It was about midnight, little after, maybe. We'd seen some action during the night, but it'd been quiet for about an hour or so.

"Anyways, we humped down the side of the hill, and about halfway down we come on some local rebels—the guys we was supposed to be there helpin' to overthrow the regime. These guys were *mean*." He jabbed a carrot with his fork, popped it into his mouth, chewed it.

"I've seen mean before, Jessie. But these guys were really fuckin' mean. Some soldiers don't think twice about rapin' and lootin', you know—spoils of war, and all that. But these guys we found were cookin' dinner on a spit over a roaring fire. At least, when we come upon their bivouac, we *thought* it was dinner.

"That was, until we heard it screamin'."

Jessie was just about to take a bite of the chicken, which was actually very good for airplane food. She stopped the fork halfway to her mouth. Looked at it for a moment. Put the chicken back on her plate.

"Screaming?"

"They had run across some government soldiers, out there in the night. Killed a few, took the rest prisoner. Instead of lockin' 'em up, they tied 'em to poles and roasted 'em over open flame.

"We didn't hang around long enough to find out if they ate 'em, but I wouldn't have been surprised."

Jessica took a fast gulp of wine.

She left the rest of her dinner on the tray. She was glad the hum of engines and air circulation made it so the people in the other seats probably couldn't overhear.

"So, are you armed now?" she asked.

He looked at the knife and fork in his hands. "Countin' these?"

"You could kill someone with those?"

He considered for a moment. "Reckon there are eight or ten ways, easy. More if I want to get creative. Creative's usually a bad idea, though, you want to kill somebody. Straightforward's best."

"I can imagine."

"I don't have a gun, if that's what you mean. Airport security is too tight to mess with, these days, what with the goddamn terrorists and all. We need one, though, I can get one most anywhere."

"A gun was pretty much what I had in mind."

"Figured."

* * *

The next morning was crisp and cold, but Jessie cut the chill with a cup of strong coffee and a brioche at a cafe down the street from the hotel. Morgan had two cups to her one, washing down a croissant with butter and a *pain au chocolat*. The cafe was warm and smoky inside, even though some smokers braved the tables out on the sidewalk.

By the time they had reached the hotel, Jessie was too exhausted to want to see any more of Paris, even though she was thrilled to be there. She stood silently by while Morgan inspected both their rooms, connected by an adjoining door. He looked under the beds and in the closets and bathrooms, checked under the pillows and behind paintings, even unscrewed the mouthpieces from the telephones. He saw her staring at him and tossed a smile her way. "No bugs," he said.

Which, she supposed, was a good sign.

She was already getting used to his solicitous nature. He opened doors for her. He looked both ways every time they climbed out of a car or stepped through a doorway. He made her sit in corners or against walls while he took the outside seats. He did it all as if she were a precious object, or perhaps a child, in need of his protection.

She knew neither was the case—only the protection part was true.

And she began to feel, for the first time in a long while, genuinely safe.

He knew what he was doing. He understood danger, and how to avoid it. He was, as he had told her, a survivor.

He was also, he explained, better at violence than at interpersonal relations. "Long as what you're lookin' for ain't a traveling companion, we'll get along fine," he said. "I ain't much good at holdin' up my end of a conversation. I like to be alone, and I'm happiest sitting in a saddle in the middle of a deep valley somewhere's where I know the nearest human is about a hundred miles in any direction. But I can stand people for short times, and I'll keep you safe, any danger comes your way. More'n that, no guarantees."

"I take it you're not married," she said.

"Not currently. Have been."

"And?"

"Didn't take."

"Kids?"

"Nope. I got a dog, couple of horses. Some cattle. Got a woman in Ely I see sometimes, got kind of an understanding. She don't expect much, I reckon, and that's about what she gets."

"Sounds like a lonely life."

"Why I have a dog."

The rooms thoroughly vetted, she slipped between clean, starched sheets, put her head on the goose down pillow, pulled the comforter over her, and she was out. Morgan had the room next door, and was sitting up in a chair, with the connecting door open, the last time she saw him.

Until morning. He shook her awake at seven, Paris time. That made it...she didn't even want to think about it. Was she on New York time, or Iowa, or someplace between?

Caffeine...

"Let's go, Jessie," he said, his morning voice low and gruff. "Got a big day ahead."

She felt a momentary sense of unease, of confusion. She was normally one of those people who always woke up knowing just where she was, but there was nothing normal about life any more, and she couldn't remember the last time a man's rough hand had shaken her shoulder to wake her up.

She kind of liked it.

Paris, she thought. That's right. I'm in Paris.

Cool.

She slid out of bed, opened the heavy drapes. The rain had stopped during the night, but there were still puddles in the uneven gray street beyond the hotel's cobbled courtyard. The trunks of bare-limbed trees disappeared into wrought iron bases flush with the sidewalk. An ancient man in blue work clothes was sweeping the gutter with a broom that looked like it was made of sticks. Instead of the expected beret, though, he was wearing a red GMC ball cap.

Another country, no question about that.

Morgan was already showered and dressed in a faded blue denim shirt, new jeans, and boots. She sent him back to his room and then dropped her nightgown, stepped into the bathroom, and cranked on the hot water.

The shower helped invigorate her. The shower, and the knowledge that Paris was outside these walls, spurred her to hurry into a sweater and slacks so she could get out there and see the city by daylight.

She had almost forgotten that she was here to steal millions of dollars from a killer.

Morgan hadn't forgotten.

He looked at her when she stepped through the adjoining door, into his room, and nodded approvingly.

"That'll work," he said.

She felt like she was in a display case.

"What does that mean?"

"Means you look damn good," he said. "Prettier'n a September sunset. But still businesslike. The French, they like a woman who looks good. You're gonna sweet-talk a few million bucks from a French banker, helps to let him enjoy the scenery at the same time. You don't have a sweater just like that but a couple sizes smaller, do you?"

"Sorry to disappoint," Jessie said. "But, no."

"Well, this one'll do, I guess. Just stretch your arms back a couple of times, you know. Stick your chest out."

"What makes you think the banker's even a man?"

"This is France, Jessie. You're gonna be askin' for a big withdrawal. A huge withdrawal. No way a woman will be the one makin' the final decision on this. Not here."

"You make it sound like Saudi Arabia or something, Morgan. Europe isn't as provincial as that, is it?"

"Not provincial, no. But traditional. Some aspects of it. Banking is one of those aspects. Trust me."

"I guess we'll see," Jessie said. "Soon enough."

* * *

After breakfast, they made their way to the Banque de la Cité, a French affiliate of MetroBank. The building, a block off the bustling Champs Élysées on Rue Marbeuf, was huge. Gray stone outside, marble and brass inside, and the employees were all impeccably dressed in business attire. The tellers here wore nicer clothes than many executives back home. While Morgan waited outside, Jessie swallowed her nerves and walked in, straight to an information desk.

"Bonjour," a pleasant young woman said.

"Bonjour," Jessie said. "Umm, do you speak English?"

"Yes, a little." Morgan had told her everyone would say that, even if they had grown up in Kansas City.

"I need to make a withdrawal from an account here," Jessie said. "A very large withdrawal."

"I see," the young lady said. "Over one hundred thousand francs?"

"Over one million," Jessie said. "Dollars, not francs."

The woman's smile faded for a moment. "I see," she said again. "Please have a seat, while I call Monsieur Charbonneau."

Jessie sat on a Louis XIV couch and watched the pleasant young woman, all business now, pick up a telephone headset and speak tersely into it. At one point, she stopped and looked at Jessie.

"May I have your name, please?"

"Barbara Slonaker," Jessie said.

The woman repeated it into the phone. She listened for a moment longer, then put the phone down.

"M. Charbonneau will be right with you," she said. "He says he remembers you well and looks forward to seeing you."

Chapter 19

Get up and run?

Stay and bluff? Plastic surgery could do wonders these days...

He'd never buy that. Particularly if what Morgan said about French bankers was true. For all Jessie knew, he'd had slept with Barbara, or tried to.

The antique couch, never exactly comfortable to begin with, began to feel like some kind of torture implement.

As Jessie deliberated, the pretty young woman at the information desk stood, smoothing her skirt with a practiced motion. Jessie knew it was too late to do anything except face the man.

At least, she assured herself, he probably wouldn't try to push her in front of the Metro. And French prisons couldn't be all that bad, could they?

He looked like what she expected—like Morgan had predicted. A traditional, male, French banker. Three-piece gray suit with white pinstripes, silver hair slicked over a bald spot, pencil-thin mustache between a large nose and a larger smile. He held his arms wide as he approached her.

"*Bonjour*, Barbara," he said. He drew her into his arms, gave her a light kiss on each cheek.

"Hello, Henri," she said, tentative. "I'm surprised you remember me."

"How could I forget you?" he asked. His accent was noticeable, but not too strong. He released her, but took her hands in his. "We have had so many lovely conversations. It's wonderful to finally see your lovely face. You are every bit as beautiful as I knew you would be."

"Why thank you, Henri. And you're just as handsome as you sounded." She figured their phone relationship must have become fairly flirtatious—either that or everything she'd ever heard about Frenchmen was true. Either way, throwing compliments around like an old-timer scattering bread for the Central Park pigeons wouldn't hurt.

He continued to hold her hand, drawing her away from the information desk toward a bank of private offices. "Come," he said. "Tell me why you're here—and without calling first? I hope you can stay for dinner."

* * *

When she was seated in a comfortable guest chair in front of his expansive Louis XVI desk, she went into her prepared tale. She had only taken in about half of what he'd said on the way to his office, between his accent and the pulse hammering in her ears. But he didn't seem to have any clue that she wasn't the Barbara Slonaker he thought she was. She should have known that Barbara would have developed relationships with people at the banks where she had set up Cielo accounts. Relationships make people less likely to ask questions, less likely to dig beneath the surface of things. Barbara had taught her that.

Twice, now.

"Cielo Holdings is experiencing some cash flow difficulties," she began. "Of course, I'm not at liberty to discuss the specifics."

"Of course."

"But I'm afraid it means I'll have to make a very large withdrawal. Not everything. I want to leave enough here to make it worthwhile for you to continue to maintain the account. And I can guarantee you that the flow isn't drying up. There will be more deposits coming this way soon."

"That is good news," Henri said. "I'm sorry for Cielo's difficulties, but I hope we can continue to be of service to the company for many years to come."

"I'm certain that our relationship will continue," Jessie said.

"How large of a withdrawal are we discussing?"

"I need three million dollars."

Henri pressed his palms together. A little hard, Jessie thought. His face drained of color. But only for a moment, and then he was back to normal so quickly, it could have been a trick of the light, a cloud passing across the sun outside.

The amount was a guess. She was pretty sure there was about six million parked here at any given time. But she couldn't know what had happened to the Cielo accounts in the past few days, and she hadn't wanted to name a sum that was clearly ridiculous.

"I can't give you that much in cash, of course," he said.

"Of course."

"Would one hundred thousand dollars in cash suffice, with a bank draft for the remainder?"

"I think that would be just fine," Jessie said with a smile.

* * *

Outside the bank, she handed the briefcase to Morgan.

"How'd it go?" he asked.

"A breeze," she said. "Little hitch at first, but after that, nothing to it."

"What hitch?"

"He knows Barbara Slonaker."

"He does? So what'd you do?"

"He only knows her by phone. Never saw her face. Now he knows her face, but it's mine. If she ever shows up here, they're both in for a shock."

Morgan laughed.

"How much you get?"

"One hundred thousand," she said. "In francs. Bank draft for the rest. That's better anyway. We'll take it to another bank, deposit it, wire it somewhere safe. Practically untraceable."

"You know any bankers in Paris?"

"Nope. And that's for the best. As long as they never met Barbara Slonaker."

* * *

They found a multinational bank, introduced themselves as Barbara Slonaker and Frank Johns (a little joke on Morgan's part—Frank Johns was one of the many false identities he traveled under, and he liked the ring of "Frank and Jessie Johns") and deposited the check, then made arrangements to have a million dollars of it transferred to Joan's account in Clark's Grove and from there to an account Jessie had set up before leaving town. They got a bank draft from this bank and repeated the process, twice more. She would have preferred to smurf it more cautiously, but they didn't want to spend too much time in Paris. At each stop, they also converted several thousand of their cash into dollars. When they were finished, it was almost five o'clock. They were tired and hungry, and they were still carrying a briefcase full of cash.

They made one more stop, taking a cab to Galeries Lafayette, the magnificent department store on Boulevard Haussmann. Jessica's wardrobe was getting a little worse for wear, so they bought a new overnight bag, and filled it with a couple of winter dresses, new underwear and warm socks, and some new jeans and sweaters. Jessie could barely turn her gaze away from the spectacular steel and glass Art Nouveau dome, soaring ten stories over the floor, to look at clothing, but Morgan pushed and prodded until she had chosen. They paid in cash, then caught another cab back to the hotel.

They put the new suitcase in Jessie's closet. Morgan took out a few thousand francs for dinner, and hung the bag by its strap from his shoulder.

"You're bringing that?" she asked him.

"Not letting, it out of my sight," he said. "Now, if you're really hungry, I know just the spot."

They took the Metro across the Seine and got off near L'Hôtel de Ville. From there, they walked a couple of blocks to a tiny cafe that looked, to Jessie, indistinguishable from a thousand others in the city. It was called Cafe Prevôt, according to the small sign next to a peeling wooden door.

Stepping through the door, though, was like walking into God's own kitchen. The odors of fresh bread and rich wine and beef and fish and potatoes and a hundred sauces joined together in an olfactory symphony that practically lifted Jessie off her feet and wafted her to a table. They had never stopped for lunch, and she had known she was hungry, but suddenly she was really hungry, ravenous, ready to order everything on the menu just for starters.

She let Morgan order for both of them, to spare herself the embarrassment. To keep it simple, he ordered *steak frites* with *haricots vert* for both of them, accompanied by a bottle of the house red.

She was surprised he'd taken such a boring way out, until the bread came. It was hot, steam rising as they broke pieces off the *baguette* and slathered on sweet butter. Her mouth watered at the sight of it. By the time the meals came, she had eaten three pieces and couldn't imagine anything ever tasting better.

She was wrong.

The steak was perfect, medium rare, pink on the inside and tender as angel food cake. The potatoes were equally superb, and the beans were wonderfully spiced and cooked to snap when she bit into them.

They had chatted about non-essential subjects, Paris and travel and jet lag, until the food came, and then they'd set to eating like it was their last meal.

Finally, with green salads and cheese behind them, they each had a cup of strong, aromatic coffee.

"What'd you think?" Morgan asked.

"I thought maybe you could tell by the way I ate like a pig without saying a single word all through dinner."

"Figured maybe you was just hungry."

"Well, that too. I can't remember food ever tasting so good," she said. "Does this mean I'm spoiled now? I'll never be able to enjoy regular mortal cooking again?"

"That's a possibility. Once you've eaten here, you'll keep findin' reasons to come back to Paris. Now that you're not a Prevôt virgin any more, next time maybe they'll let you have some of the shellfish."

"Can't I just stay here?"

"Sure, and you could probably get in three or four more dinners before they tracked you down and killed you. I think you're in too deep, Jessie, to stay in one place for any length of time. At least until you've got the goods on old Richard Steele."

"I suppose you're right," Jessie said. "Thank you, anyway, for introducing me to the marvels of Paris. Galeries Lafayette, Cafe Prevôt... For a Nevada cowboy, you seem to know your way around."

"I said I prefer to be on my own spread, out in the country. Hard to make a livin' there, though."

"Doesn't seem to be exactly easy anywhere, these days. So tell me, oh worldly one. I've heard there's something called the Louvre. Is it in the same class as these other places?"

"You can't eat it or wear it, but it ain't bad," Morgan said. "Worth a visit on your next trip."

"I'll just have to make sure there *is* a next trip."

"My job is to make sure you live to see it. Especially now that I know you can afford me."

"So far so good."

Warm and full and content, they agreed to walk back to the hotel. It was several blocks, but not too cold, and since this was Jessie's last night in Paris, she wanted the experience of walking its nighttime streets. They were taking Rue Charlemagne at an angle toward Rue de Rivoli, intending to go a few blocks out of their way in order to see the Place de la Bastille before heading back over the river. But they had only gone a short distance when Morgan put an arm over Jessie's shoulder and drew her against him. She started to pull away, but he held her with a strength that showed he wasn't playing around.

"Keep walkin'," he said in a whisper. "Like there's nothin' wrong."

"Is there something wrong?"

"I don't want to say there is, but I can't say there ain't," he said. "Turn right here."

They hung a right at the corner of Rue St. Paul. This was a narrow street, with a couple of closed shops, a *charcuterie* with a brass horse's head over the door, a *patisserie* behind shuttered doors.

She remembered that the horse's head sculpture meant they sold horse meat in the *charcuterie*, and was just as glad the windows were dark.

"What is it?" Jessie asked.

"Someone's been behind us since we left the restaurant," Morgan said.

"But how could anyone have found us so fast?"

"Don't know that they have. Could be someone who knows you made a big cash withdrawal today. Could be he saw our wad of cash in the cafe. Either way, we have to make sure he's really after us before we do anything about it."

They hurried the couple of blocks to Quai de Celestins, which ran alongside the Seine. They were less than a block now to Pont de Sully, the bridge that led back toward their hotel. She hadn't seen their shadow since they'd turned onto Rue St. Paul.

"Is he still back there?" Jessie asked. Morgan's big arm was still wrapped around her shoulder. She found its bulk comforting.

It wouldn't stop bullets, though.

"He's not where he was," Morgan said. "He looped around the block. Runnin', most like. He's closer now."

She risked a glance back, underneath Morgan's arm. Half afraid of what she'd see.

What did a killer look like?

Hell, she already knew the answer to that. If it wasn't Richard Steele or Jake Garland, she figured, she would feel better.

The man was wearing a trench coat, Burberry, maybe, light brown, and a snap brim cap. But then he passed under a light, and she got a clear look at his face.

A baby face. Soft round cheeks, weak chin. Big doe eyes.

"Jesus Christ," she said, tensing.

"Keep goin'," Morgan said. "What is it?"

"That's the guy that shoved me in front of the subway."

"Shit," Morgan said. "Run."

Running, she was good at. They made the bridge, and were on its upward arc, toward the center, when she glanced at Morgan. He was looking at the guy behind them, who had also started to run.

"Wish I had a fuckin' gun," Morgan said.

"You know, I do too."

"Save your breath," Morgan said. "You're gonna need it."

"Hey, running is my useful skill," she said.

"How are you at ducking?" he asked.

Then she saw why.

Ahead of them, two men were coming their way. They looked like serious trouble. Short leather jackets, black jeans, boots with chains on them.

Behind them, the guy from the subway was running flat out, and he had one hand inside his camel trench coat. Then the hand came out, and it was filled with dark metal.

A gun.

He pointed it their way.

She looked at the two guys coming toward them. Surely he wouldn't shoot with witnesses there.

Unless they were accomplices, not witnesses.

They had guns in their hands, too. Pointed at her and Morgan.

"Goddammit," Morgan said. He grabbed Jessie with strong arms, lifted her up. "Sure as fuck hope you can swim."

He threw her over the side of the bridge. Right before she hit the inky, frigid water, she heard the shots.

Chapter 20

One Saturday morning in Manhattan, the previous February, Jessie had pulled on sweats and Nikes, pulled her hair back into a ponytail, and gone for a five mile run in Central Park.

It was a cold morning, the kind of cold that by late February feels like it'll be around forever, worming its way into your bones, settling there and never letting go. But the run warmed her.

She had timed it so that it would end at the Fifth Avenue entrance to the Park. She had brought three bucks for coffee, and intended to spend some time window-shopping on Fifth before heading home. Barbara Slonaker had shown her a new diamond tennis bracelet from Cartier on Thursday, and while it wasn't the kind of thing Jessie would wear, she appreciated that her jewelry choices were getting a little stale, and she could use a couple of new pieces.

But while she browsed the windows, sweat drying on her body and beginning to chill her, the skies overhead opened up with a sudden downpour. She was twenty-some blocks from home with no money for a cab, a subway, or even an umbrella. And, looking around, she realized that money wouldn't necessarily help. The shops here didn't have those cheapo folding umbrellas that were ubiquitous in other, more downscale parts of the city, and all the cabs seemed to be full.

She had already run her five miles. Running home, while not out of the question, would be a challenge.

Still, there weren't a lot of options. She headed for home at a pace somewhere between a fast walk and a slow run.

By the time she had covered six blocks, she was soaked.

By the time she reached her street, her teeth were chattering like a spastic flamenco dancer's castanets. She was shivering uncontrollably, and her breath was tearing out of her lungs with huh-huh-huh noises that worried her.

She had believed she would never feel cold like that again.

But that was nothing, she realized now.

The Seine felt like liquid ice. She plowed into it with the force of a speeding truck through fog. Sank fast, and sinking, realized that she had to maintain her focus. It would be too easy to simply let go, to give in to the cold and the impact and let the water wash her away.

She couldn't spend much time in the river, she knew, or she wouldn't have much time left.

She surfaced, carving at the water with her palms in a desperate effort to keep her head above it. She realized that her purse was clutched in one hand, interfering with her movements. She pulled the strap over her head, yanked it down so it crossed between her breasts with the purse bouncing against her hip, so she wouldn't have to worry about it.

That was when she heard another splash. She couldn't see anything at water level. Above the river, she could see spots of light, but everything was diffuse, screened by the water in her eyes.

She didn't hear any more gunshots.

Did that mean Morgan was dead? Was whatever had splashed nearby his corpse?

She bobbed with the current, straining all her senses for some sign of life.

Somewhere, she heard a gentle, persistent thrumming.

"Jess!"

Morgan's voice. She heard splashing, not far away.

"Over here!" she called.

Vaguely aware of how ridiculous that was. But how did you define "here" when you didn't know where you were?

What she'd give for one of those maps with the pointer on it. YOU ARE HERE.

"Keep talking!" Morgan shouted. "Keep paddling!"

"Where are you?" she replied.

Then she heard nothing, saw nothing. Had he gone under? She kept paddling, as instructed, trying to hold herself in one spot.

The thrumming grew louder.

The water started to not feel so cold. She thought that was probably a bad sign. Not that she was getting used to it, but that she was succumbing to hypothermia or something.

A powerful hand gripped her shoulder.

"Jess," Morgan Byrd said. "Listen!"

She listened. Just that unknown, steady sound. A motor?

"What is it?"

"It's a *Bateau Mouche*," he said. She knew what he meant: pleasure boats that cruised up and down the Seine, carrying tourists and lovers and diners. There were numerous companies providing similar services, but they were all called by the name of the originator. *Bateaux Mouche.*

"Can they see us?"

"I don't know," Morgan said. He treaded water next to her. "We might have gone over before they were close enough."

"I don't know how long I can keep this up," Jessica said. "Should we swim for the bank?"

"For all we know, they're waiting for us there," he answered. "Hold onto my belt, and swim with me."

She worked her fingers beneath his belt. He struck out in the direction of the motor, which was coming closer all the time. Jessie hung on, paddling in an effort to keep up with his powerful strokes, his long arms and legs pulling him forward, threatening to break her grip.

If she let go, she would never find him again—not with the darkness and the volume of the boat's engines, coming closer...

Suddenly it loomed ahead of them, cutting through night-black water.

Morgan shoved backwards, slamming into Jessie.

"Shit!" he shouted. "It's on us!"

And it was. The hull was big and white and shiny, and it was about to mow them down.

And presumably at the other end of that hull was a spinning propeller that would grind any remaining pieces into fish food.

To make a bad situation marginally worse, Morgan was backpedaling so fast that he was bumping into Jess, and she couldn't get out of his way quickly enough. If they became entangled, they were both doomed.

Then the boat's wake hit them, pushing them back from the hull. The roiling waves, so innocent when you were looking down at them, pounded into her face and threatened to suck her underneath.

Which, she reminded herself, was where she couldn't breathe.

Getting trapped under the hull would mean no air. It would also, if she survived it, lead to the propeller.

Then Morgan reversed direction again, striking out toward the hull, suicidally, it looked like. But he managed to pull up next to it, and then he started pounding on it with his fist.

She lost contact with him, treaded water again.

She saw the briefcase now. Like she had done with her purse, he had slung it across his chest by the strap, and it flailed behind him as he pulled himself out of the water, one palm pressing against the slick, treacherous hull of the boat as he slammed on it.

Each time he rose above the water, he shouted. "Hello! *Au secours!*"

Jessie could hear Morgan's banging and yelling, but now she could also hear the sounds of diners on the deck, silver clinking, china clanking, loud voices and louder laughter. She didn't think there was any way they would hear the noise from belowdecks. If they did, they would just think it was something bumping up against the hull.

The water was so dark, so inviting, like a long winter's night.

Maybe it was time to give up.

She closed her eyes...

Chapter 21

It was so warm in the blanket, Jessie never wanted to leave.

She vaguely remembered being hauled onto the boat. Remembered feeling very sleepy, and wanting the water to just keep gently rocking her as the world faded out.

Someone on deck must have heard Morgan's pounding and thrown a line over. By the time Jessie regained full consciousness, she was lying on a deck chair with a couple of dry blankets draped over her. As she regained her senses, the illusion of warmth faded and a deep chill gripped her.

Before she even opened her eyes, she heard laughter. Morgan's laughter, rumbling from deep in his chest, like the growl of a territorial grizzly defending its cave.

She blinked, twice, and looked at him. He was sitting up on a chair like hers, a red blanket wrapped over his shoulders. His hair was still wet. Black ribbons of...something...black, and ribbonlike, hung from his short hair and soaked clothes.

"You look like shit," he said. Laughing again.

"I can't imagine that I look any worse than you do," Jessie said.

"Probably not. But I didn't have to watch myself floppin' on the floor like a landed fish, wretchin' up half the Seine."

"That's a lovely image."

"I think some of the tourists got video," he said. "If you've a mind to watch it some night."

They were in an interior cabin, but there was a door open and she could still hear the sounds of dinner on deck, still feel the gentle bounce of the boat churning down the river.

Hot air blew from a vent, but dissipated quickly. Jessie couldn't stop shivering, in spite of the blankets.

A tuxedo-clad waiter, white jacketed and cummerbunded, came in with a silver tray. A bottle of Bordeaux and two crystal glasses balanced on the tray, and he held it high, a napkin draped over his arm. With the other hand he dragged a small table across the room, positioned it between the two chairs.

"*Comment ça va*, mademoiselle?" he asked.

"He wants to know how you are," Morgan said.

"I didn't figure he was complimenting my hairdo," she said. "Fine. Tell him I'm fine."

"*Elle est tres bien, merci*," Morgan said.

The waiter tossed her a wide smile, opened the wine, poured a little into Morgan's glass. Always a waiter, even in medicinal situations.

Morgan lifted the glass, sniffed it, sloshed it around in his mouth. Swallowed.

"*Bien*," he said.

The waiter poured the two glasses, stood there for a moment as if expecting a tip or some other instructions, then walked out.

Morgan raised his glass toward Jessica. She picked hers up in a trembling hand, managed to clink it against his without spilling the whole thing.

"*Salut*," Morgan said.

"So...this kind of thing happen to you often?" she asked.

They both laughed. She liked his laughter. It was honest, not at all self-conscious, and it involved his whole body.

"Not exactly like this, no," he said.

"Just as soon keep it that way?"

"I've had worse jobs," he said.

"Can I ask you something, Morgan? What the hell happened up there?"

"Beats the hell out of me. The one guy was followin' us. We know that much for a fact." He took a sip of the Bordeaux, smacked his lips. "Good stuff. You said he's the one threw you under a train, so we can pretty much guarantee he's not a friend of yours. Those other guys had guns, too. So the question is, did they draw to help us, because they saw your pal behind us aimin' his piece? Or were they in cahoots, tryin' to catch us in the crossfire? I expect that ain't what happened, or we wouldn't be here talkin'. Seemed like they was shootin' at each other."

"How do we tell?"

"Don't see as we can, at this point. Unless we get off this boat and all three of 'em are waitin' for us together."

"How could they have tracked us down so quickly?"

"Can't say for sure. Maybe the Barbara Slonaker name tipped 'em off. Maybe they're watchin' the money. Maybe they came to do the same thing, only to find out we beat 'em to it."

She drank her wine quietly for a moment, letting it warm her from the inside. "You sure you wouldn't rather be back in Nevada?"

Morgan chuckled. "I'll tell you what. Back there, I work as a guide sometimes for guys that fancy themselves big game hunters, goin' out into the wilderness to bring down a duck or a deer or some such. These guys, most times, can barely handle their own weapons, much less keep the safety on when it's supposed to be and take it off when they want to shoot, and they gotta wear bright orange clothes so they don't accidentally shoot each other.

"When I'm not doin' that, I run some cattle, but I've got a guy oversees most of the actual ranchin'. Still, that's a hard day's work, too. Between watchin' over hunters or cows and watchin' over you, I'll take you any time."

"Thanks, I suppose," Jessie said.

She started to say something else, but they were interrupted by a crowd filing into the room—partiers carrying bottles, plates of cheese and bread, colorful pastries and tarts. There were eight of them, men and women in equal numbers. They were dressed for an elegant evening out: long dresses and diamonds for the women, dark suits with ties for the men.

They had obviously been enjoying themselves.

"Is this where the castaways are?" one said in perfect English, with only the slightest French accent.

"Reckon that's us," Morgan said.

The English-speaker bowed deeply. "Jean-Pierre Fournier," he said. "It is a pleasure to make your acquaintance."

"Morgan Byrd. The lady is Barbara Slonaker. And likewise."

"Is the wine to your tastes, Mademoiselle Slonaker?"

"Yes, it's fine. Is it from you?"

"Yes, a small gift for our wet friends. Allow me to introduce my companions." He pointed to each one as he named them. "Sylvie Rousseau, Marc Sauro, Michelle Pascal, Emil Dupin, Charles Delacourt, Genevieve Hébert, and Christine Delaroche."

There was a round of "*bonjours*," then everyone reached around one another, shaking hands with both Jessica and Morgan. Jessie's hand was kissed three times, which she found strangely charming.

"Thank you so much," she said when the introductions were finished. "Won't you sit down?"

They did, pulling unoccupied deck chairs into a semi-circle around her and Morgan. A few of them spoke English, but Jean-Pierre's was the best and most of the conversation flowed through him.

"Are you having a party?" Jessie asked him.

"Today is my birthday," he said. "I have sixty years today."

He didn't look it. His hair was jet black and thick, his face unlined, his stomach firm. Jessie said as much.

"Thank you," he said. "But it's true. I thought that instead of mourning the loss of my youth, I should celebrate with friends the next stage of my life."

"That sounds like a very good idea," Jessie said.

"I'll have to keep that in mind in a few years," Morgan added.

"And this way, if the celebration failed and I remained depressed, I would be able to throw myself overboard," Jean-Pierre said. "At least, that was my plan. I didn't know we would be rescuing people from the river instead."

"We certainly appreciate the rescue," Jessie said.

"The captain and crew are really the ones to thank for that," Jean-Pierre said. "We only stood by and cheered them on."

"Well, thank you for that much." She raised her glass. "And for the excellent wine."

"I feel that a near-drowning is a fine reason to drink good wine."

"You think waking up in the morning is a good reason to drink wine," Michelle said, to general laughter.

"And going to sleep at night," someone added. Marc, maybe. They all laughed again, and then started talking all at once, in a combination of French and English that Jessie could hardly keep up with. Before she really understood what was happening, though, the eight French people were beginning to disrobe in front of her.

She looked at Morgan, who was doing the same thing.

"When did this turn into an orgy?" she asked.

"It's not," he said. "They want us to get out of these wet clothes. They figure between the eight of them, they can come up with enough dry stuff for us and still be dressed enough for them to get home."

"That's so nice!" Jessie said. "I thought the French hated Americans."

"That's a myth," Morgan said. "They mostly hate the obnoxious Americans. Come to think of it, so do I."

By the time the boat docked, Jessie and Morgan had shed their wet clothing (the French women considerately making themselves into a human screen around Jessie, and with a bit of ooh-la-la-ing at Morgan's rangy build) and put on an assemblage of articles offered by their newfound friends. Jessie ended up with an ensemble that would never fly on a Paris runway, but it was dry. Morgan had to settle for a pair of long johns that Emil had worn under his trousers, since none of the men wanted to give up his pants, and a starched white shirt. Coats were donated to the cause. Jessie got a luxurious real fur. Their own clothes were put into a big plastic bag, courtesy of the *Bateau Mouche* crew, along with the soaked briefcase that Morgan had somehow managed to hang onto.

"I really don't know how to thank you for all this," Jessie said as they headed toward the gangplank. She noticed that Morgan was watchful, examining both banks of the river as they disembarked.

"*De rien*," Jean-Pierre said. "Think nothing of it. Only one item of business remains—where can we drop you?"

"Hôtel Champlain," Morgan said, naming a place Jessie had never heard of. She kept her mouth shut and went along with it.

They moved en masse to the group's two parked cars, a Peugeot and a Citrôen. Morgan pulled Jessie close, put his head next to her ear.

"Anyone is watchin', they probably wouldn't be able to spot us in this mob," he said. "They'd be lookin' for our old clothes, and they expect us to be by ourselves—or maybe getting into an ambulance. This is the best cover we could ask for."

Short of a gaggle of hookers, Jessie thought. She just nodded, and then they were at the cars. She and Morgan were invited into the back seat of the Peugeot, which was Jean-Pierre's car. He was a surgeon, it turned out, and he kept the group laughing on the short ride to the hotel Morgan had picked. When they arrived, Morgan and Jessie got out, and there was a round of kissing on both cheeks in traditional French fashion. Jean-Pierre wouldn't hear of any kind of payment, but he gave Morgan a business card so the clothing could be returned when it was no longer needed. He elicited a promise to call if they were ever in Paris again, and then drove off into the night.

"What are we doing here?" Jessie asked as they stood in front of the Hôtel Champlain. It looked like a dive, little better than the one she had left behind in Manhattan.

"Can't go back to the Grande Écoles," he said. "Somebody found us this easy in Paris, they got to know where we're stayin'. So we check in here, leave in the morning. Remember those new clothes you bought?"

"Yes," she said.

"Forget 'em."

They checked in, paying with wet cash, under one of Morgan's pseudonyms. Went upstairs to a tiny room with one full size bed and a bathroom containing a bathtub, sink, toilet and bidet, all crammed so close to one another that it was hard to move between them.

She hoped the laptop could be salvaged. While she put it and the other soaked contents of her purse on top of a towel that she had spread on the dresser, Morgan draped their wet clothes over the shower curtain rod, then took the briefcase and emptied its contents, just under a hundred thousand dollars, into the tub.

"Now that," he said, "looks like laundered money."

Jessie chuckled at the lame joke, and at their situation. Morgan laughed at her—her hair completely disheveled, dressed in two borrowed slips, no panties, borrowed tights and a borrowed fur coat.

Then they were both laughing, hysterical, at anything and everything. The size of the room. The sight of one another. The wet money, the wet clothes, the narrow escape from the would-be killers. Unable to stand, they both sat on the bed, rolled on the bed.

Rolled into each other's arms.

Laughing, at first.

Then not.

Their faces ending up close together. Lips almost touching.

"Jessie," Morgan said, then broke into laughter again.

She kissed him. Tasted river water and wine and his own hypermasculine flavor. Kissed him again, using her tongue this time, drawing his into her mouth. Wanting to taste all of him.

He kissed back. Their mouths all over each other, lips necks ears shoulders, then the borrowed clothes started to come off, with gusts of laughter punctuating the removal of someone else's slip, someone else's long underwear. And the mouths moved more freely. Morgan explored the hollow beneath Jessie's shoulder, the space between her breasts, the undersides. She tensed, feeling her nipples harden, as his kisses and licks and small bites moved up from there, circling, closing in slowly. She dug her nails into his shoulder, his bicep, arched her back.

The laughing was over now, and there was a different kind of urgency in the small room.

He kissed her nipples, finally, drawing each one in turn into his mouth and flicking it gently with his tongue, closing his teeth over them, pulling. She moaned and writhed on the bed. Then he released her breasts, kissing his way further down her torso, across her stomach, pausing to nuzzle her navel for a moment and then continuing down.

And down.

She felt his breath, hot between her legs, then felt his tongue taste her wetness. It moved up, then, just the tip of it, the lightest touch. She clamped her thighs around his head involuntarily at this, then relaxed them as his tongue resumed its gentle ministrations.

After a few minutes, she came, a shuddering, powerful orgasm. She heard the sound of a condom wrapper being torn open, wondered briefly where he had got it—at least, she thought, the wrappers were waterproof, and then he moved up on the bed, moved over her, into her, hard and wanting, and she moved with him, pulled him into her, and then she started to laugh again, holding it in as much as she could so she didn't push him out of her, she wanted him inside her so much, and he said, "What's wrong?"

And she said, "I've been wet for hours, but not this way," and then he started laughing too, but moving as well, pushing into her, she rising to meet him, and then they weren't laughing at all anymore, were barely breathing, just moving and feeling and being.

Chapter 22

It was the second time recently that Jessie had awakened to hear Morgan's voice, speaking softly but with the unmistakable rasp that he blamed on one too many punches to the throat, but sounded like a long life of cigarettes, booze, and screaming too loud to her.

He didn't smoke, though. His boozing seemed to be contained to the occasional glass of wine. Just one with dinner, she realized, then another one on the boat. He had nursed them both.

Keeping himself sober, she figured. Alert for anything that might happen.

A gunfight on a bridge, say.

So maybe it really was the punches.

Muhammad Ali was a little worse for wear, wasn't he?

"Yeah, she's right here," she heard Morgan saying. "I think she had a good time. Seemed to. I know I did."

He listened for a moment. Alertness came to Jessie. Who was he talking to about this? About her?

"She's pretty," he said. "Nice rack. Yeah, I know, one track mind."

He listened again. This time, Jessie sat up in bed, looked at him. He caught her eye, smiled. "She's up," he said. Listened. "Okay."

He held his phone out toward Jessie. "Wants to talk to you."

"Who is it?" she demanded.

"Christie. I think I mentioned her. Woman back in Ely I have an understanding with."

"Interesting word," Jessie said. She held her hand out.

"Good morning," she said.

"Howdy, there," a woman's voice on the other end said. "I'm Christie."

"I'm Jessie."

"You're the client?"

"That's right."

"And you're sleeping with him, too?"

"I don't know if I'd characterize it that way. One time."

"He's usually pretty good. Attentive, concerned about your needs. You get the chance to try him out some more, I'd recommend it."

"Uhh...thanks, I guess."

"That's pretty much it. Nice to meet you."

"Same here," Jessie said. She handed the phone back to Morgan. "Very friendly," she said.

"That's Christie." He took the phone, listened for a moment. "I love you too, Christie. I'll call you. Bye."

He hung up.

"An understanding, huh?" Jessie said.

"That's right. You Easterners might call it a relationship, but I'm not sure you'd recognize our rules. When I'm home, we see a lot of each other. But neither of us owns the other. We want to play around, we do, but we respect each other and care about each other, so we tell each other what we're up to."

"I see," she said. Looked down at herself: upper body nude, sheets twisted around her hips and legs. "'Nice rack,' huh?"

"You're not as big as Christie, but not bad. Anyway, I figure, when in Rome..."

"Or Paris."

"As the case may be."

"Gee, thanks."

"Jessie, I like you. I think you're sexy. I had fun last night, and I hope you did. I also hope you're adult enough not to let it mean more than it means, you catch my drift."

"Yes, Morgan. I do. Don't worry about me, okay? I've been around the block."

He smiled. "Yeah, I could tell that."

He pulled on clothes that were still slightly damp. "I'm glad you're up," he said. "We have to get to the airport."

"Already? I thought our flight wasn't until afternoon."

"That was before we knew they were onto us," he said. "If they've figured out the Barbara Slonaker name, they'll know about the reservations and be watching that afternoon flight, at both ends. We can't be on that one, but we have to get to Geneva as quick as we can. I'd rather rent a car and drive it, but they'd be ready for us by the time we got there. At least if we get an early start we have a chance of beating them to the money."

"We can't fly smelling like the Seine, can we?"

"I'll see if there's a store along the street somewhere that's open now. Might not be much." He handed her a scrap of paper. "Write your sizes down on this, and I'll try to get something that ain't too butt-ugly."

A moment later he picked up the briefcase.

"You're taking that with you?" she asked.

"Figured it's safest with me. You'll be okay here. I'm takin' the key—don't open the door or answer the phone. I'll be back in a few."

He walked out.

She looked at her watch, which, almost miraculously, was still running. It was just after eight, Paris time.

And she was alone in a hotel room.

She had a sudden moment of panic. What if this whole thing had been a set-up? Get her to trust him, get her in a situation where he had to go out without her, carrying the money. He could go anywhere, disappear. She would stay in the room, how long? An hour? Two? Six?

At some point she would have to leave. Or wait for Richard Steele's hired guns to come.

Morgan Byrd could be on the phone right now, telling them where to find her. Tying up loose ends.

She looked at the telephone. No help there. She had no one she could call, didn't even have a cell phone of her own. She had suggested picking one up on the way to the airport, but Morgan had vetoed the idea. "Nothing that can be traced, for a while," he said. "Not if there are feds in league with Steele. No phone. No e-mail or being online unless it's absolutely necessary. No GPS or anything like that."

She was truly on her own. Unless Morgan came back.

After twenty minutes, she had serious doubts.

She took a quick, anxious shower, checked her watch as soon as she came out.

Twenty-five minutes.

Twenty-seven...

Thirty-four minutes after he had left, Jessie heard a key rattle in the lock. Braced herself for whoever came in.

It was Morgan, carrying two plastic bags, a cheap suitcase, and the briefcase.

"Put these on quick," he said. "There's a cab waiting downstairs."

She opened the bag he tossed her way.

Ugly. But serviceable, she supposed. A pea-soup green sweater, and brown polyester slacks. A new bra, strictly utilitarian. White cotton underwear. Black socks. While she dressed, he stuffed the borrowed clothes into one of the bags, explaining that the cab driver would deliver it to Jean-Pierre's office.

"Next time, Morgan," she said, "I do my own shopping."

"I thought you wanted to go outside in two slips and a fur coat again, I'd've let you do it this time," he said.

* * *

They got onto an eleven-forty flight to Geneva on Swissair—two hours earlier than the one they were booked on. Jessie kept her head buried in a magazine most of the time they were at the airport, while Morgan watched for anyone familiar or threatening.

When they were off the ground, he turned to her. "You trust me, Jessica?"

As if he could read her mind.

She started to give him the pat answer, decided that he was looking for an honest one instead.

"Now I do, yes."

"Now meanin', now we've had sex? Or now since I took a bag of money and left this morning, but came back?"

"B," she said. "Left and came back."

"That's the better answer," he said. "But the right answer should be, 'not even as far as I can throw you.'"

"I shouldn't trust you? Then what am I paying you for?"

"You haven't paid me yet. Nice to know you've got the cash for it, though. And no, you shouldn't trust me, not really. You can't afford to trust anyone, Jessie. Not where you are now."

"What do you mean?"

"This ain't your real life, Jess. In your real life, there are people you can trust. Your real life is back in New York, with friends and a job. For other people, real life is a family, a house, stability that way. Others, this could be their real life. Always on the run, people trying to kill 'em. People do live like that. Not long, usually, and maybe not all that happy. But they live, just the same.

"This is my life, Jessie. You're an Eastern career woman, liberal I expect, upper middle class. Good home. Me, I'm a warrior. Haven't voted in the last few elections, and don't know how I'd vote if I did. Can't hardly remember my mother, except as a punchin' bag. My dad, he was a rough one. Never could hold down a real job, keep a house, anything like that. Always throwin' away whatever he'd held onto in search of the next big chance, but those big chances never really came around. Drank too much, brawled, whored around. I've been fightin' my whole life, one thing or another.

"Not you, though. You're a tourist here. You need to get back to your real life, wherever that is, before you can trust again. Until you do, you need to sleep with one eye open. You need to keep track of where all the doors are, wherever you happen to be. Always figure out an escape route from anyplace—street, house, restaurant—whatever. Always know the way you came in and at least one other way out."

"You're telling me this like you're not always going to be there..."

"I'll stay as long as you need me to. I'll watch your back as close's I can. But I may not always be there. I may have to do somethin' else. We may have to be separated for a short while, like this morning. I could be in the hospital, or planted in the ground, and you'd be on your own out here again. Your real life after all this most probably won't be just like it was before. But it won't be this. It'll be something else. You want to make it back to real life, you'll pay close attention to what I'm sayin' here."

"I'm listening."

The flight attendant came by, took Jessie's order for tomato juice and Morgan's for coffee, cream and sugar. They were quiet until she had moved on.

"Then tell me who you trust."

"No one. Myself, maybe."

"You're learnin'," he said. "Tell me where you're going."

"Switzerland."

Morgan shook his head.

"Real life. Home."

"When will you get there?"

"When it's safe."

Morgan smiled. "Quick study," he said. "I like that."

Chapter 23

Between the sun and the lake and the cleanliness, Geneva fairly sparkled.

Jessie could see Lac Leman (also called Lake Geneva, Morgan had explained) from the Rue du Rhône, where BancSuisse had its offices, any time she crossed one of the streets that sloped down toward the lake and the English Garden at its shores. The bright sunlight seemed whiter and crisper here than anyplace Jessie had ever seen. A function of the altitude, she guessed. Light glinted off the lake's choppy waters and reflected from the sanitary-looking streets and the immaculate buildings. The day was cool but there was so much sun that Jessie felt overly warm in the new leather coat she had bought at an airport shop.

Morgan waited in the bank's lobby, pretending to be a customer filling out a deposit slip, while Jessie went into her routine about needing to withdraw a substantial sum of money, first to a young clean-cut, rosy-cheeked man sitting at a shiny teak desk, and then to his boss, Herr Gunter Fleck, in a bright windowed office overlooking the street.

Gunter Fleck was the epitome of German officiousness, transplanted perfectly into the staid and serious world of Swiss banking. A round man with a small round head and a big round belly, Jessie could easily picture him in *lederhosen* and a little green hat, bellying up to the bar in a *biergarten* somewhere to reach over his belly for a tall frosted stein. But in his office, he was all business.

When Jessie finished her spiel, he looked at her gravely. "I am afraid that you and Mr. Steele have, how do you say it in English, crossed your wires?"

"Excuse me?"

"Mr. Steele was here personally, just this morning. He closed out the Cielo Holdings account here and withdrew all of Cielo's funds."

Ouch.

There was only one way Jessie could look at this, and it was as a problem. Steele was here in Geneva. He would know she was coming here. He would know he'd beat her here. He had the money, and when she and Morgan walked out of the bank empty handed, they would be sitting ducks.

She thanked Herr Fleck and hurried back down the wide staircase to the lobby.

Her face must have signaled Morgan that there was something wrong. He touched her arm as she approached. "What's up?"

"Steele's been here. This morning. He closed the account, took all the money."

"Damn," he said. "Let's go."

He led her out of the bank, scouting the way ahead as they went. She didn't see any sign of Steele or anyone who looked like his thugs. She stayed close to Morgan's side.

"You think he's still here?"

"I was him, I wouldn't be," Morgan said. "I'd be on my way to the Caymans. Like we should be."

"Guess we'd better hurry if we want to beat him there," Jessie said. "Unless he stopped there before he came here."

"Only one way we're gonna find out," Morgan said. "They're not likely to tell you over the phone, are they?"

"No, they'll need to see my I.D. Such as it is."

"What I thought."

"So, straight to the airport?"

"Actually, I need to do a little business here first. I have an account at this place up the street." He pointed toward a bank called Banque du Genève. "You can come in with me, or wait in one of these shops."

Jessie looked around. Next to the bank was a chocolate shop. She didn't have a ferocious sweet tooth, but the idea of being in Switzerland for such a brief time and not checking out the chocolate seemed wrong, somehow.

"I'll be in there," she said. "Don't be too long or I won't be able to fit out the door."

"Don't think that'll be a real concern," Morgan said, looking at his watch. "It's noon. I'll be out by twelve-fifteen, latest." He headed toward the bank's double glass doors.

The chocolate shop smelled like a dream, the kind you don't want to wake up from and if you do, you try to force yourself back to sleep quickly enough to catch the tail end of it, just to linger a while longer in its particular landscape.

Behind a long glass screen two heavy-set women—but hey, what other kind would be working here? Jessie thought—were rolling, pounding, and cutting big slabs of chocolate on a gray marble work surface. They glanced up at Jessie when she came in, then went back to their efforts, pulling and slapping at the chocolate like two manic masseuses on an especially tense client.

These women were rosy-cheeked, too. Rosy cheeks were big here. The mountain air, maybe.

Another woman, built somewhat like the other two but wearing a nice dress instead of aprons and stained white work clothes, smiled at her from a counter at the back of the shop. She stood behind a cash register and in front of a wall display of chocolates in a magical variety of shapes—flowers and fish, dogs and cats, cars and trucks, balls and birds and butterflies. Behind the racks of chocolate the wall was mirrored, making the small shop appear larger. On tables between the door and the counter were boxes and bars of various European brand-name chocolates, Toblerone and Lindt and Droste, as well as plastic-wrapped bars and bricks of the chocolate made here.

"*Bonjour*," the woman said.

"Hello," Jessie said. "*Bonjour*."

"You are American?" the woman asked.

"Yes," Jessie said. "That's right."

"There is no good chocolate in America, is there?"

"I don't know," Jessie said. "There's Hershey, of course. Ghirardelli. Godiva. Dove is nice."

The woman held out a paper cup with shards of chocolate in it.

"Taste," she said.

Jessie took the cup, removed a small chunk. Placed it on her tongue. Tingled.

"Mmm," she said. "Maybe you're right."

"Of course I am," the woman said matter-of-factly. "In America they don't make it fresh for you. Everything is packaged."

"That's true, I guess," Jessie said. She put another piece of chocolate in her mouth, and ordered a quarter pound to take with her.

While she was paying, she looked past the woman at the mirror. Something outside the shop's windows had caught her eye.

Richard Steele.

Jessie was positive it was him. He had hurried past the window without glancing in. He wore a gray suit and coat and carried a brown briefcase clutched under his arm like a football. Next to him was a tall, hulking man who looked like a thug, in a black windbreaker and khaki slacks.

"I have to go," she said. She snatched up her chocolate, which the woman had put into a small paper bag, and headed for the door.

"But your change..." the woman said.

Jessie ignored her.

It *was* Steele. And the way he was carrying that briefcase—it was full of cash. If she could find him...she didn't finish the thought. She had no idea what she would do if she ran him down. Still, she wanted to find him. Wished again that she had a cell phone, some way to summon Morgan.

She looked down the street, in the direction he'd been walking. Didn't see him. Had he grabbed a cab, or gone into a shop?

She scanned the passing cars, then turned her attention to the stores and businesses lining the Rue du Rhône. Dress shops, men's clothiers, travel agencies, banks and financial services...she hurried down the street, peering into each window.

No sign of him. He'd vanished.

She looked into a cafe, didn't see him, and was starting to turn around, go back to the bank to meet Morgan, when she bumped into a man coming out the cafe door.

A man in a gray suit.

Brown leather briefcase in his hand.

Her heart stopped.

She almost couldn't raise her eyes to his face. But she couldn't not look.

"*Pardon*," the man said, in perfect French. She looked.

Not Steele.

He moved off, and she looked again at the crowded sidewalk. Lunch hour in Geneva's financial district. Gray suits were the order of the day.

She should have been looking for the big guy, the bodyguard. Steele could have been anywhere, but he was gone now.

With the money.

Chapter 24

Morgan finished his business and stepped into the sunny street.

He craned his neck, looking both ways for Jessie.

She was probably still shopping. Spending some of Steele's cash. Hell, why not? He had just deposited a healthy chunk of it himself.

Jessie was paying him two hundred and fifty dollars a day, plus expenses. She had reimbursed him for all the airplane tickets he had put on his own credit cards—he always paid off the cards that were under fake names, so they wouldn't be canceled. He'd deposited a little over four thousand dollars. Not a lot of money, but about three thousand and change more than had been in there before.

The mercenary business wasn't what it used to be, particularly for a man getting up in years.

Particularly for a man with some degree of conscience.

Morgan Byrd had killed for money. He knew that wasn't exactly socially acceptable behavior. It wouldn't get him into heaven even if he had Mother Teresa on his arm.

But a man needed a trade, and this was one he knew. He took pride in doing the best job he could at it.

It beat flipping burgers.

But even with all that, there were some things he couldn't abide. He wouldn't work for ruthless dictators whose idea of restoring order was killing everyone in their country who might be a threat, today, tomorrow, or sometime in the future.

He wouldn't work for terrorists or people known to him to be criminals—drug dealers and the like. Wouldn't take their money.

Which left him, sad to say, without a lot of choices in the modern world. Politically motivated rebels were usually too poor to hire mercenaries. The people in power could afford them, but in most places they were the bad guys, in Morgan's view, using force to keep their populations oppressed.

Morgan was a firm believer in free enterprise and the benefits of capitalism. Sometimes, he knew, capitalism needed a little push. And once in a while conflicts were political in nature, but the people on both sides were willing to follow what he considered to be reasonable rules of warfare.

It was rare, though, and getting more so.

At his age, he should have been less selective about the jobs he took. Instead, he found himself becoming ever choosier. The faces of the dead still haunted him, especially their eyes, their gazes boring into him as he slept, but applying some standards to his employment seemed to help a little.

As a result, Morgan's savings were being gradually depleted. More and more of his income was coming from other sources, but it hardly paid his bills. He needed a big paycheck, the kind he'd earned and burned through in his younger days.

It also wouldn't hurt, just once, to do a job he could look back on with some kind of pride.

Jessie didn't know it, but financially and otherwise, she was a godsend. Especially considering that the situation she found herself stuck in put her at odds with a crooked multimillionaire.

He couldn't ask for better.

* * *

Instead of giving up, Jessie kept looking, now with a new target in mind.

A guy who probably topped six-three, in a black nylon windbreaker, would be a lot easier to spot in a crowd like this. Jessie hiked several blocks down the Rue Du Rhône, then cut over on Rue D'Italie toward the lake.

At the base of this street was the English Garden, a lakefront park that seemed popular with the tourist set. A grassy sward, trees, a fountain, and what would probably be a lush flower garden if it weren't mid-December attracted strollers, artists, photographers, and families.

Looking out over the lake, Jessie could see a powerful jet of water that erupted twenty stories or more into the air.

The sky was almost cobalt blue, as clear as she had ever seen it.

But there was no sign of Steele or his friend.

She went back up to the bank. Even though it was cool outside Jessie had worked up a sweat.

Morgan Byrd stood outside his bank, hands in his pockets, looking angry. It was the first time she had seen him that way.

She didn't much like it.

"Where the hell have you been?" he asked. "I've been waitin' here, not knowin' if you had been picked up, taken into an alley and killed, what. If I'm supposed to be responsible for you, I gotta know where you are."

"Sorry, Morgan," she said. "I saw Steele, and—"

"Steele?" he interrupted. "When?"

"When I was waiting for you. I was in that store—" she pointed toward the chocolate shop "—and he passed by the window. He was with one of his thugs, carrying a briefcase."

"What'd you do?"

"I tried to find them. I figured maybe if I could see where he went, we'd have a chance to get the briefcase away from him."

He took her elbow and walked her away from the bank.

"Think about this a minute, Jessie," he said. "If you had seen him again, chances are he would have seen you. His first reaction to seein' you would be to kill you. Since he's got a gunny along, he could do it without even getting' his hands dirty.

"If we made a play for the briefcase, he would just raise a holler and get us both arrested. We'd spend a long time in a Swiss jail and he'd go home happy. Maybe while we were in jail, we'd meet with accidents, but maybe that wouldn't even be necessary.

"Any way you look at it, takin' off after him by yourself was a bad mistake, and one you can't make if you want me to work for you."

"I understand," she said, stung by his criticism. "I already apologized. What do you want me to do?"

"I'm not lookin' for an apology," he said. "I just don't want you to do it again. You understand?"

"I think I get it," she said.

"Good." He raised his arm to the street to hail a taxi. "Now let's get to the hotel, grab our stuff, and go to the airport. We got a plane to charter."

"Charter?"

A cab pulled over to the curb. As Morgan opened the door for her, he said, "Steele beat us here, and he's got a head start. If he's takin' commercial flights, we might be able to beat him to the Caymans. Anyway, we got the cash to do it—might as well live it up a little."

* * *

She was a wreck.

There weren't that many things that were important to Barbara Slonaker.

Climate change? Couldn't give a rat's ass. Deforestation? Who cared? Would Susan Lucci ever win that Emmy?

Okay, there was some small amount of intellectual curiosity over that one, she had to admit. But she had never lost any sleep over it, and now the show had been cancelled anyway.

So the list of things that she would, in fact, lose sleep over was a short one. Shortish, anyway. Poverty, that was a big one. Huge. She had never really been poor, but she had been less rich than she was right now, and she didn't like it, didn't care to fall into that particular category again.

Losing her looks bothered her occasionally, although she found as she grew older that, really, it mattered less and less.

Not getting laid, though—that was a bad one. She realized that there could be, if you wanted to make the leap, a connection between this one and the last. So far, this hadn't been a problem for her, except for the occasional stretch of a month or so, now and again. Usually she could find someone to scratch that particular itch for her.

Then—always, really—there was death.

The main one. The single worry that plagued her nights more than any other.

She was scared—no, too weak a word—absolutely terrified of dying.

Barbara Slonaker was not a woman who liked pain. She had passed, thanks, on childbirth. She'd had her ears pierced, but only reluctantly. Tattoos? Forget it.

But she thought that if she had a choice between dying and living in agony, unable to feed herself, connected to tubes and bags and wires— given that unpleasant choice, she would choose to live. Don't pull that plug, doc, I'm not ready yet!

Because she knew what it was like to live, even in pain. Dying, though—that great unknown...she didn't know what to expect. Didn't know what was there, if anything. A long tunnel with a bright light at the end? Eternal flaming torment? Bleak nothingness?

Only one way to find out.

Lately, though, there had been a new fear to add to her catalogue. A new consideration etched into her list of unpleasant thoughts that could keep her pacing the hardwood floors of her apartment at three in the morning.

Jail.

Or, to be perfectly specific, the nagging feeling that she could soon be finding out for herself what jail was like.

She thought she had an idea.

Her childhood, which an outsider might have considered fairly idyllic, was, in fact, decidedly *not*.

Her mother was a strong woman. More than strong. Determined, treacherous, utterly without mercy, devious, manipulative. Barbara liked to get her way, but she was nothing compared to dear old Ma.

Her father, on the other hand, had the backbone of an amoeba. He was the family's primary breadwinner—that was just the way it worked in those days—but he turned his checks over to his wife and never had any claim in how they were spent.

If she wanted to move, they moved. If she wanted to redecorate, they redecorated. If she wanted to vacation at the beach, well, they slathered on the suntan oil and braced themselves for sand in their pants.

And somehow, it turned out that what she wanted in a daughter was someone who would always be in the house, always within earshot of her piercing shriek.

Barbara had never figured out if it was that her mother didn't trust the outside world, and was afraid that if Barbara left the house, she might be kidnapped by gypsies or killed or eaten by tigers, or if she didn't trust Barbara, and assumed that if she was out of sight she would be getting into trouble. The only kinds of trouble Barbara could imagine, in her early days, were the same ones she thought her mom might be afraid of. Later on, she realized there were alternatives, like running away from home, getting pregnant, or maybe realizing that there was intelligent life beyond the Slonaker household.

Getting pregnant held no appeal. The others, though—especially the part about intelligent life...

When she applied to college she only chose institutions that were too far from home to commute to. She was accepted at Mount Holyoke, and moved into a dorm there.

She never lived at home again.

Spent the night once in a while. She didn't hate her mother. She just didn't want to live in the woman's house, because doing so was as close to prison as she could realistically imagine.

Which led back to jail, and her desire to keep far away therefrom.

But that bitch Jessica Cutler was gone. Vanished. With the Cielo Holdings files.

She could turn up at any time. And when she did she could wreck the whole deal. She could ruin Richard Steele. They all could be arrested.

She could end up both poor and in jail.

Only thing worse was dead, and that had also been known to happen to people in prison.

The more she thought about it, the more convinced she was that it was going to happen. Jessie would blow into town accompanied by a hundred Feds, and they would all be rounded up and locked away.

This was the stuff of nightmares, of sleepless nights spent wearing a groove in her floor.

She called Richard once a day. Called Jake Garland. Called Jim Mackie.

"We're looking," they said. "Nothing yet," they said.

Not good enough.

She suddenly realized that she had been sitting at her desk snapping a pencil into smaller and smaller pieces. Finally, the pieces wouldn't break, but there were trenches in her fingers where she had been pressing the pencil into them.

She picked up the phone, dialed Garland's number.

"It's me," she said when he answered.

"Barbara, nice to hear from you. It's been, what, twenty hours or so?"

"Can I help it if I'm nervous?" she asked.

"Isn't that what Prozac is for? Or Valium, one of those."

"Give me a break, Jake," she said. "Any news?"

"Something," he said. "Where are you?"

"I'm in my office. At my desk. Where do you think?"

"You're not in Europe?"

"Of course not. Why would I be in...oh, God, Jake..."

"There's a Barbara Slonaker in Europe," he said. She was in Paris first. Now she's in Switzerland."

"That...that fucking little—"

"Easy, Barb. Don't give yourself a stroke."

"But...she took my name?"

"Borrowed, might be more accurate. Seems she's been making some withdrawals, too."

Barbara paused. "That's nervy," she said. "I still hate her, but you've got to admit, she's got brass ones."

"You're so sexy when you talk dirty," Jake said.

"Bite me, Garland."

"We're looking for her, Barb. Now that we know what name she's using, it'll just get easier."

"Yeah, but fuck, Jake. Using my name? I really don't want to go to jail."

"Chill, Barbara. We're getting closer. She'll make a mistake. She's an amateur. She's been lucky, but she doesn't really know what she's doing."

"Pretty damn lucky, I'd say."

"Luck doesn't last. Anyway, I have a feeling I know where she's headed next."

"You do?"

"Well, she hasn't been spotted in the Caymans yet. We'll get her there."

Chapter 25

Jessie woke up to the sight of Morgan watching her over the pages of *Fortune* magazine.

"*Fortune?*" she asked. "Isn't that a little highbrow for you?"

"Well, "Morgan drawled, "they don't seem to have *Field & Stream* or *Guns & Ammo* on board."

She glanced around the plane, a Cessna C525 Citationjet. It seated five in relative luxury. "I bet not."

"You take what you can get on these no-frills flights," he said.

The no-frills flight was costing them twenty-five thousand dollars of Richard Steele's money. The fare was a little above the going rate, but they had made certain demands on Karl Bessler, the pilot they'd found at the airport in Geneva.

Virtual anonymity, for one. Immediate departure, for another. He'd had to file a flight plan and take off within a couple of hours of meeting Jessie and Morgan.

Karl Bessler was as German as they came. Blond, blue-eyed, tall and broad shouldered, he looked like a poster boy for Aryan perfection. He stank of cheap tobacco.

Schedules were damn near sacred to him.

Fortunately, dollars were ever so slightly more sacred.

"Why is it I never catch you sleeping?" Jessica asked.

"Long habit," Morgan said. "I'm a light sleeper. One eye open, and all that crap. I like to be the last one asleep and the first one awake."

"So I don't sneak up on you with a knife or anything."

"There's that. Guy tried something like that once—actually, it was a garrote."

"What happened?"

"I wasn't sleepin' as sound as he thought I was. Used it on him."

"Pleasant."

"Cut the shit out of my hands, I can tell you that."

"You tell the best stories, Byrd. How come I never went out with your type before?"

"Ain't goin' out with me now."

"Figure of speech, okay?"

"Whatever."

There was a cultural gulf between them that she would never be able to bridge. Not that she wanted to—theirs was a business relationship, with a couple of added bonus features.

She usually tried not to sleep with people she worked with. And she had always made a definite point of not risking death with any banking colleagues.

Two rules out the window. The Gospel According to Jessica grew slimmer by the day.

At this point, she wasn't sure how far she trusted him. He had been out of her sight when Richard Steele showed up in Geneva. How did she know he hadn't called Steele?

He could even have helped ensure that Steele made it to the bank before she could get there. The doubts that had begun to nag at her in Paris had grown exponentially since spotting Steele on the Rue du Rhône. Morgan had warned her not to trust, and she was taking that caution to heart.

"How can you live like that, Morgan?" she asked.

"Like what?"

"Having to worry about things like sleeping lightly so you don't get killed. Thinking about things like men with garrotes sneaking up on you. I just don't see what kind of life that is. It seems insane."

"So workin' a nine-to-five job is better?" he countered. "Bein' at the beck and call of so-called superiors, when it could be the only thing that makes them superior is they've worked there a couple of weeks longer than you have, or went to a more expensive college, or kissed the boss's ass better? Puttin' in forty years of your life at the same company, so when you're too old to be of value anymore they can give you a watch and a check and slam the door in your face. That makes more sense?"

"That's the way it's done, Morgan. It's called living a normal life."

"Your version of normal," Morgan said. "Life's not normal to me unless more days than not, I can get up and go for a ride on one of my horses, listen to birds callin', see some coyotes on their way back to their dens for the day, maybe some jackrabbits, pronghorn antelope once in a while. Normal life is spendin' a few nights each year under the stars, a little fire to keep me warm, eatin' food that hasn't been processed and preserved and irradiated. Normal life is payin' attention to my own schedule and my own needs and not worryin' about making some boss happy. Bosses, in case you haven't noticed, tend to be the biggest assholes at any given company. That's how they got to be the boss."

"You sound like you've been there."

"I know people who have. Never had what you'd call a real job, unless you count the U.S. Army."

"No," she said. "I don't think that would count."

"I don't either. But the part about bosses sure as hell applies."

Jessie looked out the window. They'd been chasing the sun across the Atlantic, but it looked like they were losing the race. The clouds beneath them were a roiling sea of purples and blues, leafed with gold at the horizon.

Morgan had spoken before about her need to return to her real life, but the distance home seemed so vast she was beginning to believe she would never cover it.

But if she didn't make it back, what would she become? Someone like Morgan, living in the moment, never knowing where she would sleep that night or if she would wake up? Maybe that had an appeal for some people, but she longed for security, for peace of mind. She wanted to know that the rent would be covered, the groceries would keep coming, the credit cards would be paid off.

She recognized that she wasn't the marrying type. She would probably always be single, childless. That was okay. She didn't need a white picket fence as long as she could maybe have a washer and dryer in her apartment someday.

"Someday" felt like it was getting farther and farther away, the harder she chased it.

***

Once again, he shook her awake.

The tang of hot coffee scented the air. She blinked, tried to roll over. His hand was firm on her shoulder.

"Gotta get going, Jessie."

She blinked again, tried to focus. A hotel room, sunlight blasting in through open shades. Wicker and blond wood furniture. Pastel wallpaper with a floral print.

They were in George Town, Grand Cayman Island.

She remembered.

They had flown in late the night before—too late to get to the bank. They'd asked a cabbie for a hotel recommendation, somewhere not too close to the airport or the bank, to reduce any possibility of running into Steele. He'd brought them here, to The Shores on Elgin Avenue, from which you couldn't actually see the shore or hear the surf.

But that was okay. They weren't here as tourists.

By the time they had checked in and fallen asleep it was after five.

"What time is it?" she asked.

"Little after eleven," he said. "There's coffee."

"Eleven! Fuck!"

"That's why there's coffee," he said. "No time for breakfast. Put yourself together. We're burnin' daylight."

She sat up in bed, snatched one of the cups off the tray. Her head was pounding, and she felt like she hadn't slept at all. Even blinking hurt.

"Sorry, Morgan. I..."

"Little jet lag?"

"Yeah, looks like it. I'll be okay."

He held his hand out to her. She put her hand up, palm open, and he dropped three ibuprofen tablets into it.

"Take these with the coffee," he said.

She put the tablets into her mouth, washed them down with a big swallow.

"Thanks."

"Come on," he said. "Take a shower. Make it a quick one."

She got out of bed, no longer the least bit self-conscious about wearing lingerie, or nothing, around him.

"One of these days," she said, "I *will* wake up first."

"Right. On the day they bury me."

"Whatever it takes." She went into the bathroom and started the shower.

Chapter 26

Morgan and Jessica took a cab from The Shores to Edward Street, where International Islands Business Bank had its main branch. The cab was an interesting affair—an aged Volkswagen Thing, painted bright yellow and decorated with peeling stickers, mostly daisies and yellow ducks. There was no roof, but then Jessie figured a roof was rarely needed here. The air was warm and even this far inland carried the faintest tang of salt water.

George Town was beautiful. It was in some ways bigger and more modern than she had anticipated, but it was definitely a Caribbean island. Black people rode bicycles, drove old beaten cars and new American ones. The whites she saw were mostly in cabs, like herself. Palm trees dotted the skyline under a sky of cloudless azure.

The tropical flavor was enhanced by the paint on many of the structures. On one block, four different buildings were painted different shades of blue, as if trying to capture the hues of sea and sky. Here there was a house of shocking pink, there one in canary, there a bright cherry red with green trim, like a structural Christmas card.

She hadn't seen the beach yet, but Morgan had guaranteed soft white sand and pure blue water, and she was hoping they'd have time for at least a quick dip.

She had a fleeting vision of Cassie standing waist-deep in the gentle surf. She'd like to bring her niece here, under different circumstances.

IIBB was in a modern, concrete and glass four-story building on Edward Street. The salt air was sharper here, Jessie noticed as the cab pulled away, and the sun felt a little warmer.

"You go on in," Morgan said. "I'll keep an eye on the street."

"Right back," Jessie said.

* * *

And she was.

"Too late?" Morgan asked when he saw her face.

"Again," she said. "And this is where the bulk of his money was. Millions and millions."

"They say when?"

"Earlier this morning."

"So he's still on the island."

"Or was. Could be on his way anywhere by now."

"Reckon so."

"And we're screwed. Couple million bucks from Paris isn't going to hurt him much."

"Could be, Jess. Fuck, I'm sorry."

They started walking, slowly, looking at the sidewalk.

Toward the ocean.

No destination in mind, but drawn by the scent of the sea, the distant rumble of surf.

"I can afford to pay you off, at least. And then maybe set myself up with a new identity somewhere. Maybe someday I'll get over the fear that Richard Steele or Jake Garland is going to put a gun barrel against the back of my head when I'm not watching."

"Couple million, you could live just about anywhere."

"Yeah, I guess. If you call that living."

By now they were at the coast. A wide stretch of clean white sand stretched to the water's edge. Foamy surf sparkled beyond the sand, lightly lapping the beach. Sails of distant boats shone white in the sun.

"Paradise for some folks," Morgan said.

"Some. I don't think for me."

"Listen, Jess. It ain't necessarily over yet."

"No? How do you figure?"

"You only lose the fight if you give up or die. You're still talkin', so I figure you're alive. That only leaves givin' up. You doin' that?"

"What options do I have left? Everything I've tried has gone wrong. The cops, the feds, the press, the money...nothing's worked. The bastard's untouchable."

"I don't necessarily know all the details of international banking law," Morgan said. "But didn't you say that Cielo Holdings is a Cayman Islands corporation?"

"That's right. So?"

"So aren't Cayman corporations supposed to have offices here in the islands?"

She looked away from the hypnotic roll of the waves.

"Yes," she said. "They're supposed to. Every business registered in the Caymans has to have a physical address. But those are usually dummy offices. A mail drop, a telephone with voicemail. No one's usually there."

"You have the address?"

"Sure, it's on all the Cielo Holdings records on my computer. And in that file I've been lugging around. Got a little wet in the Seine, but I think it's legible."

"Won't hurt us to have a look-see, will it?"

"I don't see what it would hurt. It's doubtful that we'll find anyone there, though."

"That, Jessica Cutler," Morgan said, "is what breakin' and enterin' are there for."

Standing there, her hand bumped Morgan's and he took it, wrapping his big fingers around hers. She let him, stood for a few minutes that way. He didn't feel like a lover at that moment; his smell, his big, rough fingers, his bristled chin, these all reminded Jessica of nothing so much as a bright May third morning, when she was fifteen.

Usually, her father had shaved and left for work by the time she dragged herself out of bed. But this morning, he was sitting downstairs at the breakfast table when she left for school, wearing a silk bathrobe and pajamas. He was unshaven and his hair was uncombed. A plate of bacon and eggs sat uneaten before him, and his coffee had gone cold. There was a folded newspaper on the table next to him.

"Feeling okay, Daddy?" she remembered asking him.

"Not really," he said. He mustered a wan smile for her. "Staying home today."

That was rare, almost unheard of. She put her thin schoolgirl's arms around him, and he embraced her, drawing her close in a tight, suffocating hug. His cheeks scratched her face in a way that reminded her of weekends and vacations past. She saw the folds in his neck, and later remembered thinking that he must be pretty old. Much later, she figured out that he had been fifty-nine.

Then he let her go, said, "Goodbye, Jessica. I love you," and went into his study. He closed the door, and she left for school.

Halfway through third period, the principal pulled her out of class, escorted her to the office, sat down with her behind closed doors. Nobody there but the two of them and a school counselor.

They spoke in hushed, grave tones. She knew it was bad news. Braced herself for the worst.

Her father had killed himself, they told her. She found out later that he had locked himself in the study, jammed a pistol against the roof of his mouth, and pulled the trigger. Her mother, hearing the shot, had broken into the room and found him.

There was enough damage to his head that the casket was closed at the funeral, so that was the last time she had ever seen her father. She usually thought of him in his dark pinstripe suits, banker's clothes, with his face smooth and his thinning silver hair combed and slicked back, but sometimes the memory of that May third came back all at once, in a rush of emotion and sadness.

This was one of those times.

Chapter 27

The Cielo Holdings office was in a small business park off Crewe Road, not far from Owen Roberts Airport. The business park was on a small cul-de-sac, and within the J-shaped business park, Cielo was at the far end from the road, the short end of the J. That made it pretty isolated, which was a good thing since it took a few minutes of working with his pocket pick set for Morgan to open the door.

"I always carry a pick set," he said, showing Jessie something that looked like a fountain pen. "Doesn't everybody?"

He took the thing apart. It was suddenly a collection of thin black metal parts, and he put one of those parts into the lock on Cielo's glass-and-steel door and then stuck another part in and fiddled with it for a minute, made a face, fiddled a while longer, and then there was a distinctly audible click and he pulled the door open.

Listened.

Breathed.

"No alarm," he said. "I was bankin' there wouldn't be, since probably there's nothin' in here that anybody but us would be fool enough to steal."

"I'm sure you're right about that," Jessie said.

They went inside.

Morgan was right. There wasn't much to the office. A steel desk and a broken down wooden office chair. A black filing cabinet. A telephone connected to an old answering machine and a fax machine. No computer, no typewriter. A layer of dust coated the desk.

"Well, here we are," she said. "What are we looking for?"

"Beats the hell out of me," Morgan said. "I'm good at not getting' killed, and killin' other people. There's nobody here needs killin', and nobody takin' shots at us. Kind of leaves me at a loss."

He said it with a smile, so she assumed he was kidding. But she wasn't sure.

"This was your idea, Morgan," she reminded him.

"Damn. That's right."

"Look, Morgan, if this is some kind of Socratic method thing, this just isn't the time, okay?"

He nodded, the smile gone. "Got it, Jess. Here's what I was thinkin'. You say the account at the bank here had millions in it, right?"

"That's right. This is where most of Richard's assets ended up. At least, to my knowledge. He moved them out of here, it wasn't with my help."

"So he'd probably want to do something similar to what we did in Paris. Shift it into a few smaller accounts, either to keep it here or to wire it someplace he felt safer. Maybe he'd want to cash a bunch of it out, at least for now, since he knows you're after it."

"That's probably true. Steele wouldn't risk carrying that much currency into the U.S. He'd smurf it around here first."

"And that could take a while, right? Might even take a couple of days for the bank to get all that cash together. So he's probably stayin' on the island at least overnight. I figured if anyone would know where he is, it'd be whoever runs this office. Might even have made reservations for him."

"They didn't do it online," she said. "Not from here, anyway. So we're looking for scratch paper, a faxed itinerary, anything like that."

"That's right."

She looked around the bare office. "Not many places to look."

"That's good, because neither one of us has had breakfast, and I, for one, am starvin'."

Digging through the desk revealed nothing except that someone here had opened a tube of Smarties candies and not replaced the lid tightly. The wastebasket beside the desk was empty. There were no unread faxes in the machine's incoming tray. Rodent droppings were congregated in one corner of the room, near a window.

Jessie tried looking at the bottom of the desk drawer, to see if any secret notes were taped there. There weren't.

Not even gum.

"This is pointless," she said.

Morgan looked at her. "Maybe. I have one other idea."

"Is it better than this one?"

He let that slide. "It might involve violence. You okay with that?"

"Let's see, how many times has Steele tried to kill me?"

"I know, but it's different when you're on the giving end. And Steele won't be the recipient."

"Who, then?"

"You said someone has to be the official company representative in the Caymans. He can check e-mail and voicemail from anywhere, but whoever it is who comes here once in a while, clears junk faxes from the machine, changes toner, and so on, right?"

"Yes, that's right."

"So if we can find that person, and that person knows where to find Steele, we can make that person give Steele up."

"We can? But he works for Steele."

"That doesn't matter. Believe me. He'll give Steele up within ten minutes. Might cost you some of Steele's money. Unless Steele pays him well, in which case we'll have to take a different approach. Still, one way or another."

Was he talking about torture? She couldn't even bring herself to use the word. "I don't know, Morgan. That seems kind of—"

"What? Premeditated? These folks are tryin' to kill you, Jess. You said that your own self. You want to put a crimp in Steele's operations, do him some damage, you might have to hurt somebody."

"I guess, but—"

"No buts, Jessie. Either you're serious about this or you're not. If you're not, then we can stay here and lounge on the beach for all I care. You're payin' me by the day. But if you want to get Steele, you'll let me do this."

"If we do find Steele, what then?"

"If we can, we take the money. If we can't do that, why not just kill him?"

"Are you serious?"

"Serious as can be, Jessie. That's one way to put a stop to him trying to kill you."

"But..." She didn't know what to say. The idea had occurred to her, of course. Many times. But to be presented with it as an actual possibility...and here on the island, she realized, they actually had a chance to get away with it. If the body wasn't found for a day or so, they could fly back to the States, be long gone before anyone could connect them with Steele.

Steele dead. She couldn't wrap her mind around the idea.

"Let's see if we can't leave that as a last resort," she finally said.

"Killing's always the last resort," Morgan said. "For me, anyway."

"That's reassuring."

"Killing raises the stakes. Introduces an element of risk. I don't take chances I don't have to."

"I'm not asking you to defend your chosen profession, Morgan."

"You're not going to launch into one of those 'sanctity of all life, how could you be a murderer of innocent people' speeches?"

"Believe me, I've thought about that a lot since I hired you. Before, even. But I did hire you, so I guess that would make me a ginormous hypocrite. You don't like to think of yourself as a killer, I don't like to imagine myself a hypocrite." She took a breath. "Okay?"

"Makes sense to me." Morgan said. "Let's find that address."

The filing cabinet contained copies of all the incorporation paperwork for Cielo Holdings, as well as the various documents required by the laws of the Cayman Islands.

The documents included a list of directors and officers of the company, and even though she knew it should be there, it gave Jessie a start to see the name and New York address of Barbara Slonaker listed.

Finally, at the back of the cabinet, they found a copy of the lease for the office. A new name showed up here—Barrett Fowles. Beneath that was the title "Resident Agent."

"There's our man," Jessie said. "I remember seeing that name in some of Steele's papers."

"Barrett Fowles? You sure that's a man?"

"Don't be mean."

"I'm fixin' to go over there and beat the shit out of him if I have to, and you don't want me to make fun of his name?"

Jessie couldn't hold back a dry chuckle. "I have to draw the line somewhere, Morgan."

* * *

Barrett Fowles lived in a luxurious house on Rum Point, about forty minutes from downtown George Town. An eight foot fence, draped with bougainvillea, encircled the place. Behind an iron gate, a paved drive led up to a huge white stucco two story house with a tile roof.

On the way over, they had passed neighborhoods of rank poverty, with trash piled up between houses, naked children playing in the streets, packs of dogs running wild. Jessie had been reminded of her sister's diatribe about the complicity of bankers in the world's economic problems, about the growing gulf between rich and poor. Joan had always been radical, but Jessie couldn't dismiss her complaints out of hand. Not without admitting that there was some truth to them.

"He didn't pay for this place by being Richard's Cayman Islands agent," Jessie said. They sat in a rented Jeep Wrangler, fire engine red, parked down the street from the house. They'd been there for a little over an hour, watching for any sign of activity.

"We don't know how many companies he represents here," Morgan replied. "Or if he skims from Cielo."

"Both true," Jessie said. "You think anybody's home? No one's gone in or out."

"We drove past, there was a Bentley in the driveway. You don't leave a Bentley in the drive, especially this close to the ocean, unless you're leavin' soon."

"So someone's there who owns a Bentley."

"Or Fowles owns a Bentley, or rented one, because he wants to impress the boss."

"You think Steele is in there?"

"I think if it was me, and I had just withdrawn several million dollars from a bank in cash or some other easily negotiable manner, I'd rather stay at a secure private home than in a hotel."

"Good point."

"This place looks secure."

"More or less, yeah."

"Looks secure. Isn't, but it looks good."

"Why isn't it?"

"One thing, you could drive right through that fence, you didn't mind scratchin' your car up something fierce. Or you could cut through it in about a minute. Wouldn't even bother with the gate."

"Maybe it's electrified or something."

"Could be, but I don't think so. There's some razor wire on top of it might make you think twice about goin' over, but mostly it's for show. I don't think Fowles has ever had anything in there he really had to keep safe before."

"Well, you're the expert."

"Just don't forget that," he said. "And get that map up, the gate's openin'."

They'd prearranged a camouflage system. Jessie hoped it worked, or there might be gunplay sooner than she was ready for. She raised a map they had been given at the car rental agency and buried her face in it, trying to look like a lost tourist. Morgan leaned over, pointing out random streets as the Bentley pulled out of the drive, turned onto the road, and passed them. Jessie watched through small holes torn in the map.

"That's Richard," she said. "Sitting in the passenger seat."

"Probably Fowles drivin', then," Morgan said. "Know the two women in back?"

"I've never seen them before. But the guy in the back, behind Richard, that's the one who was with him in Geneva. A bodyguard or something, I guess."

"Good. Maybe the house is unguarded."

"You still want to go in?"

"The women had dark tans, sun-bleached hair. They look like locals. Probably dinner dates for Steele and Fowles. They wouldn't take millions of dollars to dinner with them, especially with a couple of local babes they don't know that well. Might even be escorts."

"I guess so."

"So we'll go in, have a little look around, see what we come up with."

"Like I said, Morgan. You're the expert. I'm just along for the ride."

Chapter 28

They drove the Wrangler a quarter mile down the road and parked it underneath a stand of palms. From there, they followed a beaten trail to the beach.

"Now you'll see another reason I don't think the house is as secure as it looks from the road," Morgan said. "It's beachfront. No one wants to pay for beachfront property and then wall it off from the beach."

"That makes sense, I guess. I mean, I wouldn't."

"So unless you got yourself a private beach, you leave it open on that side."

Reaching the beach, they turned and walked on the edge of the sandy strip toward the house. The property rose above the beach, surrounded by spreading mangroves and a fence that stopped at the beach line. There were other houses around, but they were scattered, with at least forty or fifty yards between them.

The sand was soft and white—Jessie squatted, scooped up a fistful, and let it sift out between her fingers—and sloped gently to the water, which was emerald green for the first hundred yards or so, then a turquoise color, finally dark blue toward the horizon. A few bathers were scattered on the beach, but this wasn't a big tourist spot.

Once again, Jessie thought that it would be a lovely place to visit, under different circumstances. If she survived this whole ordeal she would have to devote more of her energies to traveling than she ever had.

If.

When they reached the beachfront facing Fowles's place, they stopped, looked at the water, keeping up their tourist act. While Jessie watched a frigate bird skimming just above the surf, Morgan turned slowly, as if scanning the skyline for nothing in particular.

"Place looks empty," he said.

"Are you sure?"

"No. Only way to be sure is to go on in. But from here I can't see anyone."

"Are we going to, then?"

"Going to what?"

"Go in."

"I thought that's what we were here for."

He led the way, walking toward the house as if he belonged there. "Anybody stops us, just follow my lead," he whispered.

Nobody did. They made it to the back of the house, which was mostly glass, to let in the light and the view. To their left was a pool, Olympic-sized or close to it, with a small pool house. Between the pool house and the house was a small walkway that led around the side of the house. They took that path, so they'd be blocked from the view of anyone who happened by on the beach. They followed it to a door that led into a service area. The door was locked, but it only took Morgan a few moments to pick the lock.

Then they were inside. There were a washer and dryer, and an inner door opened into a big, modern kitchen equipped with restaurant-quality, stainless steel appliances.

"Well, we're in," Jessie said. "Now what?"

"We'll cover the downstairs," Morgan said, his voice low. "I expect the master bedroom is upstairs facin' the ocean. A guest room would also face the ocean, but they wouldn't want it right next to the master, so they'd put it down here."

"How do you know stuff like that?" she asked.

He smiled. "I just make it up."

This time, though, he was right. They passed through a formal dining room and into a sprawling living room, all rattan and floral cushions and glass, with abstract oil paintings framed on the walls. Sliding glass doors opened right onto the beach.

Morgan let out a low whistle. "Nice," he said.

Jessie couldn't argue with that.

They continued through the living room. Another hallway led to a closed door. It was locked, but Morgan had it open in a few seconds. "Interior locks are almost always worthless," he explained.

"So I see."

Behind the door was the guest room he had predicted. There were a couple of leather suitcases at the end of the bed, a door leading into a guest bath, and a smaller door that opened toward the ocean.

"Bingo," Morgan said.

"You are good."

"I know."

"Now we look for the money?"

"Now we look for the money. And pray that Fowles didn't put it in a safe somewhere."

Jessica started with the dresser. "He wouldn't, would he? I mean, why would Richard hand over that much cash to someone he hardly knows? Fowles probably doesn't even know what Richard's doing here in George Town."

Morgan went to the suitcases, rummaged through them, felt the linings and checked the stitching.

"No, he probably doesn't. So the cash should be in here somewhere."

The dresser contained some of Steele's clothes and some spare linens, but no money. She moved on to the two small tables by the sides of the king-size bed as Morgan opened the closet door. "Never mind that," he said. "It's here."

She rushed to his side. Inside the closet were three large black bags with heavy brass locks.

"That's it?" she asked.

"I reckon so," Morgan said. "I don't know it for a fact, but those are Blackhawk bags. Even the zippers are bulletproof, and those are damn good locks on 'em. I can get 'em open, but it'll take some time. Better we just take them and haul ass out of here before someone finds us."

"If he had bearer bonds, bank checks, anything like that, you think they'd be in the bags too?"

"No way to know, Jess. We can keep searchin' the room, but the longer we look the bigger risk we run."

"Let's do it, then," she said. He handed her one of the bags, picked up the other two himself.

"Heavy," he said. "Paper weighs a lot."

"Hopefully there's a lot in these. And we're not snatching somebody's seashell collection."

"We are, I'm comin' back here to kill someone just on general principle."

"Let's hope we don't have to take that chance."

He was right, they were heavy. She adjusted the strap on her shoulder with her right hand, finally deciding the best way to carry it was with both hands up and helping to support it.

"Let's scram," he said. With a bag slung over each shoulder, he bumped his way past her, down the hall, and into the living room.

Which was where he stopped.

"Shit," he said.

* * *

"What?"

Morgan waved a hand behind him to quiet Jessie. She hadn't been spotted yet, and he hoped to keep it that way.

Be tough, though. Depended on how many of them there were. If this guy was alone, then it might work out okay for her.

If the guy wasn't alone, they were in some serious trouble.

Because the guy was big, and he didn't look like he was in an especially cheerful mood, and he had been cradling a short-barreled Ithaca twelve-gauge with a pistol grip when he passed by the living room windows. Now that he had seen Morgan inside with two stolen bags over his shoulder, he was pointing it.

At Morgan.

Hence the "shit."

Which was followed, naturally enough, by Jessie's "What?"

Morgan backstepped, into the hallway off the living room, bumping into Jessie.

"Don't ask questions," he said tersely. He shoved something into her hand. Keys. "Wait until you hear the glass door open—or shatter— then go back through that door out of the guest room. Keep the bag if you can. Run for the Jeep. Get the fuck out of Dodge and don't look back. I survive, I'll find you."

"But—"

"Go!"

He ran then, bursting out of the hallway and dashing across the living room. He wanted to make the kitchen. He made that, they both had a chance.

The big glass door exploded.

* * *

Hearing the crash, Jessie ran. Back through the bedroom and out through the door. She headed straight for the beach, with only one look over her shoulder to see the guard stepping inside through the shattered glass. Knowing his back was to her—and counting on his preoccupation with Morgan to keep it that way—she cut across the edge of the sand, toward the Jeep, the big bag thumping against her hip with every step.

So heavy.

She nearly fell a dozen times.

Even though she kept her footing, she believed that there were armed men breathing down her neck.

She didn't risk another glance back until the Jeep was in sight.

No one there.

She kept running. Hurled the bag into the open back seat of the Jeep. Leapt behind the wheel.

Shoved the key in the lock. Cranked it.

The engine started.

She hated the idea of leaving Morgan. But he was right. His job was making sure that she lived. If she had stayed there with him, chances are they would both be killed.

That wouldn't do either of them any good.

She threw the Jeep into reverse, pulled out onto the street.

* * *

When the window exploded, Morgan threw both bags forward, and let their momentum help carry him into the dining room. The doorway blocked flying glass and lead shot.

Sounded like the living room would never be the same, though.

Behind, he heard the guy crash through what was left of the glass. Morgan dodged through the dining room, knocking a chair over with one of the big Blackhawk bags. Then he darted out the kitchen door.

Over his shoulder he caught a glimpse of the guy with the shotgun, aiming at him. The kitchen door swung closed, and the guy was gone. Morgan braced himself for the blast, but it didn't come.

He continued through the kitchen and the little laundry area and out the door on the side of the house.

The guy was standing next to the pool, waiting for him.

"Went back out through the living room," Morgan said. "Smart."

"Smarter dan you, mon," the guy said.

He was a Caymanian, Morgan guessed. His accent sounded to Morgan like a cartoon Jamaican's. Skin as dark as espresso beans. A head the approximate size, shape, and color of a cannonball. He was close to six-and-a-half feet tall and muscled like a body builder, wearing a tight polo shirt and khaki shorts.

Then there was that gun.

"Let's talk about this," Morgan said.

"Dunno what dere is to talk about. Already fucked up de house, mon. Got to answer to de boss for that."

"You could let me beat you up, then say you shot at me but I overpowered you and escaped."

"Could do dat. Won't, but hey, it wort' a try, right?"

"Way I see it. Or you could beat me up and let me walk away."

"Could just beat you up, an' leave you here for de boss to kill."

"Which boss is that?" Morgan asked. "Fowles, or Steele?"

"Why you care?"

"'Cause you work for Fowles, I could give you one of these here bags. You could retire."

"Shoot you now, I could take bot'."

"You got all the answers, don't you?"

The guy smiled, baring big white teeth in pink gums. "Way I see it."

He aimed the gun at Morgan. Morgan thought about dropping the bags. He didn't think there would be any dodging the blast at this range, but at least wanted the freedom of movement to try.

But he decided against it, turned them so they were in front of him instead. Shielding him.

Nowhere for him to go anyway—he was hemmed in by the two buildings. The other guy had all the maneuvering room he needed, around the pool. Might as well take whatever protection the two Blackhawks full of money would offer.

The guy's eyes narrowed as his finger squeezed the trigger.

Then his world blew up.

Or that's how it must have seemed.

What really happened was that a red Jeep Wrangler plowed through the wood and wire fence wrapping around the property and headed right for him, its front end covered in kindling and bougainvillea.

He spun and fired, but his shot was wild, and most of it ended up in the pool. The Jeep screeched to a stop.

Morgan charged, holding one of the Blackhawks in front of him. The guy turned back toward him, swinging the gun like a club.

The butt end of the gun came down on the bag. Morgan had momentum, though, and kept coming, rolling over the guy.

Whose legs scissored out, clamped over Morgan's.

They both fell onto the paving tiles, Morgan on top, straddling the black guy.

Morgan tossed the bag aside, jabbed at the guy's throat. His punch was blocked. He threw another, which was deflected. His fist hit the tile.

He drew back bloody knuckles.

The guy bucked underneath him, trying to bring his long legs around Morgan's neck. He and Morgan were both throwing punches, blocking them.

Morgan put up his left arm to block, brought his right one back, twisting his torso. Raised his fist, to get up some speed.

Brought it down in the Caymanian's crotch.

The guy let out a wheezing gasp. Morgan got his feet under him. The guy rolled onto his side, hands at his groin.

That wouldn't keep him down for long, though. Morgan moved in. Kicked.

His boot caught the guy in the ribs. The guy bucked.

Morgan kicked again. Face, this time. The guy's head snapped back and hit the tile.

The Jeep was just sitting there, idling, Jessica behind the wheel.

"Where's his gun?" Morgan called. "Get the fuckin' gun!"

Jessie answered something but he didn't hear her. The Caymanian was dragging himself to his knees. Bastard could take a lot of punishment.

Morgan let him gain his knees, rise unsteadily to his feet. Before he had his balance, though, Morgan cocked his fist, shoulder back, then rammed it forward in a stiff-armed jab to the guy's throat.

The guy ducked, or buckled. Morgan's fist caught his cheek instead.

The guy went down. Landed on his back, head smacking the tiles again.

Morgan saw the white flash of exposed cheekbone. The guy's eye was swelling, closing fast.

"Just lay down," Morgan said.

The guy said something, spat blood. Morgan couldn't even understand him now.

He wished Jessie would get the Ithaca and finish this.

Didn't look like she was, though.

The guy pulled himself up to his hands and knees again. Morgan lashed out with another kick. The toe of his boot caught the guy's throat. He let out a strangled cry and fell over, hitting the tiles, rolling once and splashing into the pool.

Face down.

He sank, then bobbed back up. Floated.

Morgan grabbed up the two Blackhawks, carried them to the Jeep, tossed them in.

"Did you see where the shotgun went?" he asked, climbing into the passenger seat.

Jessie pointed. "It's in the pool."

"Shit."

"Is he dead?"

"I sure as hell hope so. Drive."

Chapter 29

"Didn't I tell you to get out of here?"

"Well, yeah, but—"

"No buts! I specifically gave you an order and you blatantly disregarded it and—"

"Morgan."

"—and I don't—what?"

"*You* work for *me*."

Silence.

The Caymanian scenery whipping past the open Jeep. Jessie flooring it.

"Well, that ain't the point."

"Maybe not. You're glad I came back though, right?"

"No. I would be glad to know that you could obey a simple English command. A *dog* can do that much."

"You're welcome, Morgan."

"For what?"

"For saving your life."

"Savin' my—you don't think I could've taken him?"

"I saw you take him. I'm not sure how well you'd have done if he'd shot you first."

"Well, you might could have a point there."

"I think maybe."

They left the battered Jeep in a restaurant parking lot a few blocks from the rental agency, with the keys and two thousand dollars inside the glove compartment, for the damages. "We'll call 'em later, tell 'em where they can find it," Morgan said.

"Guess you won't be using that credit card again soon."

"Hopefully the cash'll be there when they retrieve it and it'll balance out."

From the restaurant, they caught a cab most of the way back to the hotel. The last quarter mile, they walked, carrying their big Blackhawk bags.

At the hotel, they went into their room, locked the door. Sat down on the beds. It was a little after six.

Morgan tossed a smile Jessie's way.

"Some fuckin' day, huh?"

"No kidding. You have any idea how to get into these bags?"

"I'll be able to open these locks. Just gonna need some time. We might could get into 'em with a pair of bolt cutters, too. Not sure about that. Could probably snip the locks off, or shoot 'em off, we had a gun."

"Which we don't."

"Which we don't now. But I'm thinkin' we probably want to get our hands on one."

He put the Blackhawks in the room's little closet.

"Now? Why?"

"I doubt we can get off this island tonight. Especially not if you want to deposit any of this money in local banks." He pulled off his torn, bloody shirt, wadded it up and tossed it into the room's wastebasket. Tugged off his boots. His jeans followed.

"Okay."

"But by morning, this island is going to be a very inhospitable place. I killed a man today, Jess, or damn near. He shot up his own boss's house with a shotgun. His boss, far as anybody knows, is an honest businessman, and Steele, from whom we just stole a few millions bucks, is also an honest businessman."

Jessie snorted.

"As far as anybody here knows," Morgan repeated.

"So the cops will be after us."

"Cops. If Steele has any men here, they'll be looking for us. Fowles knows any more tough guys, them too." He pulled fresh clothes from his own bag, put on a pair of jeans, a cotton shirt.

"So what are you going to do, go to a sporting goods store and buy a gun?"

"There's easier ways to get them than that."

"Such as?"

"You don't need to know, Jess." Standing in front of a mirror, he rubbed a cut on his forehead, patted his hair into place. "I figure I'll be gone a couple hours. Keep the door locked behind me. Don't let anybody in for any reason. If someone tries to get in, lock yourself in the bathroom, then go out that window in there. We get separated for any reason, I'll see you tomorrow morning at seven at that beach we were at this morning. You remember which one I mean?"

She nodded. The one where she had held his hand and thought about her father. She wasn't likely to forget.

She still sat on the bed. He bent over, kissed her forehead. "Lock the door," he said.

"Don't worry about me."

"Easy for you to say."

He was gone.

Jessie locked the door, flipped the deadbolt, hung the chain.

She still didn't feel especially secure.

Not with Morgan gone, all that money—or whatever—in the room, and the entire Caymanian police force looking for them.

Not to mention whoever might be on Steele's payroll.

She didn't feel very fucking secure at all.

There was a small dresser in the room. Jessie pulled the drawers out of it.

Shoved it across the carpet until it was in front of the door.

Put the drawers back in.

She unplugged the room's TV—they didn't bolt them down here, like they did back in cheap hotels in the States, apparently—and put it on top of the dresser. Leaning against the door, so if it opened the TV would fall.

Better.

But not much.

She thought she mostly trusted Morgan now. If he was really working for Steele, he wouldn't have put himself in harm's way for her, would he?

It was just so hard to know.

She didn't trust anyone's motivations anymore. Everything she had thought she understood about human nature had been thrown out the window. The capacity of people to astonish her was endless.

She suddenly wished she could call Cassie. To hear a child's voice, try to tap into that innocent, trusting manner that kids had.

But she knew that was a bad idea. She left the phone where it was.

She looked at the unplugged TV, on top of the dresser. She looked at the Blackhawks.

She watched the digital clock radio tick the minutes off, one by one by one.

One hour.

Two.

Three.

She had memorized the emergency information card hung on the back of the door.

She'd thumbed through the George Town phone book. Memorized parts of it. Wished the paperback novel she had picked up at the airport in Iowa, so long ago, hadn't been ruined by her dip in the Seine.

Wishing, she thought, was a fucking useless waste of brain cells.

Her mood was dark.

Dark...

* * *

A knock at the door. A whispered, "Barbara, it's me."

It sounded like Morgan. Mostly. Something was off, though.

"Who?"

"Morgan, goddammit, open up!"

Now *that* sounded like Morgan.

She straightened the TV, but left it where it was. If something was wrong, she could shove it, buy herself a second or two.

She took down the chain, unlocked the dead bolt, the knob.

The door opened. An unfamiliar black face was looking at her.

She shoved the TV.

"Shit!" the black man said.

She was halfway to the bathroom when she heard Morgan's voice.

"Barb, it's okay. He's on our side!"

She stopped, turned. The black man was standing there with the TV in his arms. Morgan was behind him.

Morgan looked like hell.

"What happened?"

"Just let us into the room, for fuck's sake."

"Sure, okay."

The man handed her the TV. She set it aside, tugged on the dresser. The man pushed it from the other side and they got it out of the way. He and Morgan came in, enveloped in a cloud of blood and rank sweat.

"Did they find you?" she asked.

Morgan had a fat lower lip and a bruise on his cheekbone, under his left eye. It would be a shiner before long, she figured. The cut on his forehead was bleeding again. His words were slurring a little because of the lip.

Morgan gestured toward the black man.

"This here's Maurice."

"Hi Maurice."

"Maurice, this is Barbara."

Maurice smiled, put out a hand. Jessie shook it.

"Pleased to meet you, ma'am."

"Sorry about throwing a TV at you."

"Think nothing of it." Maurice had a faint English tinge to his accent, which made sense; the Caymans were a British Crown Colony. It made him sound dignified.

Which was probably foolish, since he was coming in with a beaten and battered Morgan.

"So what happened?"

"I was in a bar down by the water, havin' myself a perfectly civilized conversation with Maurice here about where a man could pick up some firepower," Morgan said. "When these two other guys started fightin'."

"Two other guys."

"Yeah. Only they didn't contain it so well."

"Apparently not."

"One of them threw a punch, but it landed on Maurice. I took that as an affront, and threw one of my own. Things escalated."

"As they somehow have a tendency to do when you're involved."

"I don't think you know me well enough to be talkin' like that, Barb."

"I think I do."

Morgan chuckled. "Maybe."

"So who won?"

"Who do you think?"

"Cops looking for you now?"

Morgan and Maurice exchanged glances. Jessie didn't miss it.

"They are," she said. "Good Lord."

"They could be. They sort of came in to break up the fight. Maurice and I hightailed it out of there before they started arrestin' people."

"Great. So now what?"

"Well, Maurice has made us a very generous offer. You see, he has this boat."

"And he'll let us stay on it?"

"You are both welcome on my boat," Maurice said. "For one thousand dollars each."

"Ah," Jessie said. "Now I see." So much for dignified.

"You had any better offers, sittin' in here?" Morgan asked.

"Can't say that I have, Morgan."

"What I thought."

"Let's go, then. I hope we don't need Dramamine, because I'm fresh out."

Chapter 30

Barbara left the office, pushed through the double glass doors in the lobby and stepped into an icy wind. She tugged her coat tighter, turned up its collar. Heading into the wind, she cocked her head slightly to keep the worst of it out of her eyes.

December in the city. Felt like a cold one.

The way things were going, maybe she'd slip in the slush and get run over by a cab.

Of course, there wasn't any slush yet. The last couple of weeks had been cold, but dry. There would be, though, before the winter was over. The days would be long and gray, the sky a flat pewter sheet overhead, rain would turn freezing and the stuff would pile up in the gutters and along the sidewalks. The poor and the homeless would freeze to death, prompting a call for reform, for more and better shelters, which would last for about two days until the sun broke through, and then people would play catch in the park, and everyone would think it was spring, and the concern would go away until next year's freeze.

Cynical, Slonaker? she thought.

But then, what the hell, didn't she have a right to be? She was inextricably involved in criminal activity, and there was a person running around loose who could put her behind bars. People had died, and more of that was coming. She hadn't planned for any of this, had just wanted some creature comforts, some lovely things around her.

When your life turned to shit before your eyes, you were entitled to a little cynicism, she believed.

She needed a drink.

Or ten.

Maybe she just needed to get plastered.

One good thing about Manhattan, you didn't have to go far to find a watering hole.

There was a bar on the corner. Not an especially inviting joint, but there were neon beer signs in the window. She went in.

She was right. This was no trendoid joint, but a hardcore working man's drink-yourself-to-death place. The only woman was the one behind the bar, and she looked like the unfortunate aftereffect of a bad accident. Not the kind of establishment she would ever willingly patronize.

Which made it perfect. She wouldn't run into anyone she knew here. And nobody would bother her.

She took a stool, ordered a Mai Tai.

After a while, she ordered a second one.

She was pretty well into that one when *he* walked in.

She noticed him because he, like her, was not the type of person you'd expect to see in a dump like this. And because he was the kind of guy you noticed.

He noticed her too, but then, as the only woman in the place, she would have thought something was wrong if he didn't. She had already decided the place wasn't a gay bar, just the kind of dive where oblivion is a higher aspiration than sex.

But this man wasn't like the others. He was in his early forties, professional, successful. Expensive suit. Looked like Armani. Most of the wretches in the room couldn't even *spell* Armani. His hair was cut, he was shaved, he looked like someone who smelled clean. Maybe she'd be able to find out.

She found out. He paused in the doorway just long enough to do a quick, subtle scan of the room, and then came straight over and sat on the empty stool next to hers. He smiled at her before he even acknowledged the bartender.

"Hi," he said.

"What'll it be, Romeo?" the bartender asked. Two teeth in front had gold on them; the gap between them yawned like the vacuum of space.

"I'd like a beer," he said. "Whatever's on tap."

"Comin' at ya," the bartender said, drawing him a mug.

"Thanks."

"Hello," Barbara said.

He turned back to her, offered a hand. She took it. "I'm Jordan," he said. "Pleased to meet you."

"Barbara," he said.

"A pleasure, Barbara. I won't ask if you come here often, because you look as if you still have your own liver."

"First time."

"Same here. I was looking for a drink, not slow death."

"I know what you mean."

"Listen, Barbara. I don't want you to think I'm being too pushy, but this obviously isn't the kind of scene either of us enjoys. How would you feel about getting out of here, maybe getting a real drink somewhere half decent?"

"Talked me into it," she said. "Let's go."

* * *

Three hours later they were in her apartment.

But what a three hours.

They drank, they talked. They talked some more. At some point they stopped at a Chinese restaurant and ate for a while, but there was more drinking and more talking involved there as well.

Jordan was a broker with a seat on the New York Stock Exchange. He'd been born and raised in Illinois, moved to New York after he got his MBA at Notre Dame. He lived on Central Park West. He owned a Mercedes convertible which he kept garaged a couple of blocks from his apartment—used it to go to the mountains or the shore, but not during the week. His annual income was in the mid six figures.

That was all helpful information. But after they reached her place, she found out the more important bits. Such as, he liked older women. He was hung, if not like a horse, then at least like a good-sized pony. And drinking made him amorous.

Three hours later, they got some sleep.

But what a three hours.

Chapter 31

Maurice's boat, the *Ugly Lady*, was docked at Lobster Pot Jetty, a short distance from George Town. It was a fishing boat, forty feet long and at least as many years old.

And as many years since it had been cleaned, Morgan thought. But you took what you were offered. Still, after he'd been on board for a few minutes he wondered if he would have to destroy these clothes, too. There'd be no getting the fish stink out of them.

This job was costing him more in wardrobe than he would make off it. Except that he was charging the *nouveau riche* Jessica Cutler for all expenses.

"Nice name," he said as they boarded.

"She's beastly ugly, all right," Maurice said. "But she's seaworthy."

Maurice let them have the only cabin—generous, considering the price they were paying. They closed the door and then Morgan went to work on the bags. It took half an hour to open the first lock, but the others went more quickly.

The bags held cash. Lots of it.

Not the many millions that Jessie swore were in the account. Either Steele hadn't emptied the whole account, or more likely had taken the bulk of the money in other instruments and hid them someplace else, kept them on his person, or had already deposited them into other accounts.

But millions, anyway. More than they'd taken in Paris. Five, six million, easy.

Not enough to ruin Richard Steele. Certainly enough that he'd miss it, though.

Enough to piss him off.

Jessie turned in early, so Morgan went up onto the deck and sat with Maurice. The man poured them each a drink, lit a cigarette, and sat down in the cockpit. Morgan took a seat nearby. The boat moved gently on the quiet sea.

In the distance, a building was decorated for Christmas with red and green lights and a big star made of white lights. Morgan had almost forgotten that the holidays were coming. He would have to pick something up for Christie somewhere. Hadn't had time to stop and think about it, though, much less do any gift shopping.

He had been consumed with trying to keep Jessie alive and out of trouble, and at the same time helping her come up with some kind of plan that would free her from this mess once and for all.

The woman had gumption, that was for sure. What his mom called stick-to-it-iveness. Which, in his dad, must have been a recessive trait, because he had never exhibited it once in his life.

Morgan admired it. Had spent his life trying to hone that particular trait, and being drawn to those who showed it. It seemed to come naturally to Jessie. He didn't know enough about her background to understand how she had such an advanced case of it—she was oddly reluctant, he thought, to talk much about her past, her family. But it was there, no denying it.

"You like the music?" Maurice asked.

Morgan hadn't really been listening, but now he cocked an ear toward the shore. The lit-up building was a restaurant or nightclub of some kind, and a steel drum band was playing something with a calypso beat.

He smiled. "Got a nice sound to it, I reckon."

"Once you get the music of the islands in you, you can't get it out. That's why no one who has spent time here ever wants to leave."

"More time than I spent, I reckon. I can't wait to get home."

"You are a special case, I think, Mr. Byrd."

"Been called that. And worse."

"Your woman. Barbara. She's very lovely."

"Not my woman, but yes, she is."

"You're in some serious trouble, no?" His cigarette flared in the dark.

"We're in some serious trouble yes."

"I will do whatever I can to help. I have a rifle on board. And a faster engine than you'd think. A little smuggling, now and again..."

"Whatever pays the bills. And both might come in handy. We're hopin' to fly out tomorrow morning. But it pays to have options."

"Always," Maurice agreed. He threw his cigarette butt overboard.

Morgan rose, stretched, felt his shoulder pop. "Guess I'll hit the sack," he said. "Try for an early start in the morning. Thanks for your help, Maurice."

"No problem," Maurice said.

Morgan went below, used the head, then stripped his clothes off and climbed into the narrow berth next to Jessica. She stirred, opened her eyes.

"You look like shit," she said, touching his bruised cheek.

"Thanks. Nice to know I look the same way I feel."

"I can't believe you fought that guy who was trying to kill us and hardly got a scratch, but then got beat up so badly in a stupid bar fight."

"Didn't take it quite as seriously, I guess. And there were more people, fists, feet, and so on. More things to get hit by."

"Does it hurt?"

"Nearly everywhere."

"Nearly?" She pulled his head toward her, kissed the bruise, the cut over his eye, the swollen lips.

He kissed back. Felt her tongue slipping into his mouth. Felt her shift, opening her legs. His leg went between hers and she pushed against him. His hand went to her shoulder. She wasn't wearing anything. Traced her shoulder, her arm, went to her breast.

"Expecting someone?" he asked.

"Just trying to sleep," she said. "It's kind of warm on this boat."

"Smells like fish, too."

"I noticed that."

"Wonder where I could put my head, where I wouldn't smell it."

"I'm sure I don't know."

He kissed her neck, kissed lower. Buried his head between her breasts. Put his hands on the sides of them, squeezing them against his face. Inhaling them, the skin soft against his bruised cheeks.

"That's better," he said.

"Can't understand you," she said. "You've got boobs in your face."

"That's right," he said. Not caring if she could hear or not. He let go with his left hand, drew a line down her stomach. Across her belly. Found her moist and ready.

He was ready too. He shifted, pushed her legs apart with his hand, entered her.

At one point, he wondered if the boat was really rocking or if it was just his imagination. Decided he didn't care.

Maurice would understand.

Chapter 32

The churning of the boat's engines woke Morgan up.

"The fuck...?" Morgan said. Which was what woke Jessie.

He pulled on pants and went topside. She dressed a little more thoroughly, but almost as fast. When she reached the cockpit, Morgan was looking toward the jetty. She didn't see Maurice, but the fact that the boat was under way meant he was probably up on the flying bridge.

A police car was disgorging cops. Another car—the Bentley—had pulled up next to it. Steele and the big bodyguard got out. Fowles closed his door and went to talk to one of the officers. Another car drove up and screeched to a stop, a big Ford Expedition, and five heavily muscled black men climbed out. It looked like Steele had gathered an army.

"Get down," Morgan hissed at Jessie. She ducked.

"I saw the police car coming, I cast off," Maurice said. "I hope that's all right."

"Reckon that's exactly right," Morgan said.

"But they see us."

"They don't know me," Morgan said. "Just Barb. You stay belowdecks, no matter what," he said to her.

"What's happening?" she asked climbing back down the companionway steps.

"They're looking this way," Maurice said. "Pointing."

"Shit," Morgan said. "Looks like us leavin' has attracted their attention. Make like we don't see 'em, like we're just shippin' out to catch some fish."

"Aye aye, captain," Maurice said.

"Fast engine, you said?"

"Faster than you'd think, I said. But you wouldn't think..."

Morgan looked at the ancient craft. "Yeah, I know."

Jessie watched Morgan busy himself coiling a line, pretending he wasn't paying any attention to what was going on back on the pier.

"Are we okay?" she asked.

"They're still lookin' at us and talkin'. Steele is kind of wavin' his arms, like he's pissed off about something."

"I'm sure he's got plenty to be pissed off about."

"That big guy," Morgan said. "The one you said is a bodyguard?"

"Yes?"

"He's talkin' to someone. A civilian. Who happens to be standin' in a speedboat."

"Faster than this one?"

"I said a speedboat, didn't I? Maurice, you better open 'er up."

"Done, Morgan," Maurice said from the bridge.

Jessie felt the power through the floor. The boat vibrated beneath her, then bucked forward.

She climbed the steps, looked out over the gunwale. The jetty fell behind quickly, but Steele's bodyguard and the other men were stepping into the speedboat.

She saw weapons in their hands.

Morgan saw them. too.

"You said you got a gun on this tub," he said.

"Under your berth," Maurice said. "It isn't much, but it shoots."

"Might could need it. Barb, see if you can't find it down there."

She went into the cabin, got on her hands and knees and felt around under the bed. Plenty of dust, a couple of old socks. Finally her fingers touched a leather case, and she tugged it out.

Took it topside.

"Here it is," she said. Morgan took it, unzipped the case. Pulled out a rifle.

"Savage 110-E," he said. "Well, you said it was a rifle, didn't claim it was a new one. There ammo for this?"

"It's in the galley. Over the sink," Maurice said.

"Barb."

Jessie went back down, into the galley, found a cabinet over the sink. Two boxes of bullets, marked 30.06. She didn't know what that meant, but figured it must be the right stuff because there was nothing else that looked like bullets. She carried the boxes up.

"Thanks," Morgan said. He dug some shells from the box, dropped a few in his pocket, started to load the gun.

"What's going on?" she asked.

Morgan looked over the side.

"They're comin' after us," he said. "We're movin', but we can't outrun 'em for long."

"I don't think they know that!" Maurice said, yelling to be heard over the engine and the pounding surf. "Look!"

Morgan looked. Jessie peeked out of the companionway to see what they were looking at.

In the speedboat, three of the men had rifles out. Aimed their way. They fired.

She saw the muzzle flashes, saw smoke, heard the shots. The bullets went wide.

Way past them. If they were that bad, maybe there was nothing to worry about.

The boat continued to bounce through the water.

"They missed," she said.

Stating the obvious.

Or maybe not.

"They're not shooting at us!" Maurice shouted. "They're trying to block us in!"

Morgan and Jessie turned to see what he was talking about.

Before them, a big tug was cutting almost across their path.

Lashed on the stern deck were three spare fuel barrels.

The crew—five Caymanians—jumped over the side.

"They're shooting at that," Maurice called. "Some of their shots hit the hull."

"They'll get the range, next time," Morgan said.

"I think so too."

"Then what...?"

Morgan started to say something, but another volley from the speedboat rushed past them. Over their heads, this time.

A bullet punched into one of the fuel drums.

It exploded. Flame jetted into the air, two stories high. Smaller flames burst from the sides.

She couldn't see it, blinded by the first blast, but a secondary roar meant the other drums had blown too.

The surface of the ocean was aflame.

Then a bigger boom. The tug jumped as if swatted from below, split apart at the middle, then whooshed upward in flame and sparks and smoke, as its own fuel tanks caught.

"Port!" Morgan called.

"It's too late!" Maurice shouted. "We're on top of it!"

As he spoke, the boat kicked off a wave and slammed down into the fiery water. The bow cut through a sheet of flame and oily black smoke. A deafening roar drowned out all other sound.

Bits of flaming debris rained onto the deck. Jessie covered her head, felt the hair on her arms being singed.

Glancing up, she saw a chunk of the tug—good-sized, maybe the roof of the pilothouse—spinning over their heads, wobbling end over end like a poorly thrown football.

Then the boat broke through into clear water. The flames and smoke were behind them, between them and the smaller speedboat. The roar quieted and she could hear the engine laboring.

Through the fire, she caught a glimpse of the speedboat. Closing fast. Almost to the burning water.

Then it was blotted out.

The hunk of metal, charred, smoldering, slammed down into the speedboat.

She could hear their screams over the fire's roar.

"That's gotta hurt," Morgan said.

"Right bastards!" Maurice spat. "Shooting us is one thing. Shooting an innocent tug..."

"Kinda blew up in their faces, didn't it," Morgan said. "Everyone okay?"

"Scorched, but fine," Jessie said.

"Make sure there are no fires," Maurice said. Morgan and Jessie walked from stern to bow. They found scorch marks, but nothing had caught.

The speedboat was drifting in the middle of the fiery patch. It would blow any minute now. Beyond that, Jessie could see a couple of heads, swimming for shore.

"We got lucky," Morgan said.

"That keeps happening to us," Jessie said. "Every time it does, I get more worried. It's not always going to hold."

"Got that right," Morgan said. "But let's take advantage of it while we can. Hey Maurice, where we headed?"

"I think we should aim for Cayman Brac," Maurice said. "They'll be looking for this boat. I'll have to scuttle her, buy a new one."

"We can help with that," Jessie said.

"Anyway, I have a friend on Cayman Brac," Maurice continued. "He has a fast boat. He can get you to the U.S."

"That'd work," Morgan said. "Seein' as how we're not going to make our flight."

"Won't the George Town cops just call the other islands and tell them to watch for us?" The Cayman Islands were a chain of three, with Grand Cayman the largest. The others were Cayman Brac and Little Cayman. George Town, on Grand Cayman, was the capital city.

"Sure they will," Maurice said. "But my friend will meet us on the open sea. We aren't going near the Islands again in this boat. This is the last hurrah for the *Ugly Lady*, my friends. At least you made it an exciting one."

Chapter 33

"Guy looks like a refugee from a Jimmy Buffett record," Morgan grumbled.

"You're dating yourself," Jessie said.

"What? Jimmy Buffett's still around, isn't he?"

"Sure," Jessie said. "But when's the last time you've seen a record?"

"Hey, I still have a turntable. And stacks of vinyl."

"Yes, but Morgan, in case you hadn't noticed—you're a dinosaur."

"Can't argue with that," he said.

But he was right, Jessie thought. Maurice's friend Kelly—they didn't know if it was a first name, a last name, or his only name—did in fact look like a Jimmy Buffett character. He was darkly tanned, with that mottled appearance that comes from dark skin under a coating of hairs bleached almost white from the sun. He had long blond hair tied up in a bandanna, pirate-style. His only clothes were a pair of board shorts and sockless sneakers, but he looked like the kind of guy that, should he bother to put on a shirt, would only have Hawaiian shirts or surf gear T-shirts from which to choose.

He was a little under six feet tall, broad-shouldered and solid, with the kind of stringy muscularity that comes from working rather than from working out. When he met them, he stuck out his hand to Jessie first, and announced, "Maurice says you kids need to get stateside. I haven't been above the 25th parallel in years, but I can put you ashore on the Keys somewhere."

"Kids," even though he was younger than Jessie by at least five years, she guessed.

"I'd rather land someplace we can rent a car," Morgan said. "Don't feel much like walkin'."

"I can put you down somewhere near civilization, bro," Kelly said. "But that'll cost you more. It means sacrificing my principles."

"Glad to hear your principles are fluid," Morgan said. "What's this jaunt gonna cost us?"

"I drop you on the Keys, it's five Gs," Kelly said. "You want to go someplace like Miami, it goes up to ten. I fucking hate Miami, man. Retired people strolling with their grandparents, Cubanos all over the place, idiots who think supermodel is one word and you can become one by having your picture in a fucking Spiegel catalog—"

"Ten it is, then," Morgan interrupted. "Maybe not Miami, but somewhere along that coast."

"Ten it is."

* * *

He'd met them in his power yacht, a forty-two-foot Carver called *Ariadne's Thread*, on the open sea midway between Grand Cayman and Cayman Brac. They were about five hundred miles from Miami. It was eleven in the morning.

The transfer went easily. Kelly pulled up alongside the *Ugly Lady*, and Morgan helped Jessie across to his boat. Then he handed over the Blackhawk bags to her, and jumped across right behind them.

Maurice stayed behind on the *Ugly Lady* for a while longer, but when he came over it was in a hurry.

"Full throttle, Kelly!" he shouted. "Get us away from here!"

"I'm on it, bro," Kelly said. He poured on the steam and the boat bucked, then shot forward, bouncing over the waves. "Hold onto your hats. Or your pants, if you don't wear hats."

Behind them, Jessica could see a line of black smoke starting to rise from the *Ugly Lady*. Maurice stood in the cockpit, looking back at his boat, a solemn set to his jaw.

"I hate to see her go," Maurice said. "You did say you could assist me with a new one."

"Reckon we can do that," Morgan said.

"Excellent," Maurice said. "There'll be fireworks in a moment."

He'd lit a fuse of some kind on the boat, leading to her fuel tanks. *Ariadne's Thread* was less than a mile away when they blew. First a fountain of flame shot into the air, then a moment later the sound hit them, a deep roar across the water. Behind the sound came a warm breeze that passed over the boat once and was gone.

Jessie put a hand on Maurice's arm.

"I'm sorry," she said. "We really didn't mean to bring you into our trouble."

"I knew you had troubles when I met Morgan," he said. "Some people avoid trouble, but it seems others of us are drawn to it. I must be one of those."

"I have a feeling that type isn't especially long-lived."

"Probably not, Barbara." He patted her hand, and turned away from her to watch the black smudge in the sky, all that was left of his boat.

* * *

Later they were all sitting on a settee in the flybridge, around a sun-bleached wooden table. Kelly had passed around Mexican beer in brown glass bottles. Morgan drank slowly, turning his bottle in a lazy circle on the slick tabletop between sips.

"Funny name for a boat," he said. "*Ariadne's Thread.*"

Kelly, at the helm, took a long pull. He held a cigarette between his fingers while he drank. Before he spoke, he dug into his shorts pocket for a small foil package. He unwrapped the foil, removed a couple of white pills, and put them on his tongue, washing them down with another swig from the bottle. "Might be," he said. "I kind of like it, though."

"She's a nice boat, I'll give you that." Morgan said.

"1990 Carver. Twin Cat diesels, less than a year old. Top speed is thirty-four knots." Kelly said. "She does what I need her to do, when I need it, which is more than I can say for any woman I've had." This with a special smile for Jessie. She cringed inwardly.

"So why the name?" Morgan asked.

"You know the story of Theseus and the Minotaur?" Kelly asked. "The Minotaur lived in a maze. Theseus was this Greek hero who went after the Minotaur. To make sure he could find his way back out of the maze, this chick Ariadne gave Theseus a ball of thread. He unspooled it as he went, and when he was finished with the Minotaur he followed the thread back out."

"Why'd she give him the thread?" Morgan asked. "What was Theseus to her?"

"They wanted to get married," Kelly explained. "But Zeus had other ideas. She wound up marrying this cat Dionysus instead. Good move, too, you ask me. He's the god of booze and orgies."

"Interesting fairy tale," Morgan said. "But what's it got to do with the boat?"

Kelly took a drag on his smoke and flipped the butt overboard. "Let's just say I, ahh, negotiate a lot of mazes in her. The sea, like the song says, is my lady. But I need to be able to get through the mazes out there, the reefs close to shore in some of the more out-of-the-way places I put in, you know? So if the ocean is Ariadne, then the tool I use to always find my way home again is the thread."

"Downright poetic," Morgan said.

"Fuckin' A," Kelly said.

* * *

Kelly manned the helm for most of the trip, although Maurice spelled him once in a while. Jessie and Morgan stayed belowdecks, in the master cabin. There was a shower down there, and they took turns cleaning up. Morgan went into the galley and cooked up a bunch of ground beef that he found in the freezer, boiled some pasta, and simmered the beef in a tomato sauce with a variety of spices he found tossed into a drawer. He served it all up in the saloon at dinnertime. Jessie took Kelly a dish at the helm, then went back down to the saloon. Kelly gave her the creeps.

"No law says you have to eat seafood on a boat," Morgan said.

"If we spend much more time on the water," Jessie said, "I'm never going to want to see a fish again."

"Least this one smells better than the *Ugly Lady*," Morgan said. "No offense, Maurice."

"None taken, Morgan," Maurice said. "Kelly's no fisherman."

"Sorta got that idea." Morgan slid a package across the table to the Caymanian, wrapped in a couple of plastic garbage bags he had found in the galley. "That there's a hundred thousand bucks. Ought to more than pay for your boat."

A slow smile spread across Maurice's face, revealing even white teeth. "I think that would be adequate payment, yes" he said.

"Thought so too."

A scrape at the doorway alerted Jessie to another presence. Kelly. He stood in the entryway, arms over his head against the doorjamb, leaning in.

"That's a lot of money, bro," he said.

"That's right," Morgan said.

"Makes me think you must have a lot more than that, you could come up with that much for my pal Maurice, here."

"Could be. You're gettin' your share of it."

"What keeps me from just killing the two of you and taking it all?" he asked.

"You could try," Morgan said. He didn't leave his seat, but there was something in the way he held himself, a hint of steeliness that reflected the sudden tension in the room. His voice remained calm, though. "I have no doubt you're a dangerous man. But I also figure you're not half as dangerous as I am. You come at me, I'll have to take you out, and then I'll have to drive this tub myself all the way to Florida, or have Maurice do it. Rather not, though, so I'm hopin' you'll take the reasonable approach and earn what you've been promised."

"You have to sleep sometime," Kelly said.

"Unless I take some of those pills you've got," Morgan said.

Kelly glared at him. This was turning into an elementary school staredown, Jessie feared.

She would have to blow a whistle or ring a bell or make one of them stand in the corner. Just a couple of naughty boys...except the stakes were life and death.

God, was she tired of those stakes. She would have given anything for the toughest challenge of the day to be "subway or cab?" once again. What was it about men that made them want to kill each other all the time?

And since there were so many men on the planet, why hadn't one of them already had the sense to kill Kelly?

Finally, Kelly backed down. Or at least, that was the way it looked to her. He didn't act like a loser...he just shrugged, grinned, and turned away, heading back up to his flybridge.

Chapter 34

At three forty-two AM, Jessie handed Kelly ten thousand dollars and they climbed into a dinghy. Maurice was already standing in it, and Morgan had handed the Blackhawk bags down to him. Maurice would row them to shore and then return to Kelly's boat.

"Pleasure doing business with you kids," Kelly called. "Keep it real."

Neither one answered. They had both slept briefly, fitfully, but they were tired and cranky and ready for this little adventure to be over. At least, Jessie was. For Morgan, she figured, one adventure was probably pretty much the same as the next.

Maurice rowed for a while. Jessie had basically lost track of time, so she didn't know for how long. A while later—the sky was still dark, but she thought maybe she could see a band of lighter gray at the horizon—he beached the dinghy. Morgan took two of the Blackhawks, she took the third, and they waded ashore through gently rolling surf.

There was an expanse of sandy beach. Beyond that, a road. Beyond the road, a closed restaurant, and up the block, what looked like a couple of hotels.

"Welcome to Fort Lauderdale," Maurice shouted as he pushed off. "Enjoy your stay!"

"Fort Lauderdale?" Jessie asked.

"What it looks like to me," Morgan said. "Good place to come ashore. Beach isn't as wide as Miami, or as likely to be populated this time of the morning. Plenty of hotels we can check into, places we can rent a car."

"Which one are we going to do?"

"I'd as soon put some miles under our belts before we sleep," Morgan said. They were almost to the road. "All we know, Kelly's on the radio right now tellin' someone where he dropped us."

"Why would he do that?"

"Because I pissed him off. Who knows what that shitheel might do? I'm just sayin' I'd rather not stay where he knows we are."

"Would he really have killed us for that money?"

"He'd have killed you. I don't know how tough he is, or how brave. But if it'd been just one unarmed woman, or one man who wasn't me, he'd have done it, I reckon."

"One man who wasn't you. Must be tough to live up to that kind of self-expectation."

"Anyone but me, I'd doubt their ability to do it," Morgan said. "But I know I'm capable of being me."

"You know what I mean. You always have to be the toughest, the most fearless, the best."

"Not fearless," he said. "I'm afraid of plenty. I just don't let the fear overwhelm me, or rule my decisions. Fear's a good thing. Keeps you careful."

"I know all about that," Jessie said. "More than I want to. I feel like Theseus in that maze, only no one bothered to give me a ball of yarn. I need an Ariadne to lead me back where I belong."

They stopped by the side of the road. Dropped the bags. Looked both ways, up and down the street. Street lights, palm trees, buildings up against the sidewalk. Across the street was where they had come from, beach and surf and the vastness of the Atlantic Ocean.

"Could use one right now, tell us where the nearest car rental agency is," Morgan said.

"They'd have a brochure at that hotel," Jessie said, pointing up the hill. "Or a cab, or both."

"True enough." Morgan hoisted his bags. "Let's hike."

* * *

By nine-fifteen, they had pulled into a motel outside Orlando. There was a Waffle House across the parking lot, but they were both too exhausted to eat. They checked into a room and slept until four-thirty.

Jessie woke up first.

This is different, she thought. Afternoon light from outside filtered in through curtains that gave it a yellowish cast.

Morgan was sleeping on top of the blankets, nude. His powerful body was crisscrossed by scar tissue. Some, she could recognize as probably gunshot wounds, cuts from a knife or something else sharp. Others were odd shapes that she couldn't begin to figure out.

He whimpered a little, in his sleep. Twitched, as if something was pestering him.

She put a hand on his broad back, traced a couple of the scars. He woke up. Smiled.

"You were dreaming."

"Was it bad?"

"Maybe a little. You didn't sound happy."

He reached for her hand. "I am. Mostly. I mean, considering."

"Considering."

"Right. Considering."

* * *

At five-thirty, they ate dinner at the Waffle House. Washed it down with lots of coffee. They paid cash.

After dinner, they found a used car lot—not a big dealership, but one of those places where people who need money in a hurry can be paid minimally to have their cars basically stolen from them—and picked out a nine year old Toyota Camry. Morgan used one of his false identities, that of Brian Mitchell from South Bend, Indiana.

Honest Jack, the proprietor of this particular lot, explained that he really should see proof of insurance before letting the car off the lot. Morgan slipped a couple of hundred dollar bills across his desk, smiled, and said "Proof enough?"

Jack pocketed the bills with a single practiced sweep. He had done this before.

Florida's Turnpike toll road headed north out of Orlando. After turning in their rental, they found the Turnpike, and after a while longer that became Interstate 75.

Heading home.

Wherever that was.

Chapter 35

Sure, it was whirlwind, Barbara thought. But that wasn't necessarily a bad thing.

She and Jordan had just really connected. Since that night in the bar they had seen each other several times, meeting for nooners at lunch, sleeping together most nights, having breakfast together before heading off to their separate jobs in the financial industries.

His apartment was every bit as nice as hers. A little more closet space, maybe, but his suits were numerous and expensive. Each was wrapped in plastic before it was hung in the closet.

He always paid, for everything.

He was very attentive to her needs. She'd never had so many orgasms in so few days.

He was interested in her, asking about her day, her troubles. She told him what she could. He listened intently, with a half-smile on that incredible face, as if every word that escaped from her lips was a beautiful butterfly, and he felt privileged just to be allowed to watch them flutter away.

So where was the down side?

She wanted it to last.

She had wanted plenty in her life, she knew. And look where that had gotten her.

But this—she wanted this with a hunger that made the rest of it nothing by comparison. The money, the apartment, the possessions—those things were like wanting a particular vintage of champagne.

Jordan, in these few short days, had become as important as water, as air.

And the bitch of it was, she couldn't tell him the biggest secret of her life. Not without maybe losing him.

Of course, with every day that passed that Jessica Cutler was still missing, the risk of losing him—and everything else in her life—grew anyway.

A rock and a hard place. A fire and a frying pan. She was stuck.

So what she finally decided was this: she would tell him. And then she would tell the police. She would turn state's evidence against Steele and Mackie and Garland. She would testify against them, make a deal, and get immunity for herself. Then she and Jordan could settle down without having to worry about anything beyond who was going to sleep in the wet spot.

She came to this realization at work. She should, she understood, have been doing some actual work, but she had more important things on her mind.

She tugged open the bottom drawer of her desk, reached into her purse. Took out her cell phone. She didn't trust the office phones with this kind of thing. She dialed Jordan's cell phone number.

"Hi," he said. His voice throaty, a bedroom voice.

"Hi. Listen, I just wanted to tell you—tonight, there's something serious we have to talk about, okay? Someplace quiet and private, where we won't be disturbed."

"Is everything okay, babe?" he asked.

"It's fine, sweet, really. Better than okay. Better than it's been for a long time. There's just something...something that will take some explaining. A kind of a problem I've had, but I've figured out what to do about it. I'm going to make it go away, and then it won't be a problem anymore and then there'll be nothing, sweet love, nothing at all between you and me, okay?"

"Okay, Barb, whatever you say. If there's anything I can do to—"

"I know. And no. All you have to do is listen and let me tell you about this, and then tomorrow I'll deal with it and we'll make a fresh start. How's that sound?"

"I don't know, Barb. I'm just glad that whatever it is, you've got it under control."

"Oh, it's under control," she promised him. "I feel better already."

* * *

They were meeting for dinner at her place at eight. Between five-thirty, when she left work, and then, she went for a walk.

Walking and thinking. Ignoring the evening's chill and the panhandlers and the young families, the dog-walkers and the street screamers.

Because she'd had a change of heart.

No way, she thought, was this going to work. Who would promise her immunity from prosecution? This wasn't some big federal task force crime. She could give anecdotal evidence of Richard's money laundering, but she didn't have any documentary evidence. She knew what Jessie had seen in the parking garage, but she couldn't prove that either. She could steer investigators toward Cielo Holdings, but that was about it.

In the greater scheme of things, what she knew was small potatoes. She couldn't even guarantee that anyone would end up behind bars. And if they didn't, then her life wouldn't be worth any more than Jessie's.

She had been carried away by her brainstorm in the afternoon, but now, in the cold dark of night, the truth was all too clear.

She could never talk about it. To anyone.

She would have to make something up, to explain to Jordan the "problem" she'd been talking about without giving away any details of her real situation.

She would base their relationship on a lie, because the truth was just too dangerous.

By the time she got back to her apartment, she felt better. She knew that she had to stay the course.

No one could know.

Not even Jordan. *Especially* not Jordan. He was too decent, too kind. He'd be crushed, would turn away from her.

She bathed, dressed. Some makeup, light perfume.

The doorbell rang at eight.

He was always prompt.

She opened the door, let Jordan in. They kissed: long, deep, hungry.

He closed the door. He was wearing a leather jacket, leather gloves, a black silk scarf wrapped once around his neck. Casual, expensive elegance.

"I'm sorry, Barbara," he said.

"For what?"

From underneath the jacket, he pulled a gun.

"Oh, God, Jordan, don't tell me—"

"Don't, Barbara. I—"

"—but listen, I...I'm not going to the cops. I'm not doing any—"

"—I don't want you to say any more, Barbara. It won't—"

"—thing about it, and...Jesus, Jordan, this is *me*, I'm begging—"

"—make any difference at all, Barb. The decision has been made. Richard doesn't like—"

"—you..."

"—loose ends."

The gun looked huge to Barbara, a .357 Magnum or something. Terrifying.

But she didn't have to look at it for long.

Chapter 36

They slept in motels alongside the interstates at night and drove during the day, because that's what normal people did. Morgan was adamant that if you wanted to blend in, you did what normal people did. Drive about five miles faster than the posted speed limits. Eat at roadside coffee shops. Sleep in chain motels.

"You're truly a font of survival information, aren't you?" Jessie asked him once. She was behind the wheel, heading up Interstate 24. Nashville was ahead, and the Appalachians were receding in her rearview.

"That's what I do," Morgan said. "You know about money. I know about stayin' alive."

"How long have you been doing this?"

He looked out the window at the grassy countryside before he answered. "I enlisted toward the end of Vietnam," he said finally. "Served two tours. Rangers. I won't bore you with the names of the battles I fought in, but it was nasty over there.

"After I got back to the world, I couldn't seem to hang on to a real job. My folks was from Oklahoma, had a little farm outside Norman. Tried to go back there, and it just didn't make sense. I worked in a garage for a bit, delivered mail for about two weeks, worked in a fast food place, did some construction, some road grading. Drifted.

"Finally I got a call from a guy I'd served with. Said there was some action in Africa—Angola, it was. Said they was looking for some guys knew how to fire a gun, blow shit up. I could do that.

"And the money was good. Best I'd ever seen. I went to Angola with my buddy, came back, decided there was nothing holding me to Oklahoma, and wandered until I found the spread in Nevada I have now. It's quiet, pretty, folks leave you alone for the most part. I rented it for a while, did another couple of jobs here and there and I could afford to buy it."

"And that's your life? Firing a gun, blowing shit up, and Christie?"

"Seems like it works for me."

"You can't argue with success," she said.

"Way I see it."

* * *

The miles slipped by. The landscape changed, flattening before them. The sky became a vast bowl over a perfectly level surface. The road was a black ribbon that led them and followed them and defined their world. Meals, music on the radio, motels at night. Conversation sometimes, long silences other times.

Always, the question that hung over Jessie was, what now?

They had taken some of Steele's money but not enough to cripple him. He still wanted her dead. Now more than ever, most likely. She was feeling the same way about him.

So she was back to the beginning. Not enough evidence to convince the authorities, even if she could find someone Steele didn't own. No help from the press. No help from MetroBank.

Enough money to start a new life somewhere, but that was about it.

Somehow, it didn't feel like a victory.

* * *

Four days later, they passed through Clark's Grove, turned right up the long dirt driveway, and came to a dusty halt in front of Joan's house. The storm door banged open and Cassie burst from the porch as if she'd been shot out by a cannon. She ran into Jessica's arms and twined her little girl arms around Jessie's neck.

"Aunt Jessie!" she cried. "You're home!"

"Yes, honey," Jessie said. "I'm home."

And for a brief moment she was. She looked up, toward the house, saw Joan coming down the front steps toward her with a smile on her face, wiping a bowl with a dish towel. If home is where the heart is, as they say, then she was home.

But then Morgan cleared his throat behind her, and she knew that her long journey wasn't over yet. She didn't know what her next step would be, but she had to take it.

She squeezed Cassie tightly, then let her go. The girl took her hand to lead her inside.

"Come on, Aunt Jessie," she said. "You have to see my room! I got a new bride doll while you were gone."

Jessie stopped before Joan, gave her sister a hug, then let Cassie take her inside and up the stairs.

Chapter 37

After Cassie finally went to bed—only with Jessica's promise that she would take the girl into Clark's Grove the next day for ice cream—Jessie and Morgan went into Joan's living room to tell her what they'd been doing for the past week.

With the slightest lift of her chin, Joan indicated Morgan's bruises, fading but still painting his face with a spectrum of blues and purples, with some yellow mixed in. "Looks better on you than it would on my sister."

"Between the two of us," Morgan replied, "I guess we know who can handle herself better."

Joan flashed a quick grin and handed Jessie online news articles she'd printed. "You're missing," she said. "And someone named Barbara Slonaker is dead."

Jessie felt like her legs had turned to liquid beneath her. She sat abruptly. "Dead how?"

"Murdered," Joan said. "Shot. These are from the *New York Times*, so there's not a lot of detail. Had this happened in Clark's Grove—or a disappearance, like yours, for that matter—it would be front page news for a week. Apparently these things are a just a touch more commonplace in New York."

Jessie scanned the articles, barely able to focus on them. They were short and to the point. Jessica Dawn Cutler was missing. Her employers at MetroBank implied that she had problems forming relationships and was prone to promiscuity, either of which, the story inferred, could have something to do with her disappearance.

"Promiscuity?" Jessie asked.

Joan shrugged. "You're single and over thirty. They needed to say something bad about you, so it was either spinster or slut. You show some cleavage and leg at work, so probably slut made more sense."

"Great."

"Welcome to reality in corporate America," Joan said. "Remember how we used to spell it, Jess, with a 'K?' Amerika?"

"*You* used to, maybe," Jessie said. "Before my time."

"I forget, you're a baby. So tell me what you've been up to since you left."

The telling took a little more than an hour. Joan rarely interrupted. Jessie told most of it, and once in a while, Morgan stepped in and gave his side of things.

Jessie had been hoping for a miracle—hoping that in relaying the story, something she'd missed, some tiny detail, maybe, would present itself as the answer she'd been looking for.

But it didn't happen. No sudden revelation. Those were for movies, she decided. Not real people.

Not real problems.

The whole thing struck her as more than a little absurd. She was sitting in her sister's comfortable, homey Midwestern living room with her sister and a mercenary, a man who killed for money. A fire crackled in the fireplace. A picture her niece had drawn stood, framed, on the mantel. She suddenly had millions of dollars of someone else's money— money that couldn't be traced or connected to her. She could buy anything she wanted.

Except her old life back.

And, possibly, her security.

Would Steele take a million bucks just to leave her alone?

Not likely.

Not if it had been his million to begin with.

She suspected that he was not a real forgiving type. The way he held a gun to people's heads and blew their brains out sort of gave that away.

"You could," Joan suggested, "buy a billboard in Times Square and tell the world he's a fucking creep. Or build a website with the same message."

"And get sued for libel," Jessie said. "Or slander, or whatever it is."

"That's a possibility," Joan said. "But you'd be able to afford one hell of a lawyer."

"Thanks," Jessie said. "I hope you don't mind if I back-burner that particular plan, though."

"Just a thought."

"You know," Jessie said. "I'm absolutely beat. Why don't we go to bed, get some rest, and maybe by tomorrow once of us will have had a brainstorm?"

"Can't argue with thinkin' like that," Morgan said.

Jessie rose, kissed her sister on the head. "Good night, Joan," she said. "Thanks so much for letting me stay here again. I promise, I'll be out of your hair soon."

"Whenever you're ready," Joan said. "Careful you don't wake Cassie when you go in. She's so excited you're back, you may not get her back to sleep again."

* * *

The next day Cassie woke early, determined to make sure that Jessie followed through on her promise. But Jessie slept in, exhausted from everything she'd been through, and thankful to have a place she could stay where she didn't feel like her life was in danger every minute.

After a leisurely brunch—as leisurely as it could be, with Cassie sitting in a chair pulled up almost against Jessie's, peppering her with questions about Paris and Switzerland and airplanes and boats (she'd never been on either)—Jessie took a long, hot bath in Joan's big clawfoot tub.

When the bath was over and she was dressed in a warm sweatshirt and clean jeans and a pair of Joan's big winter boots, she took Cassie by the hand. "You guys be okay for a while?" she asked Morgan and Joan, who were engaged in a political debate of some kind. "We're going into town."

"We'll be fine," Joan said. "Enjoy. Just don't spoil her too much."

"I'll try to restrain myself," Jessie said. She took Cassie out to Joan's truck, made sure the girl was belted in. "I'm a little tired of driving, but I think I can make it far enough to get some ice cream in town."

"Thanks, Aunt Jessie," Cassie said. She was quiet until they were out of the driveway and on the road toward town. Then she squirmed in her seat, turning to face her aunt. "Can I ask you a question?"

"Sure, sweetie. What is it?"

"Why don't you like my mom?"

Jessie felt her grip tighten on the wheel. Her knuckles went white.

"What makes you say that?" she said. "I like her just fine. She's my sister."

"I know she is," Cassie said. "But you've never come to see us before. Now you have, but it seems like you're in some kind of trouble."

"Well, I am." Jessie thought out her words carefully. She didn't want to lie to her niece. But neither did she want to tell her the whole story.

"Sometimes you don't really know who is important to you until you're in trouble," she said. "When you feel like you have to run away from everything, then the person you run to is a good sign of who you really need in your life."

"Why did you have to run away?"

"Never mind that, Cassie," Jessie said. "The point is, your mom and I have never been as close as some sisters are. That's partly because she's so much older than me, and was pretty much out of the house before I was really big enough to know her. But it's also because she did something a long time ago that made me angry, and it's taken me a long time to get over that anger."

"Are you over it now?"

"I don't know. I'm trying to be."

"What did she do?"

"That's another thing you don't need to worry about. It was long ago, and far away, and it's not something you should have to care about, okay?"

"Okay."

"As long as she's a good mommy to you, that's the important thing."

"Oh, she is," Cassie said. "She's the best."

"Then that's what counts. Have you started thinking about what kind of ice cream you want?"

"I will when we get there," Cassie said. "That's the best part."

Chapter 38

She had double-nut fudge with chocolate and butterscotch syrups, whipped cream, and cherries on top. Jessie felt positively conservative with her mint chocolate chip.

The ice cream parlor was called Dino's, and was as old-fashioned as Jessie could conceive, like a screen capture from "The Music Man." It was a single long, narrow room. Down one side was the counter, with a glass sneeze-guard and double rows of ice cream cartons. The counter boy wore a paper cap and a stained apron and used a heavy duty scoop, which he rinsed between flavors under a continually running tap. Behind the counter were shelves of syrups and condiments—nuts, sprinkles, chocolate chips. There was a marble slab for chopping up fruit, and brass headed spigots for sodas.

Jessie was glad this place, at least, had survived the recession that had struck Clark's Grove and so many other towns.

Afterwards, she didn't want to get right back in the truck. She needed to walk off some of the giant scoops she'd just ingested. Dino's was close to the town square, which was really done up for Christmas now, so Cassie suggested they stroll around the square looking at the decorations. It was mid-afternoon and beginning to cool down, but they were both dressed warmly.

"What do you want for Christmas, Aunt Jessie?" Cassie asked.

"World peace," Jessie said. She was only half kidding.

Personal peace would be good enough. The ability to get through Christmas day without looking over her shoulder, jumping at shadows...she would settle for that. Gladly.

Pretty pathetic, she thought. But nothing that could be bought at a shopping mall seemed particularly important to her anymore. One's values changed according to the situation, she figured. She had seen pictures of refugees on the news, people fleeing war or poverty in places like the Balkans, the Middle East, and always wondered why they would even want to keep on going, having left behind everything they owned. They piled onto trucks and tractors and headed for camps across some border, carrying maybe a pillowcase full of personal items, often just the clothes they wore.

Now, though, she thought she understood a little better. They still had their lives. As long as they had that, the rest was secondary. Reaching sanctuary had to be the first priority.

And for Jessie, Clark's Grove was sanctuary. The little town square felt safe. There was old snow on the ground, turning gray, but a new storm was on the way, according to the radio. Christmas was just a week away now, and it would definitely be a white one. Many of the buildings facing onto the square—the occupied ones, at any rate—were decorated with colored lights. Several of them had holiday scenes painted on their windows. The vacant buildings reminded her that poverty wasn't restricted to other countries, and the questions Joan had raised, about her own complicity in that, started bubbling to the surface again.

She tried to push it away. Walking through town, holding Cassie's hand, Jessie had the feeling of having stepped into a past she hadn't realized ever really existed outside the movies.

But it had, and it was right here.

Maybe, she thought, that was why she felt so safe here. Because it reminded her of a time before her troubles had started—a time when the kind of trouble she was in couldn't have been. People just didn't behave that way in the days Clark's Grove represented.

Which was why, when she saw the baby-faced man, she didn't recognize him at first.

She thought it must have been someone she'd met when she had been in town with Joan before. At the library, or the coffee shop.

But he wasn't.

He didn't see her, which was good.

He was inside the post office, talking to one of the clerks. Jessie and Cassie were passing by, enjoying a scene of elves and reindeer feasting on carrots that had been painted on the front window. A movement of some kind—the baby-faced man leaning toward the clerk, she realized—caused Jessie to look past the paint and into the building's well-lit interior.

And there he was.

Once she saw his round cheeks, the big doe eyes, the crop of brown hair, she realized who he was and looked away quickly. Tugged on Cassie's arm, pulling the girl toward the corner. From here, she couldn't be seen by anyone inside. But the truck was all the way across the square, in front of Dino's, kitty corner from the post office.

And the post office door was swinging open.

She lifted Cassie into her arms and ran.

"Shh!" she warned.

"But Aunt Jessie, I can—"

"Keep quiet and hang on, Cass" she said. With her niece's arms wrapped around her neck, she dashed down the block, to the back of the post office. An alley ran behind the building, with parking for postal vehicles. The post office was one of two buildings on this block, almost dwarfed by the courthouse.

On the next block, around the corner from the courthouse, was Grove Pharmacy, the drugstore Joan worked for. That was where Jessie headed.

At the corner, she would be exposed for a few seconds while she crossed the street. No getting around it. At least she was half a block off the main square, and she was carrying Cassie. She shifted the girl so her own head was blocked by Cassie's, to anyone looking from the square, and she raced across the street as fast as she could.

The alley continued back here, behind the drugstore. There was a small parking area, and a single glass back door to the drugstore. She went inside. A bell hanging from the door jangled, seemingly as loud as gunshots.

"Look around, Cassie," she hissed. "Do you see anyone working here that you know and trust?"

"Aunt Jessie, I—"

"I'm sorry, Cass," Jessie said. "I don't mean to scare you, but please do this."

"Him. Mr. Adams," Cassie said. She pointed to a lean man with short gray hair and a rosy complexion. He was using a pricing gun to sticker boxes of pantyhose.

"Okay. I'm going to leave you with Mr. Adams for a while," Jessie said. "Then I'll come for you, or your mom will, at his house. Don't be afraid, okay? We're going to be fine."

"I am, though," Cassie said. The girl was blinking back tears, putting up a brave front.

"That's okay, I guess," Jessie said. "I am too. But I promise you it'll be all right."

"Okay." Cassie squeezed her neck. She squeezed back, carried Cassie over to the man she'd pointed out.

"Mr. Adams?" she said. He nodded. He had kind blue eyes, and she thought the girl had chosen well. "My name's Jessie. I'm Joan Temchin's sister. You know Cassandra, right?"

"Of course," he said. He looked at the little girl. "Everything all right, Cassie?" he asked.

"No," Cassie said.

"She's right. There is a problem," Jessie said. "I'm going to ask you to do me, and Joan, a huge favor. And I'm going to do it without explaining anything to you. If you trust Joan and Cassie, then you'll have to trust me too, and do this for me."

"What is it?" he asked.

"Take Cassie. Get her out of here. Take her to your house, right now. Keep her there and keep her safe and out of sight until Joan comes for her, or I do. Can you do that?"

"I'm in the middle of my shift, but—"

"Mr. Adams, it's very important. I wouldn't be bothering you with this if it wasn't."

"I can see that, Miss," he said. "Fine, I'll take her home. Can I leave her there with Marcy until my shift is over?"

"Marcy is your wife?"

"That's right."

"If you think she'll be safe, then yes. That would be fine."

"That's what I'll do, then. My car's right in back."

"That's great. Thank you so much, Mr. Adams."

"Don't mention it," he said. "I'm happy to do what I can for Joan."

"That's good." Jessie kissed Cassie and handed her over to Mr. Adams, who took her straight out the back door without even stopping for a coat.

Jessie crossed to the front of the store, looked out through the display windows toward the square. She couldn't see the baby-faced man anywhere.

But she did see two other men, tall and broad, wearing dark coats. They could have been any two men, but they weren't. She knew that by now. The way they walked, heads swiveling so they didn't miss anything, shoulders forward with purpose, hands tucked in pockets—resting on pistols, no doubt—convinced her that they were looking for her.

Steele's men.

More of the thugs she had dodged in Manhattan.

Who knew how many more there were out there? And the baby-faced man, the one who had pushed her in front of the subway, who had shot at them on the bridge in Paris, was undoubtedly in charge.

She didn't know how they had tracked her to Clark's Grove. But they had. That was all that really mattered.

She couldn't go out the front. She would have to stay in the alleys, work her way around to Dino's and the truck, and then get home to warn Joan and Morgan. And then she needed to get a new mobile phone.

She went out the back door, turned left, headed down the alley. It passed behind a hardware store here, with a loading dock that faced onto the alley. She stayed close to the empty dock. When she got to the corner, she looked across the street, then eased herself around the corner.

And felt a hand reach out, grabbing her sleeve.

She started to shriek but the hand yanked her forward, off balance, and another hand clapped over her mouth.

She looked into the eyes of the baby-faced man.

Chapter 39

"You're a hard woman to find."

Jessie was still off-balance. The man turned her, his right hand clamped tightly over her mouth, so that her back was up against his chest. This way, he could hold her just with the hand that was on her mouth. He released her other arm.

He could, without too much effort, snap her neck in this position.

Which was probably item number one on his to-do list, she thought.

Instead, he rummaged under his coat with his left hand. Came out with a small brown leather case. Let it fall open.

A badge. And an identification card.

"My name is Zing," he said. "Special Agent John Langford Zing, FBI. If I let go of you, will you keep quiet?"

She nodded.

He released her mouth.

"FBI?" she asked. She turned to face him.

"That's right."

"But I thought—"

"Then you were wrong."

"Zing?"

"Yes—"

"No, that's your name?"

"I'm thinking of changing it," he said.

"Don't."

"What?"

"Change your name. Believe me, it's more trouble than it's worth."

"I guess you would know. Listen, Ms. Cutler, we need to get out of here. Clark's Grove is not the safest place for you right now."

"I know. I've seen them. I thought you were with—"

"I know what you thought. Or I think I do. Anyway, I've got a car parked over by the courthouse."

"I have my sister's truck, in front of the ice cream parlor."

"They'll be watching the truck by now. They don't know I exist. We'll take mine."

She didn't argue. She followed him back through the alley, behind Grove's Pharmacy, across the street. There was a little parking area behind the courthouse. A couple of police cars, a few cars belonging to courthouse employees. And a dark blue Ford Taurus.

He opened the Taurus.

"Get in," he said.

She did.

"Now get down on the floor."

She did that too.

He turned the key. Music blared from the speaker beside her head. She recognized The Clash's *London's Burning.*

"Sorry," he said, turning the music down.

She rubbed her ear. "I didn't think FBI guys were allowed to listen to stuff like that. Is punk rock on J. Edgar's approved music list?"

"You'd be surprised what the old man's ghost lets us get away with," Zing said. He backed out of the space.

"Okay, where am I going?"

"You're asking me? You're the FBI, not me."

"You have someplace here, a safe house. Someplace you're staying. Can you walk away from it, right now? Away from Iowa? That would really be best."

"No," she said. Thinking of Joan, of Morgan. Of Cassie, left in the care of a stranger from the drugstore. "I have to go back."

"I thought maybe," he said. "So where are we going?"

"Around the square to the street next to the ice cream parlor. Dino's. I don't know the name of the street. Turn right there."

"Got it," Zing said.

She felt the car lurch as he pulled out of the alley and turned toward the square. Hunched on the floor, she felt uncomfortably exposed—she couldn't see what was going on, could only feel the motion of the vehicle, and didn't even know for sure that she trusted this guy yet. He could be delivering her straight into the arms of Richard Steele. He had a FinCEN agent in his pocket, why not FBI too?

But there was something about him that caused her to believe him. The roundness of his face, topped with unruly brown hair that was probably a little longer than J. Edgar Hoover would have allowed, the set of his brown eyes, far apart and large—these things all gave him a boyish look that made him seem honest.

Stupid way to judge someone, she knew. But then, what choice did she have?

If she had tried to run, he could have killed her on the spot. Better to go along, see if he really was what he said. If not, she could try to escape later.

Or just let Morgan take care of him. The old guy would probably like that. Make him feel useful.

The car came to a stop. "Stay down," Zing said. He held his hand in front of his mouth, as if covering a cough, and barely moved his lips as he spoke. "There are a couple of them crossing the street right in front of us."

"Not going anywhere," she whispered.

After a moment, the car started moving forward again. "They're gone. There's one other team I can see, across the street by the bank."

"Who are they?" she asked. She felt the car corner, to the right.

"Okay, we're away from the square," Zing said, ignoring her question. "Heading west."

"Stay on this road for about fifteen minutes or so. Through a bunch of farmland."

"You might as well come on up and sit, then."

She pushed herself up, sat in the passenger seat, pulled the shoulder belt across her and buckled it.

"You didn't answer my question."

"I thought it was rhetorical," he said. "Those are the people Richard Steele has sent out to kill you."

"Then I guess it was rhetorical. That's who I thought they were. I was kind of hoping you'd have some other answer."

"Where are we going?"

"My sister's house."

"And who's there?"

"My sister. Another friend."

"The guy you were with in Paris? On the bridge?"

"That's right."

"He's got good instincts. Could come in handy."

"Can I ask you a question? Or maybe a hundred of them?"

"Not now," Zing said. "Soon. When we get to your sister's. I don't want to have to cover this more than once."

"Okay," she said with a sigh. "I've waited this long, I guess I can wait a few more minutes."

* * *

Zing took the country roads faster than Jessie would have, and they pulled up in front of Joan's house fifteen minutes later. On the way, Jessie gave him a bare-bones version of what she had seen that night in Manhattan. Joan came out onto the porch. Jessie could see Morgan in an upstairs window with a gun pointed down.

"It's okay," Jessie said.

"Okay?" Joan asked, her face pale. "Where's Cassandra?"

"A man named Adams," Jessie said. "Call him at home. He's got her. She's safe."

Joan ran inside, to the telephone in the kitchen. By the time she came back, Morgan had come downstairs and they'd gathered in the living room. Zing pulled off his overcoat, revealing a brown wool blazer, a maroon polo shirt, and khaki slacks.

Fed casual.

"Ben says he has Cassie there," Joan reported. He was going to leave her with Marcy, but then decided he'd stay too."

"She'll be fine," Jessie said. "Won't she?"

"She should be," Zing said. "They're not looking for a kid."

"Who isn't?" Joan asked. "Jessie, who is this guy?"

"Been wonderin' that myself," Morgan said.

"Sorry," Jessie said. "I just don't know where my manners have gone. Joan's my big sister. Morgan is my friend. Joan, Morgan, this is Special Agent John Langford Zing of the FBI."

"Surprised you remembered it all," Zing said.

"Jessie, can I see you for a minute?" Joan asked. "In the kitchen?"

"Just like on the sitcoms," Jessie said. "Sure." She followed Joan from the living room. Inside her cheerful kitchen, Joan closed the door and spun toward her.

"You brought the *FBI* here? To my house? Are you fucking *nuts*, Jessie?"

Chapter 40

"Joan, I know, I wasn't thinking about that—"

"Jessie, that isn't something you can not think about. This must be thought about, all the time, for the rest of your life. It's just part of being on the run."

"I'm hoping I won't spend the rest of my life on the run, Joan."

"Maybe you won't, Jess. But I will, you know?"

"Yes, Joan. I know. I'm sorry, but...I'm kind of in a bind here. I didn't know where else to go, and—"

The kitchen door pushed open. "Hey," Morgan said. "What's up in here? I had a deck of cards or somethin', I could entertain Special Agent Zing out there all day, but as it is he's startin' to get tired of lookin' at me, and vice versa."

Jessie scooted one of the kitchen chairs away from the yellow wooden table, sat down heavily. "I guess I should've, y'know, mentioned that my older sister was kind of a fugitive, Morgan."

He looked at Joan, smiling. "You don't say."

"Don't breathe a word of it to the fed out there," Joan said.

"Not my style," Morgan said. "I'm pretty good at keeping secrets."

"God, I hope so," Joan said.

"So what did you do?"

Joan fixed him with a steady glare. "What do you care?"

"Joan, I've trusted him with my life. He could put me in jail for decades. And I could do the same to him. It's not going to kill you to tell him. Maybe he can help."

"I can't," Joan said. "I haven't talked about it for so long, I'm just not capable anymore."

"I don't even know all the details," Jessie said. "I was just a kid at the time."

"Something from that long ago got you on the dodge still?" Morgan asked. "Must've been a bad one."

"Three people were killed," Joan said. "All right? You happy now?"

"Joan was part of a radical group. An offshoot of the Weather Underground, wasn't it? What'd you call yourselves?"

"Weather Girls," Joan said. "The movement wasn't particularly enlightened when it came to feminist issues, in those days. This was when the whole Women's Lib thing was just getting started, and most of your average campus radicals thought the chicks were only good for baking hash brownies, that sort of thing. Action was supposed to be the province of the boys.

"So we started the Weather Girls—obviously, the name was a joke—to prove different."

"And their big action was to blow up a bank," Jessie said.

"Interesting choice," Morgan said. "Didn't you say your father was a banker?"

"He managed a branch of MetroBank in Queens," Jessie said.

"I see," Morgan said. "When was this?"

"1972," Joan said.

"I wasn't born yet," Jessie added. "Joan had left home a few years before, run away, really."

"That's right. About this time of year. Right before Christmas. My theory," Joan said, "—and our folks weren't the kind of people who talk about things like this, so it's just a theory—is that they decided to get pregnant again when they realized that I was gone for good. I was sixteen when I left. I can't explain the big gap between us any other way."

"So you and the other Weather Chicks blew up a bank building. And there were people in it?"

"There shouldn't have been," Joan said. "It was supposed to be empty. It was late at night. But what we didn't know was that there were auditors coming from MetroBank's headquarters. Dad had asked these three to work late that night, making sure the books were okay, that the auditors wouldn't find any problems or mistakes. Dad prided himself on running a tight ship."

"That changes things a bit," Morgan said. "You blew up your own father's branch?"

Jessie looked at the floor, then up at Joan. Her sister didn't look sheepish or abashed in the least.

"We were trying to make a statement," Joan said. "I knew that MetroBank had huge investments in the military-industrial complex."

"Name me a bank that didn't," Jessie said. "Or doesn't."

"That's not the point," Joan said. "I didn't know for certain what other banks invested in. I knew what MetroBank did."

"Okay," Morgan said. "Your dad know it was you?"

"Not at first," Joan said. "But it didn't take long. Part of the reason we did it was to make a point, that women could be guerrillas as well as men. So people knew it was us—we wanted them to know. Once the word spread in the movement, everyone found out. The FBI had people everywhere by then, we were infiltrated...he found out I was involved. I had to go into hiding, with the other women in the group. Six of us. We split up. I went to Canada for a few years, eventually slipped back into the States. I haven't used my real name, my father's name, since then. I've had lots of identities. Joan Temchin is only the most recent, but it looked like it was going to be a safe one. I was thinking maybe I'd keep it forever."

"She went undercover," Jessie said. "To help get away with it, they—the movement—spread the word that she was dead. That the Weather Girls had been blown up in an accidental explosion, while trying to make another bomb. I spoke with her once in a while, but not often. Usually a few years would go by, then I'd hear from her under some other name. I never had her listed in any phone directory or address book, never put her down on an application, anything like that. That's why I figured it would be safe to come here—as far as the world knew, my sister had died before I was born."

"Makes sense," Morgan said.

"You want to tell him about Dad, or should I?" Jessie said.

"I can," Joan said. Her voice was thick, and for a change she looked every one of her years. "He became depressed. I guess I can't blame him. I mean, his own daughter blowing up his pride and joy, killing people he had ordered to be there. It was a mistake, the deaths, I mean, but still...he kept working, stayed in the banking business, for, how long?"

"I was fourteen," Jessie said.

"Right. And I don't know what finally set him off, really. Could have been anything, the economy, something...but one day, he just decided enough was enough. He had lived all he wanted to."

"He killed himself?"

"That's right," Joan said.

"Third of May," Jessie added. "Mom died almost to the day, three years later."

"That's not unusual," Morgan said.

"Doesn't make it any easier," Jessie said.

"Hey, I know," Morgan said. He crossed the kitchen, put an arm around Jessie's shoulders. "I'm sorry, Jess."

"Yeah. Thanks."

"I don't think she's exactly forgiven me," Joan said.

"It's not that easy to forgive," Jessie said.

"I know, Jess, but—"

She stopped mid-sentence when there was a knock at the kitchen door. She turned to it, tugged it open.

Zing was standing there.

"I don't know what's going on in here," Zing said. "But I thought you should know—a car just pulled into the drive. You expecting anyone?"

"No," Joan said.

"Then I'd guess it's trouble," Zing said. "We should brace ourselves for it, just in case."

Chapter 41

"Get ready?" Jessie asked. "How?"

"Get upstairs, for starters," Zing said.

"Why upstairs?"

"Easier to shoot down from above than it is up from below," Morgan explained.

"Shoot?" Jessie echoed.

"You got any weapons in the house?" Zing asked.

"No," Joan said.

"Yup," Morgan said.

"You do?" Jessie asked.

"Unloaded my gear this morning," Morgan said. "Just in case."

"Just in case, huh?" Joan said.

"Now ain't you glad I did?"

"We're wasting time, people," Zing said. "Let's go."

They went.

While they had talked, the sun had set. The sky outside was dark now. A few stars glittered coldly. The upstairs was mostly taken up by the two bedrooms, Cassie's and Joan's. Both had slanted ceilings and dormer windows facing onto the front. They went into Joan's room.

Jessie peeked out and saw a dark car sitting in the drive, about fifty yards from the house. Lights off, motor running.

"Jesus," she said. "I can't believe—"

"Believe it," Zing said. "It's true. Steele isn't the type to let you just walk away. Not after all the trouble you've caused him."

Morgan came in with his arms full of guns of every description. He placed the arsenal carefully on Joan's double bed.

Joan pulled open the drawer of a nightstand next to the bed. On top of it were a telephone, a lamp, and a digital alarm clock. From inside the drawer she took a revolver, a box of bullets, and another, larger box. She flipped it open. Shotgun shells.

"I thought you said you didn't have any guns," Jessie said.

"I lied," Joan said. She went to the closet, reached behind some long coats and dresses, pulled out a shotgun. "It's a way of life."

"There's just one car," Jessie said. "How many guns do we need?"

"More'n they got would be good," Morgan said.

Special Agent Zing held up a hand. "Listen."

Conversation stopped. The sound of tires on gravel could be heard clearly in the quiet night. "Another car," Zing said.

"Damn," Jessie said.

They heard a car door close, and another.

"Everybody stay down," Zing said. "Close to the floor, and away from the windows. They'll be shooting up, so their slugs will be angled toward the ceiling. They can do a lot of damage to the front half of the room, but mostly high up. If you're low, and against the back wall, worst that'll happen is getting cut by flying glass."

"Unless they've got some weapons with good long ranges," Morgan said. "Then they can move farther back, fire on a more level plane, come through the walls at floor level. Or they could lob some grenades in, maybe tear gas..."

"I was being optimistic," Zing said.

"Let's be realistic instead," Morgan said. "These ladies deserve to know their chances."

As they spoke, Morgan and Zing tore apart the room. They took the bed off its metal frame, hauled the frame out into the hallway and leaned it up against a wall. Put the heavy box spring flat on the ground, and leaned the mattress on top of it, slanting away from the window. Behind this construction they dragged a dresser, its drawers full of clothes.

"I don't suppose they could be paid off?" Jessie said when they were done.

"Reckon not," Morgan said. "Time you got out there to make 'em an offer, you'd be dead. Same for the rest of us."

"So they're just here to kill us?" Jessie asked.

"What I think," Morgan said. "Could be wrong, I guess."

"I don't think you are," Zing said. "They wanted to talk, they could've called on the phone."

"My God, the phone!" Jessie said. "Why don't we call for help?"

"Not sure who you could call," Morgan said. "But you can check, you want to."

Jessie went to the nightstand. Picked up the receiver, held it to her ear. There was no sound.

"It's dead."

"Figured," Morgan said.

"Does that mean they're already here? In the house?"

"Not necessarily," Zing answered. "The phone lines here are above ground. Line comes in off the street. They could have cut it at the pole out there, and we'd never know it."

"What about a cell phone? Don't you have a cell?" Jessie asked.

"Sure I do," Zing said. "I could use it. But Morgan's right—who are we going to call? The local cops? Bureau's nearest field office is in Dubuque, and they're not going to be able to get anyone out here soon enough to help."

"I'd rather not have a bunch of federal agents running around here, if it's all the same to anybody," Joan said.

"Anyway, I'm in the middle of an ongoing investigation of Richard Steele," Zing said. "There's a bloodbath here, that might hamper my investigation."

"If there's a bloodbath here, don't you think they're going to find out about it?" Jessie asked.

"Maybe not immediately," Zing said. "I don't think I need a lot more time."

"Seems like a pretty weak reason not to call for reinforcements," Jessie said.

"Jess," Joan said. "Let's take care of this ourselves if we can."

She sounded adamant.

"Okay, okay," Jessie said. "I'm just hoping if there's a bloodbath, it's them bleeding, not us."

"Hey," Morgan said. "I told you what I'm good at, right?"

"You've mentioned a whole array of things you're good at, Morgan. Surviving, shooting guys, blowing shit up. Isn't that the basic list?"

"Exactly what we need here," he said.

The four went quiet. And in the stillness, they heard another car approach, pull to a stop. More doors opened and closed.

"Well, they have reinforcements," Jessie said. "Even if we don't." She glanced out the window. The three cars were parked about thirty yards back now, nose to tail to nose, forming a kind of three sided box. A group of men, maybe a dozen or so, stood inside the box.

They all had guns.

She stepped away from the window.

And everything happened at once.

Guns boomed. Downstairs, the big window in the living room, which Joan always kept curtained, exploded. Bullets slammed into walls, smashed furniture, lights, the television. The hail of bullets seemed to go on and on. Jessie could hear things falling, thumping around, downstairs, as their fusillade tossed objects into the air and shattered them.

After what seemed like a long time, the gunfire tapered off.

"Everyone okay?" Zing asked. He was disregarding his own instructions, standing at the window.

"So far," Jessie said.

"If you don't count my house," Joan said.

"Got a feeling your house is gonna be a big write-off," Morgan said.

"Good thing it's rented, I guess."

Zing looked through a gap in the curtains.

"They're advancing," he said. "I make ten of them. Or a dozen. There's one off in the trees, circling around to the back of the house. Joan, there any upstairs windows in back?"

"Just one," she said. "In the bathroom. Small one."

"Which one you want, Byrd?" Zing asked. "Front or back?"

"I'll take the front," Morgan said. "Jessie's my client, I want to stay where I can keep an eye on her."

"Works for me," Zing said. "I wouldn't wait too long, if I were you. They'll be at the door in a minute."

Morgan rose from his spot next to Jessie, patted her knee. "You'll be fine," he said.

Fine, Jessie thought. My ass.

Morgan went to the window, raised an M-16 automatic rifle to his shoulder. "This'll be loud," he said. "Get behind that dresser."

He jammed the muzzle through the glass, breaking it, and squeezed the trigger at the same time. The gun seemed to go insane—roaring, fire flashing from the muzzle, brass shells flying and clinking on the walls and floor. He moved it in a steady arc, then drew it back inside, dove behind the dresser, next to Jessie.

"Cover your heads," he said.

They did. Just as the windows blew in.

It was as Zing had predicted. Most of the bullets angled up sharply, chewing up the ceiling and raining dust on them. Glass from the windows whipped through the air. Jessie's hands were lacerated by tiny shards, but she kept them where they were, thankful that it was her hands and not her face. The curtains were shredded in seconds.

Then it ended. Morgan crawled on his belly to the exterior wall, raised himself slowly, then showed his gun at the window. Fired a burst, looked out.

"Two down," he said. "But the others've gone to ground."

"Done what?" Jessie said.

"Taken cover," Morgan said. "Hopefully not in the house."

"Hopefully?"

"What I'd do," he said. "Try to get inside while we were duckin' their volley."

"How do we tell?"

"One of you could go look," Morgan said.

"No!" Jessie said.

"Then we wait a while, see if anybody shows up."

From the bathroom there was another thunder of gunfire, another shattering of glass. A moment later, Zing stuck his head into the bedroom.

"Two back there," he said. "I know I hit one."

"I dropped a couple out here too," Morgan said. "This is all of 'em, we might could have this wrapped up before too long."

"I'm going back in there, keep an eye out," Zing said. The bathroom was across the hall from the bedrooms, on the other side of the staircase.

"I got this side," Morgan said.

There was quiet.

It stretched on.

"What the hell are they doing?" Jessie asked.

"Considerin' their options," Morgan said.

"I see," Jessie said. "Agent Zing, can I ask you a question?"

"Sure." His voice was clear in the silence. The bathroom tiles lent it a slight echo.

"Did you push me in front of a subway? Because I could have sworn—"

He laughed. "No," he said. "I tried to *catch* you, when I saw you going over. Then I tried to catch the guy who did push you. He ran as soon as you fell, didn't wait around to see if you were alive or not."

"But why...why were you there, then?"

"Oh, I was following you."

"Why?"

"Morgan, trade places a minute," Zing called.

"Coming," Morgan said. He went into the bathroom. Zing came into the bedroom, took Morgan's position at the window.

"My guy's back by the barn," Zing said.

"Three behind the cars," Morgan said. "A couple more in those trees over to the left. I ain't entirely sure about the others."

"I'll have a look," Zing said. He peered out the window, through the tattered strips of fabric that had been gingham curtains.

"So why?" Jessie asked.

"I've been after Richard Steele for more than a year," Zing said. "I know he's dirty, but I've never been able to come up with enough evidence to make a case."

"He's shooting at us," Joan said. "That good enough?"

"Oh, he won't be out there himself," Zing said. "There will be three or four layers between him and whoever is pulling those triggers. So anyway, I figured if I could follow his money, maybe I could get the goods on him that way."

"Follow the money. The old standby."

"That's right, Jessie. Only in this case, the money was pretty well protected."

"I hope you don't mind if I take a perverse professional pride in that."

"Not at all. But with the money out of reach, I figured the next best thing might be to watch the banker. If I could prove you were dirty, maybe I'd have something I could use to turn you against Steele."

"But I wasn't."

"Apparently not. You did, however, do the next best thing. You saw or heard or found out something that scared Steele. That made him decide you needed to be taken out of the picture."

"I saw him kill five men. Well, him and Jake Garland, a Treasury agent assigned to FinCEN."

"Swell," Zing said. "That'd do it. Anyway, you went off the radar, after that. So did Steele. I was stuck. I knew—hang on. Heads down."

He squeezed off a ten-second burst and then dropped to the floor. A returning volley destroyed what was left of the window, driving into the ceiling and the far wall.

From the bathroom, they heard Morgan firing again.

Then it was quiet.

"Is this how it always is?" Jessie asked. "On TV, the shooting just goes on until somebody's the winner."

"This isn't TV," Zing pointed out. "Nobody really wants to get shot. Makes people tend to stay behind cover, and only fire when they really think they can get away with it."

"Great. So we'll be here a while."

"Could be."

"Don't you have neighbors, Joan?"

"Half a mile away," Joan said. "More. They can probably hear. But if they come over, those guys'll just kill them, so I hope they're smart enough to stay away."

"Anyway," Zing continued, "I knew Steele had an account in Paris. When both of you had faded out of sight, I decided to watch the bank."

"He had other accounts in other cities."

"I know that. But I didn't know which cities, and I didn't know what banks. I knew Paris, and I knew the bank. I went with what I had. And I saw you, and Byrd, there. Followed you around. Hoping you were dirty, still, and that you'd lead me to Steele."

"But I didn't."

"No, you didn't. But you almost walked into an ambush."

"On the bridge?"

"That's right. Steele had guys in Paris, too. Either they figured out what hotel you were at, or they were watching the bank like I was. They found out where you went for dinner, and planned to meet you on your way back. It would have been easy to shoot you, dump your bodies into the Seine, and poof! Problem solved. But you'd made me, so you and Morgan were on edge, guarded, hopped up on adrenaline. I saw the guys before you did, because you were focused on me. They were drawing weapons, so I pulled mine and fired first, past you. They returned fire, but by then you were already in the drink."

"What happened to them?"

"They're dead," he said, matter of factly. "There was nothing to tie them to me, so I left them where they were."

"Well, thanks, I guess," Jessie said. "For saving our lives. Hey Morgan," she called. "You hear that?"

"Yup," Morgan said. "Reckon we owe you one, Zing."

"We get out of this, I'll consider that thanks enough," Zing said.

"But what did you do after that?" Jessie asked. "How'd you end up here?"

"I didn't know what name you were traveling under, where you were going, anything like that," Zing explained. "But I had one advantage. My badge. That earned me some cooperation from the gendarmes, and I made the rounds to every bank in the city, just about, to see who had made large transfers that day. Preferably to the States. Then I cross-referenced the transfers. None of them, by themselves, were big enough to add up to much, but when you put them all together they did. And they pointed to Clark's Grove, Iowa. It took me a few days to do the legwork, then I hopped the first flight I could get to Chicago and high-tailed it out here. I was looking around Clark's Grove for you when you ran straight into my arms."

"I guess I'm lucky I did."

"Only if you count being alive as lucky," he said. "Those guys outside probably did the same thing, no doubt with help from Steele's friends at MetroBank. You ran into one of them, you'd be a corpsicle in the town square by now."

"And Cassie too," Joan said.

"Your sister did the right thing, handing her off," Zing said. "You wouldn't want her here now."

"No, you're right," Joan said.

"Joan," Morgan said. "You know how to shoot that Mossberg?"

"I've done it," Joan said. "Not at live targets."

"You still a pacifist?"

"Is that some kind of joke?"

"Never mind. I want to take a look around downstairs, make sure we're still alone here. You watch this back window for me?"

"Sure," she said. "But I think I want something that'll hold more than two shells."

She leaned the shotgun against the wall, chose a Heckler & Koch automatic rifle from the bed, checked to make sure it was loaded, and pocketed an extra clip.

Jessie watched her go. "That's my sister," she said.

Chapter 42

Morgan knew that his greatest exposure would be on the stairs, on his way down, when his legs would come into view before he could cover himself.

To better his odds, he went down at a crouch, head and weapon at knee level. He moved slowly, silently, testing each step as he went, even though he'd already walked them up and down and committed each squeak and groan to memory.

The downstairs was dark—the first flurries of gunfire had taken out every light bulb. The only illumination came from the moon outside, a few days past full, and the moon's reflection off snow in the yard.

The front door was a wreck. Morgan figured the porch was totaled. And the living room had been hit hard. The curtains hung in strips that fluttered in the breeze that passed through the glassless window. Lamps and knickknacks were shattered, the TV and stereo trashed, the wall opposite the window pocked and cracking. A light fixture had been blown off the ceiling and lay half on top of the coffee table, half on the floor.

The dolls were ruined. It gave him a creepy feeling—eyeballs scattered across the floor, here a slice of cheek, there an entire head or an intact face in the middle of assorted carnage.

It reminded him of his ghosts.

He checked the kitchen next. Since it faced the back of the house, it wasn't too bad.

There didn't seem to be anyone inside yet. Morgan looked out the windows, careful not to silhouette himself against open space. No movement. But they were still out there. He took a seat in a chair that faced the window, a big, overstuffed chair that had stuffing spewing from a dozen bullet holes, and he waited.

* * *

"Have you ever fired a gun?" Zing asked.

"No," Jessie said.

He reached under his blazer, pulled out a silvery pistol with dark grips. He handed it to her by the barrel.

"This is a Springfield Armory 1911-A1," he said. "Custom made for the Bureau."

She took the gun. It was heavier than she'd expected, but fit comfortably into her right hand.

"Here's what you have to know. This is the trigger, obviously," he said, pointing to it. "It's a semi-auto, so squeeze, release, squeeze, and so on. It'll shoot as fast as you can pull it. It'll kick some, so hold it firmly, with your arm locked, and steady your gun hand with the other one. Here, give it back."

She did. He showed her how to eject the clip and insert a new one, handed it back to her. "The most important thing is making sure you hit something when you fire. Aim for the center of the chest. That way, even if you're off by a few inches in any direction, you'll still do some damage."

"And you're telling me all this because...?"

"Because there's always the chance that Morgan and your sister and I might not survive tonight. If things get bad, I want you to be able to defend yourself. You're the one who'll have to testify against Steele."

"Let's hope it doesn't come to that. Me having to win any gunfights, I mean."

"Let's hope. And let's move into the other room."

"Why?" Jessie asked.

"Because we haven't fired from those windows," he said. "Doesn't mean they'll be lazy, but they might be. They could be paying more attention to the window we've been at, and it could give us some kind of edge later."

"I guess that's a good thing."

"You take every edge you can get," he said. They left Joan's room and went into Cassie's. This room had taken some hits, but there was still some glass in the window and it wasn't as cold as Joan's.

They worked together, recreating the bed and dresser shield with Cassie's furniture that he and Morgan had done in Joan's room.

"So just what is it Steele's involved in?" Jessie asked. "I haven't been able to figure that out."

Zing stood at the window, looking between the frame and the curtain. "What hasn't he been? He's the kind of dirtbag I hate, because he's been lucky and smart. He's skated on murders, beatings, robberies and an assortment of other crimes, most of which include a level of violent behavior that would turn your stomach. He's a garden-variety sociopath, able to pretend to be a human being. But that's an act. Inside he's as empty as a champagne bottle on New Year's morning. As far as I've been able to tell, he was strictly second-rate until he fell into his current game. It's not the kind of thing your major crime figures bother with, but there's a lot of cash passing through his hands."

"I knew that much."

"Right. You would. I'm not sure what all he's got his hands in—I know he bought into a casino, real estate, trying to diversify his portfolio, as it were. But the bankroll for all of it is this charity scam he has going. He hires homeless people, vagrants, and so on—and I use the term 'hires' loosely, because that implies that they get paid some kind of a decent wage. They go out collecting donations for charities, usually homeless shelters. Makes it believable. You've seen them at airports, supermarket parking lots, and so on. Carrying a bucket or a container of some kind. They have some kind of official looking letter or ID badge, to show that they're working for a registered charity. People are more likely to give them a buck or two than they are to a street panhandler.

"But the cash goes through Steele's operation before it ever goes to the shelters or soup kitchens. Steele's people skim off most of it. Maybe a couple of pennies from every dollar goes to pay the workers, same to the shelters. The rest of it goes into accounts in the various cities, and eventually into Steele's accounts. From there, you or someone like you would disperse it so it can't easily be traced."

"Nice," Jessie said. Thinking about the long-term unemployed people Joan had described. People in a troubled economy who needed every kind of help they could get. "Makes me want to take a long hot shower."

"I know the feeling. Not only do the shelters only get a few cents on the dollar, but then people who might have given to legitimate charities feel like they've already done their part. So he's hurting the real charities all the way around. And the people those charities serve. All to rake in a few bucks."

"Can he really generate millions of dollars with this scam?"

"Last I was able to determine, he had this going in seventeen cities up and down the East Coast. Other players have similar operations in various places, but no single individual has franchised it like this. Individually, none of these people collects a whole lot of money. But if they take in, say, an average of fifty bucks a day, and he's got maybe thirty guys working in any city, that's fifteen hundred from each city. Times seventeen cities, you're up over twenty-five grand a day. Or about a quarter of a million every ten days. Some days are worse, some better, but it averages about that. It's not sexy, but the pay's good."

"Bastard," Jessie said. Her stomach heaved at the thought that she'd been part of that process.

"That's one way to put it. He can be charming if he thinks he can use you, but he's vicious if you're in his way. Steele had been keeping the business at arm's reach—not playing the game in New York. But greed caught up to him. He tried to move in on the people who were running it there. New York's the most lucrative territory there is for this kind of racket. That's what the shootout you saw was all about—some of those guys trying to discourage his expansion. Their bodies haven't turned up yet."

"And that Treasury agent, Garland, is in on this with him?"

"I'm sure Steele saw the potential advantages of controlling the people who could be the biggest threat to him. A FinCEN agent assigned to Manhattan would be a natural ally. He's probably paying Garland his annual government salary every month."

"As well as paying off various people at MetroBank."

"Most likely. At a certain point, the bank is going to want to protect itself anyway. They could lose their banking license for this, so even the people too high up for Steele to have paid off individually have a vested

260 - Jeffrey J. Mariotte

interest in keeping it quiet. Not that they know what he's really up to—I'm sure they don't, and they don't want to know because they want the business. And the Treasury Department wants to avoid any more big bank failures, so they don't want MetroBank to go belly-up. Damn!"

"What?"

"Listen," he said. After a moment, she heard it—a distant siren, coming closer. "I can see the lights already," he added.

"Police?" Jessie asked. "Why is that a bad thing?"

Joan came in from the bathroom. "I heard a siren."

"They're almost here," Zing said from his post at the window. "Coming from the direction of town. Local sheriff, probably."

Jessie and Joan crowded around him at the window.

"They don't know what they're walking into," Zing said.

The squad car almost missed the drive, braked to a sudden stop, then backed up a few feet, turned, and nosed down the dirt lane.

"Turn back, you idiot," Zing muttered. Jessie looked at him, saw the tension cording his neck, tightening his jaw.

The car came to a stop behind the three cars already parked down the drive, spotlight shining on the cars. The driver's door opened and a uniformed officer climbed out, shotgun in his hand. Another one came out the passenger side.

"Sheriff!" the passenger called. "Hello?"

"That's Lonnie," Joan said.

"Friend of yours?" Zing asked.

"As good as someone can be who doesn't even know your real name."

"Can you reach him on a direct line? Cell phone?"

"Not direct. I could call the department."

"Too late for that." Zing leaned out past the broken glass. "Sheriff, take cover!" he shouted.

A moment of absolute silence passed. Then the quiet was split by thunder. The two officers were torn open by the barrage, the light bar on top of their car was destroyed, the car rocked and riddled.

Zing opened fire toward the muzzle flashes. From downstairs, they could hear Morgan doing the same.

Then Zing shoved Jessie and Joan to the floor, threw himself on top of them.

Another spray of bullets filled the window. Glass rained down. Plaster exploded, the air was thick with plaster and smoke.

Quiet again.

Zing shifted. Moved off the women. "You okay?" he asked.

"I am," Jessie said.

"Sure," Joan said. "Except Lonnie Briggs out there was a friend of mine, and now he's dead and there wasn't a fucking thing I could do about it."

"I'm so sorry, Joanie," Jessie said.

"Not your fault," Joan said. "Well, it really is, but what the fuck, right?"

"I never meant to bring this down on you."

"I know, Jess. I know."

Zing went to the bedroom doorway. "Hey, Byrd!" he called.

"Hey!" came up from downstairs.

"You okay?"

"Fine." They heard the sounds of his feet on the stairs, less cautious than when he'd gone down.

A moment later he was standing in the door, gun in his hands, shoulders slumped. He looked tired, old.

"I been thinking," he said. "Sitting in here's no good."

"Yeah," Zing said. "I've had the same thought."

"We need to go out there. Take the fight to them. Otherwise they can last forever."

"We're under siege," Zing said. "And they have all the advantages."

"Yep. You up for some wet work?"

"Beats sitting around waiting for them."

"Let's go, then." Morgan looked at Jessie and Joan. "You ladies stick close together. Stay upstairs. Away from the windows. Anyone comes through the door doesn't announce himself first, kill him."

"Gladly," Joan said.

Zing brought in more of the weaponry from Joan's room. "You can hold off a regiment with this stuff, if you need to," he said. He handed an Uzi to Zing, kept a Mac-10 for himself, doled out a couple of wicked-looking knives. He dumped other guns on the bed for Jessie and Joan.

"Shouldn't be necessary," Morgan added. "But just in case."

"Right," Jessie said. "Just in case."

Morgan Byrd and John Langford Zing gave some final instructions, left, and the sisters were alone in the room.

"Some fun, huh?" Joan said.

Chapter 43

When Morgan said "now," Jessie and Joan, stationed at both bedroom windows upstairs, opened fire toward the parked cars. As instructed, they fired for fifteen seconds and then ducked behind the furniture shields. Return fire flew over their heads.

When they started shooting, Morgan kicked out a window on the side of the house farthest from the action, a small window set over the washing machine in Joan's little utility room. It was big enough to fit through, though. Morgan threw himself to the ground, and Zing followed.

As soon as they were both out, they rose to low crouches, turning in three hundred and sixty-degree circles, Morgan clockwise and Zing counter-clockwise.

This side of the house was clear. So far.

Morgan had thought it would be. There was a row of trees close to the house here. No doors opened onto this side. No reason anyone would come out this way.

Which was why they had.

Morgan had a feeling that, at some point, they would have to split up. But they were both safer if they could cover each other's backs for as long as possible. So he gestured to the north, toward the back of the house.

So far, they had only seen the one guy heading back that way. Morgan knew that by now, chances were that there were considerably more than that.

Chance they'd have to take.

They went into the trees. It was the right season—whatever leaves were still on the ground from the fall were frozen solid to the soil. The greater danger was the crunch of snow and the cracking sound of the hard earth under their feet, but they would just have to deal with that, try to keep it quieter than the night breeze.

Most of the actual wars he'd fought in had taken place in warmer climes, he realized. The Gulf, Latin America, Africa...there had been a bodyguard job in the Balkans, though. He had spent almost forty hours standing guard in a ravine south of Sarajevo while the city was being shelled. Freezing rain had turned to ice, and he had to keep moving, bending his joints so his clothes would crack. One of the guys working with him got frostbite so severe he couldn't walk for most of a year. Another one didn't pull through.

That was cold.

Iowa in December, he could handle.

He hoped the bad guys didn't have night vision goggles, because he didn't. He had pretty good night eyes, though, for an old guy. No telling about the fed—they weren't necessarily trained for all combat situations.

But you took your chances when you were partnered up with someone you didn't know. So far, Zing seemed like a guy who could carry his weight.

Moving amidst the trees, they covered a little over two hundred yards in ten minutes or so. Well past the barn. At Morgan's signal, they struck out across the furrowed field toward an imaginary line extending from the far corner of the barn. The grooves cut into the land gave them a little bit of cover, and the fact that anyone standing near the barn would be watching the house, not the fields, gave them more.

Once they were even with the barn, they started moving closer to it. So far, they hadn't spoken. All communication was done with hand signals and nods, and Zing had responded like a soldier.

From here, they could see two men. One stood at each corner of the barn, on the side nearest the house. The barn's roof reflected silver moonlight, but the bulk of it was a big block of shadow. From the house, the men would have blended into the shadows of the barn's structure and been invisible. But at this angle, they were distinct from the barn's walls.

Somewhere out there was the body of one Morgan had already shot. Morgan hoped he was dead, not wounded.

What they couldn't tell from here was who might be on the side of the barn they couldn't see. The front side, facing the house. That was where the big door was, and there could have been a tank and a platoon of infantry in there.

That was a question they would have to answer.

* * *

Their diversion over, Joan had returned to Cassie's room to wait with Jessie, as Morgan had suggested. For a while, they were quiet. The tension of the situation kept them from making small talk, and nothing else seemed appropriate to the moment.

Besides, what kind of small talk would you make under these circumstances? "Gee, that's a chilly wind blowing through the shot-out windows..."

But the minutes ticked by on Cassie's Beauty and the Beast wall clock, which had been miraculously spared. As they did, Jessie felt more and more uncomfortable with the long silence—a silence that, when she really thought about it, had stretched for most of her life.

Too long.

And hell, if facing death together didn't open Joan up, what would?

"Joan?"

"Mmm?"

"Do you blame yourself, ever? You know, for Dad—Dad's death? And Mom's, I guess."

Joan shifted. She was at the window, watching. Jessie sat, leaning against the far wall.

"I don't...no, that's not right. Sure. I mean, I pretty much have to, I think."

"Yeah, I guess."

"He didn't have to go and kill himself, though. I still think that was a little extreme. Especially since it had been so long. Since the bombing, I mean."

"I know. But he was never, while I knew him, you know, really alive. Other kids had dads who did things with them, took them to the park, the playground, skating. Stuff like that. Dad never did that, after you were gone. I don't know if he did when you were little."

"Yeah, he did, Jess. Sometimes. He worked a lot too. But on weekends, he'd rake leaves in the yard into a big pile, and let me jump into them even though that scattered them all over the place and he had to rake them all over again. He took me to Atlantic City, to the boardwalk there once—just me and him. Bought me cotton candy, let me pick the rides we went on."

"That sounds nice. I never got that."

"Isn't that kind of an overreaction, though? I mean, sure, what I did was probably stupid rebellious teenage behavior—"

"You killed three people, Joan."

"Okay, so worse than your average stupid teenager. But for him to just shut down like that, to die inside, as you say...and then to keep on walking around dead for so long after that. What's that all about?"

"Maybe he was trying to come alive again. And he finally realized it just wasn't going to happen."

"Yeah, I don't know. I guess so. I was doing what I thought I had to do, Jess. We were trying to end a war. We were trying to end racism and injustice. Sacrifices had to be made."

"That's a lovely sentiment."

"You weren't there, Jess. You don't know what it was like in those days. Our intentions were good."

"I know what I've read. The most privileged class in the history of the world—before or since—felt like it had to make its mark. You chose social protest because everything else had already been handed to you on a platter."

"It wasn't quite that simple."

"No? You were a banker's only daughter. You lived in a big house, you had your own room with a huge canopy bed and all the toys and books a kid could want—your room was still there after you were gone, the door was locked and no one ever went into it, but I did. You even had dolls back then, lots of them. I never got to play with those, though. They stayed in your old room. And you just said Dad did stuff with you, took you places, and Mom must have, too. She was always the maternal type, right?"

"Yes, but—we weren't so focused on our own possessions, our own happiness, Jess. We were also concerned with what was going on around us, with the problems of those who had less than we did."

"I'm sure you were. Because you could afford to be."

"That's an easy way to say it, Jessie, but yes. That's true, to some extent. The poor, the oppressed—they had a hard enough time just scraping by from day to day. They needed those of us with the luxury of some free time, some spending money, to help them."

"Or you thought they did."

"Which is close enough to the same thing."

"I guess."

"Trade places?"

It took Jessie a moment to realize what she was asking. "Sure," she said, pushing herself off the wall with the palms of her hands.

She went to the window, and Joan shook her legs out, then slid down the wall to the floor.

"It's been quiet," she said. "I don't know what they're waiting for. I just wish they'd do something."

"Or go away," Jessie said.

"Or that."

* * *

There was a door at the back of the barn, a regular-sized door that a person could walk through. Morgan eased it open.

Once again, he wished for night vision goggles. Make this job a hell of a lot easier.

He slipped through the narrow opening. Zing followed.

The barn's front doors were open. A band of moonlight fell on Morgan's Raider, and parked behind that, the Camry he and Jessica had bought in Florida.

Beyond the Camry, empty floor, stars outside, the house in the distance. They couldn't see any more people.

Which probably meant that the only two back here were the ones they'd seen at the corners. Posted here to make sure no one escaped in the vehicles.

Which meant all the others were closing in on the house from the front. Moving, Morgan reckoned, just as slowly and cautiously as he and Special Agent Zing were.

Which, given the amount of time they had taken to get here, would put them just about at the house. He hoped the ladies were keeping a close eye out.

What it didn't give them was a lot of time to mop up out here. If Steele's men reached the house, it would be dicey for Jessie. He had no doubt she could pull the trigger, and he knew Joan could, but the two of them would be no match for experienced gunmen.

They approached the big barn door.

Morgan pointed at Zing, then pointed to the right. He touched his own chest and pointed left. Zing nodded his agreement.

Morgan drew a Ka-bar knife from his boot. Sharp blade, serrated upper edge, solid leather grip. Slinging his Mac-10 across his back, with the strap snug against his chest, he raised the knife to Zing. Zing drew a similar one that he'd strapped on in the bedroom, slung his Uzi in a similar fashion.

This had to be fast.

And quiet.

Morgan counted down three on his fingers.

At three, they both ran in their predetermined directions.

Which was when the guns started going off.

Chapter 44

"I see one," Jessie said.

"Shoot him!" Joan replied.

Jessie pulled the trigger of the semi-automatic. Her first shot kicked up dirt about ten feet from the guy she'd spotted, hunched over and making a dash for the house.

He zigzagged, changing course at a forty-five degree angle from where he'd been headed before. She brought the gun back to the window, fired again, three times, in rapid succession.

And felt herself being hurled to the floor.

By the time she realized Joan had tackled her, bullets were whipping over her head, fluttering the curtains like a hurricane wind, smacking into the walls.

"You can't just hang around there after you shoot," Joan reminded her.

"Right," Jessie said.

The return volley went on for what seemed like forever. A minute, at least.

"Stay here," Joan said. "Stay down. Behind the bed."

"Where are you—" Jessie started, but Joan was already gone.

Then she heard gunfire from the other bedroom. Joan must have decided that if everyone was shooting at this window, she could return fire from the other one. There was a fifteen-second burst, then Jessie heard bullets flying into the other room.

She went back to the window. Peeked out. Fired at the muzzle flashes she saw and hit the floor again.

This time, they didn't just fire at the window. Chunks blew out of the wall, all the way to the floor.

Nothing made it through the structure she was hiding behind. This time.

But they were getting smarter, or losing patience.

Either way was probably bad news.

"I hit one," Joan said. She had come back into the room, ducked behind the bed with Jessie.

"Good," Jessie said. "But while we're here instead of at the windows, how do we know they're not coming into the house?"

"Shit," Joan said.

She went back to the window.

Turned away.

"Too late," she said.

* * *

At the sound of gunfire from the house, both of the thugs beside the barn dropped into defensive positions, raising their weapons and pointing them toward the house. Every iota of their beings seemed to be focused on the house, on the gunfire.

So when Morgan reached his, the guy had no idea he was there. Morgan looped his left arm around the guy's throat from behind, yanking him off-balance. With his arm snaking just under the guy's chin, Morgan twisted his head back and brought the blade of the Ka-Bar across his throat in one smooth killing stroke.

Blood splashed onto the packed snow.

The guy went limp in his arms. Morgan dropped him, turned toward Zing.

The fed was good. He'd buried his own knife in the back of his man's neck, pushing it down with the heel of his right hand. Before the man could scream or speak, Zing had reached around with his left, grabbed the guy's throat, and squeezed it toward the knife. The guy twitched and gurgled, then stopped and Zing let him fall onto the snow.

They traded thumbs ups.

Morgan rifled through his guy's pockets. No wallet, no ID of any kind. Just a smart phone and some spare ammo.

He pocketed the phone and pointed toward the house.

* * *

"Are you sure?" Jessie asked.

"I saw one of them at the porch," Joan whispered. "Then he was gone."

"Just one?"

"That's all I saw, yes. That doesn't mean there aren't others."

Jessie went to the window. "I don't see anyone else in the yard. I think they're all back by the cars again."

"Except the one who's downstairs."

"Right, except him."

"Okay, keep an eye on the window. Keep talking, like we don't know he's in the house." Joan sprawled on the floor, facing the doorway. She held a shotgun from the arsenal on the bed, pointed out the door, at the stairs. "Put a blanket over me."

Jessie grabbed one from the pile of discarded linens, draped it over Joan so only the shotgun barrel was sticking out. "Can you see?"

"It's fine," Joan said. "He shows his head on those stairs, he'll lose it."

"Okay. Keep talking?" Jess said. "About what?"

"Whatever. Weren't you in the middle of bitching me out about our folks?"

Right, Jessie thought. Blaming my sister for our father's suicide, almost twenty years after she'd run away from home.

Some people could sure nurse a grudge.

Which was, she realized, what she'd been doing.

"I guess I've always blamed you, Joan," she said. "For not being around when I was growing up. Once I learned what had happened, I blamed you for running away, for making Mom and Dad feel like they had to have another kid if they wanted one at all. During that time that Mom was so sad, before she died, and even after, I blamed you for my being born at all. And I hated you for it."

"I'm sorry to hear that, Jess."

"What, did you think I'd be happy about it? Born into a hugely dysfunctional family where the golden child, the first-born, broke my parents' hearts before I even got a chance to know them. That's not a pleasant feeling, I can assure you."

"I guess not."

"You ripped our family apart and you weren't even there to take the heat. I had to deal with it all. I was the replacement you, the one who was supposed to make it all okay again. But I didn't know that was my job, and I couldn't have done it even if I had."

"Life sucks, huh?"

"I know, yours was no picnic either. God, I know that now. On the run all the time, hiding your true identity from everyone. It must be awful to know there's no going back."

"I hope you don't have to find out first hand."

"I'm just doing what I've always done, I think. Reacting. The way I grew up in that dead household, I didn't ever realize I could act. I could only react to everything else, to your abandonment, to Dad's suicide, to Mom's sorrow.

"I never have made my own decisions. What did I do after Mom died? I went to college, became a banker, lived in Manhattan. As if Dad's footsteps were so big I couldn't climb out of them.

"Now I'm still reacting. Running from the city, from Steele. Bouncing around like a pinball from bumper to bumper. Steele's here, I go there. None of the decisions I've made lately have been what I would choose to do—it's all been what I feel like I'm forced to do. The only direction I can bounce off that particular bumper."

"Uh huh," Joan said. She made a scuffling sound. Jessie turned toward her as she pulled the trigger.

The shotgun's roar was deafening. The room filled with its smoke, its pungent stink.

As the echo died, over the ringing in her ears, Jessie could hear the thumping of a corpse falling wetly down the stairs. The patter of plaster falling after it.

"Got the bastard," Joan said. "You were saying?"

Jessie touched her cheeks, surprised to find them wet with tears. "Thanks, Joan," she said.

"No problem."

Jessie looked out the window again. Saw a couple of men sprinting across the lawn. Fired. Missed, but they dodged back into the shadows instead of coming forward.

"Down!" she cried.

She and Joan hit the deck. Another minute of lying behind the big bed while the room was systematically chewed apart by flying lead.

Then it stopped. Joan was in her arms.

"I was saying..." Jessie said.

"Yes?"

"I was..." Her voice caught. She felt her eyes well up again, swallowed a sob. Decided that was pointless, and let it out. Between sobs, she continued. "...I was saying that I don't want to live that way anymore. I want to call my own shots. Choose my own goals." She sniffed. The tears were flowing again, and there was no stopping them. "That's okay, isn't it?"

"Yeah, sis," Joan said, drawing her close. Her own eyes were wet, her cheeks slick. "I think that's okay."

Chapter 45

"Came from inside," Morgan said. "Twelve-gauge, sounded like." His voice sounded odd to him after his self-imposed silence of the past several minutes.

"Yeah," Zing agreed.

Morgan pointed along the back side of the house. "You go around that way," he whispered. "Close to the house, and around the far corner. I'll head out toward the road, come in behind their cars. When I start shooting, any luck they'll head for the house."

"If they're not already there."

"Yeah, that. Anyway, they go for the house, you'll be there to pick them off. We'll get 'em in a crossfire. Just remember I'll be out there—but at an angle to you, not right on the other side of them. Any luck, we should be able to pull this off without shootin' each other."

Zing nodded and took off at a run. Morgan went the other way, out to the tree line that bounded the western edge of the property. Once through the trees, he ran south, toward the main road that headed into Clark's Grove. When he was sure he was beyond where Steele's men had parked their cars, he slowed, walked in a circle for a moment to settle his breathing and heartbeat.

When he was back to normal, he worked his way through the trees. Looked back toward the house.

He was about twenty-five yards out. In the moonlight, he could see a group of men, seven or eight, it looked like, huddled behind the cars.

He could open fire on them, pick off some. But there was no cover here at all. He'd have to be moving, if he hoped to survive.

And that was something he always hoped for.

Because he was watching for Zing, he was able to see the agent arrive at the far corner of the house. He was just a dark blur against the shadows, nothing that would attract the attention of the men at the cars. But it was enough to let Morgan know that Zing was ready.

Still he needed some kind of edge.

He remembered the cell phone.

He readied the Mac-10, wrapping the weapon's strap around his right arm to help provide one-handed stability. At a careful crouch, he moved away from the trees, cutting across so that he was almost right behind the cars.

With his left hand, he punched the POWER button on the cell phone. The display screen lit up. He pushed REDIAL.

Heard a ringing sound by the cars. A voice said, "Fuck. What is it?"

While they were all looking at the guy with the phone, Morgan opened fire.

He ran as he did, west to east, dropping to the dirt sometimes, rolling, pushing off, leaping into the air. Kept the Mac-10 pointed at where the men were standing by the cars, boxed in by their own protective shield.

Zing started shooting, too, from beside the house.

Morgan heard screams. Saw, as he ran, guys scrambling over each other to return fire. But he was in constant motion, his gun spitting fire and lead. Zing backing him up.

By the time he reached the eastern tree line, there was no more return fire. He shoved another hundred-round clip into place anyway.

There was no more sound from the cars.

They were down.

But, he realized, there had only been seven or eight there. Even with the ones he knew had been hit before, he didn't think they were all accounted for.

So they had to be inside.

He ran. Zing had come to the same conclusion, it appeared, and was already heading toward the porch.

* * *

Both women stood at the window, watching the fireworks.

Jessie felt empty, used up. Emotionally drained. Decades of anger, frustration, resentment had bubbled up inside her, a bitter brew that she had been powerless to stop. But it had passed. She stood with her hand on Joan's shoulder. Their hips pressed against one another. An easy familiarity had developed in the room, the kind of thing she suspected other sisters had always known.

It was brand new to her.

She watched Morgan run across the yard. Saw that no one was shooting at him.

"That's good, isn't it?" she asked.

"I'd say so."

* * *

Zing hit the porch first. Kicked in the door, weapon at the ready.

Sensed, rather than saw, the guy drawing down on him from the dark living room. Heard the heavy chuff of the man's breath, the click of his weapon's strap.

Flattened.

The blast went over his head. He raised his own gun and squeezed the trigger. Held it.

The man's head jerked back with the first hit. Zing kept his finger on the trigger, watched the guy's body dance with the multiple impacts.

Behind him, the porch step creaked. He swung the gun around. Almost blew Morgan Byrd's head off. Byrd raised a hand, and Zing recognized him.

"Hey, Special Agent Zing," Morgan said. "I think that son of a bitch is dead."

* * *

They gathered in the kitchen.

"Take fifteen minutes," Morgan said. "Gather anything you can't live without. Anything your daughter needs, too, Joan. Jessie, J.L., try to wipe any surfaces you might conceivably have touched."

"You okay with this, Joan?" Jessie asked.

Joan glanced around the room. It was no longer the same happy kitchen. But there were memories there, Jessie knew.

"I guess I always knew I'd have to leave it some time," she said. "This is the longest I've lived in one place since I was sixteen. But it couldn't last. Nothing good does."

"Don't know as I agree with that," Morgan said. "But I ain't gonna argue with you."

"There are a couple of cans of gasoline in the carriage house," Joan said. "If you want to burn the place down."

"Might not be a bad idea," Morgan said. "Make it a little harder to lift any prints."

"Knock yourself out," Joan said. "Landlord will be pissed, but he's insured.

*** * ***

Exactly twenty minutes later the vehicles—Joan's truck, Morgan's Raider, and Zing's Taurus—were parked in front of the house. Morgan and Zing had gone back inside to spread gasoline.

Jessie and her sister stood in front of the house. Bodies were scattered about in the snow. Bloody splashes marred the white here and there, black and glistening in the moonlight.

"Guess this has been an adventure, huh?" Joan said.

"More than I bargained for. Listen, I'm really sorry about the house and...well, everything."

"Don't be, Jessica. There's nothing to be gained from that."

"I know, but..." Jessie felt tears fighting to the surface again. Pushed them away. Leaned into her sister, pulled her close for a tight hug.

Joan still had her revolver tucked in the waistband of her jeans.

"Ow," Jessie said. "Think you still need—"

But Joan was shoving her, hard, backwards. Jessie tripped, fell sprawling in the yard.

And Joan snatched the gun from her pants, raised it, already tugging on the trigger as she did.

She fired four times.

Jessie hadn't even seen him. He was inside one of the cars—probably wounded in the early shooting. But he was still capable of holding a semi-automatic pistol at the window and pulling the trigger.

Joan's second and third shots hit him, chest and head. He slammed back against the seat, slumped forward.

And Joan fell.

Morgan and Zing were out the door in a second. Zing helped Jessie to her feet. Morgan knelt beside Joan, turned her over. Felt the side of her neck.

Looked in her eyes.

He turned her back over.

"Fuck. I'm sorry, Jess, I really am."

"She's—"

"Nothing you can do. Let's—"

"Can I hold her?"

"Jessie, she's a mess."

"I just want..." Jessie went to her sister's side, dropped to her knees. She put her hands on Joan's shoulders. Her sister was still warm. It was impossible to believe that she had been there a moment ago, and now she wasn't.

Zing had gone inside, came out with a blanket. Morgan drew Jessie aside, held her in his strong arms, letting her cry against his chest in a recreation of that old movie cliché she had always hated, while Zing wrapped Joan in the blanket.

"We can bury her, Jess," Morgan said. "But that'll take time we really can't spare. Or we can put her in the house, and let her burn."

Jessie thought of the house—Joan's house. Her books, her photos, the life she'd built here with Cassie.

Her dolls.

"Put her in the house," she said.

Chapter 46

By the time they had finished loading the cars and setting fire to Joan's home, the first fingers of sunlight were reaching up from the eastern horizon.

"The kid'll be okay with those folks, you think?" Zing asked.

"No," Jessie said. "Absolutely not. We go get her right now, before anything else."

"But Ms. Cutler, she's a little girl—this is no situation to bring a kid into. She'll slow us down, and we'd be endangering her."

"Her mother was just murdered," Jessie said. Her voice was flat, without noticeable emotion. "She's my niece. I'm not leaving her here."

"I expect she means it, Zing," Morgan said.

"Damn right I do, cowboy."

"I'm not going to argue," Zing said. "I've said my piece, and you know what I think."

"This isn't a democracy," Jessie said. "This is my show. I say we pick her up. Now."

"I got a mule back home you could give stubborn lessons to, Jessie," Morgan said. "Let's do it. Daylight's on the way. I'd like to be a thousand miles from here by the time that fire really catches."

He helped Jessie into the Raider, climbed behind the wheel. All his weaponry had been stashed in a custom-built compartment under a false floor in back. With the rear seat folded up, you could access the hatch, but with the seat in place there was no way to tell it was there.

They left the Camry behind. It had been purchased under a phony name; only a few fingerprints inside could reveal who had driven it last.

Zing followed in his Taurus. They drove into town, got Ben Adams's address from a phone booth outside a quiet Circle K, and followed Zing's map a few blocks to his ranch-style house.

Jessie went to the door alone. Before she got out of the car, she wiped her eyes, blew her nose, fluffed her hair. "I don't look like I've been crying, do I?" she asked.

"Not if he don't turn the lights on."

"What should I do?"

"He'll be half asleep, unless she's been keepin' him up yakkin' or some such," Morgan said. "Either way, he won't want to stand there socializing with you."

"Yeah, you're right," she said. "I'm just being stupid."

"Jessie, don't—"

"Don't worry, Morgan. I'll be able to keep myself together long enough to get through this. I'm just not making any guarantees about what'll happen afterwards."

She went up the walk to the front door, rang the bell, and waited. After a couple of minutes the peephole went dark, and she stood in front of it trying to look as if her life weren't collapsing around her.

The door opened and Ben looked out, groggy, a bathrobe wrapped around him. "You're Joan's friend."

"Sister," she said. "Yes. Friend, too."

"Is everything okay?"

"As okay as it's going to get. Can I take Cassie now?"

"She's sleeping, on a couch in my den. I'll get her."

"That'd be great."

He was gone for a minute. Jessie had a sudden vision of him dialing the police, hearing that Joan's house was blazing outside of town. But then he came back, a bundle in his arms. Cassie was wrapped in a blanket.

Just like her mother had been, the last time Jessie saw her. She felt tears rising up, did her best to blink them back.

"Thanks," she managed.

"If there's anything else I can do..."

"No, you've been great. Really," she said. "Really."

She took Cassie. The girl woke slightly at the transition, opened her blue eyes and saw Jessie there, and a dreamy smile broke over her face like dawn after a storm.

"Aunt Jessie," she said.

"I'm here, Cassie. I've got you now."

She hurried from the house before she broke down for good.

*　*　*

They were heading for Chicago, so they could fly out of bustling O'Hare airport instead of anyplace in Iowa. But around eight, they decided to stop for breakfast. Cassie, who had been drifting in and out of sleep for a while, finally woke up for real.

"I have to go to the bathroom," she said first. Followed quickly by, "Where are we going? And where's my mom?"

Morgan parked the SUV on the sprawling blacktop of a roadside truck stop, with multiple gas pumps, a coffee shop, showers and facilities for the truckers. Zing pulled up a few spaces away.

"You guys go ahead in," Jessie said. "Cassie and I have to talk. We'll be there in a little bit."

"We'll be there soon," Cassie said. "I really need to go pee."

"Soon, baby," Jessie said. "I just have to tell you something first."

Morgan and Zing headed for the coffee shop. Jessie took Cassandra by the hand and walked her away from the cars, toward a grassy strip at the edge of the lot. It was a cold morning, and they could see their breath.

"I don't know a good way to tell you this, honey," Jessie started. "Probably there isn't one. I don't see how there could be."

Cassie's face darkened at this prelude, as if she could smell bad news coming.

"What?" she asked. "Something about Mom?"

"That's right," Jessie said. She took a deep breath, let it out. "I'm really sorry, honey. Your mom..." She caught Cassie's gaze with her own, held it. Touched the girl's wispy hair. "She died, Cassie."

The tears broke free then. She felt them on her cheek, the sides of her nose. Cassie blurred.

And the girl was crying too. "What do you mean?" Cassie asked. "She couldn't!"

"I'm afraid so," Jessie said. "You were right, I was in trouble. I thought your mom's house was someplace where trouble couldn't find me, but it did. Some bad men came. Your mother helped fight them away. But in the end, one of them...one killed her. She was saving my life and...I am so sorry—if I had known that could ever happen in a million years I would have stayed away forever. I would never have known you, which would be terrible, but at least your mom..."

The words tangled themselves up in her throat and she couldn't continue. She dropped to her knees in the damp grass. Cassie looked at her, rage clouding her tender face. She stepped towards Jessie, fists clenched, every muscle in her body tense. There was a moment when it didn't seem as if she knew how she wanted to react, but then her arms started to flail, her fists landing on Jessie in a flurry.

"Why?" she shouted. "Why? Why, why why?"

Jessie let her hit. The punches stung, but they weren't hard enough to do any damage.

The damage was already done.

Then Cassie's face fell apart, mouth dropping open in a huge sob, lower lip twitching, eyes overflowing, and she stopped hitting.

She put her fist over Jessie's shoulder.

Brought her face close to her aunt's.

Jessie felt the small fist light on her shoulder blade. Felt a wet cheek against her own. The thin body quaked, heaving with sobs. Then the fist opened and Cassie pressed the flat of her hand against Jessie, brought her other hand around.

"I have a suitcase full of some of your stuff in the back of Morgan's car," Jessie said. "And another bag with some toys, your new bride doll. I also grabbed a bunch of pictures of your mom. You should always remember what she looked like, and who she was. She was a good woman and a great mother."

They held each other for a long time there in the cold Midwestern morning. Trucks rumbled past them, gear changes and diesel fumes assailing their senses, but they ignored it all, focused only on the loss and sorrow they shared.

Finally, hand in hand, they went inside.

Chapter 47

Manhattan the week before Christmas was like Manhattan at any other time, only more so.

The streets were a little more crowded, and the pace at which people moved and walked was stepped up a notch or two from its frenetic norm.

Shops overflowed. Everyone carried bags and more bags.

The air smelled like exhaust and sweat and tension, only cut with pine spray.

Traffic moved more slowly than usual, because there were more cars on the road, more people jamming intersections. "Don't Block The Box" was a joke, even more roundly ignored than usual.

The weather was sunny and dry, but cold. It might not be a white Christmas, but it wouldn't be a warm one either.

Jessie felt like she was home at last.

It felt great.

All things considered.

* * *

Her homecoming was marred, of course, by the death of her sister, and by the fact that she had brought her niece into the city. Cassie was fine on the flight from Chicago, but since then had suffered from regular crying jags, broken by moody spells in which she wouldn't eat or speak.

It had only been a few days, though. Jessie knew it would take much more time than that for the girl to get over her loss. And in those two days, there had been flashes of the old Cassie—infrequent, but occasional. Her smile would come back, flashing across her face at a remark, a joke, and then vanishing again when her memories returned.

She would heal. But it would be a slow process. Jessie wondered a few times if she should seek counseling for the girl. It would probably help. But Cassie would have to tell her therapist why she was so depressed, and Jessie wasn't sure that there wouldn't be any legal consequences. Did shrinks have to keep quiet when told about gun battles with multiple casualties?

There had been times when Jessie figured she would almost certainly end up in jail because of the mess she'd gotten into. In jail, or dead. Now that Cassie had no one in the world except her, she was determined to live and to remain free, so she could take care of Cassie. Going to jail was out of the question.

Dying had never been an acceptable option.

She suggested to Morgan and Zing the idea of negotiating a truce with Richard Steele. Zing was opposed to it, but Morgan gave it some thought.

And came up with a spin of his own.

So on their fourth day in New York, she was at Columbus Circle with a Glock automatic in her jacket pocket and Morgan by her side. She wore sunglasses, jeans, athletic shoes, and a sweater under a leather jacket. Her hair was pulled back into a tight ponytail.

She had called Richard Steele that morning on his private office line, from a pay phone in Times Square. Told him to come alone and unarmed if he had any interest in talking about their situation.

"Absolutely, Jessica," he said. "I'm so glad you called."

"I just bet you are," she said.

"No, really. I've been very concerned about you. It sounds like you're willing to listen to reason now, and that's great."

"We're going to meet someplace very public," she said. "So you don't just kill me."

"I wouldn't dream of it."

"Let's not bullshit each other, Richard."

"Believe what you want, Jessie."

"Don't worry about that."

"I'll have to check you to make sure you're not wired," he said.

"I'll check you too. I will have someone there with me, to check you and make sure you're not carrying. After we've looked each other over, he'll leave us. You and I will walk alone, through the Park, so we both know we're not sitting in a bugged restaurant or anything."

"That'll work."

"We both need to be able to speak freely."

"Makes sense to me."

"One more thing, Richard. I will be armed. I don't trust you, and I'm not giving up my gun."

There was a pause on the other end of the line.

"That's not negotiable, Richard. Remember, I've seen you kill. Mine's just for self defense, but I'll use it if I have to."

"Very well. I'll see you in a few hours, then."

So that afternoon, she and Morgan stood beneath the statue of Columbus until Richard crossed the street toward them. They stepped away from the statue. Cassie was safe with a friend of Zing's from the Bureau, and Zing himself was somewhere nearby, though Jessie hadn't seen him since they got there. Snow was coming down and starting to stick, as if white sky and white earth were merging, one flake at a time.

Morgan's gaze took in everything. "Looks alone," Morgan whispered. "He ain't—I'd as soon shoot my balls off as believe he'd come alone—but damned if I can see who he's with."

"I'll be careful," Jessie said. She remembered what Zing had told her about Steele's history, his predilection for violence.

"You do that. I'll be listening."

Then Steele joined them. He looked fit and healthy, as if all of Jessie's efforts hadn't cost him a minute of sleep.

"Jessie," he said, showing a big smile. For an instant, the past weeks seemed to fade away, and she saw the old Richard, the one she would have invited into her bed. She made herself think about Joan, dying in the snow, and the moment passed. "It's really great to see you." He spread his arms.

"I hope you don't think you're getting a hug, Richard," she said. "But as long as you've got 'em spread you might as well keep 'em that way. My friend here will search you."

Richard held his arms out to his sides.

"Be my guest. As you asked, I've come unarmed and unwired."

Morgan moved in close. "Lady's got a gun on you, so don't try anything," he muttered. He patted Steele down, paying extra attention to the places people usually tended to hide weapons and wires on the theory that searchers would be hesitant to linger there—the crotch and rear areas, specifically.

"He's clean," he announced after a moment.

"My turn," Steele said.

"Remember, I do have a gun. Right jacket pocket," Jessie said.

"Do you suppose your friend could hold it for a moment?" Steele asked. "So I can frisk there without you thinking I'm going for your weapon?"

"I guess that would be okay," she said. She slipped the Glock from her pocket, handed it to Morgan. Nobody passing by seemed to take any special note of the ritual that was going on here. Everyone was concerned with his or her own life.

And, hey—it was Manhattan. You minded your own business.

Richard ran his hands down Jessie's body and up again. She ignored the close attention he paid to her breasts and crotch, figuring he was using the same logic that Morgan had applied and not getting his jollies at her expense.

"You seem okay to me," he said.

"Shall we go for a stroll, then?"

"Let's."

Morgan gave her back the gun and stayed behind, watched them walk into the park. She stuck the Glock back in her coat pocket and kept her hand on it.

"So what's this really about, Jessie?"

"I'm tired, Richard. Tired of running, of hiding. Tired of your thugs trying to kill me."

"I guess I can see how that would grow wearisome."

"Always the master of understatement."

"So what are you proposing?"

"A truce of some kind? A negotiated peace settlement, maybe."

"I can go you one better, Jessie. You've proven to be a very expensive thorn in my side. But I also appreciate that you're good at your job, and I value your experience. How would you like to work for me?"

"You're joking, right?"

"Not at all. I need good money managers. Maybe now more than ever."

"I don't think that would work, Richard. I don't think I could sleep at night, knowing that I was participating in—well, just what is it you do, anyway?"

Richard smiled. "A little bit of this, a little bit of that. You know, Jessie. Nothing terribly evil."

"I don't know about that. You were never willing to tell me. And you're still not, even though you're offering me a job. Ripping off charities, isn't that it? Diverting money that should go to help the needy into your own pockets?"

"Well, I could answer that," he said with a grin. He looked around them casually. The park was busy, but people could see the snowfall growing heavier. They had been walking dogs, pushing strollers, jogging, skating. There had been a football game under way on an expanse of grass. Now the game was wrapping up, players hurrying for parked cars; the other people were taking off as well. "But you know what they say."

"Then you'd have to kill me."

"That's how it goes, I think."

"Been there, done that. That's another saying that applies here."

"You're a very resourceful woman. More so than you even realized, I suspect."

"When someone's trying to kill you, it seems like a healthy trait to cultivate."

* * *

"He's slick," Zing said. "Not giving us a thing."

He and Morgan were about two hundred yards away, paralleling their path through the park but staying at a good distance. They'd gone to the Spy Shop and paid cash for a long-range parabolic microphone. It had a transparent reflector dish, so from any distance at all it was hard to tell what Zing held in his hand. He was listening on a headphone and recording the conversation at the same time. As long as he could keep Jessie and Richard in sight, he could pick up their words.

"What's he saying?" Morgan asked.

"He's talking around everything, but not getting into specifics. We need specifics. We need him to admit to a crime. He doesn't do that, we just bought ourselves a very expensive plaything."

"One thing that's not a problem right now," Morgan said, "it's cash flow."

* * *

"I admire it in you, Jessie, I really do," Richard went on. "That's why I'd like to have you on my team."

Jessie raised her hands in an exaggerated shrug. "That's just not in the cards, Richard. I'm willing to talk, see what we can work out, if anything. But being on your payroll? Not happening."

"You know, I was afraid you'd take that stance," Richard said. He lunged at her, taking her by surprise, and pinned her arms against her sides. She couldn't get at the Glock in her pocket. She knew Morgan and Zing weren't far off, though, so she wasn't too worried.

Then two men came out of nearby bushes, rushing toward them. Two men who weren't Morgan or Zing.

They were smiling.

Maybe this hadn't been such a great idea after all.

Chapter 48

One of the men—a reasonably handsome man, she found herself thinking, for a gangster, though he was no Richard Steele—stuck a gun barrel against her stomach, smiling like an old friend as he did. Richard held her right arm away, and the other guy, who couldn't have been more than five and a half feet tall, yanked the Glock from her pocket. They were standing around her in such a way that no passersby would see the guns.

"Take her someplace private and kill her," Richard said.

"Got it," the handsome one said. "Be a pleasure."

"Sorry, Jessie," Richard said. "This wasn't the way I wanted it to be. You don't leave me any choice."

"Let's go, sweetheart," the handsome one said. He took her right arm and the little guy grabbed her left. "A little too public to do you here. But you try to make a fuss, or contact anyone, and I'll overlook that."

They started walking her toward Eighth Avenue, running alongside the Park. Steele followed, a few paces behind. The way the park was emptying out, Jessie wondered how long it would remain "too public."

Not long, she guessed.

* * *

"He just ordered those guys to kill her," Zing said.

"Let's move," Morgan said.

"They're heading for that parked Lincoln," Zing said. "We'll have to hurry." They were already jogging toward Jessie and the men.

"We could start shooting."

"And hit Jessie."

"They see us coming, they'll shoot her anyway."

"You're right," Zing said. "We need to distract them."

"Why don't you call for backup? You've got him on tape now, threatening her life, right?"

"I wish it was that easy, Morgan."

"Why isn't it?"

"Because I'm not with the Bureau."

"What?"

"I'll tell you later," Zing said. "It's just not an option right now, okay?"

"Fine, whatever," Morgan said. "I've got an idea." He changed course, headed toward where a ragtag group of vagrants, homeless men, sat on park benches. There must have been twenty-five of them, spread between eight benches on both sides of the path. Some were wrapped in blankets, others in layers of coats.

Zing followed him, eyes on Jessie the whole time.

"Hey, guys," Morgan said. "Who wants to make some easy money?"

The men perked up.

Morgan reached into his pocket, pulled out a fistful of bills.

"There's a ten here for each of you. I got something I want you do to. Could be dangerous, but I don't think so. When it's over, you come back to me and everyone who helps out gets another forty to go with the tens."

"Whaddya want?" one of the men asked.

Morgan pointed. "There's two men over there, got a lady by the arms. They've got guns. I want you guys to get in their way, block their path. I don't think they'll start shootin' with all of you there. They couldn't get all of you, and the noise would attract attention. And I doubt they'll shoot the lady, with you all as witnesses. What I want is for her to get free of them. Think you can handle that?"

"Fifty bucks each, we'll chop 'em into little pieces and feed 'em to the pigeons," the homeless guy said. He had long blond hair and a matted beard, wore a desert camo army jacket with black jeans.

"You got to hurry," Morgan said. "Intersect them before they're out of the park." He started handing out tens from the stash he'd brought along.

"On our way," army jacket said.

The men lurched from their seats. Pigeons scattered. A couple of bottles wrapped in paper bags clattered to the path. As one, the men started to run, heading for a point midway between Jessie and her captors and the street. They looked like a group heading out for an impromptu football game.

Or that's what Morgan hoped they looked like.

He knew that if he and Zing approached Jessie's captors, they'd be spotted for what they were—particularly since he had no doubt been seen with Jessie outside the park. But maybe this homeless brigade could get between the men and the car long enough for him to figure something out.

Then he'd have to deal with Special Agent John Langford Zing, who wasn't a special agent at all.

Of course.

He had been, he would never have shown up in Iowa alone. He'd never have been able to get through an all-night gun battle without calling the Bureau a dozen times.

The homeless brigade was a long shot, Morgan knew. But it was just stupid enough to work.

Or he hoped it was.

Plus, there was that whole poetic justice angle.

* * *

Jessie could see the black Town Car idling at the sidewalk, and knew that's where they were going. She couldn't really turn her head, but she didn't see Zing or Morgan anywhere. They had been listening—were supposed to be, anyway. And Zing had told her the gizmo would only work in a line-of-sight situation, so if they could hear, they could see.

Where the hell were they?

She felt the little guy's hand tense on her arm.

"What the fuck?" he asked.

She looked past him.

A band of homeless men was heading to a point that would intersect their path before they reached the street. The men looked casual, bantering back and forth, a couple of them passing bottles around. Jessie wondered if they worked for Richard, some of his collectors.

They reached the spot where they would have to run into Jessie and the men holding her.

And stopped there. Their casual demeanor disappeared. They looked determined, even angry.

"Go around them," Steele hissed from behind.

The men holding Jessie diverted their course, to the left.

The homeless men moved to block them.

"Go through them, then," Steele ordered.

It wasn't that easy.

When they neared the group of men, the ones in front leapt at them. Grabbing, reaching, hands everywhere.

"Get offa me," the little guy snarled. "You stink."

The handsome one hit a toothless old man in the gut and the guy went down in the grass. But another took his place, a broad-shouldered black guy.

And there were plenty more behind him.

"Get outta here, you freakin' losers," the little guy said.

"I don't think so," a tall blond homeless guy said. He held a bottle in his fist like a club.

"Let her go."

"Kill them!" Steele ordered.

"There's an awful lot of 'em," the handsome guy said.

"I don't care," Steele said.

"Try it," the blond guy said. "You can't get all of us. We'll tear you apart."

"He's right," the big guy said. "We had us some real firepower, some automatics, we could cut through these guys. But we thought we were only coming for the one chick, you know. I just got me a pocket piece."

Jessie expected Steele to reply, but there was nothing from him. She looked back, and he was on his way across the park in the other direction. He'd given up on this plan.

Then she looked back and saw Morgan and Zing approaching.

They had guns in their hands.

Her captors saw them too.

"Shit," the little guy said.

"Just turn me loose," Jessie said. "This has gone to hell for you. Steele's cut out. You can too."

The guys released her arms.

"Let 'em go, boys," Morgan called.

The handsome one winked at Jessie. "You and me, we'll meet again," he said. He walked away from the homeless men, up the slope to Eighth Avenue and the waiting Lincoln. The little guy was right behind him. They climbed into the car and it pulled away from the curb.

Jessie spun. Steele was walking swiftly toward the other side of the park.

"Give me your gun," she demanded, holding a hand toward Zing.

"But—"

"Give it to her," Morgan said. "She's got to finish this."

Zing reached under his coat, took his Springfield out, handed it to her.

"Be careful," he said.

She took off at a run.

Chapter 49

Richard glanced over his shoulder once. Jessie followed his gaze. First, he saw the Town Car driving away. Next, he saw the band of homeless men breaking up, as Morgan shoved money into their hands.

Finally, he spotted her. From his body language, she was pretty sure he'd had no idea that she was on his trail, much less how close she was.

Not close enough to shoot yet. But he didn't know how well or how badly she aimed a gun.

He began to run.

She poured on the juice.

Running in this park came as naturally to her as breathing. She had been doing it for years.

Two miles, four days a week. Five miles on Sunday.

If there was one thing she could do...

She was gaining on him. But they would run out of park before too long. On city streets, he'd have the advantage. She would be hesitant to shoot on a busy street.

She tugged the Springfield from her pocket.

He left the path, started across a wide grassy swath.

There was hardly anybody around.

She lifted the gun before her, tried to aim as she ran.

Squeezed the trigger, mid-stride.

The kick nearly knocked her over, since her balance was precarious. She stumbled, regained her footing. Kept running.

Richard was down.

He pushed to his feet again, this time holding his left arm with his right hand.

Winged him, then.

Not great. But it was a start. At least she had hit the right guy. Better than she'd expected.

He trudged up a slope. She suddenly realized what was coming up. The Pond. Beyond that, Fifth Avenue.

He'd be out of the park in a couple of minutes.

He gained the path beyond the grassy section. He could go faster now. She was still running on grass, where it was hard to gain traction. The stuff slipped under her shoes.

And there were people on the path. Some had stopped at the sound of her gunshot, looking at her.

She didn't care. She wanted this to be over.

She wanted Steele. Dead or in prison didn't matter anymore.

Prison was looking less likely with every step.

Just stop, you son of a bitch, she thought.

Just stop.

Stop.

He stopped.

About three feet from a woman, mid-sixties, maybe, small and gray, who hadn't gotten out of the snow fast enough.

He looked at her, looked at Jessie, closing the gap.

Grabbed the woman around the neck, from behind.

And struck out across the Pond.

It was iced over, Jessie realized. The fastest way out of the park was across the Pond. If he circled around it, he'd be well within Jessie's range for too long.

So he was going across the ice, backwards, stiff-legged, and he was holding this woman in front of him so Jessie wouldn't shoot.

When he reached the far side of the ice he'd toss her aside, go over the wall, and be safely away.

To come back and kill her some other time. Like he killed her sister.

He didn't pull the trigger on Joan. He probably wouldn't pull it on Jessie. But he was behind it all.

A lot of people were in for some rough holidays. Because of what the bankers and other titans of finance had done, to them and to the economy. And more personally, because of what Richard had done— what Jessie had helped him get away with, however inadvertent that assistance.

And he was less than a hundred feet from the city. From being out of her reach.

Then the Lincoln—the fucking Lincoln—pulled up at the curb. Waiting on Fifth to spirit him away.

She knew she wasn't a good enough shot to miss the woman and hit him. The woman was trying to scream, but he was holding her across the throat, cutting her air off. She was kicking, her clunky shoes slamming into the ice.

Richard's steps were tentative. The last thing he would want would be to end up flat on his back.

Jessie reached the edge of the ice. Stepped past a NO SKATING sign. Felt the ice give a little under her feet.

Richard was backing toward a DANGER – THIN ICE sign.

But he knew it was there. He slowed even more. The woman kicked again and he shook her like a rag doll.

"Cut it out, bitch!" Jessie heard him say.

Then she heard the ice groan.

And crack.

Richard heard it too. He couldn't have missed it.

"Damn it," he said. He pushed the woman away from him. He must have figured their combined weight was too much.

The woman fell, skidding on her hands and knees, sliding in a gentle arc.

And the ice gave another cracking sound.

Richard turned his back to Jessie. He was most of the way across. He was going to run for it.

She raised the gun.

Aimed.

Fired.

Saw blood burst from his right leg.

He went down.

Hard.

Gave a startled yelp, and disappeared.

The Lincoln sped away. Its driver had written Steele off.

She kept going. There were ladders across the ice, in spots, for just such emergencies.

Jessie found one and shoved it across the thin ice to the woman. She caught it, and Jessie dragged her to where the ice was thicker.

When she was able to regain her footing again, she looked at Jessie—Springfield jammed half into her jacket pocket, with the butt hanging out—shrieked, and hurried back to the path.

Calling for the police.

They'd be coming now anyway, Jessie knew.

She took the ladder again. Went looking for Steele. She put it down near where he had gone under. Crawled on her belly, holding onto the ladder, to distribute her weight.

Cold bit at her skin through the jeans, the sweater, pressed flat against the ice.

She reached the jagged hole in the ice. Felt it creaking around her.

There was no sign of him. She hadn't fired a killing shot, but maybe he had been too weak to swim, too wounded to get his bearings under the ice. The Pond wasn't deep here, she knew.

Deep enough, apparently.

She was crying, the tears hot on her face.

She wanted Steele dead. But not this way. Trapped under a sheet of ice, drowning in freezing water. It was too horrible, even for the worst man she'd ever known.

Then she felt hands on her legs, pulling her away from the dangerous ice.

Morgan.

Zing waited on the path. Showing his badge, breaking up little clots of onlookers.

In the distance, sirens wailed.

Morgan put an arm over her shoulders, led her quickly down the path.

Out of the park.

No words were spoken. Or needed.

Steele was gone. Joan was gone.

Hardly a fair trade.

Chapter 50

Two days later—Christmas Eve—Jessie sat in the living room of a furnished house in Queens that she had rented on a weekly basis, reading the *New York Times* for the first time in what seemed like forever.

Cassie was in the kitchen with a peanut butter sandwich and a glass of milk.

They had gone into the city for a matinee performance of *The Lion King* at Times Square. Cassie had been enthralled by the costumes and sets, and Jessie had caught her singing along with a couple of the songs. She had burst into tears when Simba's father was killed. But the tears had passed, and she left the theater with a genuine smile on her face.

Healing wouldn't happen all at once. It would never be perfect. But it was a start.

Jessie was exhausted, but Morgan and Zing had promised to come by and she was determined to stay awake for them.

At five minutes before six, the doorbell rang.

Jessie put the paper down and went to the door. Looked through the peephole to ascertain that it was them.

Morgan stood in front, Zing behind him.

Jessie unlocked the door, pulled it open. "You have no idea how refreshing it is to have a doorbell, and to have people use it instead of just bursting in with guns in their hands," she said.

As she hugged Morgan, Zing said, "If you like that sort of thing, you might want to think about moving to a better neighborhood."

"This is just temporary," Jessie said. "We're not staying here."

She gave him a hug too.

"You got a TV here?" Zing asked.

"Sure, why—?"

"Turn it on," Morgan said. "The news. Something you'll want to see. We heard it on the radio on the way over."

She went to the set and switched it on. Cassie heard the commotion and came out of the kitchen, eyes drooping, a faint milk mustache lining her lip. Morgan wiped it with his hand when he picked her up.

"Morgan," she said, wrapping her arms around his strong neck. "You did come."

"Couldn't leave town without seeing Miss Cassie again," he said.

"Thanks, Morgan."

Morgan passed her to Zing, who got the same kind of attention.

"Hugs from two beautiful women," he said. "I like coming here."

"Shh," Jessie said. The news was starting. Thirty seconds of quick cuts of the news crew and helicopters, and then the anchor outlined the evening's headlines.

"You might want to go into the other room," Morgan said to Cassie.

"I'm going to get ready for bed anyway," Cassie said. "I'm really tired." She left the room with a backhanded wave at the men.

"A prominent banker's suicide note has implicated himself and a number of other people in a huge international money-laundering scandal," the anchorwoman said.

"Oh my God," Jessie said. She sank onto the couch. Morgan sat next to her, held her hand between his.

"MetroBank Vice President Jim Mackie apparently took his own life this afternoon, at his East Hamptons residence. Before he died, though, he wrote a long letter detailing a money laundering scheme that involved officers of MetroBank, as well as businessman Richard Steele, who was killed in Central Park just two days ago, and an unnamed Treasury agent. Federal authorities are currently seeking out the Treasury agent, and are said to be closing the net on him even now.

"This case may also involve MetroBank officer Barbara Slonaker, who was found slain in her apartment last week, and MetroBank employee Jessica Cutler, missing for several weeks now. Mackie's letter described in detail how Steele's illicitly gained funds were laundered through MetroBank accounts, ending up in a variety of foreign banks. Ramifications may be far-reaching, but we'll have to wait for results of an ongoing federal investigation to know for sure. Mackie is survived by his wife and two sons. In other news…"

Zing clicked the set off.

Jessie was pale.

"God, poor Jim…"

"He didn't look well when Morgan and I paid him a visit," Zing said. "I have a feeling that as soon as he heard Steele was dead, he knew it was all collapsing in on him. It's almost as if he just stayed alive long enough to tell someone what he knew."

"Have you seen that letter they're talking about?"

"No. He was working at a computer in his home office, so he might have been writing it." Zing took a folded sheet of paper from inside his blazer, handed it to Jessie. "He wanted us to give you this."

She unfolded the paper. A list of numbers.

"These are bank accounts," she said. "And access codes…"

"Belonging to the late Richard Steele," Zing said. "Apparently a loyal MetroBank customer to the bitter end."

"But—"

"His money will to be tied up legally for months, maybe years," Zing said. "Mackie thought you might be able to put some of it to better use. Just don't take so much that you raise any red flags."

"But—aren't you a federal agent? Couldn't you get in a lot of trouble if…?"

"That's something Mr. Zing's been meaning to talk to you about," Morgan said.

Zing sat in an armchair, kitty-corner from the couch.

"I sort of lied about that part," he said. "I was with the Bureau. For nine years. A little over a year ago, I was looking into the phony donation racket—Steele's scam—out in Pittsburgh. I came across a case where a homeless guy had gone to a shelter—one of those that Steele funded—looking for a bed because it was cold and he was sick. But the shelter had closed, suddenly. Steele had skimmed off so much money that it couldn't afford to keep the doors open.

"Turns out, this guy was a high school friend of mine. I hadn't even known that he'd fallen on hard times. We had lost touch with each other. But he was a good friend for a lot of years.

"My friend died three days later, from pneumonia.

"I wanted to investigate. I'd been on the case before that, but now I started shoving everything else aside. I wanted Steele. I was sure it was him.

"Eventually, my other cases suffered. My boss didn't want me to focus on Steele to the detriment of everything else. He wanted to push me into counter-terror. It was looking hard, or impossible, to get enough evidence against Steele to get a conviction. Something had to give.

"So I quit the Bureau. I couldn't give it my all, and I wouldn't let go of Steele. I pretended I'd lost my badge and ID, got them replaced, and then gave my notice. I think my boss knew I wasn't going to drop the case, but there wasn't much he could do at that point.

"I spent everything I had, maxed out my last credit card getting that ticket to Paris. I'm broke and unemployed. Like you, I think, I'd lost everything that told me who I was, and I needed to get that back. Or I needed to find out that the things that make you who you are are the things you've always got, even when you have nothing. Either way, I'm grateful to you for helping."

"By showing you that it could always get worse?"

"Partly. Now, having said all that, as glad as I am that Steele has been wiped off the face of the planet, I'm even sorrier that he didn't live to stand trial. I believe in our system of justice, and I would have loved to have seen him convicted and hung out to dry."

Jessie let his words sink in for a minute. "I'm sorry, too," she said finally. "I almost got through this whole ordeal without killing anyone, and I would rather have kept it that way. But if I had to kill someone, he was at the top of my list."

"I understand, Jessie," Zing said. "I'm not blaming you for that. You did fine—no law enforcement officer could have done better. Once he was in the drink, I don't think I would have tried to save him."

"That's her squishy liberal side comin' out," Morgan said with a chuckle.

"Must be," Zing agreed. He fished a brown envelope from his jacket. "Here's something else for you."

Jessie took the envelope, opened it. A driver's license, three credit cards, two Social Security cards, two passports. All in the names of Jessica and Cassandra Temchin.

"It's all legit," Zing said. "The real goods. You won't have any problems."

"Thank you, John."

"Hey, I do still have some connections. And a little money goes a long way."

"Listen, Jess," Morgan said. "Me and J. L. here, we got a plane to catch, so we really should be hittin' the trail."

"Both of you?"

"Like I said," Zing said. "I don't have a job or much else to keep me here. Thought maybe I'd hang out with Morgan for a bit, see if we can't get into some trouble together."

"I wonder if the state of Nevada is ready for this," Jessie said.

"Reckon we'll find out."

Jessie walked them to the door. Zing gave her another hug and a kiss on the cheek. "Merry Christmas," he said.

"Thanks to you two. Merry Christmas to you."

Then she turned to Morgan. Moved close, inside his arms. Felt his strength enveloping her again, his scent, the bristle of his whiskers on her cheek.

After a minute, she said, "You hold me any tighter, cowboy, you're going to have to call Christie when we're done."

"It'd be worth a little long distance, Jessie," he said. "You take care, now. You got my number, anything comes up. Anything at all."

"Thank you, Morgan Byrd. Thank you for everything."

"We had us a time," Morgan said.

"That we did."

He held her hand as long as their arms could reach, but finally he was out the door and headed toward the street where a taxi waited. Her fingertips touched his one last time, and then they were gone.

Morgan Byrd and John Langford Zing climbed into the cab. It pulled away from the curb and drove away down the quiet residential street. Jessica Dawn Cutler stood in the doorway, watching it go.

And then Cassie was standing next to her, her small fingers twining with Jessie's.

"Yes we did," Jessie said softly. "We had us a time."

Epilogue

The week after Christmas, a large package was delivered to Morgan Byrd's ranch outside Winnemucca. It contained two bundles of cash, each totaling one million dollars. One was marked M.B., and the other J.L.Z.

John Langford Zing didn't want to pay taxes on the money because he would have to declare its source. So he got a series of cashier's checks and money orders adding up to four hundred thousand dollars, made out to the Internal Revenue Service, and mailed them in envelopes with no return addresses over the next several months.

Morgan Byrd bought a Christmas present for Christie—a fully loaded four-wheel drive Lincoln Navigator, with a note that said "to cover the distance quicker," and a key to his house.

On January second, homeless shelters in seventeen Eastern cities found that their bank accounts had been enhanced by a million dollars each. There was no cards received, and never any indication of whom the anonymous benefactor had been.

By the time spring greened the leaves and melted the snows and warmed the currents off Martha's Vineyard, a new business had been opened there, a shop that specialized in rare and collectible dolls, but also carried an extensive stock of new and popular dolls for all ages.

The shop was called *Joan's Place*.

Once in a while, tourists would ask the proprietor if she was Joan. She never bothered to dissuade them.

And that summer, Jessie taught her niece how to swim in the ocean.

The End

About the Author

Jeffrey J. Mariotte has written more than forty novels, including original supernatural thrillers *Cold Black Hearts*, *River Runs Red* and *Missing White Girl*, horror epic *The Slab*, and Stoker Award nominated teen horror series *Dark Vengeance*. Two of his novels have won the Scribe Award for Best Original Novel, presented by the International Association of Media Tie-In Writers.

His nonfiction work includes the true crime book *Criminal Minds: Sociopaths, Serial Killers and Other Deviants*, as well as official series companions to *Buffy the Vampire Slayer* and *Angel*. He is also the author of many comic books, including the original Western series *Desperadoes*, some of which have been nominated for Stoker and International Horror Guild awards. The miniseries *Desperadoes: Buffalo Dreams* was chosen as the Best Western Comic Book of 2007 by *True West Magazine*. Other comics work includes the horror series *Fade to Black*, action-adventure series *Garrison*, the bestselling *Presidential Material: Barack Obama*, and original graphic novel *Zombie Cop*.

He is a member of the International Thriller Writers, the Western Writers of America, and the International Association of Media Tie-in Writers. With his wife, Maryelizabeth Hart, and partner Terry Gilman, he co-owns Mysterious Galaxy, a bookstore specializing in mystery, science fiction, fantasy, and horror. He lives on the Flying M Ranch in the American southwest with his family and pets in a home filled with books, music, toys, and other relics of American pop culture.

Find him online at http://www.jeffmariotte.com and http://www.facebook.com/pages/Jeffrey-J-Mariotte.

www.ingramcontent.com/pod-product-compliance
Lightning Source LLC
Chambersburg PA
CBHW021204250626
47155CB00008B/2666